THE
PERSIAN
GAMBIT

TIM READMAN

Copyright © 2011 Tim Readman.

The right of Tim Readman to be identified as the Author of the Work has been asserted by him in accordance with the Copyright, Designs and Patents Act 1988.

First published in 2011 by Tim Readman.

All rights reserved. No part of this publication may be reproduced, stored in a retrieval system, or transmitted, in any form or by any means without the prior written permission of the publisher, nor be otherwise circulated in any form of binding or cover other than that in which it is published and without a similar condition being imposed on the subsequent purchaser. All characters in this publication are fictitious and any resemblance to real persons, living or dead, is purely coincidental.

ISBN 978-0-9570534-0-3

Design and typesetting by Pentacor Book Design, High Wycombe.

PROLOGUE

SATURDAY 19TH APRIL
'Iranian Club' dinner, Rue Vernet, Paris 8e

It was going to be another of those 'Iranian mafia' dinners as Jules insisted upon calling them whenever his mother was in earshot.

An Iranian exile herself who had married into one of France's great dynasties, Jamileh de Villarosa was accorded a senior profile by the Parisian ex-pat community. People whispered that her brother, Hamid, was increasingly involved in the politics of the Iranian diaspora and she thought that her family at least should be solid in its support for him. Hence her insistence that Jules attend the party being given by one of Dr Bakhtiar's ex ministers and his wife. For Jules, it was a duty he did his best to avoid as the Iranian soirées were normally melodramatic affairs where bluster and complaint competed for attention among a group of introspective, gilded refugees.

More than politely late, but still in time for dinner, Jules rang the bell in the apartment block in Rue Vernet. He really had no excuse as his office was just the other side of the Champs-Elysées in Rue de Berri but, as a socio-political journalist, he had long since perfected the excuse of an emerging crisis somewhere on the planet that required his immediate attention – even at weekends. Journalists he'd met tended to be impossible to pin down to any schedule and it suited him well tonight. Still blaming tribal violence in some part of Africa, which his hostess would be unlikely to have heard of, he was shown into the *salon* just as dinner was about to be served.

The room was crowded but a quick scan revealed a couple of familiar faces of people with whom he was on nodding terms, so he started to squeeze in their direction, past the over-decorated women who collectively emitted an aroma that would have overwhelmed any perfumery in Rue Faubourg Saint-Honoré.

Down the centuries, France had cultivated a glittering array of creative traditions, most of which were designed to appeal to man's sensibilities and natural desire for self-indulgence and pleasure. Opulent architecture, cutting-edge engineering, exuberant art, bohemian fashion and, perhaps most widely acknowledged, culinary excellence were conspicuous and applauded.

If France was a treasure trove of beautiful experiences, then Paris had immersed those experiences into a way of life which refused to acknowledge the unpleasant realities of mundanity such that Paris had become the centre of the *'bon chic, bon genre'* society where visual impression is everything, and opulent superficiality the result. This is the Paris where well-heeled Iranian exiles were drawn together, determined to out-class the Parisians at their own game.

Shuffling to his right, Jules found himself momentarily in an open space to one side of a heavily decorated Empire fireplace just as the party started to make its way into dinner. On the other side of the fireplace, a girl in a neat, well-cut black dress was standing on her own clutching a discrete evening bag. While everyone around them was hastening to the doorway, he and the girl stood still and their eyes met in a moment enhanced by their own stillness. The girl was tall with a slim, athletic figure, smooth olive skin, and long, dark hair worn straight as if to frame her fresh face accented by grey-green eyes, a long, slightly snub nose and a generous mouth. She looked unpretentious, uninhibited, warm and wholly out of place in this ornate gathering.

The moment was quickly broken by their hostess urging them

into dinner. Jules gave the girl a glancing smile, and found himself mesmerised by her watchful eyes. 'We will talk after dinner, I promise' he said, surprised by his own crude audacity.

The girl paused briefly, then, returning his smile, said softly 'That would be really nice'.

Jules felt as though he had tripped clumsily over both his feet at once. This was hardly the 'take it or leave it' approach that a suave, sophisticated, fearless, young Turk of a journalist should adopt. But so what, she was different, she looked amazing and there was something about her which was instantly irresistible – the eyes and the intensity of their focus.

So now, covered in unaccustomed confusion, Jules found his place at dinner next to an overbearing, middle-aged lady who clearly considered herself something of a *grande dame*, theatrically made up and laden with expensive fake jewellery. On his other side was a rather overweight, art student type in a generous blue dress that covered most things. Introducing herself as Dorri, she had a big smile, slightly chubby fingers and badly bitten nails.

Searching around, he saw the girl with the grey-green eyes on the other side of the table, about a third of the way down. He smiled at her again furtively as he adjusted his seat and noticed her glance over at him but his fleeting smile disappeared as the boy on her right engaged her in conversation.

The *grande dame* began explaining that she was a cousin of the late Shah and had been forced to flee after Dr Bakhtiar had so shamefully failed the royal family. Did Jules realise how difficult her life was; almost no servants and such a pokey little house, virtually in the *banlieu*, oh yes, her father would have been so sad.

None of which cut any ice with Jules. He sensed that it would only risk greater acquaintance if he were to mention that his grandfather had been a minister in Mossadeq's 1953 democracy and had actually been butchered by the mob in the American inspired coup that had put *her* puppet Shah back on the throne. There was always potential tension between the successive waves of people who had fled Iran.

He glanced again over towards the girl to find her also looking at him again. He raised his eyebrows nodding towards the *grande dame* and the girl smiled and looked away. Jules thought she was stunning but there was something more, something almost ethereal about her he told himself.

'She's beautiful isn't she' said the girl in the blue dress on his right, jolting him out of his fascination. Embarrassed, Jules reddened slightly and apologised for being so inattentive.

'She doesn't often come to these sort of things' Dorri continued. 'You know her?' she asked. Jules shook his head.

'Her name is Zahra Mousavi. She and I used to know each other a bit when we were at the International School together. Then she went off to Exeter University in England after her *Baccalaureat* and someone told me that she's at business school at INSEAD now. Her mother died some years ago and I hear that her poor father keeps himself very much to himself nowadays. I'll introduce you if you like' she said kindly.

'That's very sweet of you' said Jules 'but we sort of met just before dinner and agreed to continue our conversation later. But I'm being very rude; tell me about you Dorri.'

'Oh dear, I'm afraid that I'm not at all brainy like Zahra. I never even got my *Bac* – took up art instead; my father wasn't at all impressed! Actually, he's much happier now as I've met a wonderful, hunky Croatian sculptor called Andro and, in two months, we'll be married. Then I will be permanently out of Dad's hair! He doesn't think that I reflect too well on him in these circles, you see! Personally, I can't wait to get out of Paris so that's fine by me!' she added with a giggle.

'What sort of things does your sculptor do?' inquired Jules taking a mouthful of the *tarte aux fraises* and catching another glance from the girl he now knew as Zahra.

'Oh huge statues of anything anyone will pay him for mostly. Actually, he's coming over in three weeks time and, well, I'm probably jumping the gun here but perhaps the four of us could go out to dinner or something.' Dorri rambled on about their plans and the number of children they were going to have and how Croatia was so arid but also beautiful and the food that could be truly delicious if you liked hot things of course, which she did. All the while, Jules could see Zahra listening to her neighbour, stirring her coffee, and shooting glances back at him with the guarded flicker of a smile as she caught his eye. The thread that joined them was feeling ever more tangible and Jules was now eager for the meal to finish.

Eventually their hostess stood up to leave the table and, along with the other guests, Jules escorted Dorri back towards the *salon* where Zahra was talking to Georges Gayou who had been at the same school as Jules in Orleans.

'Jules, my old friend, just the man! Some of us are going on to Chez Christine for a nightcap. I am persuading Zahra to come along and you should come too. It's months since I saw you!'

Jules and Zahra looked at each other, smiled, shrugged and agreed.

'I'm going with Antoine and we'll take Zahra and a couple of others. Can you bring Dorri? She's all on her own you know.'

Jules did know but it wasn't what he had had in mind. But

Georges had probably done him a favour as he had now unwittingly provided the opportunity for him to get closer to Zahra at the nightclub without having to expose himself to a rebuff so soon in their acquaintance. They had after all only exchanged one short sentence each.

Chez Christine was the current place where the fashionable young chic of Paris congregated. It was dark, overcrowded, hot and expensive but it was the place to be so the dance floor itself was grid-locked like the Périphérique at the height of rush hour. Dorri made straight for Zahra when they arrived giving her, at huge speed, the benefit of all the happenings in her life since they last met and telling her that when Andro arrived the four of them (already a *fait accompli*) were going out to celebrate. Then, without pausing for breath, she turned to Georges claiming that she hadn't danced for absolutely ages and insisted that they do so immediately as they were playing her favourite song. Jules loved her for it.

Throughout Dorri's update on her life, Zahra had listened with interest and a sympathetic half-smile but had said nothing. Now, Jules approached her, holding out his hand which she took quite naturally, squeezing it instinctively as they moved through the crowd.

Pausing at a gap on the dance floor, they found themselves already beyond casual conversation but with little common ground upon which to advance. So they just began dancing allowing their bodies to yield a subtle intimacy which they were unable to put into words.

After what seemed a brief moment, Georges tapped Jules on the shoulder to say that it was 2:15 in the morning and he was going to take Dorri home. Outside, for April, it was surprisingly cold as Jules opened the door of his car for Zahra. The chill air also seemed to shatter the intimate bubble in which they had been immersed on the dance floor. So, as he drove her home, they stuck to the polite pleasantries used by new acquaintances.

'Dorri tells me that you went to Exeter University' Jules said.

'Yes' she replied 'Georges told me that you're a journalist so where did you study?'

'Ah, you see Zahra, already we have loads in common! I went to Oxford so the Académie Française would be shocked that we both abandoned *la belle France* for 'perfidious Albion'.' he laughed. 'Did you enjoy Exeter?'

'Yes' she said. 'It was great to get away from everything here and breathe a little. It was awfully wet though!' They both giggled.

'Well, it wasn't much better in Oxford. But tell me, do you get involved in this Iranian mafia thing much, I mean like tonight?'

'No, not too much' she said reflectively. 'My father is rather a private person and avoids most of the Iranians here. Actually, tonight was my first time at a formal Iranian evening. Did you like Oxford?'

'Yeah, it was really good. I actually found the English surprisingly easy and I still have lots of friends there. In fact, I even have a small apartment in London. I go over there whenever I can find a good excuse.'

And so their conversation continued, in casual exchanges without delving deeply into anything – as if to avoid discussing what had really passed between them that evening. When they reached her house, he turned the engine off as she slowly turned towards him fixing her ethereal gaze on him with her lips slightly parted. He moved towards her and they kissed, gently at first, then with increasing force, exploring each others lips and mouths in rising passion.

'Jules, it's no good' she said as she pulled away. 'My father is at home but please can we see each other again very soon. I have my last course break from INSEAD coming up so I'll be back on Wednesday evening. Promise me you'll ring.'

Jules kissed her again. He smiled into the magnetic grey-green eyes and kissed her on the forehead. 'Just one problem' he quipped, 'I don't have your number!'

She handed him a small visiting card from her evening bag. 'No excuses now, that's my mobile!' She laughed and turning away from him she got out of the car.

WEDNESDAY 21ST APRIL
Restaurant François 1er, Avenue Marceau, Paris 8e

The following morning, Jules awoke with a feeling that life had changed. Yes, the trees were dressed in their new spring green, and bright flowers shone all over Paris but to Jules everything was glowing around him as if he was being carried on a wave of exhilaration. Sure, he had been in love before but he had never encountered anything quite like the latent magic exuded by this girl. Not only did she have the most hypnotic eyes he had ever seen and a figure to match, she was clearly intelligent with an honesty that seemed at once direct and totally inclusive. There were no frills.

Jules resisted calling her until the afternoon.

'Oh, hi Jules' she said, sounding efficient he thought. 'I was hoping that you might ring. I'm here with my father who is right beside me' she said with emphasis, 'and he says that, if it were possible, he would very much like to meet you but actually, you never gave me a number.'

'The thing is, I'm going down to INSEAD this afternoon but I will be coming up from Fontainbleau on Wednesday evening as Papa and I have to go to Brussels on Thursday. He flies to Iran early on Friday morning so Wednesday is the only time that seems to fit. Short notice but is there any chance that you could join us then?'

Parental approval sounded a bit of an ordeal but Zahra was already more than worth the inquisition. Zahra said that her father would book a table for eight o'clock at the François 1er. Jules knew that would be a gastronomic treat as it was somewhere he had already been a couple of times with his newspaper boss. For their first evening together though, it wasn't exactly what he had had in mind or, indeed, been planning all morning. But he agreed.

'That'll be brilliant' she said concluding the arrangements with the capable tone of someone used to organising things. 'Bye Jules;' she paused adding, 'and I really can't wait to see you!'

OK, thought Jules, that sounded better and, with her father sitting right by her, to say all that, there must already have been quite a conversation between them. All of which simply confirmed the honesty and directness that had so attracted him the night before.

She obviously wasn't scared of exposing her feelings but, equally, neither did the intent feel grasping nor the effect cloying. She must have said something committal to her father about last night. She must have done, otherwise he wouldn't be insisting on meeting him – and so soon. And yet Jules didn't feel threatened by that, rather, he felt elated that perhaps she felt the same as him. At this stage, there was no reason to doubt his instincts and certainly not because she had sounded so efficient and unemotional about making the arrangements.

The Villarosa family were originally of Swiss-Jewish extraction from Geneva but, sensing richer opportunities, three of the four brothers had moved to Paris after the armistice that ended the Prussian siege of the city in February 1871. The original Banque Villarosa (founded in 1789) still maintains discrete, private offices in Geneva, a refuge for reticent French tax payers and a strategic but fiscally separate asset in the firmament of today's Paris-based group. Jules's great grandfather and his great uncles had quickly established themselves in banking and finance by making recovery loans to individuals they judged as potentially useful for the future.

They found themselves in the happy position of being cash-rich at a time of plummeting asset values. As a result, their interests expanded quickly into a substantial residential property portfolio in Paris and Lyon, vineyards in Champagne and Burgundy and chemical factories in Alsace-Lorraine and Chile. In 1910, Jules's grandfather had acquired a large estate with a small chateau south of Selles-sur-Cher. Weekends there became famous in Parisian circles for lavish hospitality and some of the highest pheasants in the Sologne area. Long before the outbreak of war in 1939, Jules's grandfather had converted to Catholicism and was therefore indistinguishable from any other Frenchmen during the persecution of French Jews under the Vichy government. Minor accommodations had to be made with the German occupying forces but the family managed to preserve much of its fortune and re-emerged at the end of the war sanitised and as pillars of French establishment.

Jules's father, Hugo had shown his own streak of non-conformity. Surfacing from the grandest passion of their youths, he and Jalileh Saiyeidi, a Persian exile and fellow student at the Sorbonne, had found themselves irretrievably dedicated to each other.

That posed an awkward problem for some of the stiffer elements of Parisian society. The daughter of a rich Iranian widow, a refugee who had pointedly chosen not to grace their salons, Jalileh was considered not quite *'comme il faut'* and caused some of the thicker applications of expensive eyebrow pencil to flake.

Jalileh, coming from an austere background with no contrived refinement, was not therefore a natural Parisian. Radiant skin, dark hair, high cheekbones that hinted at origins still further east than Iran, perfect French, a quick, natural sense of humour and an open, easy smile – she was difficult to miss even in a crowd.

For her, Paris with its heady mixture of open, architectural grandeur, fashion, gastronomy and latent student power was a magnet and acted as an antidote to the relative gloom of her mother's apartment, an exile's prison. Thus, with the passage of time, her inherent *joie de vivre* and her exiled family's whispered riches, Jalileh herself became more than acceptable to Parisian society – even if her mother remained aloof, now re-cast as odd – an eccentric.

So, blessed by the pages of *Paris Match* and eventually their parents (each side still harbouring unspoken doubts about the other), the young Villarosas were married and soon enriched their bliss with the arrival of Jules Aref, the first of four children and symbol of their multicultural union.

For most of Jules's early years, home had been the chateau in Selles-sur-Cher as his parents felt the countryside was a better environment in which to bring up their children than the sophisticated strictures of Paris. His father was often away in Paris or abroad during the week but tried to make a point of being home on a Friday night if it was at all possible. He was a committed believer in the power and stability of the family as a unit.

To this extent, Jules had been somewhat cut off in his early years from the opposite sex, partly because Chateau Marzotte was locked within the 5,500 hectares of its own estates and, in consequence, he was therefore cut off from the more sophisticated amusements available to other local children in the Loir et Cher district. The family seldom went to the Paris house unless there was a pre-arranged event. He had survived the disappointment of an experimental 'kiss' aged twelve when the ploughman's daughter, the acknowledged local expert, had prescribed touching tongues as an expression of love. Jules had to wait a further three years before being overwhelmed behind the tractor shed during the Bastille Day celebrations.

Life at home was down-to-earth with a strong work ethic pervading the family as a prerequisite for the responsibilities that it had inherited. His father's principal precept was that it was their duty to leave things better than they found them and they must all be committed servants to their duty. Consideration for other people came before their own happiness but self-righteousness and pomposity was absolutely banned at pain of merciless ridicule.

Not that home life was in any way dull, not at all. As children, they had ponies from an early age that were followed by horses and hunting; the head gamekeeper adopted Jules as his personal protégé teaching him to shoot and to fish and how to encourage the stock of wild pheasants. They all had their bicycles and then of course there was the tribe of yellow Labradors that Hugo de Villarosa bred himself (two national field trial champions among them) to which the family were unfailingly attentive.

Aged 18, he left the *Ecole Marie-Baspiste* in Orleans with high enough grades in his *baccalauréat* to qualify him to follow in his Uncle Hamid's footsteps to Brasenose College, Oxford, a path that conveniently exempted him from *service militaire.*

Jules's arrival in Oxford marked something of a turning point in his life. Away from the social paucity of Chateau Marzotte, a new world beckoned among the beautiful antiquity of the university. His first two terms saw Jules spread his wings and indulge in all the freedoms that the anonymity of life as a foreign student offered him. By the end of the Michaelmas term, his good initial intentions regarding regular attendance at lectures had been overtaken by the wealth of distractions that surrounded him. To the student fraternity, he was French, quite good looking and seemed to have an ample allowance that set his style slightly apart from the run of the mill. The girls loved it and Jules began to make up for the lost years of his country upbringing.

By the middle of the Hilary term, it was apparent that things were starting to slip. As an assiduous alumnus, Uncle Hamid was on the development committee of the BNC Society that was, among other things, charged with coordinating the 'Gaudy of Gaudies' for the 500th anniversary of the college. He had come over for a meeting in college and had asked Jules to join him for dinner at the Rose Revived on the banks of the river Thames at Newbridge, a discrete distance from Oxford.

As they lingered over their coffee and a single malt whisky, his uncle had looked at him carefully. 'You know Jules, I have a deep affection for this place, for the peace and charm of the countryside around here, for its proximity to Oxford and in turn, for all that BNC means to me. I don't have a son but you are *de facto*, following in my footsteps and that means a great deal to me. It is a common and unique bond between us and I don't want it besmirched or tainted in any way.'

'Jules' he said looking serious now, 'I know the code under which you were brought up and I both applaud and respect it. I equally know that the possibilities that you enjoy here are in stark contrast to life in Selles-sur-Cher and it is only right that you make the most of what is available. At some point down the road though, you may find yourself hemmed in by responsibilities and when that arises you will need to be equipped to rise to the occasion. So Jules, I offer you a simple maxim – get the job done first and then go and enjoy yourself. Make sure that you've done your best and then you can relax – not the other way round.'

Jules looked quizzically at him, 'I don't understand what are you saying, uncle Where is all this coming from?'

'Jules, perhaps you need to understand how people and institutions work. Venerable institutions such as our college have ways of communicating and because of their conservative nature, they look naturally to protect their own people, staff and their alumni – and of course, BNC's own reputation. Let's just say that I have been getting pleasant but unmistakable vibes that you have been so busy enjoying yourself that the job you came here to do is not getting done at the moment. A 2:2 would not be an achievement for a man of your capabilities and from what I'm hearing, even that is looking unobtainable on your present levels of commitment.'

This was a clear rebuke from the uncle he loved most, a warning pure and simple. Jules starred at him, for a moment wrong-footed.

'I hear what you say Uncle Hamid' he replied seething with inner indignation, 'and I concede that you may have a point. But, just for the record, I have every intention of leaving here with something that I can call respectable. I'll need it if I am going to strike out on my own! You talk about 'responsibilities down the road' but, at this stage, I don't even want to think about taking up the family cudgels! I want to make my own mark on my own terms and that is what I intend to do.'

Jules felt embarrassed by his outburst as soon as he had finished but wisely, his uncle chose not to pursue the matter further. Hamid knew that Hugo, his brother-in-law, remained quietly confident that Jules would come to his family responsibilities once the forces of his youth had been spent. If Jules fulfilled his stated ambition to become a journalist, it would stand him in good stead not least because he would have achieved it under his own steam and seen a bit of the dark side of the world while doing it.

Tonight, however, as Jules now anticipated a meticulous inquisition from Zahra's father and, despite his fiercely won independence, he prepared for the worst dressing as conservatively and smartly as the occasion demanded – dark blue suit, cream shirt, Hermes tie and clean, black English brogues.

At first sight, Khalîl Mousavi resembled a tall and slightly greying version of Omar Sharif, the same intense eyes but without the moustache. He greeted Jules with disarming ebullience as the waiter showed him to the table. Mousavi shook his hand warmly as Zahra came round the table and, squeezing his hand, kissed him on the cheek. The hypnotic eyes were on fire.

'Jules, thank you so much for humouring an old father's request. You probably think it's rather old fashioned of me to want to meet you but I have a couple of good reasons' said Khalîl smiling slightly enigmatically.

'Certainly not, monsieur.' said Jules politely, holding his gaze and smiling as well, 'If I had a daughter half as beautiful as Zahra, I wouldn't let her out of my sight.'

'Well, I hope I'm not that bad and I certainly wouldn't want a bolshy daughter aged nearly twenty-six on my hands!' Khalîl laughed. 'I was anxious to meet you Jules, oh and do please, for heaven's sake call me Khalîl, I particularly wanted to meet you as I do take my only daughter's happiness very seriously. But, more importantly and, at the risk of embarrassing her, I can tell you that I have never seen her as ecstatic as she was when she came home last Saturday. So, quite naturally, I wanted to meet the man who was responsible for this transformation.' Jules felt his soul and body lift.

'Secondly, I also wanted to meet you because unless I'm very much mistaken I think that your mother may be the sister of my long-standing and very dear friend, Hamid Saiyeidi. Am I correct?'

'You certainly are!' said Jules, his exhilaration turning to surprise.

Zahra looked stunned, even slightly irritated, 'You never mentioned a word of this Jules!' she accused.

'Zahra,' Jules parried, 'if you remember, we have hardly discussed anything at all!' and both he and her father laughed in friendly unison.

'No, don't worry,' Khalîl continued, 'there's no reason your uncle would have mentioned me. I very much keep my own counsel around here and the things that we are engaged in are purely, shall we say, 'business'.'

The waiter took their order. Jules followed Khalîl's advice and had the first of the new season's Charentais melon with fresh raspberries followed by the *ris de veau* in a Madeira and truffle sauce

– delicious but too rich.

The conversation moved through a gentle and nicely orchestrated third-degree on Jules's life; the moral clarity of his country upbringing that Khalîl said he would have also wished for Zahra, the pros and cons of the open Anglo-Saxon system versus the interventionism in France, the added perspective of attending foreign universities and a brief discussion of the plight of Iran today under the mullahs. Jules knew he was being tested but Khalîl was also extremely forthcoming himself so it passed as more of an exchange of views than an interrogation. Indeed, Khalîl seemed to want Jules to be fully aware of how they had come to be in Paris.

'It got to the point where the family was obliged to leave our agricultural estate in the shadow of the hills north of Tehran. The alternative, Jules, was simple – certain execution at Ayatollah Khomeini's hands. '

'As a writer, I had been a regular contributor to the Mojahedin's daily publication, *Mojahed* which had a circulation of over 600,000. By mid-1981, Ayatollah Khomeini saw us as an increasing threat to his newly established regime. So he simply set out to crush us. Literally hundreds were killed and some 3,000 of us were arrested between 1979 and 1981. Eventually, on June 20th 1981, we organised a massive demonstration in Tehran but Khomeini ordered his guards to open fire on the crowds killing hundreds of us. That night, hundreds more were summarily executed in Evin prison and it became crystal clear that it was time for us to leave.'

'I had already made precautionary arrangements and so my wife and I came to Paris where I have continued to write my articles in defiance of the clerics and one day, I intend to return to Iran. For that reason, we have chosen to keep ourselves to ourselves. Zahra, like you, has never been to Iran and sadly Zahra's mother died when she was just 12 – which is why I may be a little over protective of her.'

Jules was left with the impression that, for an Iranian living in Paris, Khalîl had remarkably Anglo-Saxon reactions which was probably why he had sent Zahra off to Exeter.

As a journalist, Jules had genuinely enjoyed meeting Khalîl and reflected that the only other person, 25 years older than himself, with whom he had these sorts of discussion, was his Uncle Hamid although, just like Khalîl, his uncle always habitually veered away from any deep analysis of Iran today lest the angle got too personal. Khalîl had certainly been slightly mysterious about their 'business' together but no doubt, all would become clear in time, especially now there would be a two-pronged attack.

'Jules,' said Khalîl looking at his watch 'as Zahra knows, I don't get out that much so this has been a real pleasure for me. I see and hear much of your uncle in you and so I look forward to our next discussion. Who knows, perhaps we might even get Zahra to cook for us! Oh and one last thing, a very big thank you. I gather that you have saved me from eternal damnation and are very kindly taking Zahra down to see your parents this weekend after I leave for Jordan on Friday.'

Jules tried to show no reaction but caught Zahra now staring intently at the ceiling.

'It's her 26th birthday on Saturday, as you know' continued Khalîl 'and I really hate missing it. It would have been awful if she had been stuck all alone at INSEAD!'

Jules shook Khalîl Mousavi's hand warmly as they parted after dinner, thanking him for what he really did hope would be the first of many pleasant evenings together. Pecking Zahra summarily on the cheek, he whispered emphatically 'Call me!'

And she did, minutes after he got back to the family apartment. She was under her bedclothes on her mobile, giggling like a teenager. Didn't he think she'd been clever? A whole weekend all to themselves and no questions asked!

'You set me up!' he said teasing her.

'But wasn't it worth it!' she insisted. 'You don't know my father well yet. He's absurdly protective of me still and always worried about the threat from his enemies back in Iran. Anyway,' she continued, 'you were wonderful and I could tell that he really liked you. He's normally never as open with strangers as he was tonight and, when he said goodnight to me just now, all he asked was when was I going to get that supper organised? But I'm really sorry we couldn't talk; there's so much I want to say. I'm just counting the minutes till Friday.'

Jules suggested they meet at the Moulin de Grez, a small, comfortable hotel with an excellent kitchen about 15 minutes south of Fontainebleau and therefore close to INSEAD. He needed to see a man in Nemours but, if she turned up in time for lunch, they'd take it from there – 'oh and on Sunday, don't forget, it'll be your turn to be grilled by my parents!'

FRIDAY 26TH APRIL, 12:15PM
Moulin de Grez, Seine et Marne, France

Jules sat on the sofa by the front door, dipping impatiently but without apparent purpose into a copy of last week's *Economist*. At every sound of approaching wheels on the gravel outside, he glanced up expectantly. After each disappointment, he looked at his watch and the blond receptionist smirked at the bellboy.

Grez-sur-Loing is a place for romantics as Jules knew well. Home in the 13th century to the Blanche of Castille, queen of France and a garrison of the Knights Templar, it was razed to the ground by the English in the Hundred Years War but later became a magnet for artists and writers attracted by its wooded position on the banks of the limpid river Loing. Frederic Delius's house still stands today in the shadow of the church of Notre Dame; Corot, Karl Larson and Seïki Kuroda all painted here.

The Moulin is a converted 16th century mill, well known for its exposed beams, its rough stone walls hung with tapestries and its excellent restaurant. It nestles on the banks of the Loing just downstream from the old, buttressed stone bridge where Robert Louis Stevenson proposed to Fanny Osbourne. The high walls around the courtyard on one side and the river on the other lend the Moulin a sense of privacy that encourages intimacy among its guests.

Behind the reception desk, Claudine, the youngest daughter of a long line of *Grezois*, was mildly confused. She had found herself warming to him instinctively but his *carte d'identité* declared him to be just 28 and she had a slight but inbuilt resentment that one so young was able to afford the best room in the house. She had noted by contrast, the somewhat scruffy, green Triumph TR4 sports car with the steering wheel on the wrong side, littering the front of the inn. Probably one of those jet-set students from the big business school in Fontainbleau, she thought.

Claudine found him striking rather than good-looking; fashionably untidy, thick dark hair, a pink Oxford, button-down shirt with sleeves unevenly rolled up, khaki chinos straight from the dry cleaners and brown deck shoes that hadn't seen too much polish recently. Unnervingly, he had a natural warmth and easy familiarity that had wholly disarmed her by the time she had finished signing him in.

Returning from the room, he had thanked her with a broad smile. 'It's her birthday tomorrow and the flowers are really gorgeous!' he said, as if she knew who he was talking about. 'It was nothing, monsieur' she lied self-consciously. Claudine had watched him position himself by the door again and, in the absence of anything more pressing, had herself begun to speculate fancifully about a weekend alone with him.

'Lucky girl!' Claudine thought as she watched Jules's mounting expectation. Three more skimmed paragraphs of the newspaper and suddenly Jules was out of his seat as a dusty old Deux Chevaux crunched to a halt outside. Claudine couldn't see the young couple greeting each other but they were already inseparable as they came through the front door. Although Jules smiled at the reception desk, Claudine doubted whether he was aware of her as, deeply engrossed in his companion, they disappeared upstairs.

Fifteen minutes later, Claudine was surprised to observe the couple re-emerge from their sanctuary, making for the restaurant. Immaculate blue jeans covered well-polished, ankle-length, brown boots, a plain cream silk shirt and a beige linen coat. A flat-woven gold chain around her neck and a family signet ring was all that outwardly adorned her – all simple but classically chic. Jules had a protective arm around her shoulder, again waving to Claudine as they passed. Claudine smiled back.

The waiter showed them to a table with a view over the terrace with the mill wheel and the river beyond. After spreading the white napkins across their laps, he handed them their menus and withdrew.

Zahra smiled steadily into Jules's eyes, leant forward and took his left hand in both of hers, kissed it and held it tight. 'I don't believe this;' she beamed wistfully, 'it's like a fairytale, all of it. It's been less than a week and yet it seems an age. Everything is understood but almost nothing has been said.'

But now they were together, at last in their own time, at the very beginning of what they both already sensed would be something very different, something already magnetic for each of them.

Aware of the decorous nature of their surrounding and as yet unsure of the true depth of Jules's commitment, Zahra insisted light-heartedly and with feigned childishness that she wasn't letting go of his hand, so there! Thus shackled and happily wrong-footed, Jules had no choice but to succumb. So, to the amusement of the waiters and uncertain looks of the other guests, they ate the langoustines with their one free hand, after which Zahra relented in time for the arrival of the roast veal. Halfway through the crème brûlée with liquorice and milk ice cream, however, the anticipation all became too much and thanking the waiters, they both laughed nervously and left the dining room, Zahra once again clinging resolutely to Jules's hand.

Their vaulted room was indeed something out of the 16th century and, with the heavy silk damask curtains restricting the afternoon light, the room had a surreal air to it. Zahra stopped giggling as Jules closed the door.

Neither of them spoke as he held her at arms length for a few slow seconds, his hands on her shoulders, her fingers hitching into his belt. Their eyes consumed each other and the distance between them. Her lips melted with a low sigh of anticipation as he brushed them with his fingers. Turning her round, his hands moved over her body as it arched to meet them. Jules kissed the nape of her neck, gently undoing the buttons of the white silk shirt as he did so. She turned more urgently and kissed him as deeply as she could as he laid her slender, athletic body softly on the bed. Slipping his clothes off, he lowered himself beside her, smiling into her eyes as she lay next to him, now turning onto her front in contrived shyness.

Straddling her back, he massaged the tension in her shoulders until the muscles became pliant and relaxed in his fingers. Her eyes were closed but a smile played on the visible side of her mouth. Leaning forward, he kissed the nape of her neck at the same time sliding his leg gently over the fullness of her firm buttocks and down her thigh. With his tongue, he followed the line of her backbone down to the soft, golden hairs at the base of her spine.

He turned her to face him and kissed her again as he ran his hands purposefully but slowly over her shoulders, over her breasts, small but now hardening to his touch, on down to the narrowness of her waist and the softness of her tummy. His hand pressed the top of her mound as she felt him touch her with his fingers, probing gently, sending out the first tremors of the tempest to come. She caught her breath as he moved all the way up her body to look deep into her eyes once more, his fingers softly kneading her temples, caressing a small scar above her right eye, his lips parting hers, pulling her top lip forward, passing it with his tongue. Fire was igniting as she raised her mouth to meet his, her arms now round his neck pulling him to her. He kissed her deeply as he moved over her and then gently down her, his tongue now rousing her nipples as it played over one breast then the other, his eyes all the while kissing hers with their glow as hers turned trance-like with unwavering welcome.

She heard herself inhale audibly as he entered her, feeling his hardness penetrating her, smooth, deeply, tingling, exhaling from the back of her throat as he withdrew, her breath shaking as he swelled upwards once more, departing, returning, retreating, filling again with slow, sensual thrusts. She moved involuntarily to meet them, her nipples now warm, moving against his skin, her fingernails beginning to seek out his back for expression. He felt the muscles of her inner thigh twitch randomly as he moved forwards and back in the tightness of her youth, sensation now filling the anticipation of the last week, light spreading from his groin, healing his hunger, calling him in. She was quickening now with small cries, not wanting to come as she fought for control against the wave of surging, joyful sensation. But the moment exploded as exhilaration rushed over her, propelling her through the ceiling of her inner awareness as she cried for it not to end.

As the river of warmth swept over her, she felt his strength still forging rhythmically through her, calling her back, inviting her to fresh heights. She tried to catch her breath but now she was being tossed again wonderfully on a sea surging with waves of light washing over her. He was moving faster inside her as they danced now together, higher and higher, on and up until the final explosion swept through them, passion expanding, overwhelming them both.

Still within her, she held him close wanting never to let the moment go, to feel him inside her, forever in this union, their breathing still coming fast, together, mixing the emotion with the pleasure, with the gratitude for the love and the bond now wrought between them. He kissed her gently but with a tenderness that was for her alone. As they lay, warm together in the half-light of the room, Zahra knew she was no longer just a father's daughter, alone. Now she had her champion, her mentor, her lover, her guide, her life to come and her source of strength to drive forward her duty and chosen endeavour.

They lay together for a warm eternity in silence and in love, with gleaming eyes and fondness, no distance between them, being now as one until their very closeness rekindled their passion and they danced again but now to the unhurried harmony of shared intimacy and uninhibited carnal pleasure of each in the other.

As evening started to fall across the banks of daffodils among the trees, Zahra kissed his forehead and whispered 'Never change, my darling love. Nothing prepared me for the glory of this passion and now I can't think of a life without you.'

Smiling, Jules ran his fingers slowly through her tousled hair. 'We'll just have make it our business to see that it never happens – except when your father's around of course!' he laughed slightly self-consciously.

When finally they woke on Saturday morning, still entwined, the rain was clattering on the windows and the wind billowing in the curtains. Jules kissed her and wished her 'happy birthday'. They made love again and decided that the warmth of their nest would shelter them at least until lunchtime. Breakfast seemed as superfluous as dinner had the night before.

Somewhere close to midday, Zahra said that her conscience was getting the better of her as they had been in bed, locked in their room for nearly a day. She went to the window and parted the curtains.

'Come on Jules, look it's stopped raining and it's clearing up. I'm going to have a shower. Come and wash my back!' she giggled.

The combination of cascading hot water, the sensuality of liquid lavender soap lubricating the smoothness of skin against skin called them back to one last bout of athletic pleasure after which, clean and glowing, Jules wrapped her in a large white towel and hugged her dry.

They dressed quickly. Zahra was blow-drying her hair when Jules took her left wrist and slipped on a gold-link bracelet with a single heart pendant. Engraved on it was simply 'Zahra' and the date. 'Happy birthday' he said and kissed her neck.

'Jules! Thank you, that's fantastic. When on earth did you manage to do this?' said Zahra with unfeigned delight.

'I told you I had to see a man in Nemours, didn't I?' he laughed.

Claudine watched them appear, heading for the dining room looking fresh, clean and completely absorbed in each other. Damn it, she thought; she was jealous! Not so much of the girl herself but of what they so obviously had together.

As requested, the waiter brought them two glasses of champagne and the menu. Zahra asked Jules to choose for both of them while she studied him and played with her present.

'Nothing too heavy' Jules pondered to the waiter, 'your asparagus followed by grilled turbot with a mousseline sauce for both of us. Thank you' he said.

Jules raised his glass 'Happy birthday again' he smiled.

Zahra beamed at him and raised her glass to him. 'Thank you my darling love, for being you, for everything – for the best birthday ever! And after lunch, I want to show you my favourite walk along the river, not far from here. It's the place I go to get away from everything.'

'So, down to the serious stuff' said Jules smiling. 'Tell me again how it was that a nice girl like you found herself at an English university.'

'You might well ask!' Zahra chortled, 'But you met my father, who you were brilliant with – you're definitely a good guy in his books! I love him hugely, he's always been there for me and I owe everything to him, except you perhaps, but dear Papa suffers from a combination of a father's protectiveness and his involvement with the politics of Iran which makes him permanently vigilant and has given him a reticence to assimilate here. He's determined that he's going back one day and I suspect that's what he and your uncle are up to.

Anyway, I guess that's why he sent me to the International School in Paris rather than the Lycée and later to university at Exeter although that was also partly to get my English fluent.'

'And you really enjoyed it you said?' asked Jules.

'Yeah, it was great. In many respects, Exeter offered me a window on the world and people in a way that my chaperoned existence here never did. I loved the new freedom, the humour and the camaraderie. And what's more, I'll have you know' she boasted with exaggerated smugness, 'that's where I found my first boyfriend'.

'Want to tell me about him?' asked Jules with a hint of something in his voice.

'It wasn't like this at all Jules! Looking back now, it was puppy love really I suppose. We had a great time together, loads of friends and we spent most of my last year together. He was lovely, kind, gentle and a great lover' Zahra paused for effect, 'but not on the same planet as you, just in case you're wondering!' she teased.

Jules laughed, 'So what happened?'

'I was heartbroken for a bit when I first came back here. I missed him horribly. But it was too far to keep seeing each other and I found being an investment analyst demanded more and more of my time. The *agent de change* I worked for had a highly rated research department and life became very competitive. We're still friends but I guess the passion just petered out.'

'And so now, what comes after INSEAD?' Jules said.

'Papa has always drummed into me that I need to be the best of the best for when we go back to Iran, to have skills not readily available there and so I must have a good MBA coming out of INSEAD.'

'And how does that look?' asked Jules

'It'll be OK' Zahra said hopefully, 'with a bit of luck, I may just make the Dean's List; we'll just have to see. For Papa though, that would be the icing on the cake!'

'No kidding!' said Jules, sincerely impressed.

Lunch over, Zahra took Jules on her favourite walk along the Loing.

Hand in hand, they walked down the track to the river. Spring adorned their path along the bank with oceans of small daffodils and bluebells stretching before them into the fresh, sparkling air, with warm shards of sunlight breaking through the tall poplars onto the rain-sodden ground below.

Approaching a small run where the river narrowed, Zahra steered them to the trunk of a fallen tree. Light flickered on the patchwork of yellow and blue around them; Zahra's fingers twined into the hair above Jules's neck and pulled his lips gently to hers. Feeling anew the glide of her tongue, Jules pulled back and smiled into her eyes. 'Here? We're going to get awfully wet you know!'

'No stupid, I just want to thank you' she grinned, her grey-green eyes on fire again. 'I wish I could put into words how very much I love you already. I had no conception of what it could be like to feel like this. I told you about Peter at Exeter partly because

I wanted you to know that I'll never keep a secret from you but also because this is so completely different for me, so all-embracing, something total.'

'Darling Zahra, I'm not very good at expressing my emotions but I promise you that I have never felt like this before about anything, so don't worry, we'll build on what we have and we'll do it together.'

'Then we'll be alright' she said seriously. 'But we do have a massive problem coming up just down the road Jules.'

'None that I'm aware of' said Jules trying to exude trivial confidence.

'You're forgetting that at some stage, my father is going home, maybe sooner than later and I shall be going with him. I cannot do otherwise! And then you'll forget me just as I forgot Peter. That's our problem and it scares me already.'

'Well,' he said smiling at her again, 'you worry far too much; let's enjoy the moment. We've got time to work things out; something's bound to turn up and, even if it doesn't, there are planes and telephones and, to put it bluntly, if we love each other enough, we'll find a way!'

She didn't reply but buried her head in his chest. She could hear his heart and the steadiness of its beat was reassuring. After a while she lifted her eyes to his once more.

SUNDAY, 28TH APRIL, 17:15

Chateau Marzotte, Selles-sur-Cher, Loir et Cher

Coming out of the tall, black metal gates that guarded the front drive of the chateau, Jules laughed shaking his head. 'You were great with them but then I knew they'd like you. And you took my uncle by storm!'

'They were lovely' said Zahra looking back at the chateau though the gates. 'I wondered about you mother to start with but I think she was OK by the end.'

'Zahra, she's like all mothers! Anyone who comes through the door looking like a threat to her 28-year-old little darling represents a danger. She actually told me that you were 'genuinely' intelligent – 'quite unlike anyone else I'd produced' was her description! No, she liked you alright.' Jules laughed again.

'Jules, you know, it's the most magical place. It must have been amazing to have been brought up here. The freedom must have been immense for children.'

'Well, there's plenty to show you another time. It appears a little grand from the outside but, as you saw, it's really a great family home and today we only came for lunch – and only because you used it as an excuse to your father!'

After a couple of minutes contemplation, Zahra turned to Jules, beaming again. 'You know Jules, I'm so glad that we met the way we met. If I'd known the full background to the man I have fallen in love with, I might have mistrusted my instincts. But I was lucky. I met the unadorned man, a man whose uncle is up to something with my father. That made it an unexpected coincidence and a special one all by itself.'

'I understand what you're saying Zahra but please remember

that I'm my own man. I'm not dependent on my father or family; I'm going my own way. I hope that I am truly therefore that 'unadorned man' as you put it' Jules insisted.

'Your spirit is free – yes my darling love but your psyche is inevitably the product of the unit that is behind you and nurtured you – and that is your family.

You don't realise how lucky you are to have that. It's not the money, it's the stability; the platform it provides you with that is so special. It's something you know that you can always inherently rely on. You probably don't even realise it but it's built in and will give you the confidence to make decisions in an uncertain world.'

'I don't disagree Zahra. What you've said is inescapable and is almost certainly the base for everyone until something like this week occurs and the tectonic plates of one's world shift.'

'I have every intention of proving myself as an incisive journalist capable of letting people see things in a new light. I need to find a way to project a new perspective on events, to reinvigorate the staleness of today's politics. It can be done and must be done. We in Europe need somehow to capture the dynamism of American wealth creation and blend it with the best of our European traditions. The treasure trove of our Europe is in danger of becoming a State-regulated museum rather than the launching pad of great enterprises that it was in the past. Politics itself is sullied by the modern democratic imperative of bribing the people before each election. And they come around too fast in any case!'

'No, journalism is probably the only way to shape things over the length of time that it takes to affect or influence change. It is the platform that can provoke peoples' minds and change attitudes. Politicians are really just periodic salesmen today. My father knows what I am trying to do and, to his credit, he has never tried to stop me.'

'Please don't misunderstand me, Jules. There's nothing wrong with what you're doing or the reasons why you're doing it. As you say, your father is absolutely aware of what you're doing and he's astute enough to realise that you must follow where your drive takes you – in his own words, so long as it is 'constructive'. Anyway, I really enjoyed meeting your parents and it'll be fun to see what Papa comes up with once he has compared notes with your uncle!'

As the TR4 neared the Moulin de Grez where they had left Zahra's Deux Chevaux, their silences grew heavier as the end of the weekend confronted them. Coming off the autoroute at Nemours, Jules looked across at Zahra and asked wistfully what time her first class was in the morning.

'I don't have one until the afternoon but I've got a huge amount of preparation that I should have got done on Friday.' Zahra replied.

'So I could actually give you dinner at the Moulin and then we could see if perhaps they would give us our room back?' Jules asked tentatively.

Zahra looked at him and giggled. 'I really couldn't eat another thing Jules, not after that huge lunch. But' she said and paused, 'Marissa who shares the house with me is away this week and there might be something in the fridge if you are genuinely hungry.'

Zahra leant across and kissed him. 'But, my darling love, you really will have to be out by seven in the morning.'

PROLOGUE

THURSDAY, 14TH AUGUST 20:15
Mousavi's apartment, Rue l' Admiral Roussin, Paris 15e

Paris is not the place to be in a hot August. Scores of the smaller shops and restaurants close for most of the month as many of their customers flee the heat for beaches and mountains hundreds of kilometres away.

Having only joined the corporate finance department of Union des Banques Françaises in July after INSEAD, Zahra felt she couldn't justify a holiday and so Jules volunteered not to take one either. Zahra's perception of everything was now regulated by the all-encompassing power of her love for Jules. Her unquestioning confidence in the strength of their relationship had quickly propelled it to become the centre of her existence, the point from which she judged all else including, for that matter, her father and their long-laid dreams of Persian renewal.

Zahra had the ability to express their feelings for them both, the gift of emotional fluency which her journalist lover was discomfited to admit he lacked in equal measure. Nevertheless, Jules's attachment was clear and absolute for all to see, unwavering and complete. Life went on as before; he loved his family and friends as before; he pursued his interests as before, but everything started and finished from a new place that was his own as part of her, and hers too, as part of him. For each, nothing surpassed the other; everything now existed only in the context of their union.

Any doubts that family and friends may have had were quickly erased by Zahra's vivacity and the confident happiness that they both radiated together. Their coming together was viewed with special hope by his Uncle Hamid who had confided to Jules after a few months observation that, despite her tender age, she was the sort of inspirational character that he had never met and that was why he was still a bachelor.

Despite the fact that Jules and Zahra were aware that something was afoot, both Khalîl and Hamid had carefully avoided being caught together since the young couple had met and they had therefore avoided a spotlight being shone onto their 'business' activities together. Tonight was different and portentous. The conspirators had themselves asked Zahra to prepare something for dinner and neither she nor Jules should mention the liaison to anyone else, please. They would understand why when it was explained but no one was to know.

It was 32 degrees Celsius outside and the through draught in the apartment really only helped a little. In the kitchen, Zahra had made iced mint and watercress soup to be followed by a generous selection of *fruits de mer* that she had collected on her way home from the bank. Her father had two bottles of Meursault on ice and was opening a special bottle of Taittinger when Jules let himself in together with his uncle. Handshakes, kisses and drinks followed.

'Dinner won't spoil' declared Khalîl, 'so why don't we sit in the *salon* for a bit?'

So they did, the old facing the young.

'First of all, we're not going to get too sentimental about this' began Khalîl 'but I'm sure that you will understand, after you have heard what we have to say, that we are both hugely thankful and genuinely full of joy that you two have found each other. I'm not going to say the obvious but we love you both and what you have together and when all of this is over, well, let's see what happens!'

Zahra looked quizzically at Jules and took his hand in hers.

PROLOGUE

She could see her father was getting unusually emotional.

'So, to the point! Neither of you is stupid and we have been at pains to hide from you the project upon which we have been engaged for so long. In a nutshell, what we are seeking to do is to unite all the democratic forces opposing the Islamic regime in our homeland in order to overthrow the regime and then rebuild a stable and prosperous country in its place. It will be a country capable of playing a leading role in securing real independence and stability for the Persian Gulf. If you like, we want to pick up at the point where Mossadeq was pushed out in 1953.'

'The economy of Iran is in tatters today. The oil price has halved this year, unemployment is at 18% and rising, large parts of State-run industries cannot even pay wages and, just last week, we heard that the mullahs have suspended all social security payments.'

'It is time therefore to put into action over two years of careful, detailed planning.'

Zahra glanced nervously at Jules.

'Tomorrow, student protests will be ignited all over Iran. They will march in solidarity with the unemployed and the unpaid, demanding what is owed to them. The day after tomorrow, a strategic group of army officers that we have been grooming for 18 months, commanding key units of the army, will take it upon themselves to 'restore order'. To do this, the people will be promised a new and properly funded, democratic government, underwritten in the first instance by loans from China. Hamid has negotiated these and they are secured on supplying the Chinese oil at $55 a barrel.'

'So you see, for all sorts of reasons, not least practical, we couldn't say anything to you both before but we needed to tell you tonight. If all our information is correct, the mullahs are on their last legs and will collapse quickly. If all goes to plan Jules, your uncle will be president-in-waiting by the end of next week.'

There was a stunned silence from the young until Zahra burst into tears.

TUESDAY, 6TH SEPTEMBER
Sofitel Athens Airport, Suite 6,

The meeting was scheduled for 14:30hrs and, like old security hands, the two senior Israelis had entered their suite some thirty minutes before to check everything was in order and scan the room for bugs, bombs or anything else unwanted. They didn't expect to find anything and nothing was found. They had been through this same routine together a number of times before but this time was different. The purpose of the meeting was increasingly urgent.

The Iranian Mojahedin, who had been given sanctuary by Saddam Hussein after their expulsion from France, were not normal bedfellows of such prominent Zionists. The overthrow of the mullahs in Tehran in August had been greeted initially with universal joy until it emerged that the nationalists' vision of the Middle East and Iran's position as a dominant force within it was very different to expectations. The nuclear threat to Israel was strategic and therefore remained the same.

The senior protagonists in Tel Aviv had recognised that there was no more than a narrow window before the democratic elections in November during which Iranian defences might be less coordinated and the nuclear installations at Isfahan and Natanz could possibly be vulnerable to attack. It was particularly important because Hamid Saiyeidi, the new president-in-waiting, had already publicly linked the termination of Iranian nuclear weapons programmes to the removal of Israel's own, long-denied, nuclear arsenal.

Joe Kleiner was the senior of the two Zionists. He was a radical and passionate believer in *Eretz Yisrael Hashlemah*, King David's Greater Israel as defined by God to Abraham in the book of Genesis.

Like many of his generation, Joe had never recognised the 1948 boundaries of the modern Jewish State or any other since then, particularly as none contained oil. His favourite quip 'our ancestors followed Moses around for 40 years and he led them to the only place in the Middle East without any oil' belied a deep-felt outrage with Jewish history.

The family had been bankers and financiers arriving in Palestine in the 1890s from Berlin. His father had been a senior member of the Haganah fighting alongside the British during the Arab revolt in the 1930s. As a young soldier, Joe had served with Ariel Sharon's 202nd Brigade and later in campaigns in Sinai and Lebanon before joining the Likud Party in the Knesset for a few years. The family business was one of the more notable success stories in the financial services sector and Joe had run it until recently handing the reins to his second son, Simon. His eldest son had been killed aged 18, fighting in Lebanon, just before the withdrawal in 1985.

Today, Joe is an elder statesman, a tried and tested *eminence grise*, no longer elected but widely accepted and wholly trusted by the right wing of the Israeli establishment. With no formal role or position in the government, he has a free hand to exercise a trusted discretion in particular affairs but also, of course, is wholly deniable by government ministers when it is expedient to do so.

Ariel Ben-Ezra, Mossad's chief spymaster, is a younger but no less committed Zionist and while he is essentially the bag carrier on high-level occasions, he provides both security and anonymity for the operations and authenticity for prospective partners. Even after years of working together, their relationship remained businesslike with little more than a hint of cordiality. Ben-Ezra knew who was boss. Together, they were an effective team often credited by those who knew of 'setting things up for the Knesset to rubber-stamp'.

At 2.25pm reception informs them that three visitors are on their way up as expected and, at exactly 2.30pm, there is a knock at the door. After checking their identities through the spy-hole, Ariel ushers Hossein Motamed and his two cohorts, Arjomand and Farid into the presence of Mr. Kleiner.

'Gentlemen,' begins Joe having shaken their hands and directed them to seats, 'you have asked for this meeting and while my colleague has briefed me to an extent, why don't you take me through what is it that you want from us.'

Joe makes a show of opening his notebook and adjusting an expensive looking propelling pencil as Motamed retrieves a single, typed sheet with a list of bullet points clearly visible.

'Mr. Kleiner, thank you for seeing us and let me say immediately that it's not so much what we want from you but what we believe we can do together.'

Joe nods, expressionless.

'You will be aware from Mr. Ben-Ezra of the broad points of our proposal but I would like to emphasise that we believe we have a unique but limited opportunity to change the course of things in Iran and therefore the whole Middle East, before the elections take place in November and Saiyeidi's regime is legitimised. Our assertion is that after years of servitude to the Shah and then the clerics, the country is not yet ready for full-blown democracy and will, as a result, fall into a dangerously nationalistic dictatorship. It will be a dictatorship with serious regional, if not global ambitions and, most importantly, it will have an unabashed finger on a nuclear trigger.'

'After all, the country itself has in the past survived everything that the West could throw at it in the way of sanctions. So the new regime now sees no constraints to regional supremacy and is further emboldened in its potential as a nuclear player.'

'The idea is simple: you provide the means and we'll provide the men. We will take out the nuclear threat, bring order and structure to the country, open its oil to Israel and the West and then, together, we can put a stop to militant Islam in the region. Our countries cooperated during the Shah's time and, with new horizons, we can do so again for the good of the region.' Motamed finished in a conciliatory tone.

'We are here, Mr. Motamed, to satisfy ourselves that you can provide the resources that you say you can to complete the job. Obviously, we can provide the materiel you require but, without the confidence that you can use it effectively, we would simply be opening ourselves to international condemnation and the wrath of our American friends for no good reason. I want you to take me through precisely what you have in mind and the resources that you think you have to do it with or will need.' Joe commanded.

Over the course of the next 25 minutes, Motamed outlined the resources at his disposal for each of the three main objectives – the nuclear installations, the presidential and interim government compound and the main broadcasting networks. He described how these goals would be achieved and the initial plan for the aftermath. He outlined measures to eliminate the current leadership in Tehran and all their principal agents around the world and, finally, their plans to re-establish ties with Israel, the Unites States and the West. Saiyeidi would be history.

'Well, it sounds feasible thus far,' Joe admitted, as if reluctant, 'but I must warn you that our agreement to be any part of this will be strictly subject to Mr. Ben-Ezra's inspection of the units you intend to use in the operation and the precise shopping list you have for us. It will also be dependent upon a team from our nuclear agency accompanying the forces eliminating the nuclear installations. Do you have a problem with that?'

He knew that the presence of an Israeli surveillance team was a demand that they couldn't refuse. It was risky though. If things went wrong, Israeli involvement would be amplified. But the State of Israel had been in that position before many times and Joe knew that the world always preferred to ignore the reality of any uncomfortable Israeli excesses – always, of course, perpetrated 'in self-defence'.

For that, he knew with confidence that he could rely on the Jewish lobby in the US and its friends.

TUESDAY, 16TH SEPTEMBER 10:45AM
Villa Cerva, Brancoli, Lucca, Italy

Zahra had called Jules in the office on her mobile a week ago saying that the bank's Director of Eastern Affairs, which basically covered everything from Ankara to Auckland, had called her into his office 'to talk about her future'.

He had told her that he did of course know that her father was terribly well connected with the new regime in Tehran and it had also been quite impossible to avoid the fact that she was herself seeing rather a lot of the nephew of the president-in-waiting of the new democratic republic, bravo for him! Apparently her friend was also the dauphin of one of France's great dynastic families too!

Coincidently, the Supervisory Board was keen to extend the bank's remit in the area and, given her exemplary performance as an analyst, and then at INSEAD (Dean's list eh!) and now in the corporate finance section, they thought (and he agreed!) that she would make the perfect choice to open their first office in Tehran! Why didn't she take 10 days off and think about it? Big increase in salary incidentally; oh, and a generous share option scheme too!

Jules had just finished working on a long and rather tedious exposé on the black market traffic in medicines in Mauritania commissioned by a glossy Paris magazine and was keen for a break anyway. Also they had hardly enjoyed any real time together since the INSEAD summer ball at the end of May. The timing was perfect and they wouldn't be bothered by the career decision which was a no-brainer and was obviously meant to be just that. Politics!

How well did Zahra know Italy? Well, he had an older Italian cousin who lived most of the time in Rome whose husband had access to a family hunting lodge up in the hills above Lucca – meant to be very romantic. She had always said that he would be very welcome to use it. 'Go for it!' she exclaimed in English. 'Done deal!' he retorted.

But Jules recognised for real now what he had known all along. Zahra was the archetypal big achiever and while their passion thus far had been of almost teenage proportions, that was about to change. The cosy, protective cocoon within which they had luxuriated in each other would be exposed to the light of day and distance and they were going to have to evolve a *modus operandi* to accommodate the transition to the real world. But not until after Lucca.

The cousin was thrilled but very sad to miss them as they had just finished their annual retreat there, escaping the heat of the Roman streets in August and early September. The caretaker, Pina would still be around to look after them and in lieu of rent (only joking eh!), it would be very nice if they would take her brother-in-law, the other co-owner, and his nice American wife out for a meal. He had lost his job and they needed cheering up – poor relations and all that!

They had flown down to Pisa and hired a car on Saturday morning. It was only 45 minutes drive from the airport – east along the autostrada to Lucca, north leaving the main road at Vinchiana and then up the steep road which wound its way round the hillside with deep, dry ravines below until they found the turning to the hunting lodge. The drive itself was even narrower and steeper with some vicious hairpin bends that would have tested even a motorcycle.

The house itself was splendid with high Tuscan ceilings, vast hanging tapestries, open spaces, ruddy-tiled roofs and a master bedroom with huge views over the olive trees, across to a small village and its church and on beyond to the valley below.

Pina was round and smiling, very willing and completely incomprehensible. She spoke only what seemed like a local dialect, extremely fast and showed no reaction to French or English at all. With gestures and pointing, Pina showed them how the boiler worked for hot water, how the kitchen appliances worked and where the fuse box was. Using the calendar on the kitchen wall, they established that she would be in again on Wednesday and she hadleft them her telephone number which was obviously going to be very useful! Waving and still smiling, she turned towards her bicycle only to stop after 10 yards or so, still smiling to wave again.

As Pina freewheeled down the hairpins, Jules and Zahra hurried upstairs to grab their swimming things and wash away the journey. The infinity pool was set into the side of the hill offering nearly the same view as their bedroom but through verdant hibiscus bushes with pinky-white trumpet flowers. After a few fast lengths, they flopped about in the warm water until they were refreshed. Going back to the kitchen, they hungrily ate the anti pasti, cold meat and salad that Pina had prepared for them and, when suitably sated, they took the last of the Pinot Grigio and their glasses upstairs to complete the decompression process, to recapture the lost weeks, to release their mutual yearning, fusing their souls once more, recharging their passion, purifying their love.

So time had flowed, swimming, sleeping, eating, always entwined until the shrill sound of the telephone dragged them back to the world about them. It was a full two days later and Jules was instantly embarrassed. It was Becky di Fabbri, the American wife of Salvatore, the other co-owner of the house, whom he had promised to ring when they arrived. Ashamed at his bad manners, Jules stuttered apologies and insisted that they would take Becky and Salvatore out the following day. It emerged that Salvatore was away for a few days for a job interview but Becky offered to come up to the house and show them round. She'd book a table at her favourite little restaurant and they could argue about the bill later.

The Thursday morning was bright but fresh for the middle of September. After a trip to the bank and the post office, Jules had thought to get in a quick espresso before Zahra finished shopping but she was already standing on the corner expectantly. Shopping bored him unless it was in the country food markets or it terrified him if he was buying something special as a natural generosity normally overcame his prudent upbringing.

He walked up behind her, put his arm round her shoulder and lightly kissed her cheek. 'You're early,' he said smiling. 'Couldn't wait' she beamed back, her fingers digging into his waist. 'Can we go home now, please? I think we've got quite a lot of time before Becky arrives.'

Zahra raced him upstairs pulling her tee-shirt off as she went, kicking her flip-flops into the corner and bouncing Jules onto the bed. When their passion was spent, she slid her body on top of his, wrapping both arms tightly round his neck, rubbing her nose gently across his and growling like a tigress. 'Why can't we just stay here forever?' she pleaded. But it was already too late. The sound of a car was even now audible coming up the vicious hairpins.

As Becky rounded the last bend, she saw Jules and Zahra spilling out of the house to greet her. She knew instinctively the way they were, it radiated from them and it swept her back to her first visit to the villa with Sal so many years ago. Looking at these two today, it suddenly seemed like yesterday again. She could see the passion and almost touch their intensity.

All smiles and understanding, she showed them the quirks of the house that Pina had omitted – like the washing machine that flooded the hall if the knob wasn't fully depressed – probing gently all the time, gauging their response to her, feeling their mutual confidence and easy trust. As Jules handed her a glass of Pinot Grigio, she looked at them both for a moment in silence and then laughed in open friendship. 'Oh, it's ridiculous, you two! It can't be more than 20 years since Sal and I were in this house, alone and consumed with passion, wondering about our own future. Looking at you two, it could be us all over again!'

'Well, it must obviously be something in the water then, it can't be us!' retorted Jules picking up Zahra's hand.

'Obviously the water,' said Becky raising her glass, 'but if you are as much in love as we were, you're going to have a wonderful 20 years, that I can promise you. Don't waste it!' Zahra looked up at Jules and kissed him. They all laughed.

Becky had had a miserable time at home, she told them. Her father was a banker with strong political connections and her mother, a writer and artist, daughter of a big rancher from Texas. Until she had been 15 or so, things had been OK in an impersonal sort of way that busy, rich people use as protection for their ambitions and the thoughts and deeds they find increasingly difficult to share with each other. Then things came unstuck. The father had a messy and ever more obvious affair. Rows, separation, rancour, divorce all followed. Both parents used Becky and her sister maliciously in the emotional and legal end game and then largely ignored them when the battle was over.

Becky had seen a promising academic career nose-dive. As her results deteriorated, she had started experimenting with boys and soft drugs and was eventually asked to leave before her exams to avoid several scandals becoming public.

Consequently, her father effectively locked her up for 18 months in a strict Italian boarding school near Florence to perfect her Italian and develop her art. It was a logical choice as they were the only subjects in which she had shown any lasting promise. After that, she had spent an aimless period with her embittered mother in Baltimore with a job in a contemporary art gallery, the gay owner of which had amassed the sum of all his knowledge in Southern California. Plastic friends, meaningless and repeated excesses, no real colour, nothing going anywhere. She badly wanted out and had jumped at the opportunity of accompanying the daughter of one of her mother's friends to summer school outside Florence. Becky was just 20.

With just one week of the course now remaining she had been poleaxed, sitting outside a café in Lucca, watching this stunning Italian eating his lunch a couple of tables away. She had known instantly that he was the one. 'It was like a thunderbolt, just completely out of the blue. I looked at him and just knew.' Becky said.

Zahra glowed in friendship, 'We were across a wide, crowded table at a dinner party in Paris,' she chipped in, 'but essentially exactly the same thing happened to me! So what happened next?'

'Oh well,' sighed Becky, 'without going into the details which still make me weak behind the knees with embarrassment, I made a complete fool of myself but, fortunately, it turned out that my perception of Sal was spot on. He just took me under his wing and I've thrived there ever since.'

PROLOGUE

'So what was the story about this house then?' continued Zahra, now anxious for further parallels.

'That was nice,' Becky smiled remembering, 'The day after I'd made such a fool of myself, Sal took me off to meet his parents on the off-chance that they were there. It was summer and, as it turned out, they'd gone off to visit an aunt of his for the day. Anyway, he showed me round his parents' house, the Villa Fabbri, about 20 kilometres from here. It was falling apart even in those days but there he showed me what it is to make love to the soul of the person, not just the body. It was a complete and wondrous revelation that simply blew all my old perceptions away!'

'We left the Villa Fabbri before his parents returned and Sal drove me the long way back to Lucca, through the hills north of here and then down to the *belle époque* spa at Bagni di Lucca. He talked about skiing in the Tuscan Alps, the drives we would do, the restaurants and secluded walks with enormous views. Then we came here. I have always assumed that Sal could not resist the urge to show me the house where he and his brother normally spent their summer weekends. And thank God he didn't' concluded Becky.

'Yes Becky,' continued Zahra 'but what was so special?'

Becky paused, looking at them both. 'OK, down to the brass tacks! I suppose this is where my life finally changed. We'd made love again when we got here which I remember just confirmed how wonderful the whole thing was and then suddenly, as the evening set in, I panicked. I freaked out. Suddenly it was midnight and Cinderella had to return to her scullery. In one short weekend, I'd been shown what life could really be like by the man I already knew I was destined for. My life had turned a corner. Now it was time to go home, back to the States and I was going to be alone

49

again. It's hard to explain but I was absolutely scared out of my wits, terrified!'

'I remember he whispered 'Relax, trust your instincts.' Then he told me that something extraordinary had happened for both of us that weekend, something I should build my plans around. I shouldn't be worried, 'We'll both be there for each other' he said. I remember hugging him as tightly as I could so that he couldn't see the tears streaming down my face.'

'And I never did go back, at least not until long after we were married!' Becky smiled in distant gratitude.

'Now you know! And the only reason I am telling you my inner secrets is because I knew as soon as I saw you both coming out of the door that you had the same bond as Sal and I. You're younger and I just hope you'll to be as lucky as we have been.'

'What a lovely story' said Zahra, 'but I'm so glad that it has obviously worked out so well for you' she said. 'We've got lots of a different sorts of problems to get sorted, all logistics and distance!'

'Oh, come on, get real' scolded Becky. 'Don't worry about that, that's just details and you'll find a way to sort those out. The important thing is the solid ground of your relationship on which you both stand with total confidence and from which you view everything else around you' said Becky with authority.

Jules smiled at them both and suggested that this was all quite heady stuff on an empty stomach, something they should perhaps do something about before the restaurant closed.

Mecenate was Becky's favourite restaurant. Close to San Michele di Moriano, it was in a tall, five-storied villa that was in some obvious need of repair. The old terrace where they were given a glass of white wine bore all the signs of faded grandeur but the view over the crumbling balustrade was compellingly huge. There was no menu – you just ate what you were given at lunchtime. Becky said that the family had fallen on hard times after the war and had opened the restaurant rather than sell the family house. The old Contessa had done the cooking herself until her arthritis forced her to make way for the children.

The son emerged to say that they were ready for them. 'The helpings are generous so don't overdo it,' warned Becky 'or you'll not be able to walk until next week! Just one of the reasons why we love this place.'

The antipasti was all home grown and a little vinegary for Zahra's taste, a minor disappointment overwhelmed by three large bowls of different sorts of freshly made pasta. Each by itself would have been sufficient for a whole meal.

Jules said how sorry they were to have missed meeting Sal. Becky was sorry too as they would have liked him – but then she was biased.

Poor Sal, she explained had been having a very tough time since he was made redundant in April. He'd been quite senior in American Foods over here until they decided to switch their European headquarters to Germany and then used it as an excuse to ditch about half their senior and therefore well-paid staff.

'Beware the horrors of middle age!' she intoned. 'Worse still', she went on, 'the old Count had died leaving his affairs in one hell of a mess and poor Sal had been sorting it out ever since. The combination of the two meant that they might well have to move to somewhere else, certainly smaller. 'But then, what the hell! That's just details and as I said,' she added gazing over the view, 'it's what you are together that really counts in life!'

So would they have time to meet Sal before they left? Well,

sadly no as Becky was off to the States tomorrow to join him and spend the weekend with her mother in Texas. It was her mother's birthday and she was having a clam bake on Sunday with all the rich and rare of the district. Paula Wilmington, the new American President's wife was an old friend and so they'd been given no option but to be there. 'We may be poor but boy, are we well connected!' joked Becky with facetious irony.

Becky dropped them back at the villa and they said their goodbyes with all the fondness of an age-gap bridged by the new intimacy of open souls.

Jules put his arm round Zahra's shoulders and walked her round to the terrace overlooking the valley. 'You know' he said, 'that lady makes a lot of sense and I liked the way she put it. I know that you have been fretting about what Becky referred to as 'details' my darling, but she's right. That's exactly what they are, just transitory details. And with your new job, we already have the beginnings of a solution. The Bank will let you come back and forth very regularly and I shall have to see a bit of Uncle Hamid now that he's so important! It'll work out just fine, you'll see.'

'Jules,' said Zahra seriously 'of course I know you're both right, my darling love. But, up until today, I've played a sort of silly, teenage game of make-believe that I'll never have to be really separated from you. Like sticking my head in the sand, I suppose.'

'But now I know that the time I've dreaded is upon us, when we're going to be apart more than we're together, so we'll just have to be committed to making sure we take every opportunity. There will be a huge challenge when I get to Iran, it's what Papa has wanted for me, it's what I have to do and I suppose, if you like, it's time for me to face reality and earn my keep in every sense.'

PROLOGUE

TUESDAY 2ND NOVEMBER
Khalîl Mousavi's apartment, Farmaniyeh, Tehran

Once she had cleared the unexpectedly long immigration procedures, Zahra took a taxi from Imam Khomeini International airport some 30 kilometres south of Tehran. She specifically asked the driver to take her through the centre of the city, as this would give her a first glimpse of the main downtown areas, and would he please point out particular points of interest as they went.

Her father had warned her that it was not the most striking of cities but nevertheless she felt a shiver of excitement as some of the better-known historical landmarks were pointed out. This was, after all, the destination that had been so long-talked about; this was the beginning of a new and exciting chapter of fulfilment for her father and a challenge for herself. The opportunity was wide open and it was all there to play for.

The concierge let Zahra into her father's rented apartment in the northern suburb of Tehran and handed her an envelope containing a spare key. Khalîl was expected to be in China for a couple of weeks longer at least before returning to Paris for a few days to mothball their apartment. She would join him there to help with the shipment of most of their effects to Tehran. They were genuine immigrants.

Their temporary apartment was owned by a minor oil Sheik from Abu Dhabi with connections in the Iranian oil business that had been put on hold by the democratic coup. Furnished, it offered two bedrooms and was modern and comfortably appointed in keeping with the owner's paradoxical aspirations for a western lifestyle in the heart of the then Islamic republic.

Khalîl had chosen it for three reasons. Firstly, it was a sort-after area with quiet streets and well-constructed villas. Secondly, it was on the road to their old estate in the foothills to the north and, finally, it was just 200 yards away from Hamid Saiyeidi's own private apartment. It was also a 10-minute walk to the northern end of the metro system that offered an alternative to the chaotic traffic to and from the downtown areas.

Zahra unpacked and adjusted her alarm clock back the two and a half hours to Tehran time. Settling into the sofa, she called Jules's mobile which he answered almost immediately. He tried to sound upbeat but, by the time she got into bed, Zahra began to lament the distance now between them. For the first time, she felt genuinely separated from Jules, alone and a little bereft. He would be out in a couple of weeks time on an assignment which he had conveniently organised, seeing the leaders of the oil-producing companies, but now he felt on the other side of the world.

Two weeks suddenly seemed a long time but tomorrow was another day and, arguably, the start of the most meaningful period of her career to date. She had plenty to think about and went to sleep prioritising her 'to do list' once more.

The operations department of the Union des Banques Françaises in Paris had hired a small, serviced suite of offices for her to start with downtown between the Tehran Stock Exchange and the Glassware Museum. It gave her an immediate and ready-made working base together with secretarial back-up if she needed it and a conference room. It would do until Zahra could find more suitable space and the people to fill it.

Her first meeting on the Wednesday was scheduled at 16:00 with the lady who was the new Director of Bank Supervision, Farideh Hosseini, at the Central Bank of Iran. It was nearly three months on from the overthrow of the Mullahs but, sitting in the entrance hall awaiting her summons, it was clear from the number of files, filing cabinets, desks and chairs being manoeuvred past her that the installation of the new guard was still very much a work-in-progress.

After some ten minutes, she was ushered into an austere office where the Director of Banking Supervision received her with just a flicker of a smile as Zahra took her seat on the metal-framed chair in front of Hosseini's desk. There were no pictures on the walls and the Director had a solitary file in front of her on the desk.

'Welcome Mademoiselle Mousavi. The Central Bank of Iran was very pleased to receive the application from the Union des Banques Françaises together which its proposal for operations here in Iran. As you will probably be aware, we have received applications from many of the major international banking groups. At this time, however, the CBI proposes to extend banking licences to just eight foreign banks and I would therefore welcome your proposal and a slightly fuller explanation of what UBF can bring us than is contained in the file that has already been submitted.' Hosseini leaned back and looked at Zahra impassively.

'Indeed Madam Director' Zahra began, 'and on behalf of my bank, I welcome this opportunity to set out the spirit of what we hope to achieve here.' Zahra felt a glow of confidence. She knew every word of the proposal backwards but, more importantly, she clearly understood every aspect of the proposed plan as she had been its principal author.

'The core of our proposal rests on two principal elements, namely, facilitating inward investment in the form of both debt and equity finance, and assisting Iran's successful participation in the international energy markets.

Building on France's long-standing involvement with Iran and our own experience and presence in international financial markets, we will seek to offer a roadmap for Iran's institutions and companies to access the best possible international investors and partners.

There was a time, Madam Director, before the business world marched to the drumbeat of capital, when the most successful banks built their reputations on the strength of their client relationships and the clients themselves knew that their bankers first interest was the client's success and not their own immediate fee income.

It was a model built on trust and integrity that was, to a large extent, swept away in the first phase of the globalisation of the banking system – a phase that ended in the demise and well-documented destruction of some of the key players such as Lehman Brothers and other major banks around the world. While we of course have always had excellent access to capital resources, UBF stuck to its business model of relationship banking, at some cost to its expansion and potential profits during that phase. Consequently, it was among those global financial institutions which did not over-extend itself and, indeed, did not need to be bailed out by its government.

We have always prided ourselves on an in-depth understanding of each of our clients' strategies and business models, and their consequent banking requirements, whether that means identifying opportunities for the client, finding the right acquisitions or partners, or simply providing timely and appropriate funding to underwrite their progress. Moreover, it is an unchangeable policy that we will not take on a client unless we feel we can add value. At the same time, our relationships with the various markets are equally

PROLOGUE

important. We undertake to protect our counterparties' interests in the context of what they do with us, and we do not mislead our market partners so now they have confidence to rely on our reputation and integrity that we have built over many years of trading. Our philosophy is therefore based on close involvement with the day-to-day affairs of our clients, offering them excellent access to all the markets in which we specialise.

As you of course will be aware, we have a particular specialisation in the energy sector that stretches from the futures markets to financing stocks of crude oil. We have developed an in-depth knowledge of the global environmental sector which we believe is going to be a key driving force for at least the next 25 years and, through our US subsidiaries, we have a clear view of various technology and medical sectors to which we pay particular attention.

Madame Director, these sectors are also of key importance to Iran's development and we hope to work closely with the people here who need the knowledge and experience we can offer to help them make the right decisions. To that end, as relationships develop, we will commit more senior people on the ground here, constantly backed up by our full, integrated and global resources encompassing market research, development and trade finance and syndication.

You have the details of our phased plan in the file in front of you and I would be happy to expand on any aspect of it that needs further explanation. Personally, as I'm sure you are aware, I am deeply committed to Iran's successful economic development in order to fulfil the potential that we have in this country and to repair the travesties of the last 50 years. You can therefore count on me personally to make sure that all UBF's resources will be brought to bear on achieving that goal.' Zahra opened her palms to signify her pledge.

Farideh Hosseini regarded Zahra without emotion for a few seconds, motionless supporting her chin on both fists. Then she leaned forward.

'Mademoiselle Mousavi, we need a number of different elements from our international banking partners, some of which support the State itself, some of which provide services for our people that we cannot offer ourselves, and some of which enrich our economy and trade. I have read your detailed submission of course but I place far greater importance on the spirit behind any plan and the expansion of the many aspects of trade that it can encourage. I therefore value in particular, your personal commitment to Iran which I know to be real and the clarity of your own purpose. I will therefore now pass the dossier to the Deputy Director with the appropriate recommendation. It has been a pleasure to meet you; please keep in touch.'

With that, Farideh Hosseini stood up and smiled warmly as she came round the desk to shake Zahra's hand. 'We will meet again!'

As Zahra walked up the street towards the metro station to go home, she felt a fresh zing of relief, achievement and fulfilment. Her baby was on the its way; she had her hands on the wheel!

It was a clear, dry evening and, consulting her map quickly, she decided to walk an extra stop before taking the train. This was her town now, her stage to play on and, after all the years of study and application, her platform for success. She wanted to drink in the people and the atmosphere, try to touch the excitement of the new freedom that people now enjoyed after more than 50 years of one form of oppressive regime or another, to luxuriate in her pride in her father's contribution for bringing all of it to reality.

PROLOGUE

There was so much to do here now, so many fields needed ploughing, surely there must be a place for Jules in all this, surely his uncle, their dear friend and supporter, would want Jules to be a part of all this!

She half-jokingly put it down to telepathy when, after she had been back in the flat for no more than five minutes, Hamid called to apologise for not having picked her up from the airport the previous evening. Had she spoken to Jules? How had the meeting with the Central Bank gone? What were her immediate plans? Sorry that her father was away, Hamid too was somewhat tied up for the next two days but what about meeting on Sunday evening? Just two blocks up the hill. They had to be vigilant, he stressed. It was important that was no hint of either nepotism or cronyism. Therefore no favours, no special treatment, nothing that could be used against them politically. Zahra was more than capable of excelling on her own without anyone's help. So much to build! Shouldn't they persuade Jules to join them in the cause?

TUESDAY 20TH NOVEMBER
Zahra's temporary Offices, Tehran

From the mundanity of looking at potential office space, interviewing a receptionist or a bookkeeper, to setting up initial appointments with chief executives or financial officers of the companies UBF needed to target, Zahra thrived on the process of creation. Because that's what it was, from scratch.

Each appointment made, each hand shaken, was all progress.

Zahra always knew that she had an advantage in the contacts and connections that she had that other people would crave but she hadn't traded on that nor did she intend to now. She didn't need to, she had her own message.

There was a world outside Iran that people here needed to recognise for what it could do for them. And she could bring it to them. She'd been there but she was on their side and so she could help them. It was a kind of crusade. After all the years of the West being demonised, myths had to be shattered, bubbles burst and harmony and trust re-established. The long nights listening to her father's recriminations about the destruction of hope in Iran, her own experiences of France and Britain, and the multi-national melee at INSEAD, had all reinforced her belief that she could be an instrument of reconciliation, that she could bring together differing views, within a kind of tower of Babel set in the midst of cultural and economic mistrust, a beacon of Abrahamic compromise.

Her father had always told her that to be a true entrepreneur, she needed zeal! Her time had come and now it consumed her.

Khalîl Mousavi was in Beijing tying up the paperwork associated with the deal Hamid had struck that linked their loans to Iranian supply of oil. The loans were effectively prepayments based on a fixed oil price. Interest was also paid in kind thereby nominally satisfying Islamic law. It was all routine but her father had called her over the weekend to say that the Chinese had approached him about the possibility of them making further direct loans to finance infrastructure programmes in Iran. He had suggested they call Zahra directly as he was not a banker himself and felt that any direct involvement could have political ramifications down the line.

PROLOGUE

By the time Mr Li Tong, a personal assistant to one of the Assistant Ministers at the Chinese Finance Ministry, called her later in the morning, Zahra had already pencilled out a potential structure.

After the usual pleasantries, Mr Tong came to the point. The Chinese were very happy with the oil-based structure that President Saiyeidi had come up with for the initial loans and would be interested to increase their commitment substantially if the opportunity arose. They would be particularly interested if Mademoiselle Mousavi could come up with a similar type of format.

Mademoiselle Mousavi replied that she would be delighted to consider appropriate ideas and get back to them within 48 hours with some initial suggestions.

Zahra's father had said that the Chinese economy was already motoring again after the 'recession' years when it only grew at 5% and the central Chinese concern was securing guaranteed sources of supply for their burgeoning energy needs. Price was a secondary consideration.

When she called his number, Mr Tong answered the phone directly with a great and lengthy expression of gratitude for her swift reply. Zahra outlined her thoughts which she had already passed by her boss in Paris and, unofficially, Uncle Hamid as well.

Iran's oil exports are targeted to reach 5m *barrels per day* by the end of the next year. China's consumption is currently scheduled to reach 10m *bpd* by the same time, of which 60% will be imported. Iran would set up a new agency, the Iran Oil Corporation, and would guarantee it a minimum supply of 2m *bpd*. China would buy a contracted minimum of 2m *bpd* at a 2.5% discount to the prevailing market price with a floor at $40. Anything over

2m *bpd* would be at the prevailing market price (same floor).

Zahra said she believed that this would underwrite 20% of China's current import requirements while committing nearly 40% of Iranian oil exports. She believed that this reflected the growing, special relationship with China. Payment would be one calendar quarter in advance i.e. a prepayment of at least $9bn a quarter.

'Thank you. Most interesting proposal, most interesting Mademoiselle Mousavi. Much talking here now to be achieved,' he said simply. 'How soon you must know?'

'Ah, Mr Tong!' exclaimed Zahra (wondering now who was this supposed personal assistant giving his own instant opinion on a $36bn deal), 'This is just the broad outline of what we think we can achieve for you Mr Tong, just the broad principles you understand. There will need to be much discussion of the detail.

I am going back to Paris at the end of the week. Perhaps you can let me know whether you think such an arrangement would be of interest in principle when I return seven days from now and, if so, the detailed discussions can then commence at once.'

'Good, very good Mademoiselle Mousavi. Will call personally by end of seven days as suggested' Mr Tong said and immediately rang off.

Zahra put down the phone and smiled. There was obviously a very long way to go before the ink was dry on a deal like this but they had a definite starting point now around which discussions would follow. Zahra had previously worked out that, if it went ahead, the deal would represent approximately 17% of Iranian GNP. Not bad for starters! The downside of course, if UBF managed to pull it off, was that it would be an impossibly hard act to follow.

Best of all though, she thought returning to immediate matters, Jules arrived tonight on assignment to interview the major oil industry players starting in the morning, so it would be interesting to compare notes when they were back in Paris together – one way traffic only of course – all being fair in love and war!

Ironically, given the last three weeks of separation, Zahra was leaving Tehran early tomorrow for meetings back at head office. Georges Dufour, her *President Directeur Général* had phoned her personally to ask her to lunch with him alone on Friday before making a presentation on her progress to the Management Board in the afternoon.

But tonight would have nothing to do with work. She was on a roll but it still seemed an aching age since she had seen Jules and she needed him badly. He had promised to be there by 19:30 at the very latest. Now, just like a teenager again, she couldn't wait.

THURSDAY 22ND NOVEMBER 11:15
Hamid Saiyeidi's apartment, Farmaniyeh, Tehran

Hamid's private apartment here was not far removed from the former royal palaces of the Qajar dynasty and in some ways reflected the survival of the wider Saiyeidi family fortunes through all the vicissitudes of the Shah's police State and the purges of the Ayatollah's that had followed. Iran was not blessed with one of the world's loveliest capitals, he reflected sadly. Pollution, traffic jams, chronic overcrowding and a lack of responsible planning had all helped to make Tehran a metropolis that even the most effusive travel agent had difficulty praising. Nevertheless, this had now become the forum for his life's ambitions.

It was really his mother's country. She had never accepted Paris as anything but a gilded exile and yearned for the dry, barren hills of her childhood. He remembered that she had startled him one day, years back, after an Iran Air airbus had been shot down by the USS Vincennes, by saying that if she had been allowed to be on it, at least she would have been on her way to Mecca and would have died in the company of other Iranian pilgrims, at least 'among her own'.

Brought up immersed in his mother's corrosive bitterness created by the American betrayal of Mossadeq's democracy in 1953 and the subsequent massacre of his father, Hamid himself had few strong religious impulses. He had acquired a working appreciation of French Catholicism by association during his years in the Paris Lyceé but had never got involved; Anglican Protestantism barely impinged on his university years at Oxford, save that is for a couple of his friends whose own insecurities had driven them into the arms of the evangelicals. Their unquestioning commitment, he later recognised, had significant parallels with fanatical elements of the mullah's Islamic regime in Iran. Both doctrines were able to command extreme loyalty until the harsher realities of life or economic hardship punctured the adherents' fervour.

From their exile in Paris, Hamid had taken up the reins of the family property portfolio, liquidating many of the physical assets that his murdered father had acquired. The portfolio had done well but Hamid had recognised that the real estate market was now global and that he had neither the time nor local expertise to take best advantage of it. Instead, as the physical assets in France were liquidated, he selected a small number of professionals in Europe and the US with proven records in running diversified property portfolios. Their brief was to take the proceeds and re-invest with a target of producing a smoothed, internal return of over 10%. Hamid had chosen well and the portfolios had substantially outperformed the targets so that by the 1990s, the Saiyeidi family future was already financially secure for generations to come – exactly what Hamid had always taken to be his father's original intention.

It was, however, an enduring irony for the bachelor Hamid that the Saiyeidi family looked unlikely to survive as such, let alone for generations, thus removing the need for sustainable financial security which had never once seemed even remotely an issue.

He was the sole surviving male and despite his forays with the ladies of Parisian society, he had never felt able to commit to marriage and so, in a sense, his sister and her family took on a more central role in his private life.

Hamid's association with Khalîl also went back many years now.

Uncomfortable with some of the increasingly extreme aspirations of the Mojahedin's leadership, Khalîl had declined to join the move to Iraq in 1986 demanded by the French government after it had concluded a lucrative trade deal with the Ayatollahs. He ostensibly broke away from the movement at the same time that he began to build his friendship with Hamid. The two had immediately forged an understanding as gilded refugees, trusting each other's seriousness and, together, unconsciously developed a mutual yearning to become citizens of a liberated, democratic and fully independent Iran. Their Persian dream had been crafted over many months of careful, unseen planning. In the end, Hamid's leadership of their cause came down simply to his wider circle of the right people and the fact that his grandfather had already established the family's political credentials as one of Mossadeq's ministers. That said, he had long maintained that Khalîl's virtuosity as a political writer could just as easily have held sway.

It seemed a long road already trod but here they now were on the brink of the first democratic elections since 1953. Khalîl would be permanently by his side once he had concluded matters in Paris which would happen any day now and, to their mutual delight, his daughter had immediately made her mark with everyone she had met since her arrival just a few weeks ago. And Jules? There was so much for him here now but Hamid was certainly not going to tread on his brother-in-law's toes. Jules already had his family duty mapped out for him back in France when he chose to cease being a journalist. But who knows? Hamid needed an heir and he was sure that Jules understood his unspoken ambition for him. Jules was here on his first visit to the homeland and obviously keen to find ways of spending time here with Zahra. Just give it time, he mused as he listened now to his nephew digging for information about his girlfriend's activities.

'Yes uncle, she said that you knew all about it and if I really wanted to know, I'd better ask you!' Jules said slightly indignantly.

'Well Jules, wearing my official hat, I am delighted but not surprised that Zahra has lived up to my expectations as far as discretion is concerned. There has to be a strict separation between work and pleasure and frankly, I would have been astounded if Zahra had chosen to discuss sensitive details of her work with anyone outside it – including you! To you journalists, information is a tradable commodity, to those whose livelihoods or existence depends on it, it is private!'

'That's a bit harsh uncle! You know I am a model of discretion.

Anyway, she's clearly had an encouraging start and seems now totally committed to the project.'

'Jules, I haven't said anything to her yet but frankly I am bursting with pride. I've tried a couple of times to talk to Khalîl who's been in China to tell him about the feedback I've had because, for him, it would really be the partial fulfilment of his dream. From a business and, indeed, a political standpoint, Zahra looks like one of those very rare people who can excel across the board.

There is nothing that gives me greater pleasure than hearing good things about either of you from unbiased, unconnected individuals. Suffice it to say that, if either the Ministry of Finance or Energy, or the Central Bank could employ her, they'd do it like a shot. She has attracted attention wherever she has gone as being personable, relaxed, intelligent, and effective at her job, but, above all, she is straightforward and patently honest. All rare qualities that make her uniquely popular here already. I know I'm biased but I'm also thrilled for both of us. Don't ever lose her!'

Jules was pleased that she was doing so well but the force of his uncle's eulogy took him by surprise and, for a second, raised his competitive hackles.

'No uncle, don't you worry, I have no intention of doing so! So anyway, Zahra apart, how's it going?'

'Jules, it is really very exciting. It's early days but the enthusiasm in the streets, in the media – everywhere, is almost tangible. It feels like a dam has burst letting loose a torrent of rejoicing and hope. It won't last of course. Freedom brings its own challenges but at least the innate fear on the streets has evaporated.

Nearly that is. Apparently there is an unfolding Israeli plot to attack us before the elections and destroy our nuclear installations as well as murdering half the government-in-waiting. It will be fronted by a group of disaffected Mojahedin but it is really Israel who is behind it and financing it.'

'How long have you known?' asked Jules with immediate concern.

'Oh, we've known for a bit as (completely off the record) one of the Mojahedin is an agent of ours. So we are ready for them, we're just not sure exactly when yet but it could be as soon as this weekend. So, just as well you and the Mousavi's are going to be in Paris!

Now look Jules, I'm really sorry but because of all this business something has come up and I can't have lunch with you. It's all on the table there waiting for you and I have asked my personal driver to take you to the airport. Your mother would kill me if you missed your plane as I know you've got a big weekend ahead of you at home!'

With that Hamid embraced his nephew and made for the door. Opening it, he stopped and turned back to Jules. 'You know, you really should think about spending a bit of time out here. There are going to be huge opportunities and we could use someone like you Jules – joking apart. Talk to Zahra about it. She understands exactly!'

PROLOGUE

SUNDAY 25TH NOVEMBER, 19:30HRS
Jules de Villarosa's apartment – Rue de la Faisanderie, Paris 16ème

The traffic on the autoroute from Orleans had been heavy and almost static on the Périphérique from the Porte de Versailles onwards. It always was on Sunday nights as if the whole of Paris was trying to return from the weekend simultaneously. Orleans was only just over an hour by train but someone would have to fetch him and take him back to the station and Jules particularly disliked the Metro on a Sunday night – it was always deserted except for tramps and tourists.

He had told Zahra that he would be back at seven o'clock and had expected her to be there before him. Zahra had been meant to go down to his parents with him that weekend for the first pheasant shoot of the season but she had had an important meeting at UBF on Friday and today, her father had wanted her to meet a professor visiting from Tehran. He had been a friend of his farm manager and wanted help in establishing a student exchange programme with France. She had said that it was very much a formal duty so she'd have supper ready by the time he arrived.

It had been a busy weekend of entertaining. On Friday night, his father had about half the guns and their wives staying in the chateau for the shoot on the Saturday morning. Jules had raced directly down to the Chateau after his plane landed at 18:30 and he thanked the Lord that it came into Orly allowing him to miss the traffic coming from Charles de Gaulle. There was a large dinner party attended by some local friends who would also be shooting the following day as his father liked to make sure everyone already knew each other beforehand. It made the day itself so much more relaxed.

None of the house party had left until after tea this afternoon and Jules had apologised to his parents for rushing off at the same time as the guests but 'Zahra would be waiting for him'.

Throwing his weekend bag into the bedroom, Jules plugged his laptop back in and checked his answerphone. A message from Zahra calmed the apprehension he always felt if she was not exactly where she said she would be, given the situation in Tehran. Left on Saturday evening, the message explained that apparently the professor would be a little later than planned but she should be with him by nine o'clock and she'd make passionate love to him when she arrived to make up for being late.

He smiled and looked in the fridge. Zahra had already prepared a ratatouille and pasta salad for their Sunday night tryst, so he returned to his computer and checked his emails with an open a bottle of white wine when the telephone rang.

'Jules, is Zahra with you? his uncle asked anxiously without preamble. 'You've seen the reports?!'

Hamid explained urgently that the rumours of a coup attempt had proved spot on and the last pockets of the Mojahedin group they had talked about were being rounded up at that moment. There had indeed been an Israeli team of nuclear scientists with the group that had attacked the nuclear installations so Israel was definitely behind it. But where were Zahra and her father. He'd tried to reach Khalîl but could get no reply. Was Zahra with Jules?

'No, she's with Khalîl, but why?' Jules asked, alarm now flooding his voice.

Hamid said that they already had received reports that some of the principal members of the interim administration and some key associates around the world had been assassinated and Khalîl wasn't answering! Could he leave it with Jules?

In quick succession, Jules tried Khalîl's apartment, his mobile and then Zahra's mobile. No answer from any of them, just the usual message service, so he left Zahra a message. Now, five minutes on and close to a state of shock, Jules decided to go and find her, something was very wrong. He could feel fear gripping his throat when the door bell rang.

Thank the Lord, he thought, glancing at the clock, noting that, not only had she obviously forgotten her key, she was also a quarter of an hour ahead of herself – which was rare. Relieved and preparing to comment on the unreliability of ladies' timekeeping and their forgetfulness, Jules was stunned as he opened the door to find a dark-suited man outside. Surprise turned instantly to alarm as the man produced his police ID.

'Good evening monsieur, I am Inspector Lépine from the Prefecture of Police. I am afraid there has been a very unpleasant incident and, I'm sorry but we believe you may be able to help us.'

The next passage of time, 15 minutes probably, passed for Jules in a strange kind of mental echo chamber that twisted everything into an unreal, detached kaleidoscope. It was probably the shock of his worst nightmare materialising so quickly and unexpectedly. Accustomary, comfortable normality suddenly shattering into hideous shards of this new reality. He could function but he could not react. He had fetched his jacket. He checked that he had his keys, his *carte d'identité*, his mobile phone and his diary. He checked the lights, he checked his keys again. Leaving the apartment, he remembered the keys to Zahra's apartment as well. So he carried out all his checks once more.

The inspector led him to the car which pulled away from the curb heading east. Jules exclaimed that he needed to call his father but Inspector Lépine assured him that it would not be necessary as his father was on his way to meet them. Lépine explained that they had found Jules's name in Zahra's diary listing him as her fiancée and next of kin but there was no address so they had traced him through his father at home.

Struggling to maintain his self-control, Jules tried to prepare himself for what was coming, checking his reactions, stifling his emotions and the shock. He asked Lépine calmly to take him through precisely what had happened before he had to confront the physical horror of the consequences head-on.

Lépine sensed his anxiety and did not disguise the facts.

In the early hours of the morning, the Associated Press office had received a handwritten fax claiming that the *Sons of Islam* had carried out the execution of two Mojahedin traitors and that their bodies could be found on the Pont Alexandre. Naturally, AP correspondents stole a march on the police. 'They were already swarming over the scene like locusts when I arrived' Lépine said, with the deep-felt distaste of someone forced to deal with the tabloid appetites of the press too frequently.

The machine-gunned and deliberately mutilated bodies had been stripped naked, tied together, booby-trapped and then hung 15 metres below the bridge to create maximum publicity and also maximum inconvenience to the authorities. Lépine apologised for his bluntness but felt it was best; it might mitigate the inevitable impact of what was to come. The man, he said, had had a note tied round his neck identifying him as the traitor Khalîl Mousavi. The rest was simple deduction.

Jules pursed his lips together hard and looked straight ahead.

As the black Citroen swept under the arch and into an inner courtyard on the Ile de la Cité, Jules saw his father waiting for them outside the double doors of the entrance. The car slowed and he felt his stomach heave and his resolve implode Biting his lower lip hard to staunch the tears as they suddenly welled up, loosened by the proximity of his father's embrace, and only half succeeding, he got out of the car and clasped his father in a tight hug, unable to speak lest the words themselves burst the dam. His father held him tight, just as he used to as a boy and then, with his arm round Jules's shoulder, guided him after the Inspector into the building.

While they sat in an ante room waiting for the Inspector to return, his father finally spoke. 'Jules,' he said softly 'let me spare you this; let me do this for you.' Jules tried to force his mouth into a grateful smile, shaking his head, still unable to speak.

When the Inspector returned, he led Jules gently into the viewing area. Jules starred vacantly at the horror before him on the mortuary slab and simply nodded.

Before him lay the embodiment of his aspirations, his future, his life's hopes – all horrifically mutilated. But as he stared at the shrouded corpses, rage unconsciously kindled a passionate fire within him. Whimpering sorrow was definitely not what Zahra deserved from him now. The bastards, the ranting, fanatical, half-human bastards! Neanderthal sick creatures! But if they wanted a fight, well now they would have one. It would be his fight and he would have vengeance in her name and bloodier the better! He would personally punish those who had perpetrated this obscenity, these Mojahedin scum, their meddling Israeli mentors and collaborators and anyone who henceforth gave them succour.

His father watched as Jules turned, jaw fixed, grim faced, away from the bodies. There was no sorrow in his eyes, just a lifeless stare of rigid determination. He still had said nothing. It wasn't a normal reaction.

By the time that Hugo de Villarosa got his son back to his apartment, he knew that anger was the only force preventing his son's collapse and that his insistence on speaking to his uncle was probably as good a way to channel it as any.

It was late, the middle of the night in Tehran but he knew that Hamid would still be in the thick of it and would be horrified if he were not called, president or not. He had a deep fondness for his brother-in-law and was well aware that Hamid had always regarded Jules like a son and the Mousavis almost as family. Jules in turn had never hidden the veneration in which he held his uncle. He would need him now. The irony of the whole situation was macabre.

When he got through, he congratulated Hamid briefly on the crushing of the coup attempt and then gave the outline of the murders on the Pont Alexandre. He could instantly sense the rage emanating from the other end of the line and swiftly agreed to put Jules on. Jules listened to his uncle for a few minutes, nodding occasionally.

'That's all fine Uncle but now we have to formulate an appropriate response. I want to be a part of that and so I'll come out as soon as I have sorted out the Mousavi's affairs.' He nodded a couple more times and said good-bye.

Jules turned to his father fighting back the tears again. 'Papi, thanks for being there. I know what you're going to say but please understand that this is something I have to do and that I will do. After that, life may begin again and then we'll look at everything, and I do mean everything – but when I get back.'

PROLOGUE

FRIDAY, 30TH NOVEMBER: 12 NOON
King's Reach, West End, Tortola, British Virgin Islands

King's Reach is a private place. The estate occupies nearly 10 acres of mostly wooded hilltop surrounded by a 12-foot, electrified fence backed up by motion sensors placed randomly round the perimeter. As an iconic, British, oil entrepreneur whose successes had stirred envy and resentment around the globe, Sir Jeremy Reynolds liked his privacy.

The telephone rang quietly in a corner of the room.

'Ah! At last, it seems that our American friends are just coming in. Look, you can see the chopper to the left of that peak' said Sir Jeremy excusing himself. Putting down his glass, he walked through the coolness of the echoing stone hall to the front door and out into the shimmering heat of the helipad behind the stables.

Jeremy had taken an unexplained call from an old American friend, Walter Baumgartner, while on a routine visit to Oslo two days ago. Walter knew King's Reach from old and suggested it would be an ideally discrete venue for a meeting that Dean Armitage wanted to set up with some high-level Israeli contacts of his.

'Jeremy, I'm so sorry, we're a little behind schedule. The plane was held up getting into Puerto Rica but we're here now and I trust no damage was done. Our Israeli colleagues arrived OK? Oh, do excuse me, Jeremy, could I introduce my good friend Dean Armitage whose law firm has looked after our family for ever and now keeps me straight as well – that is, when he's not doing the same for Defense.' Baumgartner paused as Armitage shook his host's hand.

Dean Armitage was a distinguished looking man, probably

in his 70s, a patrician who exuded quiet charm and understated good taste. His handshake was firm without being forceful, a true American cousin. 'Jeremy, it's very good to meet you. Walter has told me lots about you.'

'Nothing good I trust' Jeremy replied 'but you're very welcome all the same! Your Israeli colleagues have preceded you by some 20 minutes and I suggest we join them before they finish the rest of the Bloody Mary. Made especially for you of course – no clam juice down here though I'm afraid!'

'Dean, you take it from here,' said Walter as they crossed the hall, 'it's your show now, we'll just be good ol' oil boys.'

The Israelis rose correctly as they entered the room, Joseph Kleiner's hand outstretched. 'Dean, good to see you again; it's so very kind of you to come down at such short notice,' he began 'and this must be your friend from the Institute you told me about. May I present my close friend and colleague Ariel Ben-Ezra who is a prominent member of our defense community? I particularly wanted him to meet you as it was really as a result of his assessment of the emerging Iranian threat that we decided that we must finally take action.

Holding the tall crystal jug of Bloody Mary, Jeremy intervened to fill the Americans' glasses. 'Gentlemen, I thought you might want to use my study which has a small conference table where you can spread yourselves out a bit and get started. As it's Saturday anyway, I've given the staff the day off but our old housekeeper will bring you some sandwiches up in due course. I can assure you that she's 100% reliable.'

Jeremy led the party a couple of doors down the hall to a room fitted with pine shelves crammed with old and new books of all descriptions. The darkness of the books enveloping the room seemed to intensify the bright light from the window. An imposing knee-hole desk stood in front of it. An inlayed oval mahogany table occupied the centre of the room with six matching chairs. Six notepads and pencils lay ready for use.

'Let me know if there is anything you need gentlemen' said Sir Jeremy making for the door, 'I'll be in the drawing room catching up on some paperwork.'

The Americans and Israelis sat down either side of the table and Dean Armitage arranged his notepad in front of him. He looked at Joseph Kleiner expectantly, 'Well Joe, you've got us all the way down here, so what can we do for you?'

'Well Dean, as you cannot have missed' began Kleiner, 'we have just suffered something of a reverse in Iran as the Mojahedin group that we backed proved inadequate to the task of decommissioning the Iranian nuclear facilities, let alone overthrowing the interim regime. Things are now set in stone over there as Saiyeidi was duly installed as democratically elected President yesterday with a massive vote of public confidence as we all know. Ironically, he probably owes much of that to us or rather our failure! But I will get straight to the point as I know that we are all under time pressure.

As a result of intelligence coordinated in recent months by Ariel, we are persuaded that Iran now represents a substantial nuclear threat to Israel and a rapidly growing threat to even the US mainland itself. We passed most of this on to CIA so you may already be aware of it.'

Dean interrupted him, 'Joe, you know that I am just a consultant to Defense. Edwin Rich, our Secretary of Defense has been a confidant of mine for years but even he doesn't give me access to all those secret papers.'

'Yes, yes,' Joe continued, 'that may be the case but what you do have is intimate access to the Wilmington family and, in this case, that is what we need most. The point is that no one on your side seems to be taking our intelligence seriously!

It appears that the new regime in Tehran is under Saiyeidi, however democratic and fine their domestic programmes may appear – and we all remember the Hamas experience – the country still appears intent on developing its nuclear capability that confers not only huge regional power but also, already, the ability to strike directly at our major cities in Israel. This is an intolerable situation for us but, because of the distances involved, our problem is that we cannot guarantee the same comprehensive outcome as say, we achieved at Osiraq back in '81. If we try to take out all their missile sites ourselves and fail, they would respond. That was why we were prepared to sanction the close-quarters, Mojahedin operation.'

'Bet that took a bit of rapid spin to sort out in the Knesset when it broke!' laughed Dean somewhat maliciously.

'Dean' Joe pressed on ignoring the dig, 'you and I have discussed the evolving nuclear problem for some time now, always with the same conclusion. What's changed now is that, as of last week, we understand that the Shahab-8 ICBM can be expected to be deployed in the next 12 to 18 months. Our intelligence affirms that it will be capable of a payload of nuclear warheads and, with the new North Korean guidance systems, could be capable of reaching all parts of the USA.

This therefore is the point of no return – the tipping point. Either we find a way to neutralise the Iranian nuclear programme before its destructive threat is irreversible or we will enter a new type of cold war where 'mutually assured destruction' in the Middle East will severely inhibit Israel's scope of operations and, just as important – as of last week, the security of homeland USA itself.

It has to be stopped well before that point which means action now.' Joe paused laying his hands, palms upwards on the table for effect, 'And bluntly, that means that it has to be you Americans. They can hit us but they can't reach you – yet' Joe ended decisively

'How much incontrovertible evidence do we actually have to support all this because what the US simply couldn't risk is another intelligence catastrophe like Iraq?' asked Dean seriously.

'Mossad says that all aspects of the intelligence have been cross-checked and corroborated independently – it's rock solid Dean and we can supply chapter and verse whenever you need it' replied Joe. 'But Dean, this time I need you. We want you personally to make sure that the message gets delivered right to the President's fireside and is properly understood by him.'

'Well' reflected Dean, 'I know that it won't take much to get Wilmington on board despite his woolly views at the time of the invasion of Iraq. I think that you should get Rich leading the charge from Defence while I go round the back to make sure the message is getting through. For good measure, we'll organise a couple of authoritative papers from our friends on the National Security Council. If your estimates are even half right, the security of the United States is under direct threat again. We simply could not afford not to act!'

'Gentlemen,' said Joe Kleiner looking at his watch, 'I know that we can rely on you to get things done – just as we always do. We'll supply the evidence and you make sure it's presented effectively. In the meantime, we'll make sure that the Lobby is galvanised into action.'

TUESDAY 6TH DECEMBER, 12 NOON.
Steps of the White House, Washington DC

Its was a mild December day in Washington when President Wilmington and the Prime Minister of Israel emerged through the bow windows to stand at the top of the steps before the assembled Press corps. Behind them, senior members of the Cabinet filed out led by Edwin Rich the hawkish Secretary of Defense and his deputy followed by the Israeli ambassador and senior members of AIPAC and the Jewish lobby in Washington.

Approaching the bank of microphones, the President addressed the world.

'Ladies and Gentlemen,' he began, 'I am proud today to stand before you, shoulder to shoulder with our great friend and ally here from Israel. The conflict that Israel faces is all part of a struggle that we in the Unites States are engaged in too. The modern United States is shaped today in no mean part by generations of Jewish achievement and blood.'

The free world is now in peril as never before! The struggle today is clearly between radical, extremist Islamic forces throughout the world, particularly in the Middle East, and Western values, standards and beliefs – everything that we stand for.

As you all know, Iran has been determined to build nuclear weapons for some years now. There is no doubt that the principal threat of these weapons in the past was directed towards the State of Israel. But now it has become clear that Iran will shortly have the capability to strike at will anywhere in the world and I have no illusions that that means us here in the Unites States of America.

For Israel, it already presents a daily peril that menaces its citizens and families in their homes and in their streets. For us here, that peril is also about to become a daily reality too. Unless we act.

The new government in Iran has stated that it has no intention of giving up these deadly weapons that so threaten to destabilise the region and now the whole world and, as we have said in the past, that is fundamentally unacceptable. That has never been truer than today.

As Hamas has shown us in Palestine, democracy by itself is not the panacea to evil. We had hoped that the 'Arab Spring' would produce progress towards real democracy in the Middle East but we are still waiting. Democracy by itself is only a first step to full citizenship of the world community but much more progress is needed if a country is to earn the lasting trust of its peers.

In confirming the existence of its nuclear weapons, Iran has, in effect, announced its aggressive intent towards the State of Israel and no one should believe that this country will allow such aggression, or the threat of it, to stand.

The world is aware that recent attempts by freedom-loving members of the Mojahedin to overthrow the Tehran regime were repulsed. I wish to make clear here today that we applaud Israel's backing to the operation that promised to free the region from the tyranny of this new regime.'

Wilmington paused and looked directly at the cameras. Raising his right hand as someone might taking an oath, he continued, 'In recognition of the rightness of their cause, I pledge today that if, by the end of June this coming year, Iran refuses to dismantle its nuclear arsenal and submit to scrutiny by international inspectors to verify their destruction, this country will take on and execute that responsibility itself and by force of arms if necessary.

We cannot in all conscience do otherwise.

Thank you' the President finished abruptly.

Without affording the journalists time for any questions, Wilmington shook the Prime Minister's hand and, unsmiling, turned and retreated inside the White House.

It was as close to a public declaration of war that most people had heard in recent history. The President had intended the message, in support of his chief Middle East ally, to be loud and clear. It was.

In Jerusalem, Joe Kleiner turned off his television and smiled. The pincer grip of the embittered neo-conservative remnants of the old Bush era and of the Jewish Lobby was still breathtaking. Just days after the humiliating calamity in Iran, Israel now had absolute backing, with guarantees, that the Iranian threat would be made to disappear one way or the other. It was a comfortable position to be in. Ironic though, he thought, the United States could still make this statement with complete impunity. Even if Iran's missiles could now reach Tel Aviv, they would probably not have the full missile technology to reach Washington for at least another decade – no matter what Ariel had suggested to Dean Armitage.

In Paris, Jules also turned off his television. He had spent all day collecting most of Zahra's clothes that remained in the apartment and a few possessions ready to go to charity. Wilmington's open support for her murderers was both painful and repugnant. Worse still was the arrogance of the assumption that he could simply direct policy around the globe without serious consequence at home. As the rest of the evening wore on, it began to dawn on Jules that Wilmington's assumption of impunity might just be the weakness that could be exploited to avenge Zahra's butchers and begin to assuage his burning anger.

PROLOGUE

TUESDAY, 15TH DECEMBER, 17:45
Hamid Saiyeidi's apartment, Farmaniyeh, Tehran

In the dying embers of a cloudless December dusk, Hamid Saiyeidi gazed on the Plane trees now shorn of their palmately lobed leaves that gathered in rustling drifts in the street below. Older bark had peeled off in thin strips revealing patches of pale yellow within, a sight that could be found right across Europe. It was the same sight that that had greeted him from the family apartment overlooking the Bois de Boulogne in Paris, his home for a lifetime – the same trees that had greeted him from his house close to Grosvenor Square in London.

As he pondered in the gloaming, he was keenly aware of the enormity of the challenge the US threat now represented. The challenge was magnified by the personal vacuum that had been left by the hideous murder of his closest friend, his co-architect of Iran's new democracy and his kinsman, Khalîl, together with his adored daughter. It was as if the inner sanctum of all their hopes had been violated and both Jules and he had been manacled and forced to watch. It was never said between Khalîl and himself but, together, they been a peerless team and the young were surely going to unite them as family. The sheer horror of their massacre made the loss so much more emotional, so much more poignant and hard to deal with.

As he was now horribly aware, it had been at his own suggestion that Khalîl had kept precautionary channels open to the MEK's headquarters in Iraq at Camp Ashraf – a decision that, together with meticulous observation of their activities by the Pasdaran agent in Paris, had proved to be fatal. It was a guilt that Hamid would never assuage.

However, he was the newly elected President with an overwhelming mandate. He had been given the unique opportunity to unlock his mother country's latent potential; something that few people are privileged to do in a lifetime. But first, the country had to be secured from outside intervention and, following the aggressive tone of Wilmington's speech, that danger was now imminent and real.

The Ayatollahs had been able to fight off Saddam's attempts for regional aggrandisement and Sunni advancement back in the 1980s but at a huge cost in lives. Now his people were faced again with the military might of the world's only superpower. If, notwithstanding the welcome easing of tensions during the Obama era, America now really refused to heed the lessons of Iraq, his senior military commanders pointed out that Iran could be facing invasion by a country whose defense budget was now running at more than $500 billion annually – twice as much as the rest of the world put together!

George W. Bush was effectively defeated in Iraq by the combination of appalling post-conflict planning, a catastrophic haemorrhaging of support at home and the near universal disapproval outside his small group of allies internationally. Wilmington, the newly elected Republican president, was unlikely to make the same mistake at the planning level even if his Defense Secretary, Edwin Rich, had a reputation for self-belief every bit as gung-ho as Donald Rumsfeld, if not more so. However, Hamid realised that reaching the hearts and minds of the American people was going to be his most formidable challenge as they seldom reacted to events beyond the psychological barrier of the oceans that shielded them from the rest of the world. Not until the body-bags started coming home, that is. But if American body bags were to start coming home from any conflict with Iran – from actual fighting on the ground, what state of ruin would his own country have suffered by that point?

There was a knock on the door and one of his two private bodyguards announced Jules's arrival. The moment he had been dreading had arrived. Hamid despised public displays of emotion and had therefore insisted on receiving Jules here in the privacy of his own private apartment again.

He was hugely fond of his nephew whom he had really come to regard as he might a son. Jules's agony now mixed with his own, the more so as he had been entranced by Zahra's nature and genuinely moved by her commitment to building a new Iran. In many ways, she embodied the woman that he had never found and he had therefore basked personally in the extraordinary bond that she and Jules had wrought in so short a time.

Hamid could not avoid the truth that their destruction would never have occurred had he eschewed the political path. It was the price of his own albeit noble ambition that still remained to be paid and most painfully by Jules.

Hamid's guilt devoured him. He wrapped his arms around Jules's shoulders and clasped his nephew to him. The embrace was firm, reciprocal and out of time.

Eventually he whispered hoarsely 'No words Jules! I have no words.'

'Me neither, uncle!' Jules responded, drawing back from comfort of his uncle's embrace, 'There is so much to say but words hold so little relevance now. We can't undo what's done.'

Jules smiled weakly. 'There will be time for grief. I know that will come but now is the time to right the wrong that was done to Zahra and to Khalîl and that's what I have to do. That's why I'm here. I'm not irrational or emotional, I simply intend to even the score on this thing. I also think that I may have an idea of how it can be done, by me – with your help.'

Hamid poured them both a single malt whisky and added a little water. It was a personal ritual of theirs left over from the Oxford experience, a symbol of the common, private ground which they both shared.

'Jules, you're not a fool' his uncle said handing him a glass, 'but I wonder if you even begin to appreciate the challenge we face here. You are as close to my flesh and blood as I'm likely to have in this world and your mother will never speak to me again if anything happens to you. Personally, I have complete confidence in you to do whatever you put your mind to but, in this case, I just don't think you realise the near impossibility for you, as an untrained operative, to be much more than an unguided nuisance to our enemies.'

'Uncle, I'm not stupid you know,' said Jules indignantly, determination glinting in his eye, 'I know that I'm going to need some very intensive training. I know I need to be toughened up both physically and mentally, conditioned and taught things that most people will never need to contemplate in their normal lives. But then my life is not normal any more and will never be again until I have exorcised the demons.'

His uncle looked at him in silent angst. This was a particularly shrill, naïve madness but then the world was a dangerous place and his nephew had been badly burnt. That fire might be enough to drive him to success, to hone his awareness and caution. It was certainly blazing and trying to contain it and so divert it might simply produce another sort of explosion.

'No promises' Hamid said after a while. 'And I mean that. This is not what you were brought up to or cut out for and, if you want my help as President of Iran rather than my support as your uncle, I will need to be convinced that you have both a genuinely viable plan and the personal ability to execute it. This is no time for some kind of James Bond spectacular. The American threat is deadly serious and there is much more at stake here you know, than just you and I.' He paused to underline the Rubicon that Jules was seeking to cross.

Jules nodded.

'Alright, so, give me some idea of what you have in mind' he commanded.

'OK fine' began Jules purposefully. 'Let's start with three simple questions. Do you think Wilmington and some of those unreconstructed, neo-conservative hawks around him would have been so aggressive or threatening if they believed that we actually had the nuclear capability to retaliate in kind if attacked?'

'It would certainly have been strangely un-diplomatic' replied his uncle cautiously.

'And if they knew, for sure, that we would respond with nuclear weapons if they either invaded our sovereign territory or bombed our nuclear installations, do you think that they would be any keener to launch such strikes than say Khrushchev was over Cuba?

'Probably not Jules but they know that we have no submarines capable of launching nuclear missiles – we have no delivery system as yet that is intercontinental.'

'So, final question' Jules persisted. 'Do we have enough fissile material to make nuclear bombs? '

Hamid paused looking at his nephew quizzically. 'I don't know exactly Jules; I'd have to check but my guess would be yes – a few. As the U.N. knew back in 2009, we had enough for at least one bomb but, in fact, the enrichment programme was much more successful in the last couple of years than the Mullahs ever let on. And now, in any case, we could probably supplement any shortfall from our friends.'

'OK uncle, then there could be number of angles to it' said Jules sipping his whisky, 'but, during the Second World War, there was a famous British ruse employed to make the Germans think that the Allies were going to invade Sardinia and not Sicily. It became known as *'The Man who never was'* – they even made a movie of it. My plan is a derivation of that. It rests on the predictable frailty of human nature and the political imperative in a democracy to bow to serious and manifest risks perceived by its voters.

If it succeeds, it will alter Iran's relations with US forever and the balance of power here in the Middle East as well. If we can achieve that and trounce Israel's remaining Mojahedin friends in the process, Zahra will be avenged.'

WEDNESDAY, 3RD JANUARY, 19:45
Hamid Saiyeidi's apartment, Farmaniyeh, Tehran

It was three weeks since Jules had last seen his uncle. It had been a gruelling, hard, challenging three weeks for Jules that had shown him a side of life that had not existed for him before and a mentality that he had found instinctively alien. But it had also started to imbue him with physical and mental strength that he had never envisioned previously, combined with a confident aggression to pursue his judgement.

The manservant opened the apartment door to him and showed him into the room where his uncle was again contemplating the now leafless Plane trees through the large double windows.

'So Jules, I hear good things from my people about your progress. How has it been for you?' asked Hamid.

'Well uncle' said Jules smiling wryly, 'it was just as physically awful as I had feared to begin with and certainly very tough from a standing start. But at the same time, the other half of the day is taken up with research and planning and I have found working with Farid Karzam fascinating. Actually, I suppose about ten days ago, the unusual combination of the hard physical training and the intense, creative planning produced such a stimulus as I have never experienced before.

The physical training has been split between the usual field techniques for optimising communications, sabotage, poison and explosives, plus firearms training and self-defence overlaid by an appalling fitness and strength programme. At your insistence I gather, I was subjected to an intensive schedule that would surely have caused many Foreign Legionnaires to wilt but, to my surprise, I seemed to thrive on it. I reasoned that as I had volunteered for this, initiated it in fact, there seemed no point in not throwing myself into it fully.

And it worked. The more I put into the training the better I seemed to feel, the more energy I seemed to have, the more confident, the more optimistic. The instructors were somewhat tight lipped at first. Their resentment at being asked to do 'special favours' for the politicians, however senior, was almost audible. I think that they intentionally made the whole of the programme as tough as they could make it. So I just worked hard and kept a smile on my face.

Now after just three weeks, with my grasp of fieldcraft and firearms, I reckon that I would make a very passable field agent!

Seriously though, I suppose also that I had never known what it was to be truly physically fit. It's great and I am going to keep it going just to hang onto the sense of well being it produces, a kind of high if you like! And, if I survive all this, the girls just might fancy my new physique.' Jules said laughing.

'The way you put it, perhaps we should all be subjected to the same regime' his uncle said sardonically, 'but tell be about the planning.'

Hamid had ordered Farid Karzam, the new deputy chief of the Iranian intelligence to work closely with his nephew. Karzam was a devout Muslim but a man with wide international experience and had also been a first-class and resourceful field officer, a combination that had driven him to his current position.

'I think that is coming on remarkably well' said Jules with a degree f confidence. 'Farid has a brilliant mind and his experience in Europe and the Balkans is priceless. I will take care of operations outside Europe and Farid will get things set up and rolling here. To confuse and confound our enemies, we are developing a two-pronged strategy intended to sow doubt, confusion and uncertainty. The starting gun will be the death, by natural causes I hasten to add, of an old man we have identified in Lausanne who used to be one of Italy's major players in olive oil. We don't know when it will happen but we are assured by insiders that it will be very soon.

As far as the operation goes, all the funding and paperwork is complete, and we have pretty much identified our targets and dates. As a cover for the whole of the period that I am out of France, your friends at *Le Monde* will have me on their books travelling round the Pacific looking at nuclear attitudes for an in-depth article. Oh, and we are also currently working on a fail-safe strategy that will hopefully protect my identity operationally.'

'Yes' observed his uncle, 'that is one aspect of this whole thing that deeply concerns me. The connection between us is as good as a death sentence for you if it ever emerges. If you were to be caught and identified as my agent, you would be very unlikely to be offered the luxury of a cell by the CIA. You do really realise that don't you Jules?'

'I know all that uncle, but, if the worst came to the worst,' said Jules now solemn, 'I will have done something positive for you and what you are trying to achieve so it will not have been entirely without purpose and, you must remember, with my great respect and love for you and the family, that the central *raison d'être* of my life has already been shattered.'

Moving on quickly from his unexpected attack of emotion, Jules returned to the detail, 'In any case, your intelligence services have spent days checking all the information available, the official records in Tehran as well as Paris and any SAVAK files which had not been destroyed in the Islamic revolution. They have also combed all press reports covering your return to Tehran and your political background for any mention of your immediate family. There seems to be none.

Publicly, you have always claimed that Granny fled to Paris after the US conspiracy in 1953, after Grandfather's brutal assassination. But you have never given an interview that we could find on your private life and, curiously, there was no indication anywhere of any records in France of you even having a sister.

My French passport carries no hint of mother's origins and discrete enquiries have revealed that no records here in Tehran, even of Granny's escape to Paris, survived the upheaval of the Islamic revolution. Perhaps you were never asked about a sister but, as things stand, there is nothing to connect the new President of Iran and Jules de Villarosa.

How do you think things are going at an official level?'

'Well I pray that you are right Jules' said his uncle gravely.

'On the official front, I think we have made significant progress in creating a diplomatic shield, some of which you will have seen. We are forming an *Islamic Defense Organisation* for mutual self protection and encouraging affiliation from all Muslim States, Shias and Sunnis alike. Envoys have been dispatched and I have systematically backed them up by telephone calls at the highest levels.

As you know, I spent two days in Moscow to strengthen the existing ballistic missile programme with Russia and, in the context of additional supplies of fissile material, we have renewed defense treaties with China and North Korea in return for oil at guaranteed prices – something Zahra had initiated before it happened.

All this creates a bulwark against outright American aggression that would in itself effectively isolate the US and Israel diplomatically if they were to try and pursue Wilmington's threats. The Europeans, we are told, after the Iraq experience, will want to sit on the sidelines, no doubt in a state of confused ambivalence.

Anyway, taken together, I believe that it will at least buy us time to extend the US deadline.'

Jules spent a further ten minutes outlining some of the other elements of their planning before the impending arrival of the Interior Minister was announced. Hamid quickly reiterated that the cabinet was intentionally being kept in the dark about the covert part of his defense planning so Jules would have to disappear before his presence required an explanation.

Out on the street again, Jules made his way towards his rendezvous with Farid to further refine the final the operational elements of their strategy over dinner.

The restaurant was in a small cul-de-sac that ran parallel to the main shopping street. When later they emerged from the restaurant, the street was deserted except for three drunks apparently considerably the worse for wear.

As they approached them, they suddenly stiffened up and advanced on Farid and Jules brandishing knives. The leader demanded cash, car keys and credit cards but Farid told them what they could do with themselves in very explicit language whereupon the man hurled himself at Farid.

Jules reacted almost involuntarily with trained simplicity. Grabbing the man's arm and knife hand as he passed him, he redirected the assailant's own weight so that he slammed into the lamppost behind him, face first and collapsed, unconscious and bleeding profusely. The second man was now upon him as Jules ducked, using the man's own momentum to send him somersaulting over his back into the gutter. The man rose, turning to face him just as Jules landed a flying kick to the man's neck causing him to fall back hard into the gutter, his knife skidding off down the street. The third assailant had seen enough by now and, as Jules yanked the man out of the gutter into a fierce arm lock, he fled. Despite the arm lock, the man unwisely attempted to break free with a massive lurch at a summersault. Jules instantly altered and intensified his grip resulting in an audible crack as the man's forearm broke cleanly under the pressure of his own weight. He sank to the pavement groaning in total submission.

After the police had taken the wounded men into custody, Farid insisted on seeing Jules home. Turning to shake his hand, he smiled at Jules with a kind of paternal admiration. 'Not bad at all for a beginner!' he joked, 'The guys really taught you the stuff didn't they. Let's hope you never have to use it but welcome to the fraternity all the same.'

As Jules lay in the darkness that night, he reflected on the attack. It was the first time in his life he had ever been assaulted physically and he was astonished that the aggression of his training had come through so forcefully. The final stages of his training were still ahead of him but he already felt that he was as ready as he would ever be.

Steeped in reflection, Jules felt the glow of fulfilment but even as he reflected, his awareness seemed suddenly to expand into something altogether wider and more encompassing. It was as he imagined an out-of-body experience might be except that he was not floating. With it came a sense of serene happiness that he had not enjoyed since Zahra and he were last alone together in Tehran.

In the encroaching shadows of the night, he could see her beaming at him and, once more he could feel the hypnotic radiance of her eyes. Now, from nowhere, Zahra was suddenly with him again, she had come back to him and she lightened his path into the gentle balm of sleep.

It had been so long; it had been so bitter but now, reunited, he slid eagerly into her fathomless dominion.

THE SEEDING

MONDAY, 8TH JANUARY, 21:20HRS
Hospital of All Saints, Lausanne, Switzerland

A clinical calm encompassed the darkened room. With their dancing screens and beeps, banks of monitors alone suggested activity. A nurse sat in front of them, motionless. On the opposite side of the room, the frail figure in bed was also motionless, having long since slid into a peaceful nether land of deep dreams.

Aged 97, Enrico Bardolini, the youngest of his family and the only son, had outlived his sisters only to linger within the renowned clinic for the last 18 months. He had never married but having also outlasted the few people he really trusted in his life, he had, in truth, been widowed when American General Foods had outbid his ambitions nearly 35 years ago now, taking control of his life's work.

For generations the Bardolinis had never known poverty and his father had run a successful import/export business from Genoa with growing ties across the New World and the Eastern Seaboard in particular. Young Enrico had been energised by the voyages to America when he was allowed to accompany his father on business and had soon recognised that a substantial opportunity existed among the throngs of Italians flocking to the land of opportunity. In the swirling melting pot of immigrant America, people clung to the things that reminded them of the good things they had left behind. It was a simple idea.

At the age of 20, he persuaded his father to lend him enough money to buy 215 hectares of good Tuscan olive groves and to build a pressing mill. His father's network of retailers and wholesalers across America provided a ready made and hungry channel for his production with its packaging that exuded Italian excellence.

Within months, demand surpassed supply and Enrico had started buying in particular olive varieties from other growers, pressing and blending them into an oil that, from the first pressings, was green and slightly nutty with a hint of pepper. Above all, the aim was to produce an olive oil that was not only good but had sufficiently distinctive features to enable his customers to recognise easily and adhere to the Bardolini standard.

It worked. Within a matter of years, Bardolini had grown into one of the leading brands in America. Enrico now had more than 20 pressing mills and was becoming a major factor in Italian exports of olive oil. Seizing the opportunity, he expanded his product list to include Parma ham and other dried meats, salamis, hard cheeses such as Parmesan and his own label Balsamic vinegar. The same customers bought the new Bardolini products through the same channels trusting in the name. And he made it his business not to disappoint them.

It was the eternal story of the truly committed entrepreneur evolving with the emerging pattern of demand as it coalesced into the greatest consumer market the world had ever seen. By the age of 52, his success and consequent Italian fiscal pressures dictated that he move his domicile and the executive management to Geneva. But the move shattered the intimacy of his management style that had always been close-up and hands-on. It was that closeness that had stimulated him and had driven him on and, in the end, it was the lack of it and the offer from American General Foods Inc. that stretched well beyond the bounds of ordinary avarice, that led him to relinquish what had been for so long his consuming passion.

Now hemmed in by the claustrophobia of financial abundance, stuck among the secretive and closed Genovese, with no friends of longstanding at hand, he had increasingly turned inwards to his books and to art. His problem was that he simply had found it hard to take much pleasure out of merely acquiring things; he had spent all his life creating endeavours and now that crucial joy of successful fruition seemed gone forever.

And so his life had descended. It wasn't that he was lonely; he had never been a social animal – there had never been time. He had travelled to the places he had known but almost all the faces he knew had moved on or were dead. As were his sisters, the last of whom he managed to see shortly before she died at the age of 92. It had confirmed his own mortality and sapped his ambition to bring together further literary collections. What was the point; they could only be left to institutions in nations that were not his own or in the country of his birth that he had abandoned.

The pointlessness of his existence had seemed to him so ironic and such a contrast to the life he had known as a younger man. He was not a recluse but he never saw anyone; he was not antisocial but no one knew him and he never accepted invitations from strangers. He had lost touch with the world as he dropped below its radar.

Now, with a murmuring heart and a failing digestive system, he lay waiting for death, dreaming deeply of lost enterprises.

A wailing beep pierced the nurse's empty concentration and caused running feet to clatter down the corridor. There was little they could do. The patient had had his lawyer issue a formal notice that he did not wish to be revived unnaturally and, this time around, the body had reached its natural and last state.

The lawyer was informed immediately and set to work bringing his client's affairs to the tidy conclusion that had already been well rehearsed.

TUESDAY, 10TH JANUARY, 17:45, TRAVNIK, CENTRAL BOSNIA
The office of the chief of police, Colonel Marinko Perovic

Turning to what remained in his in-tray, Colonel Petrovic noticed the handwritten envelope – no stamp so it had been delivered personally. Having survived the collapse of communism, he was well versed in the culture and habits of informants and would have bet his monthly salary, such as it was, that he would not be surprised by the contents of the slightly shabby envelope.

Most people informed on their neighbours or friends for either revenge or monetary gain. Uninvited, this was likely to be revenge.

The handwritten note inside was brief and to the point, written in stubby capitals in blue biro:

'RADIN IVANOVIC IS IRANIAN AGENT. HE IS GOING EVERY MONTH TO AIROT TO TRAIN PALESTINIANS IN BOMBS AND FIGHTING. ISRAELIS USED TO REWARD CHIEF BEFORE YOU FOR SUCH NEWS. CONTACT HAMDIJA AT FARM NEAR TURBE.'

Ivanovic was a dangerous gangster with some unpleasant Islamic fundamentalist friends who had used his services until success had neutered him. The Colonel was already something of an expert on the man.

Radin Ivanovic was a natural fighter. Thickset and square, his weather-beaten face was always slightly unshaven – even on Sundays when it received its weekly going-over, the rippled folds of flesh denied his blunted razor easy access. Calloused skin, ingrained with long-term dirt, heightened the impression of Radin's hands as unfeeling, blunt instruments while tousled, self-cut hair and fiery eyes completed the daunting first-time impression for strangers. Few ever felt compelled to press deeper into his acquaintance.

Radin was the bastard son of a brief encounter in Sarajevo. His mother was a laundry worker, his father an itinerant builder's assistant living where he could find work. Together they had committed an irreparable sin in the minds of local people as she was an orthodox Christian and he a Muslim. Their son was born into the community as an instant pariah and, having lived a hand to mouth existence with his mother until he was twelve, Radin found himself on his own when she died of pneumonia on a cold February morning. Local charity ran out after a week and an instinct for survival took him into the back street world of dog eat dog and thence onto the road.

If you come into the world with nothing, you have very little to lose and Radin had grasped early on that taking risks could probably only improve his lot. He spent his early teens shifting allegiance from one street gang to the next, killing for the first time aged just 15. After the accession of Izetbegovic as Bosnia's president in 1990, Radin attracted the attention of the Iranian Revolutionary Guard and Iran's intelligence service, VEVAK, both of whom were oiling the increase of Iran's influence in the area, covertly supplying weapons. They noted his capacity for fearlessness and harm and, at the age of 17, he was taken under VEVAK's wing to hone his skills. He thus escaped the worst of the internecine struggle within Bosnia between the Nationalists, Muslims and Croats.

After the Dayton peace accords were signed in Paris 1995, Radin had remained on the Iranian payroll, albeit on an increasingly part-time basis, interspersed with occasional technical courses to supplement his established speciality as a bomb maker. With the forum of the struggle gravitating to a political level, Radin had started to supplement his Iranian stipend with the fruits of local crime. His skills as a bomber and an assassin were a local legend by now and in a region with a legacy of unsettled scores, work was plentiful.

Successful commissions encouraged more and his reserves of cash finally grew to the predictable point where his hunger for still more money in return for unquantifiable risks started to wane. He established himself in a modest house in Travnik, the principal city and military centre of the Ottoman Empire in the Balkans, situated in the valley of the Lašva River, bordered by Vlasic Mountain to the north and Mount Vilenica to the south. This was where the Colonel had first encountered him.

Here too, his reputation brought him respect tinged with apprehension but few friends. Radin kept himself to himself when he was not working although he adopted the bar overlooking the Lašva River, some 200 yards from his old stone house. He was discrete but gradually rumours began to circulate of visits by ladies of the night after he returned from his trips. Worse, they also supplied him with the drugs that he now could afford – until his work rate dropped off about the same time as the drugs became the very thing he increasingly needed – for which he now had to take on new assignments.

Things came to a head in March 2006 when, at the Colonel's own instigation, enforcement agents of EUFOR had visited him in connection with Ratko Mladic, the missing wartime commander with whom Radin was suspected of having links. Nothing was proved but the visit triggered a heavy drugs fest that landed him in a discrete but rigid cold-turkey unit in Sarajevo financed by his friends in VEVAK, riding to his rescue.

He returned nine months later an apparently reformed if somewhat diminished man, resolved to live quietly, his only pleasure a visit to his local bar on Tuesdays and Fridays. And so things had stayed until after the democratic revolution swept Saiyeidi to power in Tehran and the old VEVAK was reformed and completely reconstructed.

As part of the process, VEVAK was known to have reviewed the various assets it had outside Iran and, if the note now before the Colonel was correct, had decided that, at least for now, it could actively use Radin's talents in bomb making and sabotage to help Israel's enemies in Palestine, no doubt as part of Iran's show of defiance to American pressure over their nuclear research, he assumed.

Colonel Perovic already knew the location of Mossad's *sayanim* and immediately saw the possibility of enhancing the meagre salary that even someone in his position of authority was obliged to accept. If the UN was serious about eliminating corruption, an admirable sentiment, then it was going to have to pay people like him properly. It wasn't his fault.

The following day after dark, the Colonel slipped up the road towards Turbe and knocked on the door of Hamdija's house. Would his friends be interested in news of Ivanovic's activities abroad, he had asked and, if so, were they interested to put the Colonel on their payroll. He was unashamedly direct.

Hamdija, as instructed, called him on his wife's mobile the following morning to confirm his appointment and establish how his remuneration would be handled. The Colonel promised a dossier on Ivanovic's recent history and ongoing surveillance. From that point on, his disappearances would be regularly logged and reported.

The Colonel's discrete inquiries revealed an emerging pattern. Absences by Radin Ivanovic were nothing new to the locals but, after an extended absence in the previous summer, they had noted a change in him. After being away for some six weeks, Radin had returned to the bar, physically restored, the menacing glint back in his eye, but just as silent as before. He also drank less and his clothes were cleaner. A series of shorter absences then ensued, ten days or two weeks at a time but still no indication of his destination. The local gossips and his own police officers had independently concurred that something had changed – he was involved in something new that had to have been dreamt up by Iran. Ivanovic had also started smoking a new brand of cigarettes that apparently came from the Palestinian territories. There was nothing that could be substantiated but all the feedback he was getting pointed to something ominous.

Colonel Perovic's report got Mossad's attention.

TUESDAY, 10TH JANUARY, 13:15HRS,
Piazza San Michele, Lucca, Italy

Count Salvatore Maria Giuseppe di Fabbri stared from the window of his first floor office on the corner of Via Vittorio Veneto and Piazza San Michele. It was still raining. The tourists that congested the Piazza from April to late October had thankfully gone and Lucca was once again left largely to itself.

THE SEEDING

It was the third day of heavy rain and the overcast skies complimented the gloomy papers on the desk behind him. Decisions that marked a further retreat of his once illustrious family would have to be taken. The weight of the past and the shortcomings of an all too aristocratic father were now bearing down on his own shoulders. It was not his fault he always told himself in the dark hours of the early morning as he lay awake wrestling with the dilemma of keeping all the balls in the air. Unfortunately, however, it was no one else's problem and increasingly, there seemed little choice but to take another step down.

His father had bought the small office suite some 10 years before he had succumbed to cancer. He told Salvatore that he kept it as a refuge from the shrillness of his wife's complaints about the inexorable decline in 'standards' as she called them. That was certainly true but, renowned for his good looks among the ladies of Lucca, he had also sought frequent but discrete relief in the arms of others. After he died, Salvatore disposed of the ample chaise longue from his father's office.

The di Fabbri family was distantly connected to the ruling House of Savoy and in his youth, his father, a staunch and vocal supporter of the diminutive Victor Emmanuel III, had devoted most of his time and what remained of the family wealth to the advancement of the king's cause. It proved to be a bad investment. After the 1943 armistice, he found himself in dangerous opposition to a number of previous friends who had allied themselves with Junio Borghese's Decima MAS together raising some 50,000 men to fight on at the side of the Nazis. Before the allies triumphed in 1945, the bulk of Italy was taken over by German forces and thousands of Italian soldiers were either killed or carried off into captivity. The Villa Fabbri, the family's home for over 400 years, in the foothills above Pescia, sustained one attack that caused serious damage but worse still, shortly thereafter, the King paid for his mistaken armistice when the Monarchy was abolished by popular vote in June 1946. Salvatore's father was now without either a cause or ready cash.

Salvatore's paternal grandmother, from another aristocratic family in Piedmont, was among the most feared *grandes dames* of the Lucchese tearooms and had always loudly maintained that Salvatore's father had married beneath himself – despite the lavish dowry that the daughter of an auto parts manufacturer brought to the union. Though she never acknowledged it, it was that dowry that kept her in faded elegance in a distant part of the Villa Fabbri until she died. It also paid for the post-war repairs to the house and allowed his father to bury his royalist wounds in the sand until the bankers started to comment on his lifestyle in the late 1960s.

That notwithstanding, his father had taken the strategic decision to broaden the family's focus into the wider world, recognising that the emerging American pre-eminence required absolute fluency in English for future success. He diverted enough of his remaining liquidity into a Swiss bank account that financed the $60,000 a year needed to put Salvatore and Giacomo, his brother, through Ampleforth, an English Catholic private school run by Benedictine monks in Yorkshire. To the genuine surprise of both parents, the boys had actually liked this strange English system that separated child from parent at an early age and Salvatore had gone on to Oxford reading French while Giacomo had plumped for the Sorbonne and Parisian ladies.

But that was pretty much the last of the family largesse and it played badly with their mother. The gradual curtailment of her various allowances was no more than a foretaste of the disaster that buried her pride of social position when the old Count died in 1994 and the full extent of the family's financial decline was revealed. After tortuous negotiations, the tax authorities were finally persuaded to take the decaying Villa Fabbri, in lieu of death duties, but there was little else left other than an apartment in Rome and an old hunting lodge up in the hills above Vinchiana, north of Lucca that had already been given to Salvatore and his brother. With few assets of her own, the widowed Contessa had moved back to the bosom of her family north of Turin.

Salvatore had always felt guilty about his mother and the distance between her and his father's sides of the family. It was their fault, their snobbery, their standoffishness and it was simultaneously both irritating and slightly embarrassing. In today's world they were certainly no better than his mother's family. His maternal grandfather and his brothers had at least worked for their success not merely inherited it.

The clanging of the bells in the towers and churches of the old city broke into the overcast skies above, signalling lunchtime, jolting him out of the morbidity of his family's demise. Time for lunch. Salvatore turned the answering machine on, descended the rickety wooden staircase pulling his father's old army trench coat over his shoulders and set off across the damp cobbles of the Piazza towards his regular table at the family run trattoria two blocks away.

After all the overpriced, soulless restaurants he had endured around the world, Da Leo's was like coming home. When he was feeling low like today, the natural warmth of the ambience with its bustle and noisy salutes to arriving regulars reminded him that life still went on, that there were still places where you could breathe out again. Since May when, out of the blue, American General Foods had made him redundant, there had been many days that he had been first in the restaurant (apart from the inevitable tourists of course who had no idea about time), reaching out for its emotional sustenance and well-being.

Today was no different as the ample waitress slammed the half carafe of red wine onto the scrubbed wood table with a chortle. 'Eating again, eh?!' she challenged as she went off without waiting. Salvatore poured some of the wine into the small Duralex tumbler, saluted other regulars close by and drank. The waitress returned with a metal basket of bread and some olive oil. 'So what's it to be today Signore di Fabbri?' she demanded.

'Thank you Maria,' he muttered scanning the day's specials, 'I'll think I'll take your homemade bean soup to warm me up and then the fried chicken and vegetables and a green salad. And a carafe of tap water please.'

'You rich people are so mean!' she scoffed agreeably, writing the order on the corner of the paper tablecloth. 'Upon my soul, who needs water on a day like this?!' Maria ripped the order from the table and sped off towards the kitchen shouting.

Salvatore smiled ironically.

The problem was that being made redundant at the age of 48, having been a deputy-general manager of the Italian subsidiary of a major American company, was a paradox for anyone who might consider taking him on. He wasn't a superstar that had a queue of international companies just waiting to parachute him into a failing part of their empire. He was an effective line manager but came with a price tag that disadvantaged him against younger men who could be trained from scratch into the particular corporate culture, to grow with the team as their careers progressed. And if he offered his services at a lower price, which indeed he had tried in order to beat the age thing, it suggested that there must be something wrong with him. No one wants to employ desperate people and, to compound matters, the sort of position that he would fit would normally be filled from internal resources in a properly run company.

So what do you do? He'd answered every possible advertisement from anywhere in the world with hardly even a single acknowledgement; he'd sent his CV off to anyone, companies or specialist headhunters, who might conceivably be interested. He had done his best at 'networking' although this was tough in Italy. He had continued extended negotiations with a local olive oil company looking to expand in the US but it all came to nothing when they decided to postpone expansion until the prospects for opening an office there became clearer after the recent US Presidential elections. But that wouldn't be until at least the Spring, so what do you do?

At that moment the chicken arrived with a crash in front of him with Maria instructing 'Enjoy' trying to imitate an American accent and failing hideously as usual. Having never met Becky, Salvatore's American wife, Maria felt free to taunt.

The chicken was delicious, peasanty and wholesome and his spirits began to lift as he ate. At least Becky seemed unshaken by the hiatus in his career and the sense of impending gloom that seemed to grip his stomach so much of the time.

Becky and Da Leo's had so far saved his sanity. Once again, he happily admitted to himself that Becky had been one of the most unexpected, surprising and fortuitous things that had occurred in his life.

From a gauche, all American, glitzed, little rich girl, an unguided missile to a sophisticated, perceptive mother and successful artist with a passionate appetite for her husband – the transformation had been truly extraordinary.

When times were bad like now, Salvatore liked to treat himself to a slow revival of the memory of their extraordinary and passionate beginning and subsequent life together. He always found it inspirational especially since the electricity between them had yet to fade despite some 20 years together, during which their relationship had become the building block upon which all of life rested.

True, redundancy was a problem but they would get through somehow, he thought as he gave Maria enough cash for a small tip as well. Da Leo's and Becky had salved his depression yet again.

And that confidence was repaid when Salvatore returned home the evening after. Becky greeted him with her usual hug and a kiss and handed him an envelope with a Zurich postmark. 'I didn't realise you were into lady gnome types' she laughed.

The address on the back of the envelope read, *Brandtburger Rechtsanwälte, Sonneggstrasse 15 Zurich* – never heard of them he thought as he opened the letter.

Dear Sir

Creation of the Bardolini Institute
The late Enrico Bardolini left instructions in his will that an Institute should be created after his death to give trainees in the olive oil industry hands-on experience and education and to further the appreciation of olive oil itself. These trainees will be drawn from both Italy and the Unites States where Mr Bardolini had many connections. He nominated a secret supervisory committee to oversee provision of funding for the institute and to recommend nominations for its director.
We have been instructed by the supervisory committee to dis-

cuss with you the post of Director and I would be grateful for the opportunity to visit you in then near future if it would be of interest. I should add that Mr Bardolini has made particularly generous financial provision for the institute and the Director will have complete autonomy in the management of its affairs, subject only to a half yearly report.
I look forward to hearing from you.

Yours faithfully

Markus Steinhoffer
Partner

Salvatore read it again and then handed it to Becky. 'Looks as though the long, dry spell could well be over at last!'

'What have I said all along, Sal – it was just a question of time before someone recognised what they were missing! And now they have' she said throwing her arms round him. 'Let's go out and celebrate!'

FRIDAY 14TH JANUARY, DUBROVNIK, CROATIA
Andro Tomac's studio

Dorri was thrilled to be Mrs Tomac – wife of the hunkiest sculptor in all of Croatia, to be away from her overbearing father and particularly, to be away from the social mores of Paris that made her feel so inadequate. High above Dubrovnik, she loved their simple stone house in the lee of the Srđ hill, surrounded by their own evergreen trees with Andro's studio within shouting distance in the garden. She loved the view down over the old city, its small, crowded harbour, its terracotta roofs and fortified walls, she loved the expanse of blue sea that stretched past the small island of Lokrum into the infinite haze.

Andro's father had been an artist before him and had moved to Dubrovnik from Split when Andro was a boy. His timing had not been good. Two years after their arrival, following Croatia's independence in 1991, the Yugoslav People's Army attacked and surrounded the city in October 1991. The siege lasted until May 1992 and, according to the Croatian Red Cross, 114 civilians were killed, among them the celebrated poet Milan Milisić.

His father always maintained that the light was more consistent in this area than around Split, an essential prerequisite for an artist, and so the family stayed despite the perpetual undercurrent of tribal tensions that ebbed and flowed. Andro absorbed all these through his school mates but, as an outgoing teenager, had grown up with a mixture of art, sport and languages. Despite limited success as an artist, Andro's father had still paid for extra lessons in English and French, insistent that his son should be able to communicate with the world. So equipped, Andro looked forward to the annual influx of girls during the tourist season. Good looking with a muscular physique and a sunny disposition, Andro was never short of entertainment and this was, after all, how he had met and vanquished Dorri.

Andro still lacked real commercial success although his work had been exhibited alongside well-established sculptors such as Josip Ivanovic or Robert Baca, both of whom he held in great esteem.

Now Dorri was claiming that she had in some way been responsible for the commission he hoped to receive from the Bardolini Institute that might put him on the international map. Dorri couldn't be precise about why she had been responsible but she was sure it was because of one of her father's banking friends in Paris. Whichever way it was, Mr Markus Steinhoffer, the lawyer to the Institute was arriving shortly and she had spent all morning cleaning and tidying.

Andro had sent Steinhoffer three alternative sketches of the statue of the Capitoline Wolf as requested. Steinhoffer had informed him that, while the statue was going to be a bequest to the Institute, the benefactor had left the artistic choice to himself. Andro wasn't going to argue especially as the specifications suggested that, whatever the choice, it would be by far the largest and most expensive work he had ever undertaken. Steinhoffer had stipulated that it needed to be ready by mid-March at the latest which left no time for delays or slip-ups. Andro had already checked that a friend would be able to get his large mobile crane down the narrow track just above the studio to lift the statue onto a transporter when the time came.

Now Andro and Dorri waited with nervous expectancy for the arrival of their conduit to international recognition.

After his visit to Salvatore di Fabbri in Lucca two days earlier, Farid Karzam felt that he was beginning to live the persona of the dour, colourless, Fritz Steinhoffer – Swiss lawyer. Now he was extending his remit to the commissioning of fine art on behalf of the Bardolini Institute. Art and sculpture were not areas to which he had enjoyed much exposure but he was drawn to the power of some modern abstract pieces and had particularly liked the most ambitious sketch that Andro had produced that seemed to combine a bulbous curvature of the body of the beast with aggressive feline features and an array of suckling equipment that would have been the pride of any wolf mother.

Dubrovnik in January is not the easiest place to get to from Milan with few direct flights mid-week that were so timed as to make it impossible to accomplish anything and return the same day. Farid had therefore been obliged to take time out as a tourist having booked himself into a small family hotel down on the bay and 10 minutes walk from the old town. After an excellent meal of prsut, a Croatian prosciutto, and freshly caught, breaded carp, he had taken unanticipated pleasure in the deserted streets around the old harbour that bore few signs of the wars it had endured.

Now, donning the lawyer's persona once more, in the clear air of the January morning, he felt refreshed as he rang the bell on the wooden gate in the wall. The taxi would wait till he'd finished his business and that should not take long.

'Good morning, Mr Steinhoffer,' said Dorri enthusiastically in her best English, 'so glad that you got here safely.'

With a flash of surprise, Herr Steinhoffer raised his eyebrows replying in a heavy, humourless Germanic accent 'Is there a reason here why I should be worried about safety?'

'No, not at all' Dorri laughed, 'let me take you straight to Andro who is waiting with some nice hot coffee. He is so excited to discuss the work with you!'

The warmth of the Tomac's greeting appeared to have little impact on the dour Swiss lawyer. Having quickly dispensed with coffee and the artistic choice, Steinhoffer got down to practicalities.

'We are going to need a material that will withstand the weather as well as having considerable strength. It has been suggested to me that a recently developed nickel-aluminium bronze used in the nuclear industry would be suitable. Can you use such a material for the statue?' asked Steinhoffer.

'If that's what you want' acquiesced Andro 'but it's certainly overkill and will be much more expensive.'

'Never mind the expense, the Bardolini Institute always gets the best. Now thickness of the material – it should be at least 45mm thick and we will also require a section to be demountable. Please have the underside, say around the teats so that it is able to be removable for maintenance and cleaning. If I am correct that will be an aperture of about 1.5 metres by a metre. Is that so?'

Andro was now puzzled but felt it simpler to just agree. The heavy specifications should not affect the artistic integrity of the statue and, if they wanted to clean the inside from time to time, who was he to object? For $150,000 he would do it their way, particularly as the profit would answer the impasse that had developed with Dorri's father over money. Furthermore, Steinhoffer was now hinting that America might be the destination for the statue, not Italy.

'Fine, Mr Steinhoffer, if that's what you want, you've got it' said Andro, just like they did on American TV.

Another ten minutes of details – bank accounts, packing materials, estimated weights and so forth and, declining even a glass of Malvasia – no, he really didn't want to try it – Herr Markus Steinhoffer, closed the heavy wooden gate behind him and got back into the waiting taxi.

Farid smiled as the taxi made its way south to the airport. For that sort of money, even after expenses, the Tomacs would do anything to avoid rocking the boat and he had put sufficient distance into the client relationship to discourage any extraneous questions. In eight weeks time the statue would be transported north along the coast to the small port of Ploče where it would be hoisted aboard a chartered Panamanian ship which would sail immediately for an unspecified destination.

FRIDAY, 14TH JANUARY, 18:50H
Andrew Jackson Apartments, Larkspur, California

Marion was becoming agitated. Everything was running late today. Brad, her boss, had warned her once again that she was not functioning as part of the team and had better get her act together or else.

There was only one new tenant this week and he was arriving today. The furniture for his three-month stay had only been delivered an hour ago which meant that she'd had to supervise its installation leaving the office unattended. One of the idiots had left a conspicuous gouge in a wall that could not be repaired before the morning and delivery men had been offensively rude to her when she had pointed that out to them. Now, with eight minutes till she closed the office for the day, it looked as though the tenant wasn't going to show either. And it was raining heavily outside – obviously, as she had forgotten her umbrella. She hated January.

With four minutes to go, Marion was just about to shut down the computers when a rain-drenched figure hassled his way through the door looking urgently in her direction.

He was very sorry to be so late but the tailback the other side of the Golden Gate Bridge had been unbelievably slow. Didn't he know that it always was, she silently chided, handing him the registration form?

'How are you paying?' she asked brusquely, 'And I'll need ID.'

The Professor stopped his accelerated scribbling and produced a small envelope from his wet jacket which he handed over. Marion counted ten $500 bills which was correct – three months at $1500 plus $500 deposit. By the time she had locked the cash in the safe and made out a receipt, the Professor had finished filling in the form and handed it back to her along with his Florida driving licence for ID. Also he then fished in his wallet and pushed over a $20 bill.

'To apologise for making you late' the man said shyly. 'Please buy yourself some nice flowers.'

Marion nodded unresponsively as she checked the signature against the driving licence and handed it back. She knew that you had to produce birth certificates signed in your parents' blood before getting one of those in Florida so it was bound to be kosher.

'Thanks, that's very considerate of you' she said almost as an afterthought. 'There's the key. Apartment 4215 is on the ground floor in E block, on the right at the end when you leave this office. You'll find your allotted parking space immediately opposite. I'm afraid there's a small mark on the wall by the door but I'll get operations to fix that in the morning.

On behalf of Equity Sure Developments, I would like to welcome you and wish to a pleasant stay with us.'

The Professor bowed slightly, scooped up his driving licence and the door key and retreated into the rain. By the time he found E Block, the office was closed and Marion was already half way to San Rafael.

Jules found the apartment clean and completely soulless. Everything seemed to work but without a sense of solid dependability. It was just the sort of unflamboyant anonymity he needed to establish the Professor's persona.

Professor Ahmad Miljabi was the result of considerable research and some good fortune by entrenched Shia elements within the Iraqi intelligence service that owed substantial favours, if not actual allegiance to Farid Karzam. Farid's brief to his Iraqi friends had been to come up with as close a twin as possible from among Iraqi citizens now residing in US to the digital three-dimensional image that he supplied them of an unnamed Jules. After boiling the possible candidates down, the most similar were located, digitally photographed again for back-testing and then profiled.

Professor Ahmad Miljabi stood out. He could have passed as a Frenchman. Although he was two inches shorter than Jules, his facial features and hair were similar, he was somewhat reclusive having recently arrived at the University of Miami from Baghdad, had a record as an active pro-Iranian Kurd but best of all had been due out of US for nearly nine months on a research trip to Manokwari in West Papua that began in the second week in January, yesterday in fact. The US operation would be mounted using his identity as a shield and a natural fail-safe for Jules. If the FBI ever got to the Professor before the operation had achieved its objectives, closure to their enquiries could be provided.

'The Professor', in the form of Jules de Villarosa, newly arrived from London on a false British passport as 'George Anstruther', had in fact already made his first cash purchase in California, just after leaving the airport – a 2007 silver Ford Expedition XLT EL with 58,000 miles on the clock from a used car lot in Sunnyvale. When Jules put $26,000 in cash on the desk, they didn't look too bothered about paperwork. They asked him where they should register it and he replied, 'James Grant, Days Inn Hotel, San Francisco'. Ten minutes later he was on his way to Larkspur.

SATURDAY, 15TH JANUARY
1st bomb location in San Francisco

Jules finally awoke from an uneven sleep just as the dawn was breaking. He wandered onto the small terrace outside the living room from which he could dimly make out the bay through the trees below him.

His brain laboured with the hollowness of jetlag and he felt his body was still in tune with European time. Why did he always react so badly to this? As a journalist, he often had to travel to different continents and his father had taught him years back that dehydration is the worst aspect of long-haul flights. He had a well-established strategy – enough alchohol to help induce sleep (he'd tried Melatonin but it always left him drowsy the following day) and then as many bottles of water as he could persuade jaded flight attendants to part with.

Only one thing really made a difference – sustained and intense exercise. He had vowed to maintain the physical transformation imposed on him during his training and tried to devote at least an hour a day to it. Donning his track suit and walkman, Jules ran rather than jogged past the San Quentin gaol and on up to the slipway to the Interstate-580 and back. The Andrew Jackson apartment complex had its own fitness circuit around the six apartment blocks and a gym that was open from 6:00am every day to cater for the downtown commuters. By 7:45am, Jules felt he had inflicted sufficient pain on his body and returned to a hot shower. For now, the jetlag was somewhat exorcised but he knew that the hollow brain syndrome would return by late afternoon.

As he walked towards the Larkspur Landing ferry terminal, the storms of the night before had passed and he was picking up the rain-drenched scent of pine and eucalyptus. The sun was hitting the hills behind him. So this was California. He felt the same thrill of the unknown that he always experienced from new places. Today though, it was reinforced with a cavernous sense of mission.

If he was going to the downtown district, Farid had suggested that he should take the 30-minute catamaran trip past Tiburon and Angel Island with the backdrop of Mount Tamalpias and into the terminal building at the bottom of Market Street. It was a way of avoiding the traffic on the Golden Gate Bridge and Jules was happy to gain the sense of geographic perspective it would offer.

It was in fact Jules's first trip to the States and his first exposure to the opulence of American high-rise architecture so magnificently illustrated by the Embarcadero Center and the soaring buildings behind it. As he walked up Pine towards the realtor's office, Jules reflected that the ferry must be the absolute best scenic route to have approached the city for the first time.

Jules and Farid had identified an apartment for rent on the Internet on Taylor, close to the intersection with Washington. They had calculated that the blast from the bomb would destroy the whole of the downtown area. In a call 'from Boston', 'Mr Ahmad' had said that he would be arriving in three days time and explained that he just wanted a six-month lease and therefore would be happy to pay everything up front and in cash when he arrived.

When he collected the keys mid-morning, the realtors seemed not to have bothered to finish the lease agreement but promised to send it on as soon as it was ready. Jules quietly wondered if they would. No documentation meant no let and the owner, whoever he was, would perhaps be none the wiser. Jules hoped it might be a tempting proposition.

Before going to the apartment, Jules dropped into Union Square and picked up some shirts and underwear from Macy's and some used designer jackets from a small store in Maiden Lane.

The apartment itself was on the 2nd floor and therefore never saw the sun. It had the utilitarian look of the 1950s about it and Jules guessed that it had not been re-painted for years, let-alone re-furbished. The access was easy with a wide lift right across the corridor from the front door and a suitable household cupboard immediately opposite the front door. Manhandling a heavy bomb should not present a problem and given the uncared for condition of the apartment, landlords or agents were unlikely to pry.

Jules hung the jackets up and put the new shirts in a chest of draws. Anyone inspecting them would assume that the tenant had left them ready for his next visit. Farid had warned him about CCTV coverage and so, giving the apartment one last glance, Jules donned a baseball hat and dark glasses and set off down to the Ferry Terminal Building for his return trip.

Arriving at Larkspur, Jules could feel the jetlag inexorably returning and so he changed and repeated his exertions of the morning. Somewhat refreshed, he set off in the SUV to explore the area along Sir Francis Drake Boulevard towards Ross and its community of desirable homes for the very successful. Farid had spent sometime there in the '90s and recommended the butcher right off

Ross Common for his excellent swordfish – a strange thing for an Iranian spy to know about, Jules had thought at the time.

The fresh swordfish, marinated in lemon and chilli and griddled along with some peppers and an excellent bottle of 2006 Stags Leap Viognier thoroughly vindicated Farid – again. The pleasure of food and wine had always been something that Jules had been brought up to appreciate and tonight was no exception. Except that it suddenly brought home to him that he was completely on his own and miles from friend or support. Climbing into bed, he felt too anxiously aware of his position to toy with the fiction of his book. It no longer seemed to hold any real weight.

Turning his light out, his mind struggled with the search for a comfort zone into which to retreat. As he wandered, he felt his mind begin to wander once more into that total serenity that had proceeded Zahra's first re-appearance in Tehran. Wilfully, he threw himself into the beckoning abyss to recapture the vision of Zahra shimmering on the banks of the Loing, beckoning to him among the yellows and blues of that wonderful spring afternoon. It was wonderful; it was as though the warmth of her welcome confirmed her very personal approbation of his crusade. He was not going to be alone.

MONDAY, 16TH JANUARY
Landfall for the bombs

The following morning, after nine hours sleep, Jules felt fresh, free from the jetlag of the previous day and full of confident, even joyous optimism. He completed his morning workout with determination, breakfasted and headed down the 101. However, his mood was dented as he sat worrying in the SUV, inching towards the Golden Gate Bridge in the rush-hour traffic. It was a contingency that he had not allowed for in his route to the airport to catch the 08:40 flight up to Eureka and he vowed never to be so lax in his planning again. Conservative by nature, he normally built some leeway into approximations and just scraped past check-in by dint of having only an attaché case. With the relative complexity of their plan, Jules knew he simply could not afford another slip up – anywhere. Every element of the plan would have some contingency built into it from now on.

As United's Embraer 120 banked above the sea-mist rolling over the coast and city below and headed north up the coast past Drakes Bay and Point Reyes, the day's project re-ignited his enthusiasm. But as he stared out of the window, his mind went back to the intensity of the vision of Zahra that had overtaken him at the point of sleeping the previous night.

Jules was not a superstitious man and, despite a healthy respect for religion and the supernatural, he had never taken matters of the mind or the subconscious too seriously. As an undergraduate, he had once played planchette at a weekend party outside Oxford where the group claimed to have got in touch with Anne Boleyn. Certainly there had been something to it, something intangible, inexplicable but no less real, and the fact that the messages were spelt out in old English lent added credence to the whole experience. It was intriguing rather than compelling but dovetailed with other stories about a mysterious radio transmitter known simply at home as 'the Black Box'. It was supposed to cure horses by identifying their natural wavelength and beaming powerful signals back down it to rectify any irregularities cause by an ailment. One of his father's horses had made an apparently miraculous recovery from a badly damaged fetlock using the device. But then you never really knew did you?; the head groom's wife was always full of weird theories.

So what was it? It was more than fixated memory, less than a physical encounter. It seemed to carry only comfort; no hint of distress, just total serenity. During the viciousness and intensity of his training in Tehran, he had brushed all other matters to one side, let alone daydreams of Zahra which he had buried under deep layers of determination. Did he now need that renewed closeness to Zahra as inner reassurance? But he had all the conviction in the world. Was he inducing these experiences or was it triggered externally somehow? He had no control over the occurrence – he had tried vainly to re-invoke it the night after the first vision but without success. He really had no idea what caused it to happen but, equally, given the bizarre nature of it, he was definitely not about to ask anyone!

As he watched the plane's wing eat up the coastline passing beneath it, Jules forced his mind back to matters in hand.

The plan involved the use of a medium-sized refrigerated truck to receive the bombs in their trunks once they were landed from the submarine off Eureka. With a few keystrokes on the Yellow Pages' Switchboard website, Farid had found eight truck dealerships within 25 miles of Eureka and eleven emails later he had purchased a converted 1999 Ford E-350 truck for $16,500. Farid had explained that he wouldn't haggle over the price provided the dealer, 101 Auto & Trucks, agreed to repaint it light grey and would hang on to it until he was ready to take it down to San Francisco in April. He would, however, be coming to Eureka on the 18th and would like to be able to use it as he was making an exploratory trip. It should be registered in the name of Professor Ahmad of Andrew Jackson Apartments, Larkspur.

For anyone wishing to remain truly anonymous and virtually untraceable, the internet was a godsend, Jules reflected.

The taxi taking him south down Highway 101 from Arcata-Eureka airport knew 101 Autos & Trucks, which was crowded together with a number of other dealerships on a strip of land between the North Coast on the Humboldt bay and a muddy creek.

For the promise of an extra $20, Jules had the taxi wait until he was satisfied that there were no problems with the truck and that he could complete the transaction. Jules told the driver that he would be needing a lift back to the airport for his return flight and Al, the driver, readily agreed to pick him up later that evening, handing him a card. 'Just ask for Al and I'll come pick you up whenever. Have nice day Professor!'

At 10:35, Jules headed off south down the 101 towards Fields Landing. The truck, newly painted an innocuous light grey and valeted, seemed to be in good condition. The heater worked and he could hear no rattles. A shame Jules thought, that it was going to be torched as a vital part of the plan.

Using Google Earth, Farid and Jules had selected what appeared to be a large and potentially deserted parking area at the end of Railway Avenue, the other side of the road from a sand and aggregates plant. Arriving in the middle of the working day, Jules was dismayed to find the chosen parking space nearly half full with trucks waiting to load from the plant. There was additional parking space only suitable for smaller trucks, such as his, on the road just before it and still less than 100 yards from the jetty where they planned to land the bombs. There was nothing else down there and Jules quickly decided that his truck was going to be less prone to get in the way or for that matter, catch anyone's attention, if it was left in the other space overnight. Jules gave a cursory inspection to the two other sites they had identified as possible back ups but was satisfied that the space for the smaller trucks was best.

Their plan called for driving into the middle of nowhere and then, he and his accomplice, their fall-guy, would take just those bombs that they needed for the California seeding and drive back to base. Jules set out to check the 60 or so mile drive to Forest Glen, the hamlet where they planned to leave the truck. It had started to pour with rain as he headed down the C36 into what the January gloom transformed into a grey, scrubby wilderness.

Forest Glen could hardly even be called a hamlet and the first two possible hiding places turned out to be too visible from the road. Crossing the stream in full winter spate and following a dirt track up to an overgrown turning, Jules found a spot that offered some miserable looking, meagre trees as protection. No one would be able to see the grey truck from the road – until Jules wanted them to.

His last port of call, back in Eureka, was the Woodley Island Marina. He established his credentials with the manager explaining that he had a client that he needed to entertain in April for a weekend, he had his ocean going certificate and wanted to hire a cruiser. That would be no problem; they always had a number available but, if Jules could email the manager, say mid-March, he could have the pick of what they had.

Al, the taxi driver, dropped him back at the airport with some 50 minutes to spare. The only food concession was already closed and Jules knew he would have to wait until he got back to Larkspur to compensate for the lack of lunch with whatever remained in the fridge.

TUESDAY, 17TH JANUARY,
Pahrump and the Nevada Test Site

Ted Airlines got Jules into Las Vegas just past 10:10. By comparison to the previous day, it had been stress-free. Learning from his mistakes, Jules had allowed an extra 30 minutes for the airport shuttle to cope with the tailback in front of the Golden Gate Bridge only to find this time that the tailback was just 150 yards long.

Jules picked up a Ford Focus from Payless Car Rental and made his way north up the CA-160 to Pahrump. Farid and his people had done most of the work on this part of the plan. All Jules had to do was turn up at Desert View Realty where an overweight, overfriendly Sabrina was waiting to show 'Professor Ahmad' from Larkspur around the Black Horse Ranch that he was expecting to rent for three months. Stopping for supplies at a 9-Eleven on the way out of town, they drove about 17 miles towards the hills before arriving at the '4-bedroom luxury ranch' that Farid had found, complete with pool and helipad. Farid said that its principal selling point was privacy.

Sabrina told him in reverent tones that this was indeed one of the finest properties they handled owing to its own private water supply that the owners had drilled 'specially'. The grass was certainly less arid looking than anywhere else for as far as the eye could see but the décor was equally as overstated as were the increasing hints from Sabrina of her cooking charms and availability. Sabrina waxed lyrical about the lost Breyfogle gold mine just up the road near the Johnnie mining settlement and told him proudly that the defunct Labbe Camp mine shafts were just 250 yards down the hill from where she was standing. The whole place was 'real historical'.

Eventually Jules began to feel claustrophobic as the sweetness of Sabrina's heavy scent clogged around him until he pointedly looked at his watch, thanked her and said he had some urgent calls to make. Sabrina looked crestfallen and withdrew with a cow-like smile but no fuss.

He unpacked his small bag and sat in the sun on the terrace with a sandwich and a cold bottle of Grolsch, waiting for the helicopter to arrive. A thermometer said 65 degrees but it felt pleasantly warmer. To the east, the hilltops were all snow clad and glistened in the sun.

About 15:10, the distinctive whump and buzz of a helicopter retrieved Jules from a gentle slide into sleep. The Schweizer 300Cbi came into sight and wheeled onto the helipad by the hanger. The little black, fly-like machine was essentially designed for training but Farid said that its size and fabrication produced one of the lowest radar profiles available.

The pilot, a Middle-Eastern looking man with greying hair called simply Bashi, descended from the cockpit, smiled broadly

THE SEEDING

and shook Jules's hand. Farid had said that the pilot would be a crack military instructor, one of the best they had. 'Understand you're still a bit wet round the ears' Bashi laughed. 'Well, I'm here to fix that!' It was a statement.

As part of his training, Jules had been given instruction on both fixed-wing aircraft and helicopters but had requested further instruction in helicopters as soon as his flying ability became integral to the success of their plans for the Nevada Test Site. Bashi told him that one of his men would be arriving any minute with a mobile platform that would allow the Schweizer be housed in the hanger, away from any possible prying eyes. 'The only problem, young man, is that you've got to be able to put the bird down right on top of it otherwise its useless. But don't worry; I'll have you doing that by the end of today!'

Half an hour later, an anonymous truck delivered the platform and two fully fuelled storage tanks and then left, but not before the driver, in dress-down kit and trainers, forgot himself entirely and gave Bashi an involuntary, stiff salute. Clearly the man commanded the respect of his men.

As soon as the truck departed, Bashi took Jules up in the Schweizer to acclimatise. Farid was right, it was comparatively easy to fly accurately and Bashi's sure hand inspired both confidence and dexterity. Returning to the ranch as the sun was setting, Bashi made Jules put it down parallel with each side of the small landing pad before finally letting him park on it.

'Not so bad eh!' Bashi said – which Jules decided to take as a pass and thanked Bashi warmly. He was now keen to fly it again. Back in the house, they cracked a couple of beers before Jules set about cooking an early supper of corn on the cob, steak and salad. Bashi said he never touched alchohol and so Jules got the freshly

131

squeezed grapefruit juice out of the fridge.

After supper, the maps came out and together they planned the best route to the area of the NTS they planned to use and the best way to get the Schweizer in and out without attracting attention. Bashi had planned a number of 'special ops' and was quick to point out the pitfalls and dangers of the three spots they identified.

The following morning, the alarm went off at 06:00 and, having demolished poached eggs on a mountain of instant hash browns and corned beef, Bashi navigated them off into the January dawn light along the optimised route that Jules would need to follow in April. Over the hill and down into Death Valley which seemed to be an uninhabited wilderness. Then banking north-east, over the hills and down over the NV-95 and into the Nevada Test Range, fast and low to avoid detection; the calm voice of Bashi beside him directing him all the while like a rally driver.

Finally they came up to the area they had pinpointed the night before and slowly surveyed the contours and folds below them for a suitable site.

'There' said Bashi finally pointing to a gully with a narrow exit, 'see if you can get in there and hover.' Jules eased the Schweizer down, conscious of the walls of the gully closing on him as he descended, wincing as windy blasts threatened to knock them sideways. 'OK, hold it there' said Bashi leaping out of the cockpit to plant a homing device. He covered it with a 2-foot square bright red cloth and pinned it to the rocky ground. Clambering back into the hovering Schweizer, Bashi re-attached his intercom. 'You'll need to be out of here having set everything up in less than five minutes so we'll just stay here a little longer to see if they have any eyes and ears that will pick us up.'

Bashi looked at his watch while Jules kept glancing up at the sky, half expecting F-15s to be swooping down on them. 'OK" he said after what seemed much longer than five minutes, 'let's get out of here. Try and follow the exact route we came in by.'

Even with the adrenalin coursing, Jules still needed a couple of minor corrections from Bashi to stick to the route. In the winter morning's light, the folds of the grey rocky ravines looked confusingly similar but, Bashi assured him, merging his memory of the map with the path Bashi was guiding him through, would allow Jules to go over it time and again in his mind later.

A little over an hour later, they had a short de-briefing session back at the ranch. 'Pretty good overall young man' Bashi said with a smile. 'We'll have one more trial run before lunch by which time we will both have a pretty good idea of the route. More importantly' Bashi said, 'I attached a clever little box to the Schweizer which we use at home for night ops. It takes the data from the flight path and can almost be used like an automatic pilot to keep you on track. Combining the data from the two trips should be foolproof, even if you contrive to lose your way!'

After their second sortie into the area, Jules said farewell to Bashi and caught a plane down to San Diego.

He had booked into an over-elaborate guest house near the Morley Field sports Complex as it gave him the chance to have his morning run and use its swimming pool as well. Settling into the spa with a glass of Zinfandel, Jules felt a degree of satisfaction. Their two trespasses into the nuclear test site were the riskiest part of the operation so far and, so far, there had been no problem.

It seemed to Jules that Zahra came when things had gone well and so he was more than ready to retire early. Tonight, however, tiredness ambushed him as he put out the light and a brief instant of longing was quickly quenched in sleep.

WEDNESDAY, JANUARY 18TH
Brewster's Boat Yard, Qualtrough Street, San Diego

Hank Brewster watched the preppy-looking man checking out his yard and the boats that he meandered past on his way towards the office. He looked like a potential client. Sure enough, he was a British investment banker from New York looking for an inexpensive boat for a little fishing.

He was going to be backwards and forwards between now and the end of the summer as they had just bought a summerhouse at Oceanside, 'the private estate at St. Malo actually'. Yes, of course Hank knew about the exclusive and eccentric 1929 development that imitated the French port of St Malo in Brittany. It was effectively a closed colony, available only to the very rich and particularly well connected.

The British investment banker also wondered about the winter arrangements, servicing facilities and provisioning. It all sounded promising but, in the end, George Anstruther had beaten him down his inventory of luxury vessels to a 1974 Acm 640 that he was selling for a friend for just $8000. The pill had been sweetened with a full maintenance contract and a stipulation that the boat should be out of the water during the winter months if it was not needed.

Anstruther paid cash from a bulging money clip, wished him well and said that he probably wouldn't see him until the Spring as he was taking his family back to Europe for their next holiday to ski. Alright for bloody bankers, thought Hank.

The yard was situated well within bomb blast of the naval base and the downtown area and, fanned by the prevailing wind, the deadly dust would be carried over a wide area inland.

THURSDAY 19TH JANUARY
*Industrial warehouse, W 21st St & Estrella Ave,
Los Angeles, California*

It was seven o'clock in the evening when Jules had reached the outskirts of the Los Angeles area. He had had thoughts of pressing on to the fabled Beverly Hills but he didn't know his way around anyway and decided instead to settle for a Best Western just off Interstate-5.

Having ploughed his way through 'tonight's special' of Beef Enchiladas in a glutinous cheese sauce washed down with some cold beer, Jules fought his way though a myriad of TV channels before falling asleep on the bed.

Farid had found small industrial warehouses hard to locate on the Internet, in the right sort of places near downtown LA. This morning though, Jules had finally got lucky after of scouring the commercial districts, concentrating on the dismal back streets adjoining the city's main arteries.

Eventually a 'To let' sign on a small unit in Estrella Street caught his eye. It was pinned to a door that was in need of a fresh coat of paint. There were a number of meat and grocery warehouses in the immediate vicinity which was useful as it gave him something to blend into. It was clearly not a much sought after position, close to the exit and entrance ramps of the Interstate-110 and continuously noisy. In addition, it turned out that it had been empty for over two and a half years.

The agent nearly buckled with gratitude that afternoon when the British Mr George Anstruther of St Malo, Oceanside put in an offer for a 2-year lease, extendable at his option for another year. Furthermore, he was even happy to pay in cash, a year in advance.

The following day, Jules had new security doors and an alarm fitted at the same time as he installed industrial shelving around most of the walls. He piled assorted tins of cheap vegetables and fruit he had bought from another wholesaler two blocks down making sure that the men fitting the new doors and the alarm had a good view of the distinctly uninteresting stock.

In the corner, he connected two large chest freezers to the electric supply but only turned one on. Into that, he loaded a full freezer of frozen vegetables and exotic fruits. The other he left ready for the one of the bombs to be installed in April.

With everything now ready in LA, Jules drove the hire car to LAX for his flight up to Seattle.

TUESDAY, 24TH JANUARY
Seattle

Farid had no knowledge of Seattle so Jules needed to come up with the final and distinct hiding place by himself. Given the pattern of the prevailing wind, he had been scouting for a location on the west side of the city but nothing suitable had shown up.

After two days, he was running down the classified section of the Seattle Times when his pencil alighted on *'2nd garage to let, fully self-contained, long term tenant preferred'*. After an initial call, it turned out that, although it was on the east side of the city, the owner was being transferred to New Zealand by his company and was looking to let the house and other garage as well. It appealed immediately as the principal tenant would be a complete stranger thereby offering him anonymous security, no interference and no complications.

Jules drove out to inspect it and shook hands with the owner after 20 minutes. The second garage was round the back of the house and not obvious from the road. It was dry and he would have the only key so long as the rent was paid six months in advance. Jules explained that he came to meetings at Microsoft once a quarter at least and had just put an offer for a car that was decrepit enough to use for the nearby skiing – his Scottish blood rebelled at the thought of always hiring cars he explained!

A day later 'Jonathan McAlistair, a consulting professor from MIT', drove a used Chevrolet Impala round the back of the house as arranged, explaining with some satisfaction that although it had 65,000 miles on the clock it was still rust free, in good working order and hadn't cost him a fortune. Jonathan handed over $5000 in cash, a generous full year in advance and received two keys and the house telephone number in return.

They had shaken hands warmly and agreed to have a beer the next time they met. They were already friends.

That afternoon, 'George Anstruther' caught a flight to Tokyo. Jules needed the period during which the statue of the Capitoline Wolf was being fashioned to set down the bones of the article that he was ostensibly writing for *Le Monde*.

TUESDAY, 14TH FEBRUARY, 17:45H
Lašva Bar, Travnik, Central Bosnia

Jasmina, an attractive, 30-year-old survivor from Srebrenica, started work at Radin's bar to the silent nods of approval from the regulars. She had been re-housed and given a fresh start by the EUFOR peacekeepers.

Since the internecine troubles, Travnik had become something of a haven for displaced refugees as the ethnic balance between Christians and Muslims was almost level with little sectarian violence. The local authorities had a publicly stated policy of maintaining that balance.

The owner of the bar claimed that she had been taken on as a favour to the local refugee authorities but no one believed that story. A mass of slightly unkempt dark brown hair festooned Jasmina's Slavic face, pale skin with a full mouth and a generous smile. For a highly competitive athlete and a successful cross-country runner, she possessed an unusually curvaceous but muscular figure. The combination stood out when compared with many of the local ladies of Travnik. Jasmina's arrival in the bar was quickly reflected in a new hat for the owner's wife to quell jealous instincts and prying eyes.

Jasmina usually greeted Radin warmly when he entered the bar and made sure that he was served quickly. He was keen to believe that she had marked him out but was repeatedly disappointed by a barrier of politeness that barred further progress as soon as he tried to delve into either her past or her immediate plans. Maybe she just had a friendly nature and was like that to all the regulars but he really hoped there might be other reasons. And, he admitted to himself, to be fair to her, he was not too forthcoming either when she would ask about him and his absences. One day maybe, one day.

THURSDAY, 5TH MARCH, PONTE À MORIANO, TUSCANY
Bardolini Institute takes shape,

Things had moved fast since Fritz Steinhoffer's visit in January.

Salvatore suspected that one probable reason why he had been approached was the 200 or so hectares of olives that came with Villa Cerva, the old family hunting lodge in the hills above Lucca. It seemed more than coincidental that Steinhoffer announced early in their meeting that the supervisory committee would look kindly on any proposal for the Bardolini Institute to acquire the olives for itself and had in fact been authorised to offer Salvatore and his brother what could only be regarded as a very full price for the land if he decided to take the job. Salvatore didn't hesitate – the proceeds comfortably took care of the looming family crisis and left them with a substantial financial cushion for the future.

Salvatore had also readily agreed to the unexpectedly generous compensation package that he was offered and had suggested that he immediately institute a three-part programme for staffing and planting in Italy and developing the Institute's reach in the US.

He acquired smart modern offices in Ponte à Moriano that was home to several good local restaurants and just 10 minutes down the hill from the hunting lodge. Fittingly, Pietro Viacci joined him after 28 years working for the Bardolini Group itself. He brought with him a comprehensive knowledge of both cultivation and production of olive oil. Together they set out new planting plans to include the olive varieties of moraiolo and divastro alongside the frantoio and leccino trees that were already established. They agreed drawings for their own pressing plant and Pietro drew together the key elements of an educational programme with a series of potential visiting speakers.

Becky had called her father two days after Steinhoffer left to begin the process of selecting a high profile list of trustees for the American Bardolini Committee which was to receive annual grants of $5m to cover students on courses at Ponte à Moriano and sponsorship of industry related schemes in the US itself. In addition, the $100m Bardolini charitable foundation would be happy to receive suitable applications through the committee.

Her father was now in his 60s, single yet again and as chauvinistic as ever. He had only met his grandchildren once on a flying visit to Rome when they had all flown down for a brief meeting in his grandiose hotel. He was jetlagged; Salvatore and Becky were guarded, and the children had been overawed and shy. It had been their only contact since Becky had announced that she was marrying 'her Italian' and not coming home. Now, however, there was something that he could exploit among his friends. His only daughter, 'the Contessa you know', suddenly had a profile that he could use to embellish his image and he set about it with relish.

Which was exactly what Becky had expected – mutual exploitation but she didn't care; he was not a real or meaningful part of her life. Add the bait of an annual trustee meeting in Ponte à Moriano in June, all expenses paid, and she had had two senior Republican senators, a judge and two high profile Chief Executives from

THE SEEDING

the US food industry as committee members inside three weeks.

The last element of the immediate task according to Steinhoffer was to install the somewhat gothic statue of a Capitoline Wolf that had been requested by Bardolini before he died as a monument to Italian American kinship.

Enrico Bardolini had enjoyed the support of the New York based *Brothers of Italy in America* and had been a significant donor to their charities. It was his wish apparently that his monument should be sited in the Little Italy area of New York. In order to meet Enrico's original installation target date of the beginning of April, the 60th anniversary of his first million-dollar quarter, Becky had fully employed all her resources to get things moving. Not only did she inform the BIA of the old man's wishes and her plans at the same time as her father and his committee but she had also explained to her mother that this might just be the bridge to reconnect with her friends in New York society, if she wanted to get involved, that was.

Now Salvatore laughed out loud as he read the somewhat formal letter from his father-in-law. It was all arranged – the date was fixed for 1st April and the unveiling was now to be sponsored jointly by his committee and the Brothers of Italy in America. The venue had been moved to City Hall Park in view of the fact that her mother's childhood friend, now the First Lady, Lucy Wilmington, had graciously agreed to her very personal request to unveil the statue herself. There would be a reception for the good and the great with which Becky's mother had been pleased to assist and the guests would also be entertained by Italy's newest tenor, Giuseppe di Francia. The event had apparently already made the social columns in New York and an exclusive interview with Becky's mother appeared in the latest edition of Vanity Fair. It was going to be an occasion everyone could be proud of.

'Nothing like a bit of creative tension to get things moving! What your parents probably don't realise is that, here in Europe, April 1st is also all fools day!' said Salvatore triumphantly congratulating Becky. The irony of it all was magnificent even if their satisfaction was just a little tinged by cynicism.

All in all, progress in the two months was beginning to look robust – the Bardolini Institute was on the map on both sides of the Atlantic but, more importantly, the family's financial problems had been resolved for the foreseeable future. Furthermore Salvatore and Pietro Viacci had begun developing plans to extend the scope of the Bardolini Institute to encompass other areas of his benefactor's considerable range of Italian food.

This time, the trip to New York would be a holiday they could really enjoy.

MONDAY, 25TH MARCH, 17:45H
Lašva Bar, Travnik, Central Bosnia

On 25th March, Jasmina observed Radin leaving his house in the afternoon with the rucksack he normally took with him when he went away for a while.

She immediately informed Hamdija, her local Mossad *katsa* and, as usual, Radin was later observed boarding a flight to Tehran. Something was going on but without corroborating evidence from Tehran, which they didn't have, it was difficult to take matters further than speculation.

Jasmina had already reported what appeared to be a Palestinian tax wrapper on a packet of Camel cigarettes he had in front of him on the bar. She was sure that she had noticed the distinctive red triangle on the black, white and green background before he put them away. Mossad was grateful for further corroboration of the Palestinian link but needed more than that before a sanction was issued for him.

THURSDAY, 1ST APRIL, 19:25PM
CITY HALL PARK, NEW YORK
American Bardolini Committee reception

Becky di Fabbri nudged her husband's arm. The First Lady had arrived and was surrounded by aspiring Republican acquaintances, some notable high rollers from Texas and a few discrete secret servicemen disguised in dark blue suits. She was scheduled to leave shortly after the unveiling of the Capitoline Wolf for a private dinner uptown. Now the flow of the good and the great through the reception line was dwindling and Becky realised that she had hardly known any of the hands she'd shaken – the price of being an ex-pat.

'I think we can get a drink and catch the crowd now' she whispered to Sal. She caught herself starring at him again. He looked so distinguished, still good looking, quietly sophisticated, exuding relaxed, confident charm. No one here tonight held a candle to him! Sal nodded and they broke away from Becky's parents in the reception group still revelling in their social renaissance.

Sal smiled, sipping a glass of cold Orvieto *Seco* that the *Brothers of Italy* had kindly donated. 'Fantastic turnout by our backers – they've really pulled in their friends too which should help us enormously down the line'.

'Quite a mixed bunch though' said Becky quietly looking around. Alongside the bankers and money men, the occasion had drawn a combination of open-necked jet-setters, politicians, fashionistas and musical celebrities, as well as a down-home Texas contingent that came to cheer on Becky's mother.

'You know Sal, coming back to something like this after so long, things look different. If I look around, sure there are the sophisticates who always blend well the world over but here, I don't know, whether it's the hair, the makeup or the clothes, the girls just look, well, over-engineered, too much of a statement!

'I mean, do look at Gerri Springer there' whispered Becky mischievously. 'She's the actress wife of that oil man my mother is always going on about. What does she look like?! I tell you, if I had those flabby arms, I would hide them in sleeves and my neckline would certainly not plunge anywhere near so low. There are cleavages for heaven's sake and then there are old cleavages!'

'Over-engineered' was probably right thought Sal, but he wasn't going to say it. They were incredibly lucky. The evening had a balmy feel to it more reminiscent of June, there was no chance of rain, and the new leaves and blossom in City Hall Park were starting to emerge with that freshness that only spring brings. 450 people were expected and, according to Becky's mother, it was the only game in town that day. She'd even had total strangers angling for an invitation.

Just then, Becky's father tapped the microphone on the speaker's platform and invited the assembled company to take a seat on the gilt chairs in front of him. When the crowd had started to settle, he introduced Carlo Benati, the president of the *Brothers of Italy*.

Carlo enthused about the extraordinary generosity of his dear friend Enrico Bardolini, his contribution to Italian culture in America and his wonderful foresight in sponsoring the *American Bardolini Committee* which was so ably led by his friend, Harvey Fairchild, to whom he would now hand back the microphone.

Becky's father then gave a warm tribute to the inherent generosity of Americans and the wonderful support that his committee and indeed the Institute itself had received from its growing band of patrons, many of whom were with them tonight. He wanted to thank the tireless efforts of his wonderful son-in-law who had achieved so much so quickly in the development of the Institute back in Italy 'So Sal, at the back there, please raise an arm so everyone can see you!' and finally how honoured he was now to turn things over to one of his wife's earliest and dearest friends, today of course 'our own First Lady of the United States of America'!'

Lucy Wilmington smiled appreciatively, uttered some plaudits about close cooperation between counties imbued with common values and how, here in New York, the first settling place of Italian immigrants into our country, it was especially apposite that the Bardolini statue should find a home. She quipped that it was probably a little 'modern' for her taste but exactly in tune with the leading edge of art today and would therefore make its own special contribution to the City Hall Park and New York in general.

With that, the First Lady pulled the lever in front of her and the white shroud that had covered Ando's creation fell to the grass to immediate and expected applause. A Texan lady sitting in front of Sal, wearing an extraordinary mauve polka dot dress with inter-planetary shoulders shouted above the clapping, 'Looks like an over-sized, bulbous hippopotamus with a scary face to me.' 'No, Martha. No!' replied the black Channel dress and glistening Cartier Tank watch beside her, 'It's Henry Moore, it's Barbara Hepworth, it's a nihilistic modern interpretation of traditional neo-realism, surely you can see that Martha?'

As the First Lady left the platform, the applause started to die which was the cue for the Italian ambassador to announce one of Italy's greatest assets, the voice of Giuseppe di Francia, the new Pavarotti, flown in specially to sing for them.

This was probably the high point of the evening as far as Sal was concerned. He'd loved opera since childhood when his penniless father had still insisted on taking both his sons to La Scala in Milan every summer. Sal turned away from the magic flowing from the tenor's soul and looked around him.

It had been a major effort by everyone even if he might not have chosen everything they'd done if left to his own devices. The clear-sided tent that enveloped the area leading to and around the Jacob Wrey Mould Fountain was decorated as a grand ballroom of a Venetian palazzo accented with crystal chandeliers that clashed horribly with the permanent, heavy, black gas lanterns on the fountain itself. Gold damask tablecloths covered the bars and the side tables with towering sprays of abundant white flowers. Swaths of white organza also fluttered from the ceiling over the hardwood floor that now covered the paving stones – lest those Jimmy Choo shoes get scuffed.

It was indeed quite a performance! Sal noticed a small plaque in the grass that read 'Do the right thing and nine out of ten times it turns out to be the right thing politically – a quote from Citizen Debs Myers'. Both of Becky's parents had probably noticed the plaque too. It would have spoken directly to the personal renaissance each hoped for. And peculiarly, Sal too hoped that the evening had provided just that renaissance for them in their separate ways.

As the guests began to drift away, the foreman of the crew that had delivered and installed the statue wandered back from inspecting the risen edifice of Freedom Tower newly completed just a block away. A shame really, thought Farid Karzam, could actually turn out to be 9/11 all over again.

SUNDAY, 4TH APRIL 12:12 PM MARSHALL, HIGHWAY 1, CALIFORNIA
Tony's Seafood restaurant en route to Eureka

Tomales Bay is a narrow, 22-mile-long inlet fed by the Pacific Ocean, 50 miles north of San Francisco. The landscape is said to resemble the rolling hills and misty moors of Scotland – a world away from commercially-clogged ribbon of Marin County shopping malls that encompass Highway 101. Oysters thrive in Tomales Bay, particularly in the open, north end where salt water from the sea meets the fresh spring water from Walker Creek. The water temperature stays cool throughout the year and the oysters thrive on a healthy population of phytoplankton.

Here in the tiny West Marin county town of Marshall (population 50), the Hog Island Oyster Company was born in 1982. A century earlier, Marshall had been a hub for commercial seafood fishing, a haven for tourists and a stop on the railway that transported lumber and seafood up and down the Northern California coast. When the marine biologists and Hog Island proprietors bought the dilapidated Marshall General store and post office in 1982, they chose the location for its aqua cultural potential. It had all the right stuff — fresh, clean, cold water, plenty of nutrients and tidal action that would help produce superior oysters. Presentation is as important as taste for half-shell oysters sold to the top restaurants and the Hog Island oyster has been meticulously bred for both.

A few paces down the street is Tony's Seafood restaurant. In Ahmad's book, it was one of the great finds of his short California experience, he explained to Radin Ivanovic as they walked towards it.

'Much of the West Coast of America suffers from over-hyped, over-glitzed superficiality, so it's refreshing to come here where the raw materials are as good as it gets and the cooking is straightforward and unpretentious. Here, it is family run and completely genuine. It doesn't look like much built out on stilts does it? Odds are we'll see one of the owners cleaning the fish outside when we arrive – then you really know it's fresh!'

They were shown to a table by a window that looked out past an old, rusting fishing boat, across the bay towards Laird's Landing on the other side. Ahmad guided Radin to Tony's barbecued oysters to start with followed by a thick tuna steak that he explained was best served raw in the middle. Ahmad himself started with mussels followed by the swordfish that their waitress, Vera, promised had been brought ashore that morning – fries, salad with blue-cheese dressing, Luna di Luna Pinot Grigio along with a large bottle of sparkling Calistoga to wash away any remnants of the previous evening's overindulgence.

Radin had arrived the previous afternoon from Tehran via Paris. Thanks to the continuing adversarial relations, there were still no direct flights between mainland USA and Tehran and for a man who had a natural and ill-disguised fear of flying, 17 hours strapped to potential death traps was a new and harrowing experience. After nearly two hours standing in line to clear US immigration, his sense of frustrated disorientation was made worse by his limited grasp of English. He was therefore glad that the girl at the Bay Autos desk seemed to have all the paperwork organised including the drop off in Los Angeles. The red Chevrolet Suburban was ready and awaited him in the third bay on the left. The car was bigger than anything Radin had ever driven before and perched on leather seats behind the surging power of the six-litre engine, Radin felt slightly regal, intoxicated by the quadraphonic sound that swept over him from the in-car sound system.

With Tehran's directions open beside him, he had carefully made the journey up to Interstate 280, across the Golden Gate bridge, along Highway 101 until Sir Francis Drake Boulevard turning right at the bottom of the slip road and then left into Larkspur Landing Circle. Cautious by nature, he had resisted the frequent boyish urges to open the throttle and see what his charger would do up the highway. He knew he was tired and he did feel genuinely strange. His chance would come.

Radin had been told that Ahmad had taken a short lease on a furnished apartment in the Andrew Jackson complex at the top of the circle. The lease expired the following week. After some minimal introductory pleasantries, a bite to eat and two litres of Semillon-Chardonnay to help him sleep, Radin had allowed his jetlag to roll over him. It was 6:30pm Pacific time.

After what seemed to Radin an endless night with patches of

light sleep and odd, repetitious dreams of crowded roads skirting into and around multi-coloured clouds, Ahmad had woken him an age later, around 11am the next morning to start their journey to meet the bombs. Radin now blinked at the hazy view across the bay and at Ahmad as they waited in silence for the first course to arrive.

Jules had a naturally outgoing nature that had suited him well to journalism and the need to encourage indiscretion in others. The fact that Radin seemed conversationally mute was in many ways a relief as projecting the image of a young college professor was not going to require constant invention.

Radin's appreciation of his barbequed oysters was a grunt with the observation that he 'no get these back home'. It was a start but Jules's further efforts extolling the virtues of his swordfish were matched only by the brief opinion on the tuna that 'this fish no cooked in middle'. It seemed pointless to try and explain again so he let it go – in fact, the bonding element of the excursion could have failed equally as well in the local MacDonald's!

For his part, Radin had run across some of these intellectual teacher types before – mostly in VERVEK. He had no use for them but they were giving him a paid and, as far as he could see, almost risk free trip to America to teach this professor something so simple that it couldn't take more than five minutes. And paying him $35,000 for his trouble. Obviously something big must be going on but Radin knew from experience when not to ask.

Once back in the privacy of the SUV, having joined the 101 heading towards Eureka, Ahmad handed Radin the map to show him where they were going, enquired after his experience on boats and then briefly outlined their tasks. Ahmad explained that he had a controller named *The Merchant* to whom they were responsible for the duration. *The Merchant* had prepared all the items they would need to complete their task.

Radin was accompanying him to Eureka to pick up the bombs. Radin would oversee the seeding of the first bomb in San Francisco and arm the demonstration bomb in the missile range. Then he was finished and would fly home. 'Nothing too testing.' Ahmad said. Radin nodded.

When they stopped for gas and a coffee, Ahmad asked briefly about the activating process that Radin was to teach him. For a man with such brutish hands, Radin drew a surprisingly sharp diagram of the arming device that triggered the detonators. He pointed to the position of the keypad for the number that had to be punched in to activate the radio receiver that could then trigger the detonation. Radin explained that once activated, the receiver operated off low-power batteries that had a life of 10 years. Radin earnestly promised that he would show him properly with the first bomb but that was really about all he had to say.

While Radin sat in pensive, almost sulky silence in the passenger seat, Jules worried about his outward ineptness that made his reactions difficult to gauge if they ran into problems. So long as Radin's eye-catching foreignness could evade any dangerous exposure to people during his brief role, he would not jeopardise anything and it was Jules's job to make sure of that.

When they pulled into the 101 Trucks & Autos, Ahmad explained that *The Merchant* had arranged for them to pick the truck up to carry the bombs and Radin should follow him back down the 101 to where they would leave it overnight ready to offload the bombs into the next morning.

The SUV pulled into Woodley Island Marina, immediately opposite Eureka, just after 7:30pm. Ahmad took all his papers and his seafaring certificates to the office and shortly emerged with the keys and maps. They collected their overnight bags and were under way within 15 minutes heading towards the mouth of Humboldt Bay, a couple of miles south. The boat was a 62ft. Dutch cabin cruiser with a cruising speed of 20 knots. Heading due west took them well into international waters by 11:30pm. Ahmad cut the engines. He explained that they were almost exactly at the rendezvous point with the submarine and then settled down to rework all his calculations to make sure that he compensated for any drift as they waited.

Jules was secretly nervous at night in situations involving other vessels at sea. His father was a keen sailor and, when Jules was 13, had once been taking the family from Sardinia to Minorca on a night passage when a huge submarine had appeared out of the blackness, broadside on about 40 yards in front. Only fast thinking by his father who was on watch with him at the time avoided a certain collision. At night, if there was no moon, like tonight, you just couldn't see.

Shortly after 00:40, the bleeper went off on the cell phone with a text message that the submarine was on the surface about a mile and a half away, had them on their radar and would be with them shortly. Ahmad acknowledged and breathed a sigh of gratitude. 'That's the waiting over.' he said 'It's always the worst bit!'

Apart from the usual Pacific swell, the sea was almost flat calm and so the chain of sailors made fast work of unloading their heavy cargo as Radin and Ahmad stored the incoming trunks below deck. Twenty minutes later, the Iranian captain saluted and closed his hatch behind him. Not a word had been spoken and they were on their own again.

Ahmad turned the cruiser round and headed for Humboldt Bay.

In the first light of the deserted dawn of Friday morning, the two of them heaved their cargo into the refrigerated truck and then Ahmad headed back out to sea and up the coast for some sleep.

Returning the cabin cruiser earlier than planned, the professor explained that his friend had to get a plane to New York but they had so enjoyed their trip and would be back next time they were up that way – July perhaps.

As they approached the grey truck again, Jules scanned the buildings, the waiting aggregate trucks and the parked cars for a sign of anything unusual, anything out of place. The area was busy with some people already leaving work for the weekend. Nothing, so with the back of the truck parked facing away from prying eyes, Ahmad retrieved the keys that had been carefully hidden between the double rear right tyres and unlocked the back. All was just as they'd left it. Ahmad climbed into the cab of the grey truck leaving Radin to follow in the SUV.

Leaving Fields Landing, they picked up Highway 101 again going south until Ahmad turned east on CA-36 and headed into the hills. The traffic was light and after about an hour and a half, Ahmad turned right across the river they had been skirting and took the dirt road up the hill until they were overlooking the road again. Ahmad parked the truck so that it couldn't be seen from below and then they manhandled the four trunks with the distinctive pink labels that they had packed at the rear of the truck, into the SUV together with one large suitcase and a smaller cardboard packet.

Ahmad rejoined Radin and took over the driving. As they retraced their steps west, he explained that *The Merchant* would distribute the other trunks; they had completed their responsibilities for the overall operation.

Some five hours later, back in the darkness of his bedroom in Lincoln Village, Jules reviewed the day's events. He mused that it was certainly the first time he had gone to bed with five nuclear bombs beside him.

The concept behind the plan rested on the in-built freedoms of the Western democracies and the strong probability that if Jules did not actually break the law overtly, did not get caught speeding, did nothing in fact to arouse local suspicion, the odds had to be strongly in favour of success as this was not a police State, it was not a country bedevilled by internecine tribal rivalry or Orwellian surveillance of its citizens. Just like home, there were no checkpoints, no surprise roadblocks and therefore little danger of detection so long as they remained innocuous and didn't draw attention to themselves. The transfer of the bombs from the submarine to the boat and then to the truck had always been acknowledged as the most exposed period of the operation when the whole project could fail but the plan had worked seamlessly thus far.

Although the trip with Radin to the Nevada Test Site would be complicated by his presence, thereafter it would just be down to himself. So, from now on, it would require some seriously unexpectedly bad luck if any of the individual elements of the plan were to be detected in the future and, from now on, the detection of any one element would no longer threaten the viability of the others – once the bombs had been hidden.

Sinking deeper into mellowness, Jules turned inward. Now surely Zahra would be with him again, now that the riskiest part of the whole operation had been completed. Jules turned his consciousness in on itself, delving towards that meeting point between consciousness and sleep where Zahra waited for him. Nothing was happening. Was he trying too hard? And as he worried, so the distraction of consciousness returned. So it went until the blackness of the void claimed him, empty-handed.

TUESDAY, 6TH APRIL 07:25
Taylor Street (near intersection with Pine), downtown San Francisco

Leaving the apartment early to avoid the traffic, they went in convoy over the Golden Gate Bridge and on down to Embarcadero 3 where Radin left his Chevrolet Suburban on level 2 of the high rise building's car park. The area was nearly deserted at that hour on a Saturday morning. From now on they would work in a team, each backing up the other.

They simply could not risk an accidental discovery of the contents of his SUV while they were unloading the first bomb at the kerbside in broad daylight and Jules had therefore made the decision to leave all but the first bomb aboard Radin's car. They planned to split the remainder once they were under way towards the Nevada Test Site if a suitable moment presented itself and, if it didn't, they would just have to be careful until they reached the Black Horse Ranch. There was nothing overtly suspicious about either them or their vehicles and they had the added tactical advantage of surprise in the event that one of them was to be threatened in any way.

Ahmad's SUV drew up close to the nondescript entrance to the grey-blue apartment block on the corner of Taylor and Pine. Ahmad lowered the heavy metal trunk onto the high-handled luggage trolley and wheeled it inside as Radin drove off to find a parking meter. On the 2nd floor, he unlocked the door to the dingy apartment. The linen cupboard with its water tank was where he had envisaged putting the trunk and it looked as though it would fit snugly into the bottom.

When Radin arrived, they opened the trunk, Ahmad activated the keypad as instructed and typed in the coded number he had received on the cell phone before they left. He re-entered the number when requested and finally the four-letter security affix known only to him. As he pressed the red activation button, the box startled him as it hummed momentarily before falling silent.

Ahmad closed and locked the trunk, pushed it flush with the back wall of the cupboard and covered it with some blankets. It all looked completely natural.

'OK, Radin, time to hit the road, let's go!'

Ahmad dropped Radin back at Embarcadero 3 car park to pick up his car and waited by the exit till it emerged. Radin knew where they were going but he was happy to let Ahmad lead. It was going to be a long and, according to Ahmad, boring drive.

It was 08:20 as they swung up onto the Bay Bridge. Crossing to Oakland, they picked up Interstate 580, past Livermore and down to where it merged with Interstate 5 and on down the kitchen garden and orchards of California to Bakersfield. Here they pulled into a shopping mall and headed for the reliable anonymity of MacDonald's.

Jules produced a map showing exactly where they were headed and rehearsed Radin on how to get to the Black Horse Ranch should anything happen to him. They would stop in Pahrump for Jules to pick up food for dinner while Radin stayed with the bombs. Jules did not want Radin exposed to human gaze more than absolutely necessary. Two Big Macs later, Jules scanned the bustling car park and abandoned the idea of splitting the cargo of bombs between them. There were just too many eyes around that might notice them moving the heavy trunks from one vehicle to the other. Even if it was not actually suspicious, it would be potentially memorable and Jules didn't want that either. Anyway, it was only another four or five hours and the areas they were heading through were increasingly empty. They'd make it and it was probably safer to have Radin guarding all the bombs in Pahrump while he bought provisions.

As the fruit trees and vegetable farms grew fewer, replaced increasingly by desert scrub, Jules reflected that it would take a particular kind of individual to want to live in these desert regions but periodic gold rushes, the Borax deposits and indeed the artesian wells that had underwritten the founding of Las Vegas had all proved powerful drivers to settlers. As literally translated, 'The Meadows' was hardly the image that the modern city brought immediately to mind with its brash lights, countless tourists and gamblers.

Nearly five hours later, Jules turned right onto the NV-160 in the middle of Pahrump and then almost immediately indicated left, turning into the parking lot of the city's Wal-Mart. Radin followed and discretely parked five spaces along in the row in front of Jules. Wandering casually over as if to address a friend he'd met by chance, Jules told Radin that he wouldn't be long, ten minutes or so, time enough to pick up some dinner for them and something to drink. He needed to stay and stand guard over their arsenal.

Radin grunted something resolutely unintelligible and watched Jules disappear. He looked at the mileage counter; 572 miles from Larkspur now and he felt it. His eyes felt hollow. He was bored and he wanted to be back home in his local bar.

Radin had thought about Jasmina quite frequently during the monotonous bouts of travel he had endured in the last week. There had been no opportunity to entangle a member of the opposite sex, it was simply not written into the plan. Apart from the girl behind the car hire desk at San Francisco airport, Jules was in fact the only other person Radin had even spoken to since he had arrived in America and Jules had made it quite clear that their relationship was strictly operational – no small talk, no personal chat. But it was the way Radin liked it too and $35,000 for doing virtually nothing was $35,000.

Radin watched the mass of evening shoppers coming and going. The girls in Travnik definitely dressed with better taste as far as he was concerned – but evidently had less money. As he watched, he began to notice a leggy looking girl in a skimpy denim skirt that was frayed at the bottom, a bare, fleshy midriff and a Jayne Mansfield cowboy hat skewed over straggly, peroxide hair. She must have walked past him three times now and the heavily-studded cowboy boots merely confirmed his impression.

He realised instinctively that she had clocked him as a possible punter staking out the ground from his car perhaps and now she also knew that he had noticed her. Radin quashed his immediate carnal reaction – had he been at home he would have run with it but not here, not now. He simply couldn't. But she could sense his interest, she was a pro and he knew that she knew. She was starting to close in on him and there was no sign of Professor Ahmad. Radin pushed the switch and closed the window as she was now making straight for him. Unperturbed, the girl sauntered directly towards the car. Radin stared straight ahead, his eyes fixed on nothing. She was knocking on the window now. Radin intensified his stare as if it might frighten her away. Unabashed, she now opened the door.

'Say lover, now you acting as if you never seen me!' she drawled 'But we knows better than that, don't we sunshine! I's got what you's a-looking for in spades an' it'll only take a short ride from here – real close.' She said sliding her hand directly over his thigh and leaving it there.

'You go away now!' hissed Radin aware that her finger tips were working their way up and over his thigh as he stared determinedly into the middle distance.

'Now you know you don't really mean that sugar: you just a shy boy now' she continued with an inane smile spreading over her face.

'You go away now!' repeated Radin with increased urgency as he scanned the store exits for the Professor.

'Oh come on baby, I can show you some real sweet music, y' know' she was kneading his crutch now.

With no sign of the Professor, Radin's helplessness and growing panic burst. He acted instinctively smashing the back of his left hand into her leering face, sending her recoiling, screaming in pain into the sharp edge of the car door, blood erupting from the wound as she hit the hard asphalt of the car park.

As Radin watched her fall, his left hand was already stretching towards the ignition key. For an eternity of probably two seconds, he continued to scour the supermarket exits for Professor Ahmad as he fired the engine into life. This was suddenly a disaster, everything had simultaneously fallen apart, his anonymity was destroyed, their entire plan was now at risk and could be exposed.

No option, he had to go, get out of here fast. But just as Radin made to slam the car door, so it was yanked wide open by a furious looking hobo screaming insults at him. The man's bare torso was covered in tattoos scarcely concealed by a leather waistcoat and he was brandishing a substantial hunting knife for immediate use. Lunging through the door space, the hobo was close to reaching Radin's throat, as Radin slammed the door on his arm causing him to drop the knife. Without pausing, Radin again slammed the door shut as hard as he could and accelerated forward, suddenly enveloped by a searing roar of anguish from the hobo as the tips of the fingers of his left hand trapped in the door were removed as the car accelerated. Surging out of the car park, Radin swung left onto the NV-160 heading north and cut his speed.

Would someone have recorded his licence plates? It was a chance he would just have to take – the hotel in San Francisco that he had used as an address for the car hire would have no record of him if questioned. He would find out soon enough when he returned the car at Los Angeles airport. Now he prayed for the delimiting sign on the edge of town so that he could begin to put some distance between himself and the disaster scene.

Emerging from Wal-Mart, Jules quickly became aware of the commotion occurring in the car park near where he had parked. As he approached his heart sank. Now, in the empty space where he had left Radin parked and unobtrusive, a blond bimbo squatted on the ground clutching her head while an urban low-life was having his hand wrapped in a makeshift bandage by a woman surrounded by five shopping bags. A security guard was speaking urgently into his handset. Jules caught snippets as he closed in '….red pickup thought to have headed south…' as he reached his car. 'No description of the man – just dark hair, swarthy.'

Instant damage control told Jules that what had appeared a catastrophe at first sight might just not be that bad if that was all that had been reported so far. He knew Radin was aware of the location of the ranch – to the north and, unless he had lost his mind in the confusion, the cops were going to be looking in the wrong direction for a red pickup truck, not Radin's 4X4 station wagon. The sound of an approaching police siren offered further clarification and, wandering up to the crowd gathering around the bloodied scene, Jules was able to glean that no one had much of a fix on what had happened and, equally, sympathy for the apparent 'victims' was limited by their patently dubious provenance and the depravity of their obvious profession. After a few unforthcoming minutes digging for new witnesses, the cops endorsed the details already given to traffic control and the pair then busied themselves assisting the 'victims' into the ambulance that had arrived.

Not knowing what had actually transpired, however, Jules was now desperate to catch up with Radin and his cache of nuclear bombs, desperate to know that he still had an operation. He swung out of the parking lot and followed Radin north up the 160. Radin was a seasoned operator, not fazed by death or gore, so at least he should be acting rationally.

But if Radin's bombs were uncovered, their strategy was dead. If they were not able to demonstrate Iran's ability to remotely set off the explosion in the Nevada Test Site, the vital element of the plan and its impact was lost. He now cursed himself for not taking a detour at lunchtime to at least give him control of the NTS bomb. It had been a glaring hole in their planning, a contingency that they'd completely overlooked.

TUESDAY, 6TH APRIL 7:05PM
Johnnie, NV-160, 16 miles north of Pahrump

It had been an unusually slow afternoon for Joe Kaldenski. The Nevada highway patrol trooper liked to stake out the NV-160 at Johnnie over the weekends. Awhile back, Joe had selected a well-sited mound at the side of the road just about where the speedsters started to slow down at the end of their run. He had perfect cover, unseen by the offenders. The boy racers from Pahrump and as far away as Vegas itself had identified the long straight strip of road as a great spot to show off their hot rods and strut their stuff. Traffic north of Pahrump was minimal at weekends and there was almost a six-mile stretch of dead straight track. In truth, they did no harm but the local community objected in principle whereas Joe simply treated it as a good hunting ground for himself.

As a younger man, Joe had revelled in the Harley-Davidson *Super Glide* that his father had left him on his death. It needed constant attention which Joe enjoyed and, really, it was that that attracted him – the mechanisms and the maintenance rather than the speed. Now 52 years of age, he therefore gloried in the machines and engines of his prey rather than just notching up speeding tickets.

As he prepared to call it a day, Joe saw the red car racing towards him. His instrumentation showed that it was doing 83 mph as it passed the mound. That was nothing exceptional in itself but he'd heard the mention of a red pickup on his radio and while this wasn't a pickup, it triggered a reaction. He gunned his motorcycle and set off after it, his lights flashing and siren wailing.

The red Chevy Suburban began to slow and Joe passed him on the left-hand bend just after the turn to Labbe Camp, signalling the driver to pull off the road into an old loading area he'd used many times before. Dismounting, he unhitched his holster as usual and walked slowly back to the Chevy, taking his time for added theatre. He could see the driver already frozen in anticipation. Joe tapped on the side window motioning him to lower it.

Joe leant his arm on the roof of the car to give himself a superior position, looking down on the victim. 'In something of a hurry ain't we, mister' he said as the window came down. The driver looked straight ahead and didn't reply. Odd, but maybe the guy was scared.

'So, where y're headed, mister?' Joe asked politely.

'Tonapah' Radin replied, inwardly relieved that he'd studied the map Jules had showed him at lunchtime.

'Driver's licence please' demanded Joe. Radin handed the cop his international driving license and sensed a momentary hiatus as he took it in.

'You got a passport mister?' Joe demanded. As he handed over his passport, Radin knew this was getting tricky. What was a Bosnian doing out here, on his own, on a Saturday evening? At the very least, the cop would report it in his notes.

'This a hired vehicle Sir? You got the papers?' asked Joe softly, his antennae alert to the unusual now.

Radin leant over to the glovebox and fished out the rental papers. The cop studied them for a few seconds.

'So, all the way from San Francisco, eh?' the cop pondered now looking carefully into the back of the vehicle. 'Lot of baggage for one man' he observed. 'You in sales or something, mister?' he continued.

'Yes, salesman' replied Radin with as much conviction as he could muster.

'Please open the back for me, Sir' Joe continued. That was it. Radin knew the man had crossed the Rubicon, the point of no return. Now it was him or me.

He got out of the car slowly, fumbling with his keys. Do nothing fast, act deliberate. He brushed past the cop; there was no sign of any traffic in either direction. Radin unlocked the back, lifting the back window above the tailgate. The cop instinctively moved forward as Joe moved aside inviting him to peer into the back. Momentarily, the cop was a fraction off balance and Radin seized his chance with precision lunging at the cop, knocking him forwards as he deftly removed his weapon from the open holster and dropped it on the ground. Seizing the man's helmet from behind in both hands, he used its leverage to execute the sharp jolt needed to break the man's neck. It was over in seconds. The cop lay motionless on the ground; still no traffic.

Radin dropped the tailgate, heaved the man into the back, pulled a cover from one of the trunks over him and slammed it again. Moving swiftly back to the motorbike, he smashed the radio with the butt of the dead man's gun and wheeled it over behind some empty oil drums that would hide it temporarily. Using the Chevy's toolkit, Radin removed the battery from the bike. He was sure that there would be a homing device somewhere on the machine but, without power, it would not transmit. After years on the streets, not much would get past him!

TUESDAY, 6TH APRIL, 17:45
Black Horse Ranch, Labbe Camp, Pahrump NV

By the time Jules had walked all the way round the house and the outbuildings, he knew there was a serious problem. The man, his car and the bombs were just not there. He was on his own, emasculated. As of right now, he had no idea what had happened, where Radin was or what had befallen him. He didn't even have an idea where to begin. He dare not call Radin's mobile phone. Radin hadn't called him and only Radin knew when it would be safe to make or take a call. He hadn't passed him as far as he knew; he'd passed one small settlement on the left but it was abandoned and visible from the road. If Radin had been followed, he must have led his pursuers past the Butch Cassidy Pass turning to Labbe Camp and gone on towards Crystal or even further.

If he'd been picked up, the operation was over anyway. Maybe Jules could improvise something with the two bombs that would not have gone down with Radin – if he could rescue the one in San Francisco and move the other out of Larkspur in time. It would depend on the length of Radin's silence. But without the NTS bomb, the rest of the plan, the weeks of work and preparation were nullified; they would have to start all over again.

How long would he give him? If Radin had been picked up, he knew that he was potentially in danger here already.

It was starting to get dark. Jules remembered that evening turned swiftly into night here but until he had some certainty about Radin, he couldn't even afford to enter the house. He would have to stake it out and wait.

At that moment, Jules heard the rumble of an approaching vehicle and threw himself behind the barn that hid the helicopter. To his relief, he saw that it was the Chevy with Radin at the wheel – and alone.

Putting his professorial hat back on, Jules listened with some sympathy but rising apprehension and anger as Radin described the chain of events. The stark fact was that, rather than conjure another solution, Radin had killed a cop and police forces around the world tended to react to that with maximum force. Jules couldn't immediately think what he might have done differently but now they were stuck with the consequences. They had to rescue the bike and hide it. Leaving it where it was raised too many questions about the specific location – their location The bike needed to disappear.

'OK Radin, the first thing to do is to conceal the body. I think the chances are that the police will check everything in the neighbourhood as soon as they realise they have a missing comrade. It would be only natural. We know that they were looking for a red pickup truck and while your car is technically not a pickup, it is still red albeit in a metallic finish. We'll leave it locked in the barn until we leave.

Let's hide the body until the morning when we'll take it with us and leave it alongside the bomb. The police will never look in the Test Site and, assuming we are successful, it will be vaporised when the demo bomb is detonated. Then, let's get down there and pick up that motorcycle.'

Having wrapped the body in the sheet that had been covering it, they laid it in a small depression ten yards from the barn and threw some random wooden planks over it and a couple of old plastic containers. Jules collected a garden rake from the shed and had Radin drive him back to the murder scene.

The motorcycle started first time and Jules led Radin back up the hill to about 200 yards short of the track that led to the house. It was getting darker by the minute but there was still enough light and, taking the sheet and the rake, Jules told Radin to wait for him. Back on the bike, Jules drove to the entrance to the disused mine. Inside, with the light from the motorcycle, he located the main shaft, removed the barbed wire with the notice warning of mortal danger attached to it and pushed the bike decisively over the edge. There was a crash as it hit the side on the way down but more of a thud at the bottom. It must have been at least 100 yards deep. Any homing signal from the bike would be lost at that depth down the mine shaft. Jules chucked the sheet in after it to obscure the view from the top. Finally, leaving the mine, Jules retraced the bike's tire track back to the Radin in the SUV obliterating the evidence behind him, like a golfer raking the sand in a bunker smooth.

Back at the house, they unloaded the two cars; it was just after 9pm. Ahmad had bought beer and wine, large New York steaks and some salad for dinner. Before cooking, Ahmad took Radin round the back of the house to the large wooden barn again and they checked the wasp-like Schweizer 300Cbi helicopter for the most unobtrusive way to transport the dead policeman.

Dinner was, as usual, a silent affair. Tonight, each man was inwardly defining the risks that now attended them after the events of the afternoon. By the time sleep claimed Jules, there had still been no sign of the police checking house to house and he was feeling slightly more confident. By the same time tomorrow, they would have vanished along with the helicopter and all the evidence of Radin's near catastrophe with the highway patrol man.

The alarm went off at 4:30am on the Sunday morning just as the cloudless dawn was ushering in another scorching day. Over breakfast of coffee, toast, Yoghurt and fruit, he explained to Radin that their route into the Nevada Missile Site would take them through Death Valley, one of the hottest places on the surface of the Earth with temperatures at the height of summer averaging well over 100 degrees Fahrenheit. The valley itself was 280 feet below sea level and the driest place in North America. Average rainfall was less than 2 inches a year. Not a place to get stuck in. Ahmad explained to Radin that the target area for the bomb was the same area that had been used for the early testing of US nuclear weapons. Radin grunted something but kept eating.

At 5:15, they pulled the helicopter out of the barn and tied the shrouded body to the inside of the legs. They then put both cars inside the barn and locked it again. To anyone coming to the house that day, everything would be locked up, consistent with normality.

The rotor blades swished into action first time and after a final check on their kit and the body, the Schweizer lifted off heading for Death Valley. With the sun rising to the East, the early morning views were spectacular. After about 45 minutes, Ahmad banked to the right, now flying almost directly into the sun. He pointed out Springdale and Hot Springs as they flew between them crossing Highway 95. 'We're now into restricted airspace,' said Ahmad as they started to slide over the hills on the east of the valley, 'so keep your eyes open and fingers crossed!'

Straight ahead and slightly to the left, Radin could see a sandy looking basin, criss-crossed with white tracks. 'That's Yucca Flats.' Said Ahmad, 'look out for a red plastic sheet that we should be coming up on. I left it as a marker.'

'Why you leave marker here?' asked Radin 'They no see?'

'Two reasons,' replied Ahmad, 'I did two test runs on a Sunday;

the first time – to pick a good, well-hidden spot at which I left the red plastic sheet as a marker and the second – to test how thorough their surveillance is, to see if they check out unusual things. The sheet was still there on the second visit and, look there it is right down there, still in place!'

He set the Schweizer down gently in the narrow gully and helped Radin remove the suitcase. It was much smaller than the trunks but still unexpectedly heavy for its size. Ahmad opened the lid and typed in the numbers he had noted on the scrap of paper plus the extra security code. Radin checked that everything was functioning and re-checked the receiver. They untied the dead policeman's body and laid it, still wrapped in its shroud, next to the suitcase. Then they covered everything with camouflage blankets and stones and earth. Ahmad started to increase power to the blades again. Radin leapt in and stuffed the red marker sheet into the locker as they lifted off. The operation had taken just over two minutes.

Back at the ranch, they shared a last cup of coffee together. Radin was anxious to get off; it was already 7:30am, the temperature was rising and they had decided that, as an extra precaution, Radin would avoid Pahrump on his way to Los Angeles airport and take the long way round skirting Las Vegas before rejoining the Interstate-15 and heading for LA.

'Thanks Radin.' said Ahmad shaking his large hand with happy finality, 'Seems we got clean away with it so far. Thanks for everything, don't talk to any strangers and have a good flight.' Radin actually smiled and again mumbled something unintelligible, presumably in his own language, before driving off. As soon as Radin disappeared over the ridge, Jules called Bashi to advise him of the new route Radin would be taking and please would they let him know when the Bosnian was securely on his flight home.

Jules felt the trauma of the previous evening and underlying tension of the past few days evaporate with Radin's departure. He was on his own again now and while the events of the previous day had uncovered a serious hole in their planning, everything was apparently still on track. Bashi was meeting him early the next morning in Barstow, just off the Interstate -15, with another hire car for his trip down to San Diego. It was just another precaution but Jules suddenly realised that he was looking forward to seeing a friendly face again.

One major element of the plan was now in place and secure. Jules had hoped that Zahra would have been there with him; perhaps she had been repressed by Radin's banality or perhaps it was his own inner distress at the murder of the policemen. He needed his reunion on a more regular basis than it was happening and he still had no clue as to what induced it or how to control it.

THURSDAY, 8TH APRIL 14:30
Brewster's Boat Yard, Qualtrough Street, San Diego

Hank had had a call to say that the Brit, George Anstruther, was having to go back east until July at the earliest and, could he could get the boat out of the water now. Anstruther would be along to stow his fishing gear and some clothes in the boat until the summer vacation. Was it secure? Of course it was, they'd never had an incident in 8 years! Anyway, if his boat came out of the water now, it could go right at the back of the yard where only a fool would risk burglary – just for old fishing tackle!

Exactly as arranged, Anstruther's station wagon came through the gates, right on time. Hank liked that in a man. He handed over the keys and pointed Mr Anstruther towards where his boat was now up on stilts until the summer. The Brit asked politely if there was anyone who could give him a hand with a trunk. For reasons he couldn't understand, his wife had insisted that he put her collection of five years worth of the *Interiors* magazine into the trunk as well as his clothes. It weighed a ton. 'No problem Mr Anstruther, I'll have one of the boys come and help you.'

Some twenty minutes later, having unloaded the trunk and stowed his gear, Anstruther thanked the unwitting bomb handler, returned to the office and paid his dues for the next 12 months in cash there and then. Hank liked cash, hated records. Twelve months was a bonus. The banker turned, smiled and waved before driving off again..

Some days later, Hank remembered that, just to cover himself, for the record, he had never checked the boat after Anstruther had left. Looking through the window, he could see the dismantled rod, a bait box and a bag, presumably for hooks, on top of the silver trunk. The sleeve of a blue jersey had got caught outside the lid as the banker had closed the trunk; well that's what happens when husbands are made to do the packing isn't it!

With the prevailing wind, Jules had calculated that a blast would destroy most of San Diego and all of the US naval facilities. President Wilmington should never have underwritten the killers of Zahra and her father.

FRIDAY, 9TH APRIL
Industrial warehouse, W 21st St & Estrella Ave, Los Angeles, California

Stopping outside the warehouse, Jules opened the new security door and checked that no one had touched the pen on top of the stock list. The chances of anyone breaking in for a few tins of fruit were minimal, particularly in that area, and he was not surprised to find the tip of the pen precisely where he had left it.

Jules now faced the problem of manhandling the bomb single handed. In anticipation, he had purchased a lightweight, foldable trolley. Checking the street for any unnatural interest from passers-by, he eased the silver trunk onto the trolley and wheeled it professionally inside. Turning the trunk and the freezer on their sides he managed to wiggle it gently into place. Righting the freezer once more, he opened the lid of the trunk, activated the receiver and extended the aerial up the back of the shelving. He tested the receiver and then submerged the metal trunk under box after box of dried fruits. On the desk, he replaced the pen exactly as it had been before, closed and double locked the new security door and set the alarm.

Jules reckoned that the blast would be within three blocks of the city centre.

Three trunks down, one to go. Now he paid the price of a long road back to Larkspur on his own having swapped the hire car for his SUV just outside Santa Clara. The January trip had been easier and he still had to manhandle the last bomb into the car on his own when he got back.

SATURDAY 10TH APRIL
The long road to Redmond, WA

Jules swapped the keys to the apartment for his untouched cash deposit in the letting office at Andrew Jackson Apartments as soon as it opened at 8:00am. He had packed up already and the SUV was all set to leave with the trunk containing the last bomb sitting openly in the back with his other few bits and pieces.

He knew that this was going to be the most tedious part of the plan but it had to be done.

It was already 9:30am by the time he got back to the grey truck with the metal trunks still inside. No one appeared to have even been up the dirt road and the area was undisturbed.

Jules now drove the truck 75 miles to the Tehama Country Sanitary Landfill site at Red Bluff where the unwanted trunks quickly blended in with the stream of other waste cascading down its sides. It was after midday by the time he got back to Forest Glen and he faced at least 11 hours of monotony on Interstate 5 ahead of him before he finally got a decent night's sleep.

Jules extracted the incendiary bomb from the cardboard package, taped it securely under the truck, and activated the detonator. The receiver attached to it was picking up a strong signal.

SUNDAY 11TH APRIL
NE 32nd Street, Northrup, Redmond, WA

Having left the SUV about a half a mile away in a quiet street, 'Jonathan' had telephoned the house to let the tenant know that he would be coming by to swap the Impala that afternoon for another car he'd bought and not to worry. The woman who had answered the phone never even emerged to greet him when he walked round the back to the garage and he saw no reason to disturb her. Sleeping dogs.

The Impala started after a couple of goes and he drove off leaving the automatic door to close itself. Fifteen minutes later, he was back but now in the SUV. Once inside the garage, he opened the trunk, attached an extra aerial to the bomb's receiver and to the car's aerial and then activated the mechanism. Still no sign of the woman, so he let things be. She probably wouldn't have noticed the difference anyway, so why explain.

Jules conceded to himself that because of the prevailing wind direction, the damage to Seattle might be limited but it would certainly put Microsoft's HQ and Research facility out of action for a meaningful period.

So the seeding programme was now complete. Each bomb had a different type of location so that the discovery of one would not jeopardise the security of another if a nationwide sweep of similar locations were made. He would not need to do anything further to any of the bombs for months – rent renewal would be next and then occasional visits if his uncle failed to make progress on the diplomatic front.

Except for probable images caught on security and traffic cameras, all traces of the past weeks had been eradicated. The apartment in Larkspur was clean, the helicopter had been sold on once more – for cash this time Farid had told him, and the SUV was permanently out of sight. In due course, the hunt would be on for the owner of the Impala, a Mr McAlistair from Larkspur, who, by then, would owe Seattle airport's long-term parking franchise a small fortune. And if anybody were to join up the all dots, they would get confirmation that the Professor had caught a flight back to Borneo.

As his plane fled West across the empty ocean before the onrushing dawn, Jules knew Zahra was with him once more. He could almost feel her presence tangibly now that his work was done, feel her pride in their endeavour; all he needed now was to reach that no-man's land on the edge of sleep.

GERMINATION

SATURDAY, 13TH APRIL, 18:30 LOCAL, (15:00 GMT)
The Great Room, President's Palace, Tehran

A press alert had been issued a day earlier announcing that President Saiyeidi would hold a press conference the following day to outline a major development in relations between Iran and the United States. It would be timed for 08:00 US Mountain Time so that as much of the world as possible would be able to listen to the President.

Many people around the world in government offices spent time discussing and debating the possible significance of the following day's pronouncement, not least in the foreign ministries. Nowhere was the activity more pronounced than in Washington where all personnel with responsibility for Iran were hastily summoned to meetings.

An air of baffled apprehension pervaded most of those meetings as Iran had fallen from top off the list of immediate concerns for the State Department and the White House since the President's ultimatum in November. A small skeleton team had been formed to produce a plan for the threatened strike but it had only met three times, each inconclusively, hoping that the stated deadline could be fudged into the middle distance.

In the Oval Office, Wilmington's key advisors all agreed that nothing new had come up to give rise to a world press conference. All they could do was to wait.

The Golestan Palace was the Qajar dynasty's royal residence and speaks of centuries of Persian power, wealth and leadership. Recently, during the Pahlavi era, the coronations of both Reza Khan on the Takht-e Marmar terrace and his son, Mohammad Reza Pahlavi, in the Museum Hall attested to the importance of the palace. It contains thirty resplendent rooms presenting everything that makes up the originality of Iranian life in the various provinces of the country. Its garden is an oasis of coolness and silence in the heart of the city and President Saiyeidi had specifically chosen it as the location for the press conference, an ancient and cultural setting that he knew nowhere in the United States of America could rival.

At exactly 6:30pm in Tehran, as noisy alarm clocks were going off in many houses in the mid-West and Pacific regions of America, President Saiyeidi strode confidently into the Great Hall and sat down at the conference table set before the assembled press and delegates from the foreign embassies in the capital.

He wore an immaculate dark blue suit adorned with the bright button of the *Legion d' Honneur* that had been hastily thrust upon him by the Quai d'Orsay upon his accession to the presidency – 'in recognition of his close personal ties to France'. A simple blue silk tie from Charvet, a cream shirt with discrete gold cufflinks carrying his family's crest, and polished black English brogues completed the vision designed to put civilizing centuries between him and the wilder Persians of long ago or, for that matter, today's hostile American rednecks.

An aide attached the microphone to his tie; Saiyeidi looked up from his notes and smiled.

'Ladies and Gentlemen' he began in flawless Oxford English, 'Thank you all for coming today. I shall speak in English as what I have to say falls almost entirely into the field of our international relations and a number of networks are relaying my words around the world. My same speech is being given to our people here in a separate, simultaneous broadcast.' He paused for emphasis and looked at his audience.

'It is now just over nine months since we restored the promise of full and universal democracy to Iran. Our domestic programme of reform and regeneration is advancing well and our economy is showing promising signs of re-birth as enterprise spreads among the grassroots of our people.

Internationally, our country is beginning to re-claim its rightful position as a force for good in our region and in the last few months we have been instrumental in forming the *Islamic Defense Organisation* to assure a common defensive system for like-minded countries in the Middle East. We have also concluded treaties with Russia, China and North Korea to ensure cooperation in a number of areas including guaranteeing their oil supplies. We believe therefore that we are moving forward both at home and abroad.

One very specific area of our international relations remains of fundamental concern to us and the measures to which I have just referred reflect that concern. That concern is our relationship with the United States of America, its allies in Europe and Israel in particular.

The enmity between Iran and America goes back a long way. It is over 50 years since the United States and the United Kingdom saw fit, in 1953, to destroy Mossadeq's first flowering of democracy here in Iran. Iranians lived and suffered under the Shah, effectively a US puppet, until 1979 when the excesses of his repressive regime provoked a religious backlash. Khomeini's resulting Islamic State simply replaced one form of tyranny for our people with another. The only difference in the latter was the complete hollowing out of Iran's economy.

During the period of Khomeini's Islamic Revolution, his regime's obsession with the US threat led to its support for international terrorism, notably Al Qaeda and consequently President George W. Bush branded Iran as a part of an 'Axis of Evil.'

Since we re-established full democracy here in Iran, the international intelligence agencies are well aware of our pro-active cooperation and energetic support in the global war on terrorism, something that no Western government has as yet chosen to acknowledge publicly. And why is that we wonder?

The answer is simple.

The re-emergence of Iran as a secular, democratic force in the region is a rallying point for the legitimate Islamic world and therefore poses a threat to the territorial ambitions of some Israeli politicians in the Likud party and their friends and supporters in dark corners in Washington. We believe that this cabal was the motivating force that led the new President of the United States to reverse the progress made with the Obama White House and pledge military intervention, war by any other name, if we do not abandon our plans for a nuclear defense capability. That pledge was not a threat, it was a promise and, as such, it is one that we cannot ignore and have a duty to take seriously.

When our democratic movement swept away the Mullah's regime, we were not surprised to find that the nuclear programme was in fact considerably more advanced than had been admitted at that time and certainly not confined to power generation. This in turn inevitably raises serious questions about our continued adherence to the Nuclear Non-Proliferation Treaty.

I want to make it absolutely clear at this point that Iran has no aggressive plans for the use of nuclear weapons. Like most nuclear nations, we regard our nuclear capability as an exclusively defensive tool, not to be used unless we ourselves are attacked – as indeed President Wilmington now pledges to do. That pledge by itself makes a mockery of the Treaty to which we are adherents.

The US uses the façade of the Nuclear Non-Proliferation Treaty as the context for its aggressive proposals. I say façade because that is what that Treaty is.

It is primarily a device to ensure that those nations that have already achieved nuclear independence can inhibit the progress of those less developed countries from attaining a similar degree of national defense, thereby prolonging their own ability to exert undo influence upon those same LDCs.

But the Treaty is also largely a sham because neither Israel, nor India, nor Pakistan nor North Korea, all of whom have significant nuclear capabilities, is currently a signatory. Indeed, one may also observe that if you are perceived as a friend or potential friend of the United States, the force of the rules are simply not applied in the same way. '

Saiyeidi pause again to emphasise what he was about to say.

'Article 10 of the Treaty allows signatories to the NPT to withdraw from it if (and I quote) 'extraordinary events, related to the subject matter of the Treaty, have jeopardized the supreme interests of its country'. North Korea withdrew from the Treaty in 2003 and, under the terms of the Treaty, I am today giving formal notice of Iran's withdrawal with immediate effect.'

Saiyeidi's flow was interrupted by spontaneous murmuring among the audience and the noise of a few journalists' feet resonating on the stone floors as they ran for the phones, unable to wait for further revelations.

Once the murmuring and clatter of running feet subsided, Saiyeidi resumed.

'We have no wish to engage in hostilities with America,' the President continued 'however, what is of grave concern to us and many others around the world is the recent, more assertive projection of American military power to satisfy various right-wing political factions close to the White House itself. It was after all, a thinly veiled ambition of regional dominance under the guise of an imposed and subservient democracy that resulted in the last pre-emptive American attack on Iraq. Following directly from that, we reject absolutely the current President's presumed right to interfere directly in the internal affairs of our own country.

In the aftermath of President Wilmington's pledge, it became an unavoidable imperative that we in Iran construct some defence against his proposed aggression. The US defence budget for the coming year will exceed $500bn. Iran's own defence budget will be something under 2% of that. Scarcely what could be described as a level playing field.

Today however, I am able to announce that we have now succeeded in constructing such a defence based on the simple principle of *'mutually assured destruction'*. Today I can announce that we have seeded all the major US cities with nuclear weapons that can and will be remotely detonated by us if President Wilmington were to carry out his aggressive threats.'

President Saiyeidi paused to let his words sink in.

'I must again stress that our motivation is purely defensive and taken for the reasons I have just outlined. I can give the world my unequivocal undertaking that we will never strike first. These of course are merely words but it should be clear to anyone who considers the reality of the situation that if we are forced, *in extremis*, to use these weapons, it is certain that not only will it be as a result of initial US aggression against us, but also, with further US retaliation certain to be triggered thereafter, Iran as we know it today will cease to exist. We already know therefore that it will be suicidal for us to use those weapons first and they will not be used unless all else has failed and we are subjected to the reality of an attack by the

United States or indeed by Israel, its proxy in this region.

Finally, we believe that there is a probable risk that many people, particularly in the Western defence community, will underestimate our current nuclear capacity and our ability to respond if so attacked. We have therefore arranged a limited demonstration of our nuclear technology on the American mainland, in the Nevada Test Site to be precise. A small nuclear device will be detonated there, harmlessly, in exactly 45 minutes from now.

We considered locating the demonstration on some distant Pacific atoll, outside the United States but rejected it as it would not confirm our ability to operate within the United States' borders and seed its major cities.

The explosion will be of a 21-kiloton bomb, of similar force to that named 'Dog' from Operation Buster in November 1951. On that occasion, US troops were in fact obliged by their government to observe the blast from a distance of just six miles with no special protection.

It is Saturday morning, 8:00am local US Mountain time and the local authorities were actually alerted 15 minutes ago. According to our agents on the ground, the area is now clear. We have therefore taken every precaution to ensure that the demonstration does not jeopardise a single innocent, American life. Our quarrel is not with the American people and never will be.

I stress once again the defensive nature of our actions. It is our real hope that the American people will recognise the consequences of their President's promised aggression. I entreat the entire world to join with us in praying that reason and respect will now prevail, with the help of God, the Merciful and Compassionate.

Thank you.'

The uproar in the Great Hall was immediate.

SATURDAY, 13TH APRIL, 10:30 LOCAL, (15:30 GMT)
The President's conference room in the White House, Washington DC

In attendance: The President of United States, Thomas Wilmington
The Vice President, George Fairburn
The Secretary of Defense, Edwin Rich
The Secretary of State, Henry Porter
The Secretary of the Treasury, Peter Faragas
The Attorney General, Luis Sanchez
The Director of CIA, Jon Miller
The Director of the FBI, Norman Watts
White House Chief of Staff, Lee Jackson

The President extinguished the TV screen and looked around the faces of his informal inner cabinet, his *counsel of last resort* as he had christened them. They had all been told to cancel any weekend engagements as soon as the Iranian press conference had been announced.

There was silence in the room as they waited for Wilmington to pronounce. The President made a low whistle as he expelled breath through teeth and taut lips. 'This SOB is not joking about is he?' It was a rhetorical question but Wilmington now turned directly to his Secretary of Defense.

'Mr President, my initial reaction is that this is simply not possible.' Edwin Rich opined. 'We did a certain amount of work once we knew what you were going to pledge to Israel last November. It is just conceivable that they might have had enough fissile material to make the demo bomb but certainly not many others.'

The phone rang at that moment. Wilmington lifted it and listened. 'Thanks' he said turning back to Rich, 'The warning sirens at the NTS are activated but as of last night, the test area was empty. The people on the ground at the Mercury base are running urgent checks to make sure that the area really is clear. The gates are still closed, no visitors are due and most of the Mercury personnel have already left for a training day at the Las Vegas facility.

Chances are, they reckon, that there will be no casualties.'

The Secretary of Defense stiffened 'Mr President, that's hardly the point, if you'll permit me. The point is that this represents a gross invasion of US sovereign territory for what is effectively an act of war and worse, in reality it's probably just pure bluff.'

'But we don't know that yet' interjected the white-haired Vice President 'and if they can succeed with this demonstration, all hell is going to break loose in every major city in this country. Americans have never been so personally threatened on their own soil by a foreign power since independence – even the Japanese never managed that!'

'Gentlemen" interrupted the President, 'the blast is due to take place in just about 30 minutes. I think that we can assume it will happen but, in the meantime, I want you each to come up with your own views on the best way to react to this. Let's reconvene to watch the explosion and then we will have to thrash out our initial response.'

As they left the meeting room, Rich gestured to the directors of the CIA and FBI to follow him while Lee Jackson, Wilmington's Chief of Staff, followed them instinctively.

Wilmington's old friend, Harvard contemporary and now Vice President, George Fairburn hung back as did Henry Porter, the Secretary of State. Wilmington remained seated.

'Mr President, Tom,' ventured the Vice President as the door closed, 'this is going to be a real hot potato. You don't go to all that trouble and then bluff and, if he is not bluffing, we are virgin territory. We'll grant him the demo but we then need to get some verification. But as I said to Ed, this is going to be a public relations minefield here and you are going to need to be ready to calm fevered brows especially in the media who will talk it up for all they're worth just as they always do.'

'I think your main problem is going to be the very plausible case Saiyeidi has just made for defensive aggression.' proffered Henry Porter, 'There can be no doubt that Iran has violated the sovereignty of our borders but the fact that it has been done in such a calculated and overt manner with this worldwide, visible demo, well, it draws the sting completely, particularly as it has, after all, been accompanied by all the safety warnings one would expect of our own government. Unfortunately, as a PR exercise, it is very professional.'

At that moment the three screens on the conference room flickered into life. One showed a satellite view of the Test Site, the next a view of the area from the Mercury base on the edge of the NTS and the right hand one, a view looking north from Las Vegas.

With five minutes to go, the Attorney General wandered back followed by the group who had been with Secretary Rich. They waited with random small talk until, right on time, the nuclear flash of the bomb cut across everything. For the President's inner counsel, it appeared slightly surreal, smaller than most latter-day test firings but yet of overwhelming, glaring significance for the safety of the country.

'Well gentlemen,' opened the President, 'he's demonstrated a capability that we didn't believe he had, so where do we go from here? Ed, you've been consulting with our intelligence chiefs here, what's your take on the situation?'

The Defense Secretary glanced at the intelligence chiefs and launched in. 'Irrespective of other considerations, the stark fact is that Iran has committed an invasive outrage on our soil that we cannot allow to stand. My instinct tells me they are bluffing. Our intelligence (which I have just checked again) swears that they must be bluffing. I think we should call their bluff. Have you any idea how much highly enriched U-235 they would need to make enough bombs. The only way they could have done it was with help from their buddies in Russia, China or North Korea and we've been monitoring that like hawks.

I think this is going to provoke most people in this country to demand quick retribution – and I think we need to be ready to respond quickly, firmly and effectively.'

'Excuse me interrupting again Ed,' rejoined George Fairburn 'but you have just explained how it might just be possible for them to have obtained their fissile material – from countries with whom they have recently announced defensive treaties, countries that we have no dependable way of trusting or tracking. If North Korea could thumb its nose at the memory of George W. Bush, I should think they would move heaven and earth! Right now, we have no way of knowing anything. We have no intelligence on the ground inside Iran and, outside it, all we have is self-interested hearsay. It's Iraq all over again in that respect!'

'Mr President, Sir,' the soldier Secretary of State asserted, 'I do really think that we are in completely virgin territory here. Clearly we cannot be seen to have a knee-jerk response to this until we have some real idea of what we are dealing with. Frankly, even if it turns out that it was a bluff, it will have so heightened the world's perception of Iranian vulnerability to our perceived image of an ugly, overbearing hegemony that any retaliatory strike could prove horribly counter productive. We need constructive diplomacy to work its passage.

And bluntly, if it turns out that the threat is real, you should be in no doubt that we will then have to totally reassess our Middle Eastern imperatives from top to bottom. Either way, Mr President, we are going to need time to assess and prepare before we react definitively.'

Wilmington pondered aloud. 'So Ed, you seem to be at the hawkish end of things, tell me, what would you do if you were Saiyeidi?'

'I would be praying that America would hesitate because that would confirm that we had taken the threat seriously, that the bluff had worked and that we Americans were trying to establish hard certainties. Saiyeidi may be a democrat but he hates America and is terrified of Israel. If I'm him and my bluff works, I get to re-write the status quo in the Middle East, just as the Secretary of State has stated and that, in my own opinion, is what this is all about.'

'So you're suggesting that we launch an immediate reprisal against Iran?' asked Wilmington.

'A token gesture, yes. Wiping out perhaps just one of their known nuclear plants' continued Rich.

'And if they then respond by say wiping out San Diego as a token destruction of just one of our naval bases?' Wilmington interjected.

'As I said Mr President, we don't think he has the capability' said the Secretary of Defense sticking to his position.

Wilmington frowned again. 'Gentlemen, even if it appears as weakness, I agree with George; we cannot just zap a couple of nukes at someone who has demonstrated that he could conceivably respond in kind. The demo was just a demo and we can't be seen to be provoked by something so publicly trailed as a non-aggressive act. Our threat to take out Saiyeidi's nuclear installations still stands and, now fully vindicated, it will proceed but only if we can be certain that he is bluffing.

So, what we need is a holding statement to buy us time, *'consulting our allies to determine a responsible reaction to the bomb that has polluted America's atmosphere'* -that type of thing. We need to use that time to dig deep and fast to try and get an accurate picture of any quantities of fissile material they could have produced or obtained from its allies and we need to see if there is any evidence of even one of their purported bombs. Frankly, the latter will be the most difficult as we have no useful leads.'

SATURDAY, 13TH APRIL 19:30 LOCAL, (18:30 GMT)
Lašva Bar, Travnik, Central Bosnia

'Radin, welcome back – yet again' chided Jasmina cheerfully. 'I am going to get it out of you one of these days. Why do you take your custom elsewhere – and for a couple of weeks at a time? I really can't believe that there can be a nicer bar or a friendlier barmaid in the whole of Travnik!' she laughed.

'That's where you may be wrong, my sweet – never really known you friendly as you might say, all a bit of a mystery see' he cooed at her, reflecting his perception of the warmth of her welcome. 'I live in hope though – always!'

'Well one of these days, we'll have to see about that won't we?' she grinned knowingly as she put beer and schnapps down beside him. Welcome back indeed thought Radin. But it was always like that and it never went any further he reminded himself as he drank the beer.

As the draught beers went down in succession chased by the icy schnapps, his optimism grew; he knew it was a waste of time but he couldn't help playing along with the notion. Was it the alchohol leading him on or was she actually warmer towards him tonight? It became an escalating, debate within him, dominating, alluring as little treats like slices of the owner's homemade sausage were produced. Maybe she had really missed him.

'So where have you been this time Radin?' she asked smirking at him seductively, more beer and another schnapps appearing. 'I'll bet it was another woman!'

'You know I never looks at anyone but you, my sweet' he said persisting in his attempts to humour her.

The badly dubbed Western showing on the TV above the bar finished followed by adverts and then the news. The lead story was a short replay of the NTS blast followed by continuing world reaction to the Iranian president's broadcast and what it might mean. Radin blinked at it as he might a favourite bedtime story.

Radin smiled as he found Jasmina quietly leaning on the bar beside him also watching the news. She seemed closer than she need be and he smiled at her again.

'All this frightens me Radin' she confided close to his ear, 'what are we to do about it all?'

'Nothing we need do, my lovely, not us. But the Americans better take heed or else they'll know all about it. And that's a fact' Radin stated with some authority in his voice.

'That so?' Jasmina replied sounding impressed. 'You always know these things Radin, I wish I understood them like you do.' She squeezed his arm gently before moving off to talk to Giorgio, the owner.

Squeezed his arm. Sshe had and never even touched him before! He could still feel her fingers on his forearm and it made his mind race. Just then Jasmina reappeared behind the bar still talking to Giorgio. She looked so warm, so comfortable even luscious really. The way her slightly unkempt, long brown hair played around her ears, full lips that parted easily into a smile, swelling her cheeks. Her dark eyelashes seemed to flatter the fineness of her nose and the clarity of her eyebrows. But she looked so warm that he could almost feel her comfort.

'So Radin, I'm off now,' she said coming round the bar, 'got a night off see, so I'll see you next time you're in.' She kissed him lightly on the cheek and walked towards the door. Radin froze, his thoughts ambushed by her sudden exit but simultaneously stunned by the kiss that tingled still on his cheek. He watched her walking towards the door, his erstwhile fantasies evaporating in her wake. He saw the slimness of her waist silhouetted in the white, body-hugging tank top she wore, the roundness of her buttocks framed in her tight blue jeans and the fullness of her breasts as she turned and smiled at him again.

He abandoned his last schnapps, untouched.

The night outside was warm but moonless with only a hint of a breeze. He caught up with her just as she threw a small pink cardigan around her shoulders. She turned at the sound of his footsteps and smiled again. 'Radin, I thought that you were stuck in for the night!' she smiled mockingly again.

'No, no,' he said too quickly, 'I was just leaving anyway see, enough's enough you know.' She let the awkward silence linger for him to fall into. 'No, no,' he stammered on, searching urgently for equilibrium. 'No, actually' he blundered on, now lost, 'no, I just was wondering if you were meeting anyone' his unrehearsed strategy now in palpable tatters.

'Yes, I was actually' she said not helping him off the hook, 'but I think I've just missed the bus and there isn't another for an hour.' There is a god, Radin told himself!

'That's awful luck,' he commiserated, 'so could I perhaps offer you a drink in the meantime, my own house is just across the bridge and I have a very fine French cognac that needs opening.'

'That would be very kind,' she said smiling again, taking his arm.

Jasmina no longer thought of sex as more than a physical aptitude – rather like running. Srebrenica had removed any sentimentality she may once have harboured about it. There you simply braced yourself and hoped to survive.

As the 16-year-old victim of two chronicled gang rapes at the hands of passing Serbian militias, she had puzzled the EUFOR do-gooders as she called them. She didn't expect or seek love or kindness. What she craved was revenge – revenge for the slaughter of her entire family – parents, two brothers and a sister – as she was made to stand and watch. They told her that night that she was the prettiest and had only been saved for their pleasure. And they took it for two endless days until she passed out, broken, filthy, bruised and bleeding and was left to die. Mossad had saved and rehabilitated her only because her grandmother had been Jewish. But now she owed them and was happy to help in any way that brought her closer to revenge.

She'd studied their files on Ivanovic detailing the cold ruthlessness of the bombings and murders that he had been paid so handsomely for. Jasmina was in no doubt about the base ferocity of the man. But he was a part of the machine that had massacred her family and this was the start of her personal retribution.

Closing the door of his stone house behind them, Radin lit the oil lamp with shaking hands and bustled to retrieve glasses and the unopened bottle of Martell. Jasmina meanwhile, dropped her pink cardigan on a chair and walked slowly to the old fireplace. Now launched on her mission, she stretched her arms up to reach the high mantelpiece, stretching unhurriedly, brazenly, hips cocked to emphasise her buttocks, knowing his eyes would be on her, knowing that he was already slipping towards the edge of control.

She heard the clink of glass behind her and, as she felt those ugly hands enfold her waist, she arched her back encouraging them up her body, waiting for them to envelop her breasts. Radin moaned quietly as his hands explored their ample fleshiness, his teeth finding the softness of the nape of her neck, unshaven bristle chafing against her skin.

Now she lowered her arms, turning to meet him to find his mouth immediately covering hers and his tongue probing staccato-like into her teeth. She felt a burst of electricity galvanise his body as he searched for a response from her. Not waiting, Radin steered them awkwardly but with urgency towards the bed in the corner of the room. Those hands were now pulling her tank top off, now opening her jeans, now working round her buttocks, easing her pants down and away.

Anticipation spawned stings of heat that in turn ignited a morbid carnality within her. Jasmina tugged at the metal button at the top of his zip, running her fingers inside his pants as it gave way, searching and finding him already hard and larger than she had expected. Releasing his trousers, she instinctively drove her fingers up his back, following the taut muscle sheathing his backbone, spreading her palms across his square shoulders, ripping his T-shirt over his head.

For an instant, they faltered on the brink, Radin fused with intent until, with his hands round her buttocks again, he lifted her further up the wooden bed, her firm, fit thighs already arching up to give him space. This was the job she had agreed to take on and despite her revulsion at the man, her physical senses mounted with a kind of perverted joy at every crudely pumped stroke of his hirsute body, the pressure building as searing sensations of pain and pleasure raced through her tummy, more encompassing than anything she'd imagined it could be until, with a last rush of vicarious pleasure, she broke through the pinnacle of a private ecstasy, basking in the sheer depravity of her own delight.

Jasmina felt Radin began to quicken frenziedly, an animal forcing harder and faster inside her. Now that he was rapt, irrevocably committed, she had control over the bastard's coming passion and she would make it her own. She had the power now, he was hers and she would destroy him. As Jasmina felt him explode inside her, she arched against him, her legs wrapping his bottom, gripping him deeper inside, thrusting hard herself, working, willing him on and on and on, her nails scalping deep wields in the coarse skin of his back.

When she was sure that she could wrestle no more from him, she released him, sliding sideways from beneath him.

Radin emitted a low groan. He was utterly spent, obliterated by her rampant persistence. Now it was time to talk.

Comfortable in her body, Jasmina wandered naked looking for the promised cognac, taking in the interior of the room. This was the abode of a solitary man, sparse, untidy, colourless. She could not see one book, just old newspapers, empty tins of processed food crowding the sink together with unwashed plates. Was this hovel the sum of his life's work?

Jasmina looked across the room at him, naked and overwhelmed by spent lust. The physicality of their encounter had actually pleased her which she found wicked and almost depraved looking at him now. Yet there was something primeval in the animal simplicity of his gutter passion, a pureness that was uncomplicated, unembellished and somehow wholesome because of it. But she was here for a purpose.

She filled two glasses with the cognac and passed one to Radin who was still slumped, exhausted in a heap. Radin took the glass, grabbing the rough blanket to appease an outburst of peasant modesty.

Still naked, uninhibited and glowing, Jasmina knelt on the hard bed in front of him, buttocks resting on ankles. Radin was utterly engulfed by her as she now moved deliberately forward, her breasts pendulous, nipples slowly brushing his hairless chest until her lips reached his briefly and then slid away again. 'You were incredible.' she murmured. Flattered, he smiled proudly. 'Such power!' she whispered sliding her hand beneath the blanket, squeezing the crumpled remains of his passion. 'We must do this again, often, but when we have more time.'

'Oh Jasmina, you are my little beauty, my dream come true' Radin waxed, raising himself to the limits of eloquence.

'So are you deserting me for another woman again soon?' she demanded half-joking, fondling him.

'Oh Jasmina, I never ever did that, it's just that I have to go away on business sometimes but that won't be for a bit now,' he reassured her.

'That's good,' she said simpering, 'because you know I really am worried about the situation, about what America might do. We're not too far from Iran here and the fallout dust cloud is bound to affect us here if they attack.' She looked disarmingly vulnerable suddenly.

'You needn't worry my sweet, honestly' Radin said bolstering her spirit, 'If the Americans have got any sense, they'll heed what the Iranian president said or else they'll discover that the other bombs are even bigger than the first one and that'll teach them. So don't you worry your head now, you just come back to bed with old Radin and everything'll be fine.'

That's it, so quick, so easy! No one unconnected could possibly have known that. Just like a lamb to the slaughter! Mossad's information was spot on she thought, now suddenly looking purposefully at her watch.

'Next time we'll have a good long go but tonight I must hurry or I'll miss that bus again, won't I?' she insisted, apologetically pulling on her jeans.

'Oh, oh, OK then. I'd quite forgot' he mused. 'You'd best hurry along then but we'll not have to wait long to see each other again, my sweet, will we?' Jasmina kissed his horny, weather-beaten forehead and made for the door. He can't even be buggered to get out of bed, she thought as she left.

Outside, the air seemed fresher than for weeks, full of unsullied, Spring-like promise suddenly and she felt elated. She'd done it and she'd probably never have to see him or play to his sordidness again.

As she waited for the bus, she called her Mossad *sayanim* on her mobile.

SATURDAY, 13TH APRIL 20:30 LOCAL, *(18:30 GMT)*
Joe Kleiner's apartment, Tel Aviv, Israel

Joe had been watching the TV commentators' reactions to Saiyeidi's broadcast flicking from ABC to CBS to Fox even to Public Service Broadcasting. The message that was coming through from all the American stations was the same and it was alarming.

Two questions recurred right across the American networks, unanswered. 'Why are the Iranians suddenly threatening to attack me, here on my own patch, in my own backyard?' And then 'Why were we threatening a country that does not even have the missile capability to reach our shores?' They came up again and again, channel after channel.

To Joe, the answer was blindingly obvious now and the trail led straight to Israel.

Generations of Americans had forgotten the unstinting sacrifice of their countrymen defending kindred values on the battlefields of Europe and the Pacific. In today's media, US foreign military adventures seemed to endlessly dwell instead on the withdrawal from Vietnam and the debacle in Iraq. 'So why the hell are we risking anything for what goes on in the Middle East?' was the view of the man-in-the-street.

Now ordinary Americans were threatened directly on their doorsteps, where they ate and slept, where they prayed, where they voted. Forget the cinematic orgy of 9/11, this was really upfront and personal and possibly already in their very own street. And so whose fault was it, why were they in this situation, what had provoked it? Kleiner suddenly had perfect recall of the TV picture of the White House steps as Wilmington bravely resolved to remove Iran's nuclear programme ostensibly in support of the State of

Israel. And now this.

The realisation of their folly caused Joe's skin to seize with a pulse of energy that rushed like crackling fire through his whole body. The reality would come out soon enough as the American press ripped the lid off years of careful, committed, well-organised work that the Jewish community led by AIPAC had done to forge an inalienable US commitment to unquestioning support for the State of Israel. How had their planning missed this cavernous mantrap?

The answer was that they had all underestimated the resourcefulness of the westernised Saiyeidi. Was it a bluff though? He doubted it. All major US cities? No way, why bother? Two or three would be enough – after that the US Administration would cave in. Racing certainty! Oh God, and then what for Israel? Our hands will now be as tied as before they were free.

Just then his secure mobile rang. It was Ben-Ezra. 'Ariel?' he said tartly 'what the fuck do we do to salvage this situation?'

'Things are bad' Ben-Ezra agreed 'but I may just have the makings of something. I've just had a call from a retired Mossad colleague. A member of the Dutch secret service he knew from their time together during the Bosnian war contacted him this evening after the blast. 'Probably nothing but you never know' was how he phrased it! He then passed on a snippet of information regarding the recent movements of a figure from their mutual past – a certain Radin Ivanovic, a bomb expert. Apparently Ivanovic had flown from Paris into San Francisco some 9 days ago and, upon checking, had flown back from Los Angeles four days later.

'OK' said Joe, 'that could just be it. Where is he now?'

'That's the extraordinary thing. I have just cross-checked with our Bosnian desk and apparently they've been monitoring him too but in Bosnia itself, suspected of training Palestinian bombers for the Iranians. They've had him under surveillance since mid-February but tonight, after the news broke, an agent managed to seduce him during which he produced a gem of information about the bombing that was not on any news bulletin. Anyway, I have a crack team of interrogators in the air right now.'

SATURDAY, 13TH APRIL, 20:00 LOCAL, (SUNDAY 14TH 01:00 GMT)
The Oval Office, the White House, Washington

President Wilmington is seated cross-legged in a leather wingchair to the right of the fireplace with the nation's flag behind him. He is casually dressed in an open necked blue shirt, khaki trousers and brown deck shoes. The look is relaxed, reassuring and reminiscent of the paternal fireside chats employed by Roosevelt to sooth the nation during the Second World War.

The President smiled, 'My fellow Americans, thank you for joining me today. I wanted to speak to you as everyone will by now be aware of the Press conference given by the President of Iran and the subsequent detonation of a nuclear device in our Nevada Test Site this morning. I shall be brief as matters are still at an early stage.

First, I want you all to know that right now every agency and organ of the US government, here and around the world is working in unprecedented harmony and determination to address the threat now posed to our country by Iran.

Secondly, I have advised the Pentagon that no immediate, direct action is to be taken in response to the situation and I want you to know that no response will be made until we have fully consulted with our allies around the world and we have a clearer picture of the exact nature of the threat we face.

Thirdly, this country has been through similar situations before during the dark days of the Cold War when both Russia and ourselves could technically have destroyed each other. As President Saiyeidi himself told you, they will not attack first as they know that it would result in the total and immediate destruction of Iran. It would therefore be an act of suicidal folly if they were to initiate an attack. So, for now, we will not respond and you therefore have nothing to fear.

Lastly, this situation is not acceptable to any of us in this country. You have my word that it will be resolved and resolved soon. Equally, if any citizen, has seen anything unusual or suspicious, however unimportant it may have seemed at the time, please do not hesitate to inform your local police.

Thank you for your attention, God bless you all and God bless America.'

SUNDAY 14TH APRIL 15:00 LOCAL, (13:00 GMT)
Hamdija's livestock farm, Turbe

Hamdija's farm lay off the road that stretches through the hills between Turbe and Vitovlje, some 14 kilometres west of Travnik. As Orthodox Jews, his grandparents had come to the province when Travnik was still a thriving industrial centre, drawn by its reputation for ethnic harmony and generous land subsidies.

Back in 2001, Hamdija had benefited from a UN programme that had given him 150 in-calf Simmental heifers and 375 Pramenka sheep. Today, with the help grants from other international NGOs and support from his friends in Mossad, he now ran nearly 550 cattle and over 1200 sheep on the hills around the secluded farm. Hamdija was a local *sayan* for Mossad. *Sayanim* offer practical support but are never put at risk operationally and are certainly not privy to classified information. Using its extensive network of *sayanim* around the world, Mossad is able to run its organisation with very few permanent staff.

Hamdija had taken Jasmina's call from the bus stop and passed her confirmation straight to his *katsa* in Sarajevo. Within an hour, he called back to congratulate him saying that a team from Israel would arrive during the night.

They had arrived four hours later in a rented VW van. Hamdija was surprised to find that there was only three of them but they immediately set to work preparing a deserted hay barn some 250 metres up the hill from the house. By 7:30am they were ready.

Just before 8:00am, a smartly dressed inspector from the water company, replete with company hat, knocked on the old wooden door of Radin Ivanovic's house just above the bridge over the Lašva river. Radin was asleep still and complained to the inspector that he should have made an appointment. The inspector unctuously apologised but the houses close to him had experienced a pressure surge that had ruptured their pipes causing serious damage to the properties and he needed to check as fast as possible to minimise potential damage to Mr Ivanovic's house.

Grudgingly, Radin, still scantily dressed, allowed the inspector in and closed the door. The inspector traced the shower and kitchen pipes back to the mains system and put down his bag to retrieve his instruments. Radin went to the cupboard to make a cup of coffee and was surprised when he turned round again to find the inspector advancing on him with what appeared to be a makeshift air pistol in his hand. The last thing he knew was the thud of the dart as it hit his neck.

Anyone watching from the bridge would have seen the smartly dressed inspector leave, thanking Mr Ivanovic and closing the door behind him. Ten minutes later, they might have been surprised to see a white VW van with Red Cross markings draw up to the house and remove Mr Ivanovic on a stretcher. In the Lašva Bar, Giorgio was engaged on the telephone trying desperately to persuade Jasmina not to take up a new job in Sarajevo and therefore missed the comings and goings – like everyone else.

As Radin slowly regained consciousness, he felt sick. Gradually, he realised that he was shackled to what seemed to be an old, solid oak chair by his arms and feet. In front of him was a table with a tape recorder and a bank of loudspeakers. Beyond the table were five large and very bight lights shining straight at him. There were another three lights either side of him. It occurred to him that it was rather like an old movie he had seen of a Nazi torture chamber.

A searing pain sliced through his eyes and brain as he moved his head to look behind him. He appeared to be in a hayloft with no way down. But then he started retching violently and that triggered further shards of pain in his eyes and brain once more. Keep still!

After a while there was a wooden clump and the sound of feet ascending stairs. Radin did not move his head. A small, chubby man in white overalls entered his field of vision as he blinked at him.

'Ah,' said the man observing the fresh stains below Radin's chin, 'I see that you have discovered what happens if you move. Not a good idea is it?'

Radin saw no point in replying.

'I shall be brief because my mission is to be so and I don't want to waste time. Radin Ivanovic, you are here because we need a few simple answers to questions that have arisen,' continued the man in white.

'We know that you flew to Tehran two weeks ago for a briefing and turned up flying from Paris to San Francisco two days later. Five days after that, having planted bombs for the Iranian government including the one in the Nevada Test Site, you flew back from Los Angeles to Paris, arriving back here yesterday.

The story is one that you clearly recognise already' the man continued calmly, 'but we want you to tell us in detail about many aspects of your trip. You may do this voluntarily – but we don't expect you to – or we may have to help you.

Ivanovic, it is only fair that I am plain with you. We are specialists; we don't break limbs or pull teeth or fingernails – nothing so physical. I'm afraid it's much worse. We torture and twist your brain and senses until you beg us to stop and then, if you don't provide the answers, we simply start all over again until you do. There is no blood, no bruising, just terror and searing pain rather greater than you have already brought on yourself. There is no mercy. There is no escape. There will just be the answers we want.

So Radin, let's try again, you flew into San Francisco where you hired a car, a red Chevrolet Trailblazer our enquiries show. I think we'd like you to take it from there to be sure we have not missed anything.'

Radin said nothing and was not about to risk moving. Silence. 'Fine Radin, no surprise, just as we expected; now I'm afraid we'll have to do it the hard way.'

So saying, the man in white overalls opened his canvas bag and produced a robust looking needle. An extra pair of hands from behind Radin'schair suddenly restrained his right forearm. A needle was inserted into the now bulging vein and taped to the skin. Next a plastic tube from behind the chair was dovetailed with the needle and it too was taped to the skin to prevent movement.

'Last chance Radin?' but the question was really rhetorical.

The man in the white overalls is Eitan, a Mossad *katsa* and an experienced interrogator particularly adept with manipulative drugs. He employs his favoured mixture of an extract of marijuana followed by a combination of LSD and a highly refined chemical terror catalyst. Using this as a third-degree tactic, a skilful interrogator can gain significant leverage over unwitting, vulnerable subjects by threatening to keep them in a crazed, tripped-out state forever unless they agree to talk. Combine that with random electronic charges to the brain that set off a searing chemical reaction and, eventually, every victim cracks.

Eitan opened the valve to let the liquefied solution into Radin's blood stream. It actually soothes the subject for the first 10 seconds or so but is almost immediately followed by a psychedelic flood of terror that plunges the subject down into new and ever more horrifying bouts of uncontrollable terror and despair combined with the searing chemical reaction every time the head is moved. The pain is one thing but mind-engulfing fear leading to recurring bouts of inescapable and hysterical terror will sap the fortitude of even the toughest. Eitan knew his trade. He had never had a failure.

After just two hours, he had all the information that he was looking for and, given the potential consequences for Israel, exactly what he had hoped not to hear.

What Eitan had heard and recorded, confirmed the very worst fears conveyed by Tel Aviv. Radin and his accomplice Ahmad had landed 26 nuclear bombs, housed in metal trunks, near Eureka. The Iranian operation had been divided into four geographic cells controlled by *'The Merchant'*. They had taken their allocation of bombs and left the rest in a van to be collected. Under Radin's supervision, Ahmad had planted and activated one bomb in San Francisco before they went on to the Nevada Test Site. Ahmad had planted their remaining three bombs after Radin had returned to Bosnia.

Radin described everything in minute detail from the winter blanket left on top of the trunk in San Francisco to the precise meal they had eaten before the dawn flight into Death Valley and the Nevada Test Site.

They had done well, the session had flowed and Eitan decided to take a short break before going on to analyse the rest of the trip.

Eitan had removed the electronic device from around Radin's neck for starters and after three hours of frank exchange, Radin had developed that not unusual relationship that sometimes emerges between captor and captive. He felt he had some elbowroom. So, as Eitan was folding his notes, Radin popped the question.

'Excuse me sir,' he said meekly, 'but how did you get onto me in the first place?'

Eitan was just at the top of the stairs but stopped. 'No harm you knowing now I suppose, Radin. The police chief first noticed your visits abroad so we installed an agent to watch you – your new barmaid at the Lašva Bar' he said continuing down the stairs. 'See you in ten minutes.'

Radin stared ahead in rapt disbelief, knowing that it must be true. The sweetness of the previous night collided repugnantly with the brutal emptiness of total deception. He found the cacophonous effect as devastating as any of Eitan's drugs.

He had always known that any form of salvation was improbable for him and had never even thought about it. Not that is until after Jasmina had closed his door last night. It had been such a strange experience for someone to respond to anything he did when he wasn't either paying for it or threatening them that it had taken him unawares. For the first time in years, perhaps ever, he had wondered what the future might be – might be, on the remote chance that he could hold on to someone like her. For him, it was only a vague and intangible concept but the first flower nevertheless that suggested something brighter might be out there somewhere if only she could lead him to it. Now the flower had been entirely crushed and he knew that there would never be another.

Suddenly, he felt alone, furious, insecure, incensed, desperate, despairing. No point in thinking about any of it, his life wasn't going to survive the interrogation anyway so he might avoid further pain and revelations, perhaps even with some honour – strange thought. Again a wisp of fragrance lost, never to be. End it now!

He reckoned that he would have 30 seconds before someone realised what was happening and Eitan was due back any moment. With the strength and determination of a man possessed, he started rocking the heavy oak chair energetically towards the edge of the hayloft. As he rocked on the edge, he heard a cry but it was too late. It was the last thing he was aware of as he plunged over the edge and onto the stone floor below, his neck broken backwards.

Eitan cursed viciously, furious with himself for such laxity. He had been on his secure phone giving exact details of the San Francisco bomb when his assistant had come running in with the news of Radin's messy departure. What they had already extracted wasn't comprehensive but at least the Americans would have the location of one of the bombs.

Two days later, the Chief of Police in Travnik reported to Mr

Hamdija that Radin Ivanovic had disappeared on another of his mysterious trips.

SUNDAY, 14TH APRIL, 19:30 LOCAL, (17:30 GMT)
Joe Kleiner's apartment, Tel Aviv, Israel

Ariel Ben-Ezra, Mossad's chief spymaster finished briefing Joe on the detailed report they had now studied from Kosovo.

'So, on the face of it, Joe, it looks as though your concerns for the predicament now faced by our country may be fully justified.

If the Iranians have indeed seeded nukes in 26 major US cities, their strategic imperatives are going to change dramatically. While before, the Americans could afford to provide us with intrinsic protection as there was no threat of mass destruction reaching their homeland, now, if the situation is as it appears, they can be reached instantly, in their backyard. And we will inevitably have to face the risk of retaliation alone now in the event of local aggression here in the Middle East. The US will no longer be able to act or impose its will with nuclear impunity.

What it means Joe, is that we will now have that state of *mutually assured destruction* that you so dreaded, right here in the Middle East. And that severely limits any plans that some have suggested for further expansion of territory – Greater Israel and so forth.

But Joe, I say *on the face of it* because we also have a number of reservations about the Iranian operation that could open the way to other possible interpretations of the situation which is why I have asked Gilad, whom you know, to come along and take you through the potential scenario.'

Gilad Zahavi, Mossad's chief strategist, smiled and cleared his throat.

'Before I start, it is important to remember that my proposition is entirely speculative and that things may indeed be just as they appear now. However, that said, we have a number of issues.' Zahavi began.

'Our starting point is inconsistency.

Why would Saiyeidi choose to use a third-rate Bosnian bomb-maker and assassin to be closely involved in almost certainly the most daring stratagem carried out by a smaller country against US in modern times? Saiyeidi's team executed a superbly detailed and well-planned coup to overthrow the crazy mullahs. In that light, does it not seem odd that someone of Radin Ivanovic's ilk would be used on such an important mission? Actually, to me it's worse than odd, it would have been totally irresponsible, crazy – two things we know that Saiyeidi isn't.

Right now the Americans are going mad looking for leads in any direction as they need a platform of certainty before they can make a decision on which way to play the situation. Right now they are lost – they have the humiliation of the exploding of a foreign nuclear device on their territory splashed live on worldwide TV, coupled with the completely unquantifiable threat of the possible destruction of their major cities – as yet undefined – if they upset the Iranians. If it were ourselves, we'd be in the same dilemma!

But that dilemma carries risk for Iran too at the moment. The Americans are pledged to take out the Iranian nuclear complexes, which, given their locations deep underground, will necessitate at least a strike by nuclear missiles. If Washington believes it is all bluff, as indeed we understand their Secretary of Defense apparently does, they will simply go ahead anyway, call it and send in the strike. So we sat on the plane coming back and thought what we might do in the Iranians' shoes.

What we don't know is the quantity of fissile material the Iranians actually have. They had enough for the limited explosion in Nevada and the chances are that they will have other reserves as well. But we believe, on the basis of all we know or could extrapolate, that there will not be much more.

If that were the case, what would you do to strengthen the bluff to the point that it deters the hotter heads in the US Administration from taking the gamble of launching a strike that you know, if you are Iranian, you could not actually respond to in kind?

If it were me, I would be ready to give them what they were looking for – proof positive that the seeding operation was genuine. So how would you do it?' Zahavi waited a couple of seconds for Kleiner to reply. None was forthcoming.

'Not too difficult really.' Zahavi cleared his throat.

'All you would need to do is set up an operation using a decoy – in this case using Radin Ivanovic and his associate. Then you would discretely have Mossad's attention drawn to Ivanovic in Bosnia so that we are already aware of his comings and goings. Involve him in the periphery of the projected plot and make sure that he witnesses the bombs unloaded and actually being activated in San Francisco and the Nevada Test Site. Then fly him out again.

When he gets back, he is inevitably picked up by us and interrogated by one of our best specialists who duly extracts the version of events as Ivanovic knows them. The fact that he managed to commit suicide before we finished with him is really irrelevant.

We inform Langley that there is a bomb in San Francisco and, voila, they then have proof positive by association of the voracity of the entirety of Saiyeidi's statement last week. After that, in all conscience of their duty to their electorate, they could never reasonably risk discounting the existence of the other 25 bombs, and their own nuclear advantage over Iran would therefore be neutralised instantly.' Zahavi sat back and let it sink in.

'And the other Iranian agent with Ivanovic? What about him?' asked Joe pensively.

'Ah, he would need to believe the story as well, deploy the other bombs which he would not know are harmless and subsequently he would have to be neutralised before the Americans could pick him up and beat the location of the bombs out of him. Or he would have to know it was a set-up; either way, he's a liability to the Iranians – dead meat!' replied Gilad.

'It's certainly an ingenious theory as well as being plausible and it probably fits the circumstances in terms of the Iranian access to fissile material as we know it. But how do we get the Americans to buy into this now?' Joe asked. 'Your theory may be right but without any proof that the threat was limited to just the two bombs, the problem for the man in the Oval Office is that you're no further on. It probably is right but you've got to prove it – prove that you're not going to lose 20 million citizens in a nuclear holocaust! In their position, you really need to prove it.'

'And that's just our sticking point' said the chief spymaster, 'we can't prove it and neither will the Americans be able to. Proving something that you can't find, isn't there, is impossible – that's why the whole gambit is so elegant and frankly likely to be inspired by the Saiyeidi team.'

Kleiner thought for a while in silence looking increasingly sombre. 'OK, we have to inform Washington of everything we know otherwise Ed Rich might get his way, in which case we might all get blown off the map if we are wrong about this bluff! All we can do is to pass on what we know together with our suspicions and try and figure out how we best protect our own nuclear resources in Israel in the inevitable shake-up that would follow US capitulation. I don't think Saiyeidi can accept anything less in the circumstances.

'Proving something that you can't find, isn't there' – that's what we're going to need to do!'

MONDAY, 15TH APRIL, WASHINGTON DC, 06:30 LOCAL, (11:30 GMT)
The President's conference room in the White House

In attendance:	*The President of Unites States, Thomas Wilmington*
	The Vice President, George Fairburn
	The Secretary of Defense, Edwin Rich
	The Secretary of State, Henry Porter
	The Secretary of the Treasury, Peter Faragas
	The Attorney General, Luis Sanchez
	The Director of CIA, Jon Miller
	The Director of the FBI, Norman Watts
	White House Chief of Staff, Lee Jackson
Guests:	*Joe Kleiner, Mossad*
	Gilad Zahavi, Mossad
	Dean Armitage, State Department

Joe Kleiner summed up after Gilad's presentation. 'So gentlemen, it's a crisis for all of us but please be assured of our absolute commitment to assist you in finding a solution as quickly as possible.'

'Thanks Joe' began Wilmington. 'First, I want to thank you and Gilad for making the very uncomfortable journey to be here with us today – supersonic is great but the military are not famed for comfort but at least I guess it was fast! Seriously though, I want to put on record our gratitude for standing shoulder to shoulder with us in this difficult time and thank you for the invaluable and exhaustive intelligence you have provided.

Unfortunately, as you put it so neatly, proving something that you can't find, isn't there, is going to be a problem. On the face of it, I have to agree with you. Our options do not look promising. We can continue to 'consult with our allies' so to speak and the news of the capture of the Bosnian can be used to buy a little media optimism.

'Henry,' he said turning to the Secretary of State, 'what are your thoughts?'

'Well Mr President, I'm not sure where it takes us but, listening to the Ivanovic interview as translated, I noticed that he said that they unloaded four large metal trunks for their own use, plus the smaller demo bomb, all of which were the same and had pink labels. The one that Ivanovic said he chose as the San Francisco bomb – and it certainly sounded as though it was a random and free choice, he said that it was simply the one closest to him of the four next morning. Furthermore, they both had to believe in the mission, so all four trunks would have had to be real nukes in case Ivanovic chose the wrong one. If the Bosnian got to make a choice, as he said he did, it would have been impossible for Tehran to risk sending three of them filled with just say stones and sawdust. They couldn't do it any other way as the Professor Ahmad did not intervene in his choice.

If that's the case and logic suggests it is, then we are looking for four bombs at least, not just one as Gilad hoped. That in itself does not discredit the theory that Ivanovic was a fall guy which actually makes solid sense to me. What it says is that we had better concentrate on finding this Professor Ahmad type and his other bombs. They were real and they are going to be hidden somewhere.'

'So, in practical terms, what you are saying' interrupted Ed Rich, 'is that once we have tied down the location of the other three trunk bombs, we may be in the clear but the problem with that is that we are potentially still short of 22 other locations in our 'major cities' to quote Saiyeidi. Unless that is, we can track down what happened to the truck and its contents.'

Just then the door opened and an aide entered picking up a telephone set as he approached the president. Wilmington listened to his whisper and picked up the phone. He listened for a couple of minutes and replaced the receiver.

'Well gentlemen, seems our Mr Ivanovic had exceptional recall. They have found the bomb in San Francisco exactly as he had described it right down to the blanket on top of it. The bad news is that it was big enough to have taken out all of the downtown area and a lot more besides.

We also now know for sure that whether it's just another three bombs or twenty-two, we have a full-blown and now confirmed crisis on our hands.'

'If I may speak, Mr President?' asked Norman Watts, Director of the FBI, 'from what our Israeli friends have said and from the material they sent us in advance, we have three main tasks for which we will need all available resources. First, we need to trace this Professor Ahmad and, second, through him locate the remaining 'pink label' bombs. Third, we urgently need to trace the truck they used and its contents. I already have my people checking locations of CCTV cameras that could help us and at least we have a reasonably good fix on times and places from Ivanovic's statement so, if there is anything out there, we'll get it quickly.'

'OK good Norman, but we do need it fast – time is what we don't have' Wilmington underlined. 'In the meantime, we have a major exercise in public relations to attend to. Properly handled and projected as a success based on international cooperation, the capture of one of the bombers and his revelations will keep the media in a state of controlled frenzy for some little time at least. It's essential that we maintain 'business as usual' while we determine our course of action. Any incidence of panic will be infectious.'

MONDAY, 15TH APRIL, 08:40 LOCAL, (13:40 GMT)
FBI Strategic Information and Operations Center, Washington

'Exemplary' was an oft-used word to describe the career of Director Norman Watts. Eldest son of a Quaker family from Idaho, he had been given an intentionally simple upbringing that emphasised obedience, duty and a compassionate responsibility for others. A model product of Yale and the Harvard Law School and a First Lieutenant in the United States Army Reserve, Watts had surprised some of his peers by opting to become an FBI Special Agent in the New York City Field Office and later at FBI Headquarters in Washington D.C. Having then spent a number of years rising to be a Deputy United States Attorney in Sacramento and then District Court Judge, he had caught the eye of the Wilmington entourage who wanted him back in the FBI as Director. Austere and not noted for his sense of humour, Norman's shirt drawer contained only white shirts, both long and short sleeved, he had never owned a pair of blue jeans and had never had need of a passport.

'OK guys, let's recap what we've got so far?' Norman Watts demanded of his assembled crisis team. He had been expressly instructed to lead the team by the President himself.

The Israelis had secure-emailed everything they had late the previous afternoon and Watts had immediately set his crisis team to analyse every last detail and construct a comprehensive, checkable map and timetable from Radin's evidence.

Fifteen hours on and they had corralled and coordinated relevant CCTV footage from all available sources, public and known private, commercial or industrial. Piecing it all together, their first fix was at 14:17 from a camera on an oyster processing plant in Marshall where Ivanovic said they'd had lunch. It showed the Ford SUV heading past it going north. Another shot put them at the Woodley Island Marina at 19:38 but then nothing in Fields Landing or anywhere else until they checked out of the Marina again at 13:52 the following day. Traffic cameras going into Fortuna picked up the Ford SUV again and, for the first time, a medium sized, grey GM truck that seemed to be following it, just as Radin had said.

The licence plates had been traced back to the truck hire company who were not expecting it back until the following week. There were no CCTV cameras out in the country where they had left the grey truck and that was the last Radin had seen of it. An 'all points bulletin' had already been put out to the police and fire services across the country on the highest priority.

Following Radin's memory of the route back to the apartment, the SUV was picked up again coming off Highway 101 at San Rafael, some 15 miles north of San Francisco later that night and leaving again early the following morning.

The police and the FBI had already woken the staff responsible for the Andrew Jackson Apartments and forced them to open their records in the middle of the night. What had seemed a minor oversight in form filling at the time, now glared at Brad, the office manager, like a wretched beacon. The Professor had paid the whole of the rent in advance plus the deposit in cash and having paid with such magnanimous swiftness, Marion, the registrations clerk had simply accepted 'Professor Ahmad – Boston' on the registration papers and couldn't therefore have checked. She had equally failed to note the number on the Florida driving licence. It was an administrative catastrophe that confirmed the wisdom of having fired her shortly thereafter.

To add insult to injury for the FBI, the hired furniture and accessories had all been removed at the end of the lease the previous week and the apartment had been thoroughly cleaned. Yes, the bombers had been there but no clues as to where they came from or went to.

It was a similar story with the Ford SUV that was registered to a James Grant with an address of 'Days Inn Hotel, San Francisco' who naturally had never heard of him. No sign of it since.

Watts exhorted his team to greater diligence and started to read the FBI reports on the apartment to double check. Some minutes later, Frank Delanie broke into his concentration, 'Pay dirt folks, we've got a face! '

It had taken time to retrieve the private CCTV footage of the entrance to the building in which the bomb had been found. It was last week's batch and, for the best of security reasons, the facilities management company did not keep old records on the premises. It was still only just past 4:00am in San Francisco and it had taken the night staff until half an hour ago to trace it.

Watts looked at the pictures of the now familiar Ford SUV drawing up outside the building. Radin and another man in a baseball hat and dark glasses unloaded a trunk onto a trolley that they had brought with them and the other man, Professor Ahmad, took it inside while Radin drove off. Some twenty minutes later, they both emerged again, the Professor still in hat and dark glasses, and walked briskly away, presumably to rejoin the SUV.

'OK Frank, get that straight to the image enhancement guys and see what they can come up with. This is the only visual fix we have on our Professor Ahmad. With all the other leads so far seemingly carefully constructed dead ends, this could be absolutely vital for stirring peoples' memories. Make sure graphics really takes on board its importance and tell them to drop everything else until they have a result.'

The rest of the team set about establishing times for Radin's journey to the Nevada Test Site but the last camera sighting was at Baker on Interstate 15, well short of Pahrump, and the three cameras there in the town drew a blank. A local realtor was more helpful – yes, a Professor Ahmad had owned a helicopter but he finally got rid of it a couple of weeks back and, yes, he had indeed hired the Black Horse Ranch for two months– no, the place was vacant again – yes, paid in cash. Further enquiries showed that the Schweizer 300Cbi had been owned by the Professor for just four weeks and been paid for by banker's draft drawn on a Liechtenstein Bank. Dead end.

The phone rang on Watts' desk. 'Yes, that's me,' Norman listened quietly, scribbling notes. 'But no licence plates? OK, that's an enormous help, make sure they buy them a beer on Uncle Sam!'

'Right gather round' shouted Watts, 'major new development. That was the fire department from a town called Hayfork in California. They were called out in the evening of April 10th, that's five days after the bombs arrived, to a blazing truck that had been abandoned in some trees off a minor road just above a place called Forest Glen. Where's the map? Here, look here,' Watts said pointing animatedly, 'must be what, about 50 to 60 miles from Fortuna. By the time the fire department got there, it was pretty much all over but two things stood out and prompted them to respond to our APB. One, the license plates had been removed and two, it appeared to have been the same type and model. And it gets better – we had supplied the engine block ID code that the hire company gave us and they matched them! The bad news is that it appears that the back of the truck was empty.

So where does that leave us now?' Watts asked the group.

'Sounds like our mystery man, *The Merchant*, must have dumped the truck but why make it so obvious?' said Frank now back again from Imaging.

Marianne, the cipher specialist chipped in 'so we'd know the trunks had been distributed. Must have had the other teams pick up their bombs – actually, when you think about it, that's the only way they could have done it and had the bombs in place and ready in time before the deadline of the NTS blast.'

'Or if the Mossad people are right,' cautioned Frank, 'and they simply disposed of the trunks to hide the fact that they had no more bangers left.'

Watts looked at them slowly. 'Son-of-a-bitch, we're actually still no further on. We know there was the San Francisco bomb and it's logical to believe that the others Ivanovic saw were genuine as well as he picked the bomb at random himself. We know the Professor disappeared for two days after the Bosnian went home giving him time to plant two other bombs but there were no sightings until he was on his way back up north. We know that he checked out of the apartment the following day and that's it – end of story. He has certainly had the opportunity to meet the deadline of the demo blast and so far, I think we have to assume that he did. Anyone any thoughts? I need to call the President – I promised to update a meeting of the inner sanctum 35 minutes from now.'

'Just thinking aloud but if I was planning their op., I'd go for San Diego, LA, San Fran and Seattle – major impact, fallout will drift to the east' suggested Jim Barber, the senior strategy analyst. 'And I know this is not helpful but, with just four bombs to hide, I'd choose a different type of hiding place each time to invalidate the hierarchical scans that we would normally employ here.'

'Thanks Jim,' said Watts with more than a hint of sarcasm, 'if that's the case, a bank of supercomputers is not going to come up with an answer in time! I'll call the President anyway.'

'Please hear me out Norman,' retorted Barber 'these guys have had the advantage of months to set this whole thing up and, as we've seen already, they haven't left any meat for us anywhere; they figured how we would come after them and planned accordingly. They thought it through properly and I'll bet that the very top guys in that new Tehran regime sanctioned it. So why don't we also try it the other way about and see what those players were doing themselves. Let's create another line of enquiry, let's invert the thing. For example, what family and friends does Saiyeidi have? Who are their friends, who did he work with to plan and execute the coup? Are there any 'interesting Iranians' who have been through US immigration at the relevant times?

In strategic terms, this is about as important for Tehran as it could be and my guess is they would only have a jerk like Ivanovic on the loose over here if his actions were very limited and highly supervised by someone Tehran trusts implicitly. So, who is this Professor Ahmad? Why don't I check out Saiyeidi and any potential leads that come from his end?'

'Sorry Jim, you're right, that could be an extremely interesting angle; run with it and grab anyone you need; now I am overdue to get back to the President – he's not going to like it any more than we do!' Watts withdrew into his private office and closed the door.

MONDAY, 15TH APRIL, 08:30 LOCAL, (13:30 GMT)
The Oval Office, the White House, Washington DC

In attendance: The President of Unites States, Thomas Wilmington
　　　　　　　　The Vice President, George Fairburn
　　　　　　　　The Secretary of Defense, Edwin Rich
　　　　　　　　The Secretary of State, Henry Porter
　　　　　　　　The Director of the FBI, Norman Watts
　　　　　　　　White House Chief of Staff, Lee Jackson

Norman Watts updated the inner cabinet on the progress SIOC had made, on the ambiguity they faced within the evidence that had emerged from the leads initiated by Ivanovic's interrogation and of the Jim Barber's assertion that the operation had been minutely planned by Tehran's top leadership and that therefore they had to have had a strong element of operational control in the field.

There was not much new there really and a pensive silence followed the end of Watts's report.

'Hmmm' nodded Wilmington. 'Plenty of evidence, plenty of noise but not much meat. I am increasingly inclined to think that Mossad's bluff theory may be right. But as Zahavi their strategist put it so succinctly, proving something you can't find, isn't there, is impossible and that's our dilemma. We will never be able to say that it doesn't exist until we can prove it and the only way of proving it will be to force the Iranians to come clean and divulge the extent of the threat. I don't suppose Saiyeidi is going to volunteer the information so we therefore desperately need to nail either the Professor or this 'Merchant' character who are the only ones outside Saiyeidi's gang who know the location of any or all of the bombs.

The white-haired Vice President looked at his friend and then around the small table.

He began in a slow, measured drawl. 'You know folks, strip it right down and ultimately this is the same old regional confrontation that we have been drawn into again and again by the Israelis and their friends in Washington. The only reason that we are actually only committed to invading Iran is because the Israelis insist that the new Shahab-8 missile could be deployed in the next 18 months and could be expected to reach our shores as well as those of Israel itself. That was the issue that prompted the last President's declaration last December.

That is particularly significant because our close support of the State of Israel over the years was, in reality, always predicated on the basis that, excluding strictly terrorist incidents like 9/11, any resulting conflict would never actually touch our shores here. Tehran is not stupid so they figured it out. Saiyeidi has now removed that rather comfortable position and we potentially face immediate retaliation on our own doorstep. All as a direct result of Israel's need for our umbrella. So let us not forget that the emerging power struggle in the Middle East was the catalyst for seeding the US mainland.'

Edwin Rich was tapping his pencil agitatedly on the notepad in front of him as he began to glower at the Vice President who continued undeterred. 'Gentlemen, I acknowledge wholeheartedly that the Israelis were the first to bring the Iranian plot to our attention but equally, they could hardly do otherwise particularly as it has such a close bearing on their own circumstances.'

'I really cannot accept that' interrupted the Secretary of Defense. 'Joe Kleiner and his friends acted expediently and with great urgency as one would expect of our closest ally in the circumstances. To suggest otherwise is almost, well anti-Semitic!'

'They could hardly have done otherwise given Saiyeidi's speech and the specific threat to Israel it contained', George Fairburn said bristling visibly from the accusation.

'Please let's stick to the issue in front of us' intervened the President quickly.

'The question now is not the why and wherefore of this situation, it's a question of how we confront, contain and neutralise the threat it poses; it's therefore a question of how we locate the bombs quickly and how we maintain public calm in the meantime. If anyone doubts the level of anxiety in the country today, all you have to do is ask my Press Secretary. Let's see how things work themselves out and then, and only then, we can turn to more arcane matters of foreign policy.

We need to recognise upfront that this is a political and not a military crisis. Having slept on it, it would be almost inconceivable for us to retaliate to Saiyeidi's actions immediately. Iran is not going to unleash the bombs that it has seeded in this country unless we provoke it – as the Secretary of State and Saiyeidi himself so aptly pointed out, their country would be reduced to smouldering, radioactive ashes in minutes. What we have to do is find a way of resolving the crisis before we in this room are swept away by a rising tide of public concern in this country. Make no mistake, we are on trial here and so far our options are exceedingly limited.

And, Edwin, please don't doubt our appreciation of Israel's help. You can reassure them that our people in this country feel that, quite apart from its strategic value to us, the Israeli people deserve our support because it is weak and surrounded by enemies' said the President tapping his finger on the table in front of him, 'because it is a democracy, which is a morally preferable and more dependable form of government and, not least, because the Jewish people have suffered horribly in the past and that, of itself, deserves our special treatment. Oh and finally, also because their conduct has in my opinion been morally superior to their enemies – which is why they were so quick to bring the matter to our attention – as you pointed out. I'm sure that I'm not alone in that view.

But equally Edwin, I'm bound to point out that you should not make the all too common mistake of assuming that our national interests are, as a result, inalienably identical with theirs. They have ruthlessly pursued their own national interest in the past without regard to us and each situation must therefore be judged on its merits and, first and foremost, on our own national interest.

'Norman' Wilmington said, turning to the Director of the FBI, 'I don't have to tell you what the stakes are here. You will have my support for anything you need, so call me at any time of the day or night. But we must have a drip feed of constructive news to satisfy the media and keep the pot from boiling over. The looming reality is that if we can't find the bombs or prove that they don't exist, our freedom of action and national policy in the Middle East will be severely affected – and I don't want to be a one-term President!'

MONDAY, 15TH APRIL, 12:15 LOCAL, (17:15 GMT)
The Press Room, the White House, Washington DC

Andrew Board, the White House Press Secretary, looked serious as he stepped up to the bank of microphones in the press room. The meeting had been called with unusually short notice but the White House Press Corps had never been far from the room since the crisis broke.

'Ladies and gentlemen, I have a short announcement from the President's office following on from his broadcast to the nation on Sunday night in the light of Iran's aggressive actions. The President is pleased to announce that thanks to unprecedented cooperation between the security arms of the Unites States and Israel, we have already been able to apprehend and question one of the two individuals responsible for planting the bomb in the Nevada Test Site. As a result of this, we have already located and disarmed another bomb that was planted in San Francisco and we are working on the information provided to accelerate our search for the others.

We remain confident of total success and urge all citizens to remain vigilant and report anything suspicious or unusual to the police.

Thank you'

TUESDAY, 16TH APRIL, 14:15 LOCAL, *(19:15 GMT)*
FBI Strategic Information and Operations Center, Washington DC

Mark Bannister from Imaging knocked and barged his way past the open plan desk units and blue desk chairs as he forged his insistent path towards Watts who was surrounded by four gesticulating analysts.

'Listen up everyone' barked Watts, 'we've got the initial analysis from imaging based on the San Francisco sightings and they are compelling! Imaging have identified two possible candidates, one of whom died three months ago, the second, well guess what folks, it's none other than a certain Professor Ahmad Miljabi from oriental linguistic studies at Miami University – not Boston!

We've got our match and now the cavalry can pick up this naturalised Iraqi!. Nice work Mark, we'll take it from here' Watts rounded off in triumph amid a wave of applause from the assembled company. That was the high point of the morning.

Within 45 minutes, the FBI radioed in that the Professor had been out of the country since January doing a study on the indigenous tribes in Indonesia and was not expected back until September.

'It's the perfect cover for God sakes!' howled Watts 'We know he was in California until he checked out of Larkspur on 10th. Someone go check all flights from the West Coast to Indonesia on 10th, 11th and 12th – he'd have to have been back under cover by the time of the Nevada blast.

Get back to your contact in Jakarta. Marianne, get hold of the CIA and find out what assets we have over there right now. Try and get a fix on where Miljabi might be. We've got to get him unharmed and in one piece – he's our only lead to the other three

West Coast bombs and he just might be able to lead us to *The Merchant*. I want him alive and talking.

WEDNESDAY, 17TH APRIL, 06:30 LOCAL, (16TH 21:00 GMT)
Manokawi Hills Hotel, Manokwari, West Papua

The rattle and buzz from Jules's Iridium satellite phone beside the bed finally dragged him out of the patchy sleep pattern that alternated between uneven dreams and anxious reality.

The incoming call was from Greg Milden who was watching the house on Valencia Avenue in Miami where Professor Ahmad Miljabi had taken a studio.

Greg had recently set up his own agency and was very keen to please particularly as the $5000 a week (plus expenses) that he was being paid went some way to securing the future for the next few months. The Englishman had paid him a month in advance at the beginning and the transfers had hit his bank account like clockwork every Friday since. Rosa Bergendorf, the owner of the house where Miljabi had his studio, was a widow in her late 70s and received almost no visitors except a middle-aged woman who seemed to come every Thursday normally for early supper. Greg supposed that she must be a daughter but, unlike the Professor's room which faced them across the street, the old lady's living space was at the back of the house and he couldn't see what passed between them.

Ben Rawlings, his English client, was a man of few words but had indicated that he was expecting someone to come and search the Professor's room – if his well laid plans worked.

'Hello Mr Rawlings! Hope those spring flowers are looking good in Shropshire this evening.'

'Fine thank you,' replied Jules looking at the dawn now rushing spectacularly over the eastern horizon. 'What have you got for me?'

'Looks like your plans have gone, well ... according to plan. Three men and a woman in a black sedan and looking every inch like Feds have just left the house. They must have talked to Mrs Bergendorf first for not more than 10 minutes and then they all showed up in the Professor's studio. They spent just over half an hour going through anything they could find and then left with a very small file of papers. Their body language said it all; they were disappointed and drove off again.'

'Excellent Greg, I know it's been a very tedious assignment but keep it up for another week and then we'll call it a day – with a $10,000 bonus for your troubles.'

Jules never heard Greg's farewell as he replaced the phone and got out of bed.

'Yes!' he hissed to himself, clenching his fist like a tennis player and wheeling out of bed. This was the proof positive that he had been waiting for that his plan had succeeded, that the Americans had swallowed the bait.

And now came the moment of truth. Now was the point in the plan at which he had to create closure in the minds of the Feds. Without closure, his knowledge of the location of the bombs would jeopardise his life forever. The Americans had connected the carefully constructed dots, now they had to be given a conclusive dead end.

TUESDAY, 16TH APRIL, 16:40 LOCAL, (17TH 00:40 GMT)
Norman Watts's office, FBI Strategic Information and Operations Center, Washington

'OK Jim, Marianne's revving up the CIA in Indonesia, so what have you got on your Saiyeidi angle so far?' asked Watts.

'Nothing that's going to set you alight, I'm afraid, Norman. There's no record of his arrival in Paris, they probably wanted to cover their tracks from the Shah and simply found the right official to bribe! Then nothing until he shows up as a pupil at the International school in Paris but the address given was in an apartment block close to the Bois de Boulogne which was later redeveloped and the record was never updated. He entered Brasenose College, Oxford when he was 19 and went on to get a 2:2 in History before taking on running the family fortune – always low key and discrete – always below the radar.'

'So are we done with that idea Jim, have you reached a cul-de-sac?'

'Hell no!' retorted Jim 'No, I've had the girls start pulling together all his known contacts and acquaintances in France, Iran or anywhere else in fact. One of the co-leaders of the coup was another exile called Khalîl Mousavi who also lived in Paris with his daughter. It seems highly unlikely that two well-healed, Iranian exiles living in Paris for that long wouldn't have known each other rather well long before starting a coup d'état together. Anyway, I'm getting all that checked out as it may be a way into Saiyeidi's life in Paris and Mousavi stands out as being the only personal friend to go back with him to Iran.'

'Has someone interviewed him?' demanded Watts.

'Unfortunately, he and his daughter were brutally murdered, supposedly by the Mojahedin as part of the Israeli's failed coup last November. But the fact that they were prepared to go to so much trouble to eliminate him suggests that Khalîl Mousavi was a key part of Saiyeidi's team and that feeds my curiosity.'

'Good job Jim, good; keep me informed' said Watts terminating the interview.

WEDNESDAY, 17TH APRIL 22:45 LOCAL, (13:45 GMT)
UNCEN Faculty of Agriculture guest facility, three miles inland from Manokwari, West Papua

Ahmad Miljabi settled himself onto the thin mattress that covered the wooden slats of the bed. The guest facility made no pretences about providing its visitors with any degree of comfort, merely a roof over their heads. Ahmad favoured the facility as there was seldom anyone else there and, at just over 1200 feet above the coastline, the nights were cooler and less plagued by mosquitoes.

A diligent, ascetic Sunni Muslim, Ahmad found the solitude enriching and the attendant peace gave him the clarity to expand his theory of eastern linguistic development. His father had been a Professor of Linguistics at Baghdad University and had pioneered a system of theoretical analysis of ancient languages with an emphasis on grammar, construction and argumentation. It was a scholarly and dry calling but one that Ahmad had embraced without hesitation. His ability had been noted soon after the demise of

Saddam Hussein and he had been pleased to accept the substantially greater funding for his research projects offered by the University of Miami than would ever have been forthcoming in Iraq.

Irian Jaya was the last Indonesian island to be touched by outsiders and provides an opportunity to witness people just now emerging from the Stone Age, a factor that had particular resonance for Ahmad.

Irian Jaya constitutes just over a fifth of Indonesia's total land mass. It has enormous diversity geographically from swampland near the southern coast, to Savannah, and snow-covered mountains. Rivers and lakes add to its beauty. Although almost all parts of the island are tropical, regionally the weather is diverse. In the mountains and tropical forest, rain falls almost all the time while, in the northern part, the rainy season occupies longer than the dry season and, at the-south-eastern area, rain falls from April through November. When Ahmad arrived in January, he had allowed himself the rare indulgence of a week off in the extraordinary islands and coral reefs that abound on the western coast around Sorong, now made famous of course by the James Bond movie.

By contrast, Irian Jaya's people and tropical rain forest are probably the most untouched on the planet and a key element that had attracted Ahmad. The population of Irian Jaya is now an estimated 2 million people, the majority of whom still live in the jungle. No one really knows the exact tancestry of Irian. The people of Irian, black-skinned and frizzy-haired, are physically very distinct from other Indonesians in the rest of the archipelago.

Today there are about 250 ethnic groups all speaking distinct languages and dialects. Most of the tribes still live a primitive life, farming, fishing and hunting for survival. Two Christian missionaries, Dutch and a German, first arrived in Manokwari in 1855.

Supported by the government, these missionaries then founded schools, simple hospitals and churches. They also helped the local people learn Bahasa Indonesia, which is spoken in many areas of Irian Jaya today.

Hatam is the language spoken by approximately 16,000 people, living in the Arfak Mountains, south of Manokwari. The language comprises five dialects: *Tinam, Miriei, Adihup, Uran* and *Moi*. Tinam is the major dialect and is easily understood and spoken by speakers of the other dialects. It is the evolution of this relationship of understanding that Ahmad is now researching at the expense of the Biltmore Foundation back in New York.

Within minutes of his head meeting the meagre pillow, Ahmad was lost in the balm that sleep brings to well-ordered and well-exercised minds. Borrowing a Christian concept, his father had always referred to it as 'the sleep of the righteous'. Ahmad never heard the sound of the car pulling up well short of the facility.

The Brown Snake's textilotoxin is one of the most potent neurotoxins known to man. Brown snake bites, even apparently trivial ones, have been associated with acute deterioration over a final five-minute period leading to death as severe cardiac depression overwhelms the victim.

The small native snake handler had already goaded his snake into something of a frenzy before lobbing it directly onto Ahmad's exposed face and shoulders. Landing on warm skin that erupted from sleep in fright, the snake instantly sank its fangs into Ahmad's neck as he flayed to rid himself of his serpentine attacker. With arms still flailing, he burst out of the door before collapsing 25 paces down the track. In less than three minutes, Ahmad lay still, his involuntary convulsions now lost.

Staring at his digital look-alike in the moonlight, Jules tried to rationalise what he had just wrought, in cold blood, to a man of intelligence whom he'd never even met. He instantly invoked the images of Zahra's bloody remains in the mortuary but his conscience pushed aside this aging defence and indelibly added Ahmad's killing to the buried reservoir of grief that awaited Jules at the end of this road.

A whistle from the snake handler and a beckoning hand brought him back to his task. Picking up the small plastic bag from the backseat of the car, he followed his hired assassin into Ahmad's room and began to sow the seeds of closure.

WEDNESDAY, 17TH APRIL, 20:45 LOCAL, (18TH 01:45 GMT)
FBI Strategic Information and Operations Center, Washington DC

The video link provided via the CIA's secure communications satellite flickered into action watched by Norman Watts and the key members of his team gathered in the executive boardroom.

Marty Doppard had called two hours previously as soon as their plane had landed at the small Sentani airport near Manokwari. They were being met, as requested, by the local chief of police to expedite the arrest of the Professor and his removal to US territory as had been hastily agreed with the Indonesian government. He would report back as and when.

Now Marty's anxious face filled the screen.

'Sir, I'm afraid that we may have something of a disaster on our hands' he started. 'When we arrived at the University's guest house where the Professor was staying, an ambulance and a doctor were already at the scene as the subject had been found dead outside the building by the cleaner a little while earlier. The doc reckons that he has been dead at least 12 hours and must have surprised a Brown Snake in his room.'

'What's a Brown Snake?' interrupted Watts.

'The police chief says that it's the second most deadly snake on the planet and they get a dozen or so deaths every year around here. It looks as though it may have been sleeping in his bed and must have been startled by him. The doc says that, even if they'd got to him immediately, there would have been little they could have done as they have no supplies of antivenom locally as it is too expensive. I'm really sorry sir but there's nothing at all we can do.'

'What a catastrophe!' moaned Watts. 'Other than *The Merchant* on whom we have absolutely nothing, he was our one and only solid lead to the bombs in California.'

'I realise that sir' said Marty trying to sound conciliatory. 'All I can do is corroborate that we have the right man here at least. Going through his things, we found a tenant guide to an apartment complex at Larkspur in northern California, a copy of *Human Traces* by Sebastian Faulks with a receipt from Borders in San Rafael which is up the road and the boarding card from Tokyo to Jakarta also tucked into it. Incidentally, from his ticket stubs, he must have stayed a night in Jakarta on his way back but we have no indication of where but he could easily have met his controller there before returning here. We also have a road map of Northern California, a box of matches from a Tony's Seaford Restaurant in Marshall and a bunch of dollars in small denomination bills.

I'm afraid he sounds like your boy sir, just sorry we were too late.'

Watts terminated the call and sat in silence.

'End of the trail!' he said with slow resignation. 'Unless anyone has any idea about who *The Merchant* is and where we might find him' he added despondently.

'Oh, we don't give up yet, Norman!' interjected Jim Barber, 'The Professor's death is clearly a substantial setback but he was controlled by someone and that someone is going to have to have been very close to Saiyeidi, one of his absolute inner circle – for secrecy's sake alone. That someone is almost certainly going to be *The Merchant* as they couldn't have risked too many chiefs in this operation.

So I come back to my own line of enquiry. And I am prepared to bet that when we can nail this guy, he or she will have spent the night that Marty Doppard was referring to, in Jakarta, debriefing the Professor. We're nowhere near the end of this yet; we need to redouble our focus on Saiyeidi and his group. That's where the key to this whole thing lies now.'

'Jim, I don't disagree,' confessed Watts, 'we just seemed to have something much more tangible in the Professor though and now we've got to start very nearly all over again.

But that's not the real problem. It's OK for us but the President has got the media crawling all over him and a number of diplomatic channels are starting to make unusual noises. He's going to need to find a resolution to all these jarring opinions and in the very near future before there is real unrest.

The clever move Saiyeidi made was the very public detonation of the explosion in the Nevada Test Site. Without that, Wilmington stood a chance of managing public perceptions but not any more.'

THURSDAY, 18TH APRIL, 18:45 LOCAL, (17:45 GMT)
The Count and Contessa di Fabbri's apartment,
Piazza San Pierino, Lucca, Italy

The doorbell rang and Becky answered it expectantly, perhaps Sal had forgotten his key.

She still got a kick each time Sal walked through the door and, nowadays, with the Institute going well, their financial problems resolved and the future of the Institute looking increasingly promising, Sal himself seemed 20 years younger and full of his old optimism; such a contrast to the days of his black demons.

She was slightly wrong-footed to find a Federal Express agent clutching a small white envelope which she duly signed for, noticing that it was from Markus Steinhoffer in Zurich.

The telephone was ringing in the kitchen and she hurriedly dismissed the FedEx man. It was her father again.

Since the blaze of publicity that had greeted the successful launch of the *American Bardolini Committee* and the unveiling of the wolf statue in City Hall Park, her father's chairmanship of the stateside team had lent him new stature and, with the blessing of the first lady herself of course, a supposed entrée to almost anywhere.

Sal had told her that she had to curb her long felt cynicism about anything altruistic emanating from her father. He was actually doing a solid job establishing funding for the whole operation and so what if he used the mantle of the foundation to inveigle his way past doors that would otherwise have been closed to him. It really didn't matter.

'Hey Becky, how's that Italian count of yours?' her father asked expecting to get the usual rise from her.

'He's fine, thank you.' she replied flatly. 'He's not back yet but what can we do for you?'

'Well, it was him I needed to speak to actually. I've got this lead into one of the great Italian technology success stories on the West Coast, see. Started his own artificial intelligence outfit 12 years ago and now he's super big here. Gene has earnestly expressed interest in getting involved in the foundation and potentially becoming a major contributor and so I was wondering how soon I could fly Sal in to see him.'

'Where's he based?' Becky asked. Perhaps Sal was right about her father but underneath, she knew it would all be self-serving.

'Gene Cantoni lives down the valley in Los Gatos, about an hour in normal traffic. And hey, guess you've heard, San Francisco is now the safest area in the US after the discovery of the bomb on Pine Street, we're clean!'

'No, I hadn't heard that Dad. Was that announced officially because there has been nothing on the Italian news?'

'Yeah, it was leaked which comes to the same thing nowadays so they'll have to confirm it officially today, I guess. Still leaves your mother under a potential mushroom cloud in Dallas though eh!' he prodded.

'That's not funny Dad' Becky said tartly.

'Yeah well, get the count to call me when gets in, eh' with which her father rang off abruptly.

Salvatore came home a few minutes later just as she had started to prepare their supper. She wiped her hands on a cloth and, as always, she threw her arms round his neck and kissed him with distinct softness on her lips. She smiled into his eyes and kissed him again.

'Anything interesting today, honey?' she asked with unfeigned interest as she returned to the cooking.

'Well, it looks probable that we may have another serious patron from Georgia this time who wants to give the foundation money so, bombs or no bombs, it looks as though I'll have to go the States again in the near future.' Sal was clearly pleased with himself.

'Well that'll put my father in his place. He was just on the phone crowing about some techno-whiz from Silicon Valley who wants to meet you and maybe give you a bucketful for the foundation apparently.

Oh, and there's a registered letter from E.T.' Becky had never met their original benefactor but she had a dark vision of some gnome from the recesses of a Zurich cellar and had simply extended it to that of the extra-terrestrial which, to her mind, seemed to fit nicely.

Sal threw his coat and tie on a chair in the hall and picked up the registered envelope. It did indeed have *Brandtburger Rechtsanwälte, Sonneggstrasse 15 Zurich* on the back of the envelope. But why would he bother to write?, Sal wondered as he grappled with the letter opener.

Dear Count di Fabbri

The Bardolini Institute

I am writing to tell you that the trustees of the Bardolini foundation discussed the future of the Institute at their recent meeting and have concluded that your management and direction of its creation and development have been excellent and they were unanimous in passing a resolution of thanks to you and your wife for the excellent job you have done.

Not least, in this context, they note that based on the endowments received from your fund raising in America alone, the future of the Institute is now secure which is an immense achievement that Senor Bardolini would himself have been proud to have been associated with.

As the Institute is now essentially self-funding, the trustees believe that their duty lies in supporting some of Senor Bardolini's other charitable interests that have not achieved the same measure of success and that, in consequence, no further funding will be forthcoming from the foundation. They feel confident that this will in no way impede your progress in the future particularly as support from the United States continues to grow.

The trustees have asked me to extend their congratulations on achieving independence and every good wish for success in the future.

Your sincerely

Markus Steinhoffer
Partner

Becky watched the look of muffled consternation grip his features as he re-read the letter.

'Unbelievable' stammered Sal slowly as read, 'unbelievable! Pietro and I have just spent weeks ... unbelievable. They can't do this! Weeks we've spent and now this, they can't do this' Sal spat as he handed Becky the letter.

'But I don't understand.' said Becky 'Why's this so bad – they've given you your independence – effectively this is your own show now, I don't see the problem.'

'Becky, my darling, I told you that Pietro and I have been working on plans to extend the scope of the Institute to pasta and cheese. To do that we are going to need to triple our funding otherwise we can't do it. Zurich knew this and suddenly they seem to be taking the commercial decisions for us which is really bizarre as we are the ones on the ground and we are the guys who have been creating the business for the Institute. But without the investment that I asked for, we're blocked.'

'And you'd discussed all this with them?' asked Becky still puzzled.

'Absolutely! I can show you all the emails that demonstrate clear commitment to our plans. They've reneged on the deal Becky!'

Sal's initial anger turned quickly to crisis management and within the hour, Sal was booked on the 06:45 Alitalia flight into Zurich the following morning having emailed Steinhoffer of his intentions. He doubted that he would have much time to prepare a defense to the onslaught he was planning for him – so much the better.

THURSDAY 18TH APRIL, WASHINGTON DC, 15:30 LOCAL, (21:30 GMT)
The President's conference room in the White House

It was only two days since Watts had last seen the President and the change in the man's bearing was immediately apparent. He no longer exuded Presidential confidence; he no longer seemed positive and directing events. Rather, Wilmington was now grappling with the growing political storm accompanying the public and media speculation. How should they best present a thorough-going, thrusting image to the world. His political future was on the line.

Wilmington sat expressionless and in silence as Watts reported the death of the Professor and Marty's verification of the evidence among his effects that confirmed him as Ivanovic's co-conspirator. He was flanked by his Vice-President, George Fairburn and Henry Porter from State, both unsmiling. The absence of the adversarial Edwin Rich from Defense and of his friend from the CIA pointed to a drawing in of horns and to Wilmington's narrowing options.

'The trouble with where we are' began the President, 'is that politically it's simply not a sustainable situation. Actually, there is no imminent military threat that we have to address. It might be a whole lot simpler if there were. In simple terms, we have taken a major position in support of our key Middle East ally, to safeguard its security and now it has come back to bite us. The Israelis failed in their earlier attempt to remove the missile threat from Iran and now the onus has been placed firmly on us, thanks to my undertaking last year.

In this room, we all know that even if there was just one hidden bomb remaining in a US city, we could not risk making good on our undertaking. Several million casualties in any major conurbation is just not an option. Equally, we all know the power of the Jewish lobby and what it could do to our prospects for a second term. It's definitely not a military problem but as long as we threaten Saiyeidi's regime, there is little chance of an accommodation that would remove the threat to our second term.'

'Seems to me Tom' opined the soldier, Henry Porter, 'that we are down to one remaining option and, however bad the odds on achieving it appear to be at this point, we just have to lay our hands on whomever *'The Merchant'* is and then try and extort the location of the bombs from him. Frankly, even if he didn't happen to know the precise location of all the goddam bombs, it probably wouldn't matter because irrespective of whether we manage to obtain the details, Saiyeidi and his friends would never be able to be sure what we had got out of him. Once we have the man, short of our actually attacking Iran, Saiyeidi isn't going to risk getting into a situation where he might have to push the button just in case it's been disarmed!'

George Fairburn shook his hand in the air. 'No Henry, you're right in one sense but it doesn't help – we'd be no further on. As Tom has just pointed out, the status quo is not sustainable politically – not only from the angle of the ongoing and ever-present threat to homeland security which can only be removed if the bombs are seen to be removed but equally the Israelis would continue to demand action in Iran or, worse still, go it alone themselves. Ultimately, we'd never be able to control them and that in itself raises more questions if this thing goes the full course.'

'It's a mess. No two ways about it' said Wilmington intervening. 'At least the stakes for Kennedy in the Cuban Missile Crisis were more clear-cut. It was either total nuclear war which would have destroyed both the Russians and us or Khrushchev had to back down. What we have here is something which is not wholly in our control because, as George points out, ultimately the Israelis will do what they want – unless we can find a tent big enough to accommodate everyone's worries and tether them inside it.

Norman, get your people working on anything that would enable us to find *'The Merchant'* before it's too late. In the meantime, I think that my friend Dean Armitage might discretely emphasise the seriousness of the situation in which we find ourselves to his friends in Israel. They can't have missed the inherent threat to their own position in all this, I'm sure.'

FRIDAY 19TH APRIL, 08:45 LOCAL, (07:45 GMT)
The offices of Brandtburger Rechtsanwälte, 15 Sonneggstrasse, Zurich, Switzerland

It was an easy trip; fifteen minutes from the airport to the Zurich Hauptbahnhof and another 15 minutes at most on foot over the River Limmat and on a bit. Sal had learnt one golden rule of travelling, particularly if you have to get up early to get to a meeting: take it easy, leave lots of time, keep the brain clear. So he took a taxi and had a quick coffee watching the good burghers of Zurich arriving for their working day.

At two minutes before 09:00, Sal retrieved Steinhoffer's business card and set off for No. 15 Sonneggstrasse. The card indicated the 6th floor but the polished nameplate suggested reception was on the 3rd floor. Entering the reception area, Sal immediately felt uncomfortable with the Spartan orderliness of the offices. These were people who didn't need to impress the client with comfortable chairs and magazines while they waited.

Sal approached the girl in the plain grey suit behind a plain wooden reception desk and explained in English that he had an appointment with Mr Steinhoffer. The plain girl merely frowned and almost out of fright Sal handed her the visiting card. The girl frowned again and disappeared. After a few minutes she reappeared and asked Sal to be seated.

Something was wrong. Glancing around the room, Sal noticed a small brochure on the firm of lawyers beside him on the table and opened it, almost involuntarily looking to see where Steinhoffer appeared in the pecking order of partners.

After three increasingly desperate glances, he was sure that Steinhoffer's name was not on the list. At which moment, a man's voice invited him to please follow him. Sal was shown into a small meeting room just off the reception area with a table and four chairs. No pictures.

'Count di Fabbri, my name is Stephan Neudorf, I am a partner in this firm. I'm afraid there has been a very disturbing mistake here and I see from your countenance that you are perhaps as confused as I am. We have no Herr Steinhoffer in this firm and, as far as I know, we never have had such a gentleman and certainly not a partner. Can I ask how you came to be here and in possession of this visiting card?'

Salvatore was stunned for a second and then aghast at the abyss opening before him.

Stephan Neudorf asked two more of his partners and the office manager to join them in the boardroom where they now all convened and listened intently and with growing puzzlement to the story.

'Count,' Neudorf said finally, 'this seems to be a victimless crime if it is a crime at all, if I have understood things correctly! And that I find very hard to understand. I don't see the motive at all. Someone clearly did some very thorough and sophisticated research before setting all this up. Enrico Bardolini did indeed die just as your Herr Steinhoffer described and he is, or was, a client of this firm and had made most of his considerable fortune exporting olive oil to America. But, for the most part, his estate has been left to various elements of the arts in Italy and an extensive series of music scholarships – most of which are actually administered by us.'

'But the money,' stuttered Salvatore, 'it must be easy to trace the source, where it was transferred from – a significant amount!'

'Not necessarily,' said Neudorf pursing his lips, 'these were international transfers and once funds have crossed a couple of borders, particularly if they used any tax havens such as Liechtenstein, the source will be completely opaque.'

'And the contact numbers?' suggested Sal hopefully.

'You said that Steinhoffer asked you always to ring his mobile phone which would not be a problem for him and I'll bet that the office phone number on his card is now out of order. But I simply don't understand why anyone would go to all this trouble and expense to create a perfectly respectable olive oil Institute in Italy for no apparent reason. There must be an ulterior motive, there has to be. That said, it sounds as though the Institute and its operations have been properly constituted and are therefore perfectly legal even if your benefactor and his or her motives remain a mystery.

So cheer up my dear Count' Neudorf said rising to terminate the meeting. 'You have your Institute and, by the sound of it, some very serious backing in the States so things could be a great deal worse!'

FRIDAY 19TH APRIL, 12:45 LOCAL, (11:45 GMT)
The Count and Contessa di Fabbri's apartment, Piazza San Pierino, Lucca, Italy

Back in the privacy of the VIP lounge in Zürich's Kloten airport, still in mental turmoil, Sal called Becky and went through the morning's extraordinary events. What were they missing? What had anyone to gain from the existence of the Institute? The Institute was constitutionally independent, the funding it had received had no strings and it had received support from a number of the good and the great in America. None of it made sense in the real world.

'Who in all conscience would want to go through all this, buy our olive groves, set up an Institute in association with some of the biggest names in US – even erecting a statue in the middle of New York, if the whole thing was just a pointless sham?' They would discuss it over dinner in the evening.

Now, some forty minutes on, alone in the apartment, Becky was just starting to prepare Sal's dinner. While she got the veal escalopes that she was going to cook with wild fungi out of the fridge, she turned on the portable Sony Trinitron TV that they used in the kitchen. The Sky News channel had yet another panel of experts discussing the ramifications of the San Francisco bomb and speculating on the search for the others. A man in a dark suit and open neck shirt was theorising on the comparative ease of mounting such an operation in any country with open borders provided the bombs were seemingly innocuous. 'If something didn't look like a bomb, why would anyone suppose it was?'

'Such as a statue' Becky said out loud.

The thought was so outrageous that it might just be real. The elaborate and ostentatious rigmarole of the Institute that had seemed pointless seconds earlier suddenly became a terrifying spectre. It fitted, it answered all Sal's questions and what better cover than having the First Lady unveil it? She dropped the potato she was peeling and picked up the phone to her mother in Texas.

FRIDAY 19TH APRIL, 08:15 LOCAL, (18:15GMT)
The Oval Office, Washington

'Hello Becky' the President said, 'I haven't seen you in years but Lucy tells me that you married an Italian Count and that you live in Lucca. I gather that you are concerned that you may both have been used in some kind of a plot. We've got a lot of it about at the moment as I expect you've seen!' said Wilmington laughing nervously.

Having listened in silence for a full two minutes to Becky's story, the President interrupted. 'Becky, I've heard enough. I want you to talk to Norman Watts immediately; he's the head of the FBI here and is coordinating things on this Iranian business. Unfortunately your suspicions sound plausible to me and even if they turn out to be wrong, I want to thank you anyway for bringing this to us. If everyone was as alert as you, things would be a whole lot easier here right now. Just stay on the line please.'

Watts was at his desk and, before transferring the call, Wilmington told him to call him as soon as he had anything definitive on the statue. Anticipating the worst, he called George Fairburn and Henry Porter to come into the Oval Office and ran them through Becky's story.

After exploring potential options for some 20 minutes, it became obvious that they had pretty much run out of road.

'So this changes everything if it's true' the Vice President summarised,.'Saiyeidi has opened a whole new front and, if the statue does turn out to be a bomb, we will no longer even know what we're looking for or where to start. It was bad enough before Tom, and this was designed to embarrass you personally. How on God's earth could they have known that Lucy would be invited to unveil it personally.'

'These people have shown themselves to be just extremely thorough all the way through' replied Wilmington. 'I suspect though that having Lucy unveil it was the cream on the cake but someone clearly did enough research to know that Becky's mother was a long-time friend of Lucy and that takes some insight. That's kind of scary. The real issue though will be the bomb itself. It blows the CIA theory of Saiyeidi's limited supplies of fissile material right out of the window and leaves us with an insoluble problem.'

The President paused, staring at the fire that had already been lit that morning. 'If it turns out to be another bomb, we've run out of options. It'll be time for realpolitik in the Middle East and the Israelis are not going to enjoy that one bit. It may cost me re-election but there will not be an option. If it's not a bomb, it is another and even more worrying harbinger of our vulnerability to covert attack'.

FRIDAY 19TH APRIL, 22:00H LOCAL, (18:30GMT)
President Saiyeidi's private apartment, Farmaniyeh, Tehran

Professor Ahmad Miljabi had been selected back in January as someone credibly capable of running the projected operation within the US. Jules and the head of Iran's new intelligence agency had pored over the file of mug shots of émigrés from Iraq to US that had been supplied by the new Iraqi secret police. Since then, Jules had been in almost continuous motion. He had been commissioned by the *Le Monde* (on behalf of a new 'international' client) to conduct a study on the nuclear aspirations of the governments of the Pacific Rim. This had given him the cover to be out of France for the critical period as well as a reason for being in various countries such as New Zealand whence he had arrived the previous evening.

He had spent most of the last day asleep in his uncle's apartment, drained and exhausted after the weeks of unrelenting tension and mortal risk. Waking in the afternoon in this totally protected sanctuary, he had started to slowly peer past the out-of-worldliness of his recent endeavours, past the perpetual motion and beyond the all-consuming immediacy of executing the plan, past all of that to a future he had been determined not to contemplate until his debt to Zahra was settled.

Zahra was indeed avenged now but as he had discovered to his profound distress, from the moment he had witnessed the writhing St. Vitas dance of the Professor's last moment on Earth, he had lost her. He knew instantly that he had compromised the wholesomeness of her vision for Iran, her integrity and her full frontal honesty of purpose by the malicious and self-serving sacrifice of a man so blamelessly innocent as the Professor. He had stooped to exactly the same level as the Mojahedin extremists who had been so free with Zahra's own body and their sharp knives. He pleaded from the bottom of his heart that she had died instantly and not in the extended agony that he had imposed on Ahmad Miljabi and indeed had been witness to. There are sins that will never shrivel with time and Miljabi would await him every time he looked into his conscience. But worse still, he knew he would never regain the paradise he had found with Zahra's visitations and the joy that they had rekindled. He faced a sterile life now with his erstwhile ambitions crushed and a minefield lurking in his every move; that was the price of his success.

Out of the morbidity of his delayed reaction, as he peered warily into the future, it seemed that it was not all bad. He was lucky by comparison to so many who did not have a family as close knit and caring as his. That would be enough for many people but having once tasted the deep contentment of true happiness nothing else would ever quite come up to it. However, unquestionably there were things to do and a family and a business to protect and develop. This was not the debt of upbringing though, of filial duty to his family and their wishes, ambitions or their encumbrances. He had always known, even if he had never admitted it to himself, that this debt had always stood before him, unavoidable and in the end inevitable.

His 'destiny' was too strong a word for it, too overblown a concept. As he now began to acknowledge, lying there in safety, looking at the ceiling, his family was both his fate and his good fortune. Hereafter, they must provide his route to salvation if it were possible. Now he needed his debt to the family to become his vocation too. *Prima genitor* dictated that he should take on the mantle of the family domain. Writing and journalism had really been a glorious escape, a red herring before the serious business started. But now that the glory of that escape had been shattered on the Pont Alexandre, it was time to address his responsibilities. Embracing them might indeed bring its own form of escape.

And he was especially lucky with his uncle. He cherished the bond with his uncle, pure, inalienable and established over so many years. With Hamid, he had never felt that there was anything to prove. A debt of closeness and support yes, but that was repayable in kind and, to a degree, he had now gone some way in that respect already, something he could perhaps feel good about.

Together now before dinner, Hamid Saiyeidi listened to his nephew's account of the last few days pouring effusive praise on his nephew's execution of the plan above all to mask his growing foreboding of Jules's defencelessness back in the real world.

'Now' Hamid said, his arm on Jules's shoulder, steering him towards the dinner table, 'let's talk about your future. I have asked the chef to prepare a proper Iranian dinner for us, something a little different and, I hope, the first of many together.'

As they sat down to a first course of *Mirza Ghasemi*, – fried eggplants, eggs, tomatoes and garlic, Jules knew that his uncle was going to advance an alternative, protective vision for him.

'No one knows better than me that France and the Villarosa empire have a strong call on your loyalty' Hamid began. 'And indeed most people in this world would give their right arm to be in your shoes with a father who has never pushed you to take up the reins but is still holding them for you until you decide otherwise. Jules, you have a highly privileged position to which considerable expectations and responsibilities are therefore attached.

But in light of the past weeks, you are no longer an ordinary individual with the freedom and anonymity of the man in the street. Today you are a potential target for the two most powerful and resourceful secret services in the world. We have tried to cover every angle to protect you from being identified or implicated and, as far as we call tell, so far there is no overt connection between any of the events and yourself. Equally, so far no one appears to have made the connection between us. Either eventuality, this side of a few years hence, would put you in considerable jeopardy as the Americans and the Israelis would be correct in assuming that, at the very least, you would know the location of the other bombs not to mention the scope of the deception that the operation has put in place.

I am told that modern drugs can achieve almost anything when it comes to extracting information and you can be sure that you would not be fit for dog meat when they'd finished with you. So I cannot impress upon you forcefully enough that you are going to run a considerable potential risk if you insist on returning to France now.'

'Uncle, let me stop you there for a second. This is obviously something that I have thought about a great deal in the last few weeks and I agree with you that it is a risk but it is a calculated one. There are actually only two people who know the location of the bombs and the extent of the remaining Iranian arsenal – you and I. They've come to a dead end with the Professor, a brick wall, and now they are going to need another line of investigation and that's bound to focus on your immediate circle and resources including the Mousavis. So what are the potential connections?

The weak points, in my analysis at least, are firstly, my parents if they were to be interviewed. That is a big 'if' because first they have to connect me – as Zahra's fiancé – with you. But if they do that, an interview can be resisted diplomatically. My father would be happy to talk to Inspector Lépine say but, in any adversarial circumstances, certainly not to the Americans or Israelis. We French are known to be chauvinistic and a crime committed by a Frenchman is French business.

Secondly, Zahra's boss knew that you and I are related – nominally at least, it was one of the reasons for promoting Zahra. But, as we know, the unhappy man died fortuitously in a car crash in the Alps sparing us the need for any nastiness.

'Lastly' Jules said tucking into the lamb *Kabab Hosseini* with onions, tomatoes and green peppers, 'lastly, there could be a tenuous connection made through the di Fabbris in Pisa but I have never actually met my cousin, the Count, and anyone investigating is going to want to talk about the 'lawyer' from Zurich who set the whole thing up. I'm satisfied that it is going to be almost impossible for Salvatore to connect me as I have never met him and Farid, who interviewed him looks nothing like me at all!

There is always a risk with the best laid plans Uncle, but I hope that we have all the points covered.'

'Well' retorted Hamid, 'you know what the English say about 'the best laid plans'! But what I wanted to suggest was an alternative strategy. I know it's not foremost in your mind right now but you are half Iranian yourself, I have no heir and I believe that if we can get through the current crisis with the Americans, the prospects here are going to be extraordinary.

You will remember that your family's most prolific period was investing in France when it was on its knees after the Prussian humiliation in 1871. That was the foundation of its fortune and I am convinced that the same sort of opportunity is going to open up here once this crisis is resolved.

Like a bent twig, Iran is bursting to make up the ground it

lost after 1953. Oil exports alone are running at 25% of the level under the Shah and yet we still have 10% of the world's reserves of crude oil; industrial production has fallen more than 50% and the infrastructure has largely crumbled. Where else on this planet can you point to such opportunities for those with vision and some money to invest?!

The Villarosa interests and those of the Saiyeidis will be merged one day anyway as I have no children. So, why not wait out the time here until the information that you have locked in your head is of no further relevance to the Americans, until they would have no use for it and the fire of their revenge has been dissipated into a new order in the Middle East?'

Hamid paused to pick up a bit of biscuity desert with almonds, honey, saffron and pistachios, his eyes never leaving his nephew's. 'Having come so far, would it not be profligate to risk the reward that you have so richly earned?'

Jules looked lost for an instant reply. 'I hear what you say, Uncle and there is plenty of good sense in it. I never said as much to her but I had already started to look at ways I could be here more, to be together with Zahra'. He paused but his uncle did not interrupt.

'But first, there are things I need to do now' Jules said eventually. 'I need to sit down with my parents now – now that this is all over. I really need to talk to them. I need to be at home to recover my true bearings but, above all, I'm afraid that I must be in Grez-sur-Loing this Thursday to honour the anniversary of our engagement. That I cannot miss, not this year. Zahra still defines who and what I am.'

FRIDAY 19TH APRIL, 15:30 LOCAL, (20:30 GMT)
FBI Strategic Information and Operations Center, Washington

'OK guys, listen up' snapped Watts as he entered the secure area now allotted to his crisis team. 'I've just come from a very difficult meeting with the President. I think it is fair to say that the crisis just escalated. Here's the situation.

The statue in City Hall Park has been confirmed. It was a 20Kt bomb with a customised antenna concealed in a nearby tree. So, we're not dealing with suitcases anymore! Two experts from the Lawrence Livermore laboratories who were on the scene have also suggested that its configuration would have made Nagasaki look like a damp squib. That's millions of lives vaporised in the New York area!

Worse still, finding this bomb was no fortuitous accident, this was planned deliberately. And arrogantly' he added. 'The truth is that we were directed to this bomb. The whole thing was a set-up, purely to underline Saiyeidi's threat. As of now, we don't know how many other larger bombs there are or where to look for them. We don't know how they were smuggled into the country or what form they take.

With as many as another 25 San Francisco type bombs still out there somewhere, Saiyeidi pretty much has us over a barrel – unless' he paused to make the point, '.........unless we can trace them conclusively within the next two or three weeks.

Now, that's a very big ask guys but we have to do it!' There was silence as he surveyed his team now clustered around him.

'For now' he continued, 'according to the White House, any surgical strikes against Iran's nuclear sites, invasion or even undercover action by Israel are all off the table. The President is going to tell the nation tonight that heroic work done by us here has resulted in the discovery and disarming of another bomb, 'in New York this time'. He will tell them that he is confident that because of our successes to date, that the Iranian threat to our national security will shortly be removed. More succinctly, he is going to start to prepare the ground for a dignified climb-down. He is also going to say that the time has now come to reach out to the people of Iran, forging new channels to their young democracy. He will therefore be proposing bi-lateral discussions aimed at preparing the ground for a security conference to be attended by all interested parties in the Middle East.

Essentially, he is running on empty. As of right now the position looks hopeless – unless we get lucky. As I say, we probably have two, maybe three weeks to come up with something to restore the America's freedom of action. If we remain under the Iranian threat when the President goes into that conference, we will lose our ability to control and direct international affairs which will in turn mean that we will have to substantially re-align the whole of US policy in the Middle East. I need hardly add that the Israelis are very keen to work hand in glove with us – they recognise that they have potentially the most to lose in all of this.

So people, we need to turn all our efforts and resources to Jim Barber's line of investigation. Who is *The Merchant?* How was the operation planned and controlled? What resources were needed? Who are Saiyeidi's immediate circle? How did Saiyeidi spend his exile in France – any relevant connections – family, friends, people he might have known? All leads, however small, need to be followed with vigour and haste. Where the hell are the bombs?

I have arranged a teleconference tomorrow morning with Kleiner and his team at 8:00am, our time, so let's have an optimised plan of action ready by then.

Jim, I want you to have Count di Fabbri interviewed soonest. The supposed lawyer that contacted and financed him must be a key link and could even turn out to be *The Merchant* himself and then we might really be motoring.'

SATURDAY 20TH APRIL, 00:30 LOCAL, (21:00 GMT FRIDAY 19TH)
President Saiyeidi's private apartment, Farmaniyeh, Tehran

Hamid Saiyeidi listened politely to his American counterpart. 'Mr President,' he said at last, 'as I said in my recent speech, our motives are entirely defensive, we have no wish for confrontation and therefore we would always welcome a new initiative on nuclear arms. We have felt for a long time that the existing Non- Proliferation Treaty had been superseded by the reality of the spread of weapons around the globe. Any new treaty therefore must recognise the possible universality of nuclear weapons with collective retribution against anyone who initiates a first strike.

But two things need to be clear. Our wholehearted co-operation will depend firstly on Israel being verifiably bound by the new treaty and secondly on you personally sponsoring a resolution to the Palestinian problem that has plagued the Middle East for more than 100 years. It must be acceptable to them, binding on the Israelis and the resulting borders explicitly guaranteed by America.

We will be happy to help in this respect in any way we can.'

Saiyeidi listened to the President Wilmington's closing thoughts. 'Yes Mr President, I want to be clear – those conditions are absolute. If you stand back from today's circumstances, I think you'll see that what we are proposing is in everyone's long-term interests, Israel included.'

Saiyeidi listened again.

'No, please never apologise for disturbing me at any hour and please do not hesitate to call me if you need further clarification. I believe that we are on the brink of a new beginning here in the Middle East and I look forward to hearing from you when you are ready to discuss your proposals in more detail. I thank you most sincerely for your call, Mr President; I look forward to working with you and I wish you a very good evening.'

Turning to Jules, Hamid Saiyeidi was stifling his elation. 'He really has no choice and I genuinely believe that if the treaties can be completed, the whole of the Middle East will have a real chance for stability at last. It doesn't matter now how we got to this position, the fact is that we are where we are tonight and that is an extraordinary and genuinely historic advance.'

Hamid hugged his nephew, his right hand patting his back earnestly. 'One day the world will know what you have achieved but not yet! Everything has to be watertight first. We need the Americans and the Israelis in a position where they can't backtrack, where they are publicly and irreversibly committed to this new beginning.'

'And what happens if somehow it all goes wrong between now and then?' asked Jules.

'There is really only one way that it can go wrong and that is if they were to discover the details of your operation and the location of the bombs. In the meantime, I have put the activation codes beyond reach of American infiltration should they try and capture me for instance. As a fail safe, I have embedded a sleeper agent somewhere outside Iran who will need to hear from me, with the appropriate password, within 60 minutes of any attack on this country. Failing that, he has standing orders to activate your remaining bombs if I am incapacitated in any way.

'But Jules, think, think!' his uncle urged returning suddenly to the dangers of Jules's trip home. 'I realise that next Thursday is a genuinely poignant moment for you but the time of the utmost danger for everything you have done is between now and the talks that Wilmington has proposed tonight. These talks could change everything and they are not more than three weeks away.

Until the moment that they are publicly and irrevocably committed to this new start, they can always retract with absolute impunity and, more importantly, you can be sure that, in the meantime, they are going to throw everything they have at safeguarding the impunity of their position as a superpower. That means, by your own analysis, finding you. They know they can't get at me, that's a given but they are bound to investigate you at some stage, if only as Zahra Mousavi's fiancé. Perhaps they are onto it already.'

'All that, I realise Uncle and believe me, I have taken it on board. But as I explained earlier, I believe that the risks are well defined and I'm afraid that this is just something that I simply have to do. As far as it goes, I have made my contribution to protecting our new democracy, Uncle Hamid and the truth is that ultimately it is those bombs that you must protect, not me. I can look after myself.

But,' he paused ruefully, 'we're both getting a bit carried away aren't we?'

HARVEST

SATURDAY 20TH APRIL, 08:30 LOCAL, (13:30 GMT – 15:30 TEL AVIV)
Teleconference Room, FBI Strategic Information and Operations Center, Washington

Norman Watts was under pressure. Everything that the FBI and the CIA had come up with so far felt as though they had been led to it, seemingly to mould or confirm the shape of the plot – as if Iran had intended them to find the evidence. As Wilmington had pointed out in a moment of frustration, Watts and his team had actually discovered nothing new and their only promising suspect was now dead. Watts himself had not been home since the Professor's body was discovered in Irian Jaya on Wednesday and had not spoken to his long-suffering wife since Thursday despite the parcel of fresh clothes that arrived for him each day.

Now his dejected President had unilaterally imposed the deadline of the upcoming Middle Eastern conference by which to solve the challenge they faced and had made life even more complicated by insisting that the Israelis must be kept in the loop. He knew Mossad's reputation for the utterly ruthless pursuit of a goal as well as the next man but he simply couldn't bring himself to trust them. The Israelis were in a worse corner than the United States and, to Norman Watts, that made them even more dangerous – ultimately, Israeli objectives always came first.

The conference screens shimmered into focus.

After an irrationally confident exchange of greetings, Watts called the electronic forum to order stressing the need for total cooperation and accelerated exchange of information to avoid the up-rushing calamity they all faced. Watts was flanked by Jim Barber and Marianne Holmes, the cipher and graphics specialist as they faced screens showing Joe Kleiner with Ariel Ben-Ezra and Rafi Hermesh of Mossad either side of him.

'So,' Watts said turning to the detail, 'what've we really got? The answer,' he continued mournfully 'is very little, if we are honest.

Based on what his university colleagues have told us, Professor Ahmad Miljabi looks an unlikely terrorist but, according to information from Iraqi intelligence, it seems that he had a reputation as a radical Kurdish student before he left Iraq. Here, he was quiet as a mouse which would fit with him being a Kurdish sleeper agent. He was apparently, according to Ivanovic, directed by a controller identified as *The Merchant*, one among a team of perhaps three leaders covering operational areas of the US. It seems likely to us that the Professor was terminated after he had debriefed *The Merchant* on the bomb locations when he passed through Jakarta. No loose ends, much cleaner for them that way but gives us nothing to go after.'

'We concur with that assessment' interjected Ben-Ezra, the Israeli spy chief, 'it's a dead-end. So we've started looking at things from the Iranian end but that is still extremely hard to penetrate so soon after the change in government. However, according to our Mojahedin contact, Hossein Motamed and the MEK were at pains to assassinate as many of Hamid Saiyeidi's inner circle as they could at the time of their failed coup, in order to weaken his power base in the country and elsewhere. That included the man always thought to have been his chief-of-staff, Khalîl Mousavi who along with his daughter, was slaughtered rather graphically in Paris. All of which means that Saiyeidi would thereafter have had to rely on a diminished group within Iran to research and execute the seeding of the nukes in the US.'

The exchange continued for another 10 minutes reviewing a series of minor, coincidental points as it became clearer that neither side had much clarity of direction. 'So,' said Norman Watts wrapping things up, 'Jim Barber is going to interview the Count and Contessa di Fabbri in Lucca tomorrow. They originally blew the whistle on the New York bomb and it seems possible that he may actually have met *The Merchant* disguised as a Swiss lawyer when the Iranians set that part of their plot in motion. I think we can all agree that from here it looks as though *The Merchant* holds the key to the entire plot. That statue was almost certainly commissioned by *The Merchant* and so Jim will also go on to Croatia to interview the sculptor in Dubrovnik.

Can we ensure that Jim and Rafi stay in close contact please? We can all reconvene once we have more hard information on *The Merchant*. In the meantime, thank you for your time gentlemen and good hunting!'

SATURDAY 20TH APRIL, 17:05 LOCAL, (15:05 GMT)
Joe Kleiner's apartment, Tel Aviv, Israel

Isaac Stern, Ariel Ben-Ezra and Rafi Hermesh, who was now charged with liaison with the FBI team, had all been summoned to a planning meeting after the teleconference. Joe looked grim faced as he produced copies of a letter in the day's *The Washington Post* which he handed on to his crisis team.

'The people of this country are in mortal danger today precisely because this president has followed the disastrous policy spawned by the neoconservative clique of unswerving support for extremist right-wing elements in Israel.

Why should we insist that Iran gets rid of its nascent nuclear capability while we never even acknowledge the substantial arsenal developed and maintained by Israel? Why should we bend the rules for India and turn a blind eye to Pakistan but object to a now fully democratic Iran having its own nuclear defense?

It's time for the American people to take off the blinkers. If successive US governments had not neglected or ducked a just resolution of the Palestinian question, who actually believes that 9/11 would have been perpetrated on us?'

'This is just the start' he said. 'Five years ago, publication of such a letter would have caused an outcry. Actually, it would probably never have been printed. We've all seen the US news coverage since the Nevada bomb. Old perceptions and loyalties become very fragile when people are being directly threatened.

Be in no doubt, if Wilmington has to acquiesce to a new nuclear treaty that would force us not only to declare our nuclear capability but worse, our weapons would be open to inspectors – no doubt the fucking UN! And that would severely pre-empt any first strike strategies we may now be able to entertain! We cannot and will not let that happen. Somehow we need to create a reason for the American people to be grateful to us – eternally. Somehow, we have to come up with the location of those bombs ourselves and the only way we are going to do that is by tapping into the innermost circle around Saiyeidi, tracking down who *The Merchant* is and taking him alive.

Someone was the architect of a very well thought out plan and it certainly wasn't Radin Ivanovic! That someone would need to be trusted by Saiyeidi with access to all the resources of the Iranian State plus the power to command them. Given the closeness of his relationship to Saiyeidi during all those years in France, Mousavi would have been an obvious choice but he was dead well before this whole operation even started. It may have been someone senior from the old VEREK and if that is the case, I'd be prepared to bet that he is also *The Merchant*.

Unfortunately, after the failed coup and the Mojahedin murders, it is difficult to know exactly what the effective Iranian command structure is anymore. Therefore we are just going to have to find a way to get inside the current hierarchy and discard every possible suspect until we get to the right answer.

Ariel, by lunchtime tomorrow say, please can you and Rafi come up with options and angles as to how we could achieve that and then we can begin to prioritise resources. One option you might want to look at is our Kurdish friends in Iraq and their blood brothers inside Iran – hard to see how they would be anywhere close to the new regime but might be worth considering.'

Ben-Ezra nodded affirmatively and looked for confirmation from Rafi. 'That's fine Mr Kleiner; I'll get right onto it. How much do I pass on to Jim Barber?'

'You pass nothing onto the Americans unless I say so!' Kleiner said with a degree of menace. 'You call me without fail Rafi, each time before you speak to him and then we decide what we pass on. That's the way we do it. You say nothing that hasn't been sanctioned by me. Is that clear?'

'As crystal, Mr Kleiner' said Rafi resisting the urge to click his heels.

'Good Rafi – and as part of your task, I also want you to draw up a detailed list of all those people close to Saiyeidi that our good friends the Mojahedin assassinated as a prelude to their fiasco – both in Iran and around the world. It may just show up a pattern or someone may stick out. What we haven't explored at all so far in any depth is the revenge motive.'

SUNDAY 21ST APRIL, 09:45 LOCAL, (08:45 GMT)
The Count and Contessa di Fabbri's apartment,
Piazza San Pierino, Lucca, Italy

Jim Barber had always been an enthusiast. It was a quality that he took with him everywhere and distinguished him from many of his peers. People warmed to him quickly and were borne along on his tide. But even for Jim, events after the teleconference had added up to an exceptional day.

Although he had learnt Italian until he was 16, he had never been to Europe before, let alone Italy. Better still, he had been transported there alone in one of the State Department's fleet of Gulfstream Vs at 560mph, dining on a beautifully rare New York steak with proper, thick fries and sleeping afterwards on a fully reclining bed. A private black limo had whisked him from the steps of the aircraft at Pisa airport, directly to the Hotel Noblesse in the centre of Lucca where he was shown to a sumptuous suite by the night porter – all formalities already taken care of. It may have been 01:30 in the morning local time but this beat the hell out of regular living!

Now, fortified by six hours sleep and rich Italian black coffee, he sat in the faded splendour of an aristocrat's salon draped with fraying tapestries and elegant Louis XV furniture. The Count had worked for an American food company and spoke excellent English which put Jim at ease. There was no TV in the room so this was not the family room and spoke of the formal nature of their interview.

That aside, the Count had been completely open recalling in considerable detail how the fairy godmother from Zurich had appeared from nowhere in his hour of need, enriched them and vanished again. In retrospect, the Count could see how the giant subterfuge made sense, simply to mask the real importance and purpose of the statue in New York. The strangest aspect of the whole affair, for the Count, was the fact that, improbably, he was now left with a fully funded, legal and functioning olive oil Institute and any family financial worries that may have afflicted him before were now removed. Unlike Cinderella, none of it had turned into a pumpkin – yet!

'Has anyone been able to ascertain the source of the funds?' Jim asked.

'That's the odd thing. It appears that the funds came through various offshore accounts, all numbered, originating in the anonymity of Liechtenstein. Someone did not want us to be able to trace the source. The police here say that this is not unusual in cases of bribery or Mafia funding but it is unique, in their experience, for something legitimate like this.'

'And so far there has been no call to return the funds to anyone

I suppose?!' exclaimed Jim, his enthusiasm for the extraordinary luck of the Count mounting.

Jim probed the Count at some length on the description of the Swiss lawyer.

The first and only time the Count had met him, he had come to the Count's office on the corner of the Piazza San Michele. With hindsight now, Salvatore recognised that it may have been a little odd as he had offered the lawyer lunch at their apartment which he had refused on the grounds that he had to get back to Zurich. He seemed to be anxious to discharge his instructions and be on his way as fast as possible. He had even kept his black Homburg hat and his overcoat on during their entire discussion. It was February and so Salvatore had put it down to Swiss lawyers in Zurich having overheated offices– unlike his.

'Well,' Salvatore enlarged 'he had grey hair under the Homburg, an unhealthy pallor despite a dark complexion and looked severely under-nourished. Probably years since he took the least form of exercise and it showed! The ghost of a man even needed a walking stick!'

'Hmm, so I suppose it's not possible that this could be your lawyer then?' Jim said sliding the picture of the Professor, taken outside the apartment building in San Francisco, across the marquetry table between them.

For a brief moment, Salvatore studied the photograph and then shook his head. 'Not a chance, I'm afraid. It's difficult to see much of the face or hair but just the shape, no way and certainly not manhandling a heavy looking trunk like that!'

'Look once more Count' urged Jim. 'It would be very helpful if it could be our man but I guess your initial description didn't fit anyway!'

'Look Jim, everyone used to call me Sal at American Foods – 'Count' makes me feel about a hundred and one! I'd really like to be even a little doubtful because I know that you've come a long way and it's very urgent but I'm afraid there's just no similarity.'

'That's really too bad, Sal' sighed Jim, 'I guess we'd hoped that the target would be just one man which would have made it much simpler given the time pressure we are all under.'

As Jim rose to leave, the front door of the apartment slammed and Salvatore called out to his wife to come and join them.

'Hi,' she said smiling, 'I'm Becky and I guess you must be from the FBI. So how's it going?'

'Not too well I'm afraid, ma'am' Jim started to reply.

'And is this your suspect?' said Becky bending down to pick up the photograph.

'Yeah, that's the guy who we believe is the leader of the team in California. We had hoped that your husband might be able to identify him as the man he met here posing as the lawyer but that's clearly not the case. We hope to have other photographs of him leaving through Seattle airport but they aren't ready yet.'

They didn't need to be, thought Becky turning quickly towards the window to hide her face which felt as though it had seized with shock. It was totally unexpected, out of context and took her completely by surprise. It wasn't a brilliant image but she realized instantly that she was probably looking at the young man she had met with his girlfriend at Villa Cerva. He had worn the same dark glasses while they waited for their lunch on the terrace at Mecenate back in September. She froze as fear swept through her followed swiftly by confusion. 'How on earth had he got mixed up in this?' She needed time to get her mind round this one. And some space.

'I'm going to make some coffee, can I get you some?' Becky said abruptly, trying to keep her tone as flat and measured as possible.

'That's very kind but unfortunately it seems that the man who came to see your husband is very different to this guy who we've been trying to trace so I'm about done here. I was really hoping that we'd get a match because that would have tied a number of things down and made our life a whole lot easier.'

'I'm really sorry' said Becky praying not to blush. She grabbed Jim's hand, shook it, forced a smile and left the room.

Momentarily taken aback by Becky's abrupt exit, Jim watched her go before turning back to Sal. 'Well, as I was saying, unfortunately that leaves us no further forward but at least I've got a good, detailed description of the lawyer who must be an integral part of the plot in any case. I think I'll give the sculptor of your statue a call to see if his description also matches – no point in going all the way down to Croatia if it was the same man, which now seems probable!

If I may, I'll send you through the other pictures of the Professor anyway just for good measure. Until then, thank you for your time, good luck with the Institute and don't fail to call me if anything comes up. The number on this card is my cell phone and will get me any time of the day or night.'

'I'll look forward to getting the pictures and I'm sorry that we were not able to help more' said Sal opening the door for the FBI Special Agent as he left.

'One last question,' said Jim turning round 'what date did you say Steinhoffer came to see you?'

'I didn't' said Sal, 'I don't think I thought to say and I don't remember anyone asking me but lets have a look' he said picking up the diary by the telephone in the hall. 'Yes, here we are, it was 12th January in the afternoon.'

'Oh well, that's that then' said Jim smiling. 'I might have saved my trip if I'd asked that before. That's the day our man in the photograph checked into California so we can be absolutely certain now that we are dealing with two players now, not just one. Thanks again.' And Jim was gone.

'You all right, Becky darling?' Sal asked supportively turning back towards his wife.

'Of course' Becky lied 'I guess the reality of what we seem to have got mixed up in didn't really hit home until just now.'

But inside she was squirming. It was the first time in 20 years that she'd told Salvatore a barefaced lie. She prayed that the next pictures would disprove what she thought she'd seen.

SUNDAY 21ST APRIL, 08:30 LOCAL, (13:30 GMT – 15:30 TEL AVIV)
Teleconference Room, FBI Strategic Information and Operations Center, Washington

The forced joviality of the previous teleconference had gone.

'We're not really getting anywhere fast over here' Watts began. 'It is now clear from Jim Barber's visit to Lucca last night that we are definitely dealing with at least two known players now – the bogus Swiss lawyer who visited the di Fabbris and then went on to the sculptor in Croatia; that was at the precisely same time that our Professor was setting things up in California. So we have two of them for sure.

So, on the face of it, we have an Iranian plan originating with Saiyeidi. It has an operational team in California that reports to *The Merchant* and perhaps the other teams Ivanovic mentioned do the same, we don't know. We have to presume that the New York bomb was the responsibility of a completely separate group, probably coordinated directly by the President himself or his immediate director of operations. It was intended to be the *coup de grace* of the whole strategy and indeed, it has proved to be.' Watts paused, 'unless, that is, we can frustrate the nuclear threat that now confronts the US and the only effective way to do that is to establish the location of the bombs and disarm them.

We know that the bombs are all on sophisticated wireless triggers like the demo bomb in Nevada and so can be detonated by someone thousands of miles away. To us, it is probable that the Iranian President has only structured access to that information and may not actually know the details himself. That would be the way we would play it – which leaves us with just one identifiable man in possession of the locations of all the bombs, probably from all the teams – *The Merchant*.

That equally means that that individual has to be 100% committed to the Iranian cause and be totally loyal to Saiyeidi himself.' We are now concentrating all our resources on trying to analyse Saiyeidi's people, as far as we know it, but we are finding hard information very sparse.'

'Interesting' interjected Kleiner, 'we too have been following a similar path and, after hours of probing and research from every angle by our best guys, we drew a blank each time – until that is, we tried a new approach and started to look for revenge as a motive. Who could have had a burning motive to seek revenge?'

'Yeah' Marianne Holmes said swiftly, as if in defence of her team's progress, 'but all of those people who were assassinated by your Mojahedin friends only had wives and, whatever else, neither the Professor nor the Swiss lawyer are women – even Saiyeidi is a bachelor. There are no male prospects that we could see that would fit.'

'Yes, that's correct' retorted Kleiner as Ben-Ezra raised his hand to speak.

'Are you aware that the Mousavi daughter had a French boyfriend who was obliged to identify the bodies,' he asked calmly. 'It must have been a horrific and deeply shattering experience for him.'

'Naturally!' rejoined Marianne defiantly. 'Jules de Villarosa is a journalist and the eldest son and heir to the Villarosa family empire. But where we came unstuck on him is establishing the motive he would have had in this case. In fact, like any of the others, any desire for revenge would surely have been directed at the MEK or just conceivably at you in Israel, not at us here in America. Where's his motive?'

'That's right,' added Watts, backing her up, 'Come on guys, Villarosa has no hot-wired connection with Iran other than his girlfriend and even if he had, he could hardly have planned and executed all this so quickly, single handed! He's a journalist for Pete's sake! Just how would he get an Iranian sub to drop off a bunch of nukes for his personal use?! You need influence for that kind of thing and unless you can prove a connection in high places, it's just another dead end.'

'We agree that without that connection, it's a straw in the wind and we have already searched unsuccessfully for a connection but with so few leads to follow.......' said Ben-Ezra shrugging his shoulders.

'Well, that's interesting' concluded Watts. 'Whatever else, we know that one person knows where at least some of the bombs are hidden because the Professor told him before he died and we still need to find that man. Whether the same man was involved in the New York bomb and any others planted by that team is not yet clear. Revenge is an interesting angle and one that we shouldn't discount but without a clear motive to attack America and the wherewithal to do it, we don't have enough to go on!'

As the screen died, Watts turned immediately to Marianne. 'What have we got in the way of photos of this Jules de Villarosa?'

'Limited I'm afraid, Norman. I checked his press corps file but it was pretty bland and the problem with the Pine Street image of the Professor, which is the only CCTV picture that we have right now, is that with dark glasses and a baseball cap, it could be made to fit most people you care to name!'

'What about any CCTV images of Miljabi leaving Seattle airport?' Watts continued.

'We asked them to check but nothing yet' advised Marianne.

'Well, ask them again, tell them it's important – no, insist that it's extremely urgent now. But well done Marianne though, I liked the fact that you had their ideas covered already. Good work! Keep me up to speed; I want to know everything that happens, night or day' he ordered. 'I'll leave it to you to brief Jim when he get's in' said Watts turning to leave 'and remind him that no one talks to the Israeli team without clearing it with me first. I don't like the Israelis being this close to what we are doing and you get the unmistakeable feeling that this is getting competitive! Just remember that they are dangerous when cornered and their hole is already deeper than ours.'

***

In Tel Aviv, Kleiner looked sternly at Hermesh. 'Rafi, I want you to start by reconstructing, as far as you can, the life and the relationship that Saiyeidi had in Paris with the Mousavis. Somehow the brutality of their death shouts to me that the father was a key man in the revolution and thereafter. Why was it necessary to make such an example of them? According to our sources, 13 others were killed quietly but certainly not Mousavi. It seems potentially like a revenge killing itself but Lord knows why. That said, with the Mousavis gone, this de Villarosa had no direct connection to the regime in Tehran.

So, see what you can come up with using the resources we have here. I think you'd better go to Paris tonight but, before you go, I want a one pager on the background of Saiyeidi, Mousavi and his daughter – and de Villarosa – birth, upbringing, education, career, anything that will give me a picture. If it was de Villarosa and he did act out of revenge, how on earth did he manage to pull it off?'

MONDAY 22ND APRIL, 07:00 LOCAL, *(12:00 GMT)*
FBI Strategic Information and Operations Center, Washington

The news of Jim's wasted journey combined with the overall lack of progress had deepened a pall of gloom that hung over the crisis team. Hoping to show solidarity with them, Norman Watts had ordered his office to be moved into secure confines of the crisis centre for the duration. Alone in his glass cage, with no glimmer of positive news appearing, Watts was beginning to feel a sense of panic eating into the façade of his 'by-the-book' management style.

Alone in his office, he was aware that ultimately this was now going to be a political crisis and not a military confrontation. Wilmington would never get endorsement from the Joint Chiefs for military intervention in Iran with the homeland nuclear threat unresolved. Even if it were, Watts had the sense that the President's old and ultimately influential friends, Vice-President Fairburn and Secretary of State Porter had already lost any enthusiasm for the Israeli inspired threat to invade. Secretary of Defense Rich had clumsily overplayed his hand to the extent that he and the neocon hawks that surrounded him were increasingly isolated – excluded even.

The only potential lead his team had produced was the possible involvement of the French boyfriend of the murdered Mousavi girl and, while it was true that he had been on assignment out of Paris for March and most of April, he was due back shortly and a well-researched and extensive article on nuclear aspirations around the Pacific Rim had actually appeared in *Le Monde* last week. It was technically possible as the timing matched but, as he'd said to Kleiner and his team, de Villarosa had no motive to go after the US and no access to support at the very highest levels in Iran. He was pretty sure that Mossad had also run its own checks as his guys had seen indications that they were following in Mossad's footsteps on occasions – and clearly they had come up with nothing either.

No, unless they got an extraordinarily lucky break, it was becoming ever more likely that the President was going to have to follow through on his proposal to recalibrate US Middle Eastern policy and that would certainly result in a new Secretary of Defence, the absolute fall from grace of the neocon tribe and an urgent reassessment of the efficacy of the US intelligence services as a whole. Watts could foresee no other outcome and had, indeed, quietly reacquainted himself with the terms of his own employment contract in respect of severance pay.

Through the glass of his private office, Watts saw Jim Barber returning and went out to greet him. 'Sorry you had a wasted trip Jim. Put your things down and come into my office and tell me about di Fabbri.'

Settling himself into the chair across the desk from his boss, Jim looked slightly part-worn. 'In my opinion, Norman, Sal di Fabbri is clean as a whistle. He does now understand how he was used but not why. I think he feels a little foolish and even embarrassed that despite the fact that they were an unwitting party to the New York bomb, he's actually left with a perfectly good job and a clean financial slate.'

'And you met his wife?' asked Watts.

'Yeah, she was a bit strange. Something about my presence seemed to startle her. She was quite abrupt – almost as if she hadn't known I was coming. Anyway, it wasn't relevant as I'd pretty much wrapped things up with her husband and she herself had never met the Swiss lawyer in any case.'

'Then she wouldn't have been any use to you anyway. You had better be aware that her mother is a good friend of the First Lady's. They went to school together or some such thing' Watts said with the disdain of someone who abhorred people who could and did pull strings based on no more than birth. 'That's how the di Fabbris managed to pull her into unveiling the statue.'

'Well, I guess that we are lucky that she was on the ball; at least it proves she's on our side!

Anything on the pictures from Seattle yet Norman? I promised to send them through to di Fabbri when they arrived' said Jim moving on.

'They came in about 15 minutes ago. Here' said Watts handing them over.

'These are certainly better. Still the dark glasses but otherwise it's a much sharper image, and, you know what Norman……,' said Jim nipping off towards his desk, '……….now these do actually look much more like this press photo of de Villarosa from an old article he wrote in *L' Expansion*' he said handing the black and white photo over to Watts. 'Shit Norman! Do you think we could be missing something here?'

'Follow that thought through Jim' encouraged Watts.

'Well, we do know that he was out of Paris at the relevant time……..revenge, revenge!' Jim said thinking aloud.

'Let's suppose that, stricken with grief, he somehow got word directly to Hamid Saiyeidi – the good and close friend of his would-be father-in-law. Let's just suppose that Saiyeidi, with his diminished inner circle, saw this young, intelligent and well-connected man as the perfect instrument around which to build a plan to neutralise the US threat of invasion. Could he leverage Jules's desire for revenge into total obedience and control?' mused Jim.

'He would have had to have loved her to distraction to have that degree of motivation, Jim. Not many people allow revenge to overtake reason and natural caution on such an extravagant scale. Tragedy, even violent tragedy normally begets remorse rather than violent revenge.

It all seems too tentative on the face of it. It's just a photographic likeness and we already have serious questions not only on de Villarosa's access to Saiyeidi but also his gut motivation to attack America. But it's an interesting idea and those are pretty rare at the moment. See what you can come up with to support the theory, anything concrete that we can actually use to join up the dots.'

MONDAY, 22ND APRIL, 16:30 LOCAL, (15:30GMT)
Union des Banques Françaises, Boulevard Haussmann, Paris 8e

Having spent most of the previous day sifting through all available sources of information and writing up his notes as ordered by Kleiner, Rafi Hermesh had caught a plane to Paris in the evening. Using the not inconsiderable efforts of the Mossad *sayan* who knew about real estate in Paris, Rafi had arranged an early morning 'viewing' of the apartment that had been owned by Khalîl Mousavi which was now up for sale. Leaving the *sayan* outside, Rafi rapidly swept the apartment for any electronic equipment that might have been hidden, tapping on the walls and floors for safes or concealed hiding places. There were none.

Things were not going well. Rafi had spent most of the previous afternoon trawling the Internet editions of all possible newspapers for any lead on Khalîl Mousavi. Apart from some limited coverage of his murder, there was absolutely nothing. Mousavi had either been something of a hermit or had purposely avoided publicity – probably both.

Separately, Mossad's banking *sayan* had pulled all his Parisian strings and managed to get Rafi an appointment with the director of human resources at Zahra Mousavi's bank. It was the best he could do as it transpired that Zahra's immediate boss had recently been killed in a car accident in the Alps.

Purporting to be from the Central Bank in Iran, he wanted to arrange to have someone talk to an Englishman, a Mr James Trenchard who was in Paris for just one day gathering material for a documentary on the attempted coup in Iran by Mojahedin and Israeli forces last November. They understood that the young lady who was to have headed up UBF's Tehran office was murdered together with her father and he hoped that the bank would be able to provide an insight into the character and career of this fine young Iranian.

It was a harmless but nevertheless deeply political request that the bank could hardly refuse with its Iranian banking licence still so freshly granted and so Rafi now found himself seated in front of Serge Martin. Monsieur Martin explained that he had never actually met M'selle Mousavi personally as he had only just taken up this post with the bank but her file provided some background material that might be useful. He had talked to the head of the International Department who had also spoken highly of her.

Taking the thin file, Rafi read the several appraisals that had been written by Zahra's deceased boss all of which attested to a bright girl, a hard worker with an excellent academic record. His eye was caught by a handwritten note – 'excellent connections at the very top in Tehran' – that was all though. She had taken a week off to consider the offer to manage the new office in Tehran. Rafi jotted down the holiday contact number that she had left. She accepted the job on her return and was murdered a few weeks later. End of file.

'So it would appear that she had a bright future ahead of her then' said Mr Trenchard handing back the file.

'Yes, it seems that she was well liked and intelligent. A tragedy really' concluded Monsieur Martin.

But not totally surprising given her connections, thought Rafi. For a banker, you couldn't get much closer to the top than her father's closest friend, the President!

TUESDAY 23RD APRIL, 08:15 LOCAL, (07:15 GMT)
The Count and Contessa di Fabbri's apartment, Piazza San Pierino, Lucca, Italy

They had overslept, something that never happened normally but somehow Sal had turned the radio alarm off. They had rushed through breakfast and Sal had left hastily for a staff meeting for which he did not wish to be late. He always believed in leading from the front and that meant being in on time in this case.

Still in her nightclothes, Becky cleared up the debris in the kitchen and wandered into the family room where the fax machine was flashing to indicate a new arrival. Picking up the cover sheet, it stated simply 'Seattle pictures attached as promised'.

Turning instinctively to the next page, Becky froze as she was hit by what she had fervently hoped she would not see. It was black and white and despite the grainy quality of the fax, she was staring at a picture of Jules de Villarosa. It was him! The baseball hat had gone and there could be no doubt this time.

This was the man the FBI were looking for in connection with the bombs in the America, her mother country; this was the man she had sat outside the Mecenate restaurant with when he was wearing the same dark glasses. This was the man whom she had made aware of her connections with the White House, of Salvatore's financial predicament. Shit! It all fitted.

Equally, this was the man who had shared a love as honest and passionate as theirs. A man who had followed in their footsteps using the Villa Cerva as a love nest.

But this was also the man who had used Salvatore and dropped them in it from a great height.

Or had he?

Hadn't Sal told her that the girl, Zahra, had been horrifically murdered alongside her father; hadn't he also explained that it was all to do with Jules's uncle who had lived in exile in France who had now returned to Iran to lead the new democracy? Hadn't they both agreed that President Saiyeidi's broadcast that they had watched together, was brave and his actions defensive?

If Jules had concocted a subterfuge involving them, they had not suffered from it.

In reality, Iranian money, if that was what it was, had rescued them and given Sal a fresh start. The Institute had money in the bank to take it through a number of years to come. Some of the US trustees would be embarrassed that they too had been used but they, like Sal and herself, had all acted in good faith, in pursuit of a good cause. And it was a good cause.

What would Sal have done if the roles had been reversed? Surely Sal, like herself, would have given up country and friends in pursuit of the inimitable centrepiece of their life together. Would he have had the same passion to propel him to seek his revenge if something so heinous had happened to her? And in some ways Jules was doing no more than allying his desire for revenge with his own Iranian birthright and in support of his own uncle.

International politics were not her domain but, cynically, it had always irked her that those countries that possessed nuclear weapons wanted to be the only ones to decide who else should be allowed to have them – and if Israel, India and Pakistan had them, then why not Iran. It was democratic now after all.

But the immediate point was that, whatever Jules had done, he had done it because he believed it to be right and justified, not only as someone who had lost the *raison d'être* of his life, the very rock upon which he stood, but he was equally acting in support of his uncle and his mother's own country.

No, she thought, Jules had actually done them no harm and now the FBI was after him.

Acting on gut instinct, Becky snatched her address book from the desk looking for the telephone number Jules had given her back in September. He was in serious trouble and she had to warn him. It was a Paris number but it didn't answer immediately. Wouldn't it be bugged? She waited until the answerphone cut in and put the phone down. Probably the parents' home would be bugged as well she reasoned, bound to be in fact.

Iran. Saiyeidi in Iran. But how do you pick up the phone and get through to the president of a foreign State? His nephew desperately needed his protection but how do you get that message through? Go through an embassy with a message they would have to relay – in France of course. Using Google, Becky quickly found the telephone number of the Iranian embassy in Paris.

'Good morning' she said when the embassy answered, 'I need to speak urgently to either the ambassador or his secretary.'

'Ambassador Badlani's office' came the voice.

'Good morning' said Becky once more, 'I need your help. I have some extremely urgent information that I need to give to President Saiyeidi in Tehran regarding the American FBI's attempts to track down the nuclear bombs in the United States. Please tell the President that he may know my name in the context of a friend of Zahra Mousavi's. Only he will understand the significance.

Please ask him to call me personally on my mobile number.'

'This is somewhat unusual, I will have to pass it by the Ambassador. Please let me have your number and I will either call you back or pass on your message.'

Less than fifteen minutes later, Becky heard her mobile ringing in her shopping bag. As she ran to get it before they rang off, she mused that the ambassador was going to turn her down.

'Contessa di Fabbri?' enquired the voice.

Oh Lord, it's the ambassador she thought uttering a tentative 'Speaking.'

'Contessa, this is Hamid Saiyeidi. I got your message and I do know your name as Jules told me about the lunch you all had together in Italy. I'm afraid we have never met although I gather your sister-in-law is a cousin of my brother-in-law.'

Becky chuckled 'Well I guess that combination saves me asking silly questions to establish that it really is you! Thank you for calling back so promptly.'

'I have the utmost regard for Jules and he said that you were, as he put it, 'special'. Apparently, you gave him and Zahra great reassurance at a moment when Zahra was worried about the future and managing the distance between Paris and Tehran. You probably met them at the pinnacle of their journey together, before the brutality of evil men cut off their future. As you can probably deduce, I was a great supporter of theirs and rather jealous that I have never found something similar. But I imagine you too must have had considerable sympathy for them otherwise we would not be talking. What is it that you needed to tell me?'

'I'm afraid that Jules is in trouble, Mr President.'

'Please, call me Hamid, you and I will never be formal.'

'Yesterday an FBI agent called Jim Barber came to see my husband to glean anything he could about the ploy that I am sure Jules must have set up for establishing the Institute as a cover for the New York bomb. He showed us a picture of the man they think is the mastermind, taken in California. It was difficult to be sure as the man was wearing dark glasses and a hat but I was pretty certain that it was Jules as soon as I saw it.

This morning however, the FBI faxed over another, much better picture of their suspect leaving Seattle airport. And then I was sure. They are strenuously looking for his identity and it can't therefore be long before they pin it down. Then Jules has real problems and I thought that you, rather than his parents, might have the resources to protect him.'

'I'm sorry to hear that. CCTV was always going to be a potential hazard' said Hamid sounding disconcerted. 'But you're right. He will be their only viable lead if they can establish his identity and then there is a high risk that all our efforts to obscure the link between us will come to nothing.'

Saiyeidi paused and Becky now detected marked anxiety in his voice. 'I warned him, even pleaded with him not to go back to France right now as the risk is so high. He's a brilliant but stubborn young man, headstrong and very determined.

How much does your husband know about any of this, apart from the FBI's call that is?'

'Nothing. It is the first time I have lied to him in 20 years I'm afraid.'

'Becky, it's unfair but please can we keep it that way for the moment. His Institute will continue to thrive, I promise you that, and when the time is right, who knows – we do have a small olive oil production in Iran, around a windy town called Rudbar. I'm sure it must have potential that needs to be unlocked!

We will meet one day and I look forward to that. You have done Iran and our new democracy a great service and I thank you. Now, if you will excuse me, I have arrangements to make.'

'Good luck Hamid. Protect him.

You know,' said Becky wistfully, closing the conversation, 'in some ways he is lucky. His love for Zahra was a huge motivator and, for him, she will always remain young, vital and passionate and therefore a reminder that he must always succeed – for her sake.'

TUESDAY 23RD APRIL, 10:00 LOCAL, (09:00 GMT)
Hotel de Calais, Rue des Capucines, Paris 8e

In the absence of an official request for information on the Mousavis which could take weeks and then still get turned down by the Quai d'Orsay shielding some French commercial interest or other, Rafi was running out of easily accessible avenues. He had come up with nothing so far and he could already hear Kleiner's recriminations. Looking at his notes from his UBF meeting, he noticed the holiday contact number Zahra had left and, just for the sake of thoroughness, he reached for his mobile phone.

'Prego!' a man said at the other end.

'Oh' said Rafi adopting his best English accent acquired during his years at Leeds University, 'do you speak English?'

'I certainly do' replied the man who now sounded American.

'Well, I am wondering if you could help me' and James Trenchard proceeded to give a brief explanation about a documentary that he was making on the violent assassination of Zahra Mousavi and her father in France and that he was looking for any material on her life in Paris. 'Oh, and to whom am I talking?'

'My name is Salvatore di Fabbri but I didn't catch the name of the girl you are trying to trace.'

As the name of the man he was talking to sank in, Rafi did a double-take trying to keep his voice level. 'The girl's name was Zahra Mousavi and I think she may have come with her boyfriend last September.'

There was a slight pause. 'Yes' Salvatore said, 'Yes, actually I never met her because I was away in America at the time but my wife met them and said they were a very nice pair, very hospitable, even gave her lunch. They stayed about a week or a little longer.

But as you know, she was horribly murdered along with her father, I believe.'

'Yes, yes, that's all part of the documentary that I'm making – it was truly shocking – that's why we want to expose those responsible for it. But do you recall the name of her boyfriend by any chance?' Rafi asked gingerly.

'Of course!' di Fabbri retorted, 'He is a distant French cousin of my sister-in-law's, Jules de Villarosa, he's a writer just like you actually.'

Rafi's mind somersaulted and then soared- at last, at long last, a real, solid connection, and a cousin no less.

'Well thank you Mr di Fabbri, that's most helpful – the bank she worked for gave me your number and I just wanted to be thorough.'

Gently placing his mobile back on the bedside table, Rafi slumped onto his back and studied the ceiling, thinking as slowly as he could. In reality, how much of a breakthrough was this?

So, the woman who had blown the whistle on the bomb in New York was married to a distant cousin of the de Villarosa's and the murdered Mousavi girl had met the wife but not the husband. But then the Mousavi connection didn't make any difference as they were already long dead by the time of the explosion in the Nevada Test Site. And as the American, Watts, had said, de Villarosa didn't have a single direct connection with Iran, his beef was not with Americans but the Mojahedin and, anyway, he couldn't have done it single handed; you can't just ring up and order a sub full of nukes.

There's something there; it's all too much of a coincidence. There's something I'm not seeing yet as the ends are just not joining up! Why had the di Fabbris been chosen by *The Merchant* as a conduit for the plan? It must have been the same man as surfaced in Irian Jaya and California. It must have been deliberate and there had to be a reason. Could de Villarosa be *The Merchant?*, that might make some sense on its own but he would still have needed Iranian support to get hold of a bomb in the statue – for which he had no real motive – and de Villarosa simply had no angle from which to bring together such powerful State intervention.

Rafi knew he had no option but to call Kleiner. At least it was progress.

TUESDAY 23RD APRIL, 07:15 LOCAL, (12:15 GMT)
FBI Strategic Information and Operations Center, Washington

As far as Jim Barber was concerned, the only advantage of the marathon analysis sessions to which the FBI system of working was prone was the well-equipped gym, sauna and steam room in the basement of the complex. Having grabbed three hours sleep in the SIOC dormitory, Jim had wanted to re-ignite the system with a vigorous work-out and now sat in the drifting fog of the steam room.

He could see no immediate answer to the question of how de Villarosa could have initiated contact with the President of Iran and kept colliding with the reality of the wall of protection that would always surround a Head of State. Jules would certainly have run straight into it. You couldn't just call them up, write to them or email them. The filtration apparatus would make achieving personal contact for something like this too chancy. Mousavi would have had a personal and highly privileged direct route into Saiyeidi but would he have passed that onto his daughter's boyfriend? He certainly wouldn't!

This whole new line of thought had come from the picture in Seattle which was at last clear enough to make a positive comparison with his earlier photo from the press office. True, but then also curious too when you thought about it. The quality of the original San Francisco photo hadn't stopped the people they'd interviewed in Larkspur or Pahrump from making a positive ID of Professor Miljabi, the man they'd seen in the picture. That was the one they'd shown everyone, even been to Italy with it. Yeah, Italy.

Jim lingered with the image of Becky di Fabbri staring at it. Running it through his mind again, she had been staring at it, hadn't she? It was the first thing she'd done after saying hello. Maybe her abruptness wasn't because she'd forgotten he was going to be there. Could she too have recognised the face? And if so how? Neither she nor the Count had asked the name of the man and he'd never said what it was. Was there a gap in his tick list?

Getting back to his desk, Jim checked the time – it would be lunchtime in Lucca –worth a try. Sal answered the phone. 'Hi Jim, you just caught me on my way back to the office.'

'Actually Sal, it was your wife I was hoping to speak to' Jim replied.

'Afraid that she always holds an art class during Thursday lunchtimes Jim, can I get her to call you?'

'No, perhaps it was nothing, but perhaps I could ask you anyway Sal, does the name Jules de Villarosa mean anything to you?'

'Of course,' laughed Sal, 'just as I was telling the English journalist who rang earlier this morning, Jules is a distant cousin of my sister-in-law. I've never actually met him but Becky had lunch with him and his girlfriend when they were staying in our house up in the hills last September.'

'No shit – if you'll excuse my French Sal' exclaimed Jim, 'that is one hell of a coincidence isn't it?'

'Coincidence of what?' asked Sal.

'Never mind Sal, tell me about the journalist who rang you.'

'Oh, he was doing a story about the attempted coup in Iran last year when the Mojahedin tried to overthrow the new government. It was strange really. He rang off as soon as I told him that Jules was a distant cousin, he seemed startled. From his research, he must have known that Jules's uncle is the new President!'

'What did you just say?' spluttered Jim in disbelief.

'That it just seemed odd, given the story he said he was writing, that he didn't seem to realise Jules's uncle is Hamid Saiyeidi, the President. He just didn't mention it, very odd really.'

'Sal you don't know how helpful you have just been. I'll call you back soon to clarify some points but thank you for now.'

Jim dropped the phone, falling over himself, running towards Watts's office.

'Norman' he cried bursting in on a conversation Watts was having with Marianne, 'Jules de Villarosa is none other than President Saiyeidi's nephew. Sal di Fabbri is a distant cousin of de Villarosa and Saiyeidi is Jules's mother's brother!'

There was a brief moment of nothing before Watts exploded. 'Well why the hell didn't you tell me this before!' Watts shouted.

'Because I didn't bloody well know myself until about 15 seconds ago! We only got the Seattle pictures through last night after all' Jim shouted back.

'This changes everything, Jim. He had the motive and now he has the means.' Watts paused thinking urgently. 'We need to pick him up immediately – if we're right and now I'm sure we are, he must be *The Merchant* or he may even have impersonated the Professor. Actually, whether he was the mastermind behind the plot or it was Saiyeidi is just semantics now. Either way, he would know where the bombs are. Grab him and we've got the bombs! Get the CIA onto it immediately; get him on ice in Guantanamo!'

'There's just one catch, Norman. I think that the Mossad people may be all over this as well although they may not know that Saiyeidi is his uncle yet. They've been asking questions, the right questions though and they are definitely on his trail. The wretched Rafi Hermesh never uttered a word to me!'

'If those fucking Zionists get to him first, you are in deep shit my friend. Not only will they then have the all the leverage with us that they need for a generation to come as we'll have no firsthand answers about the location of the bombs but we'll also have a dead Frenchman on our hands. Tell the CIA to get him under wraps before the Zionists can get to him!'

'Take it easy Norman!' Jim replied tartly. 'If I hadn't suggested this line of enquiry, we'd still be stuck where the trail ended in Manokawi.'

'That's exactly where we need to be, Jim, and I apologise, you're quite correct. Get onto Marty Doppard in Indonesia and get him to check for any Europeans leaving Manokawi about the time the Professor died or shortly after. De Villarosa would have to have been there one way or the other. That's were we start our trace. We've got to get to him before the Israelis do!'

TUESDAY 23RD APRIL, 10:15 LOCAL, (15:15 GMT) (00:15 IRIAN JAYA)

FBI Strategic Information and Operations Center, Washington

For the first time, Jim Barber had come up against the practical realities and frustration of international time zones. He had called Marty Doppard in Indonesia immediately after the near panic with which Norman Watts had received Sal di Fabbri's revelation tying de Villarosa directly to his uncle in Tehran.

It was already 10:30 at night in Indonesia. Marty, having called his new friend in the Manokawi police department, had relayed the message that even the CIA simply didn't have the political leverage to get the offices of a provincial airline in distant Manokawi raided at one o'clock in the morning. In any case, the employees capable of pinpointing the information, whoever they might be, would certainly be dispersed and at home asleep – most of them without a telephone. Washington would simply have to wait for Manokawi to open but, in the meantime, Marty would fly there personally to be on the spot and he would also alert the US embassy to get the necessary diplomatic machinery in motion.

Jim knew that he must use the intervening period constructively and probably cut some corners. So, anticipating the result of Marty's endeavours, Jim reasoned that his bird would almost certainly have flown shortly after the Professor's demise and would probably have headed either for Iran or France. But that was now nearly a week ago!

To clear up the loose ends and partly to re-engage his inquisitiveness, he called Sal di Fabbri back as promised to address the remaining question marks. The fact was that everyone had been able to identify the man in the CCTV image despite its poor quality and it was only logical therefore that Becky must have recognised the man she had lunched with as well. It would account for her strange reaction. She could have said so at the time and her failure to do so had possibly, regrettably, put them behind in the race with Mossad to get to de Villarosa. Equally, she could not have been in any way complicit in de Villarosa's plot as it was, after all, Becky herself who had blown the whistle on the statue bomb in New York in the first place. It might well be a case of over-exposure to European semantics of family or fairness – Iran being a new, fledgling democracy, Samson and Goliath and so forth. Maybe Sal would shed some light on the conundrum.

Sal sounded somewhat defensive when he answered the phone, like someone already slightly out of their depth.

'Sal, I have something of a dilemma so I need to ask you a difficult question,' Jim said trying to sound as much like an old friend as he could. 'You remember how, when I visited you and your wife saw the picture I had showed you of our suspect?'

'Yes' replied Sal nervously.

'Well, we now know that the man in the photograph was in fact your cousin, the one she had lunch with back in the summer. Can you think of any reason why she might have wanted to obfuscate? On the face of it, the inconsistency bothers me because it doesn't fit with the overriding fact that it was Becky who tipped us off about the New York bomb just as soon as she had an inkling of a suspicion.'

'Look Jim,' said Sal unbuttoning, 'it's something that I don't understand myself along with a number of other things that have happened recently – Zurich, the Institute and so forth. My guess is that Jules de Villarosa was a smart guy and thought he could use us in whatever he was up to, hiding behind our transparent ignorance. It may be that there are things Becky hasn't told me, that maybe she too guessed we'd been used when she saw the photograph, maybe she just wanted confirmation. Anyway, she's out right now but you're right, there are things that we need to sort out and not least how this all plays out for the future of the Institute.'

'Sal, I really don't think you need to be concerned about that. Your Institute is a success in its own right and, while you may have been used, you were clearly not involved in the deception or the plot in any way. That at least is obvious to everyone and in a sense we've moved on now and whatever the reason for Becky's initial reluctance, it's really no longer relevant.'

Norman Watts was striding towards him looking decisive so Jim excused himself and rang off.

'Jim, what news from Indonesia?' Watts urged.

'I'm afraid we're strung up on the hour change and lack of local communications in Irian Jaya Norman. Marty's doing his best but obviously all the offices are closed and most people are asleep' Jim replied, palms uplifted. 'There's nothing we can do until he can raise a bit more of a storm.'

TUESDAY 23RD APRIL, 11:15 LOCAL, (16:15 GMT) (001:15 WEDNESDAY, IRIAN JAYA)
FBI Strategic Information and Operations Center, Washington

The phone on Jim's desk interrupted his devil's advocate reasoning. It was Marty calling from Manokawi and Jim flicked on the speaker phone.

'Seems we managed to get things going a little ahead of schedule here as the ambassador's call galvanised the government and they got the reservations manager for the airline in Jakarta out of bed. He checked the passenger lists and guess what? He could only find one European flying out that day – a woman – but there was another more interesting passenger – Professor Ahmad Miljabi was listed on the early morning flight to Jakarta – that's in the morning after his death – even before the alarm was raised. Mr Watts Sir, I'm afraid it looks as though your bird was here but has flown. Sorry to be the harbinger of bad news yet again.'

Marty rang off and there was only a brief pause before Watts resumed his diatribe.

'I'm sorry Jim but the fact is that if de Villarosa was masquerading as the Professor all along, as he could have been as is now suggested by someone flying out of Manokawi using the Professor's name and presumably his papers, he definitely knows the location of the bombs. Definitely! Either it was de Villarosa himself all the time or, as makes no difference now, he would have been de-briefed in his role as *'The Merchant'*.

But that was nearly a week ago so he must be in either France or Iran now and from what you say, I fear the Israelis are ahead of us already. If he's in Iran, all we can do is see if the CIA can help, which I very much doubt – we are nearly blind there – otherwise it's France. You need to get over there today – a regular flight will to get you to Paris by the morning. I'll warn the CIA people to meet you and get them working on things before you arrive.'

WEDNESDAY 24TH APRIL, 09:05 LOCAL, (08:05 GMT)

Bibliographie Nationale Française, Paiis 13ᵉ

Commissioned by Francois Mitterand during the final stages of his political life to be 'one of, if not the biggest and most modern library in the world', the BnF caused outrage in many quarters for its impersonality but with the assistance of modern technology and Google's *Scholar* programme, Rafi Hermesh thought it was one of the most awe-inspiring sources of information in the world. The sheer functionality was breathtaking enabling flexible searches across scores of linked databases covering thousands of newspapers and periodicals around the world. It completely transformed the tedium of trawling for information.

Joe Kleiner had commended his diligence in unearthing the connection between Zahra Mousavi, Jules de Villarosa and the di Fabbris and instructed him to delve into the Villarosa background for anything that might give the boyfriend access to substantial Iranian official assistance.

'I think you should be aware Rafi that the Americans are onto something. Dean Armitage called me early this morning to warn me that his contact inside the FBI believed that they had a major new lead and they were sending Jim Barber over to follow it up. Whatever it is they are ahead of us by the sound of it but at least you are in the right place. If you need any back-up, just let me know. I'm pretty damn sure they will try and cut us out if they get the chance – despite what their President has said!

Now, as you're in Paris, you should make use of the BnF which is a gold mine of information nowadays' he concluded.

The fact that Rafi had done a *stage* at the library as part of his modern languages degree at Leeds University had clearly escaped Kleiner's memory.

Rafi constructed a search with the key words 'Mousavi', 'Villarosa', 'Fabbri' and 'Saiyeidi' across all the major international newspapers and magazines and a few regional French newspapers such as *La Republique d' Orleans*. There was almost nothing on the Mousavis again except coverage of their murder, a huge volume on the Villarosa empire but little on the family, almost nothing at all on the di Fabbris except for an ancient reference to Salvatore's father's extravagant hospitality to Victor Emmanuel III during the war in 1942 – and nothing at all on Hamid Saiyeidi until the overthrow of the mullahs.

Rafi couldn't put his finger on it but the results felt as though they lacked a proper balance. It seemed odd to him that there was a total absence of reference to Saiyeidi outside politics, nothing on his time in exile and, apart from a couple of mentions of his mother, nothing on his family. There were gaps where there should have been at least trivia.

Rafi's mobile started vibrating in his pocket and he scuttled quickly out of the silence of the library before it stopped. He could see it was Kleiner calling.

'Hermesh, you're an idiot!' bawled Kleiner. 'Don't you think at all, don't you concentrate on what you are doing?'

'I'm sorry Sir, you've lost me' Rafi stammered.

'Brasenose you cretin! Brasenose! They both went to Brasenose. It's in your own notes. Have you checked for a connection?'

Rafi's mind had gone a blank momentarily under the verbal onslaught. 'Err, no Sir' he stuttered.

'Well for fuck's sake man, get on with it' and the phone went dead. As soon as it did, Rafi remembered and then he cringed. Saiyeidi and de Villarosa both went to Brasenose College, Oxford. He'd put it in the one-page notes that Kleiner had asked for. They were different ages but Kleiner was right, there could be something. He should have picked that up.

Back at his laptop, he opened another Internet connection and typed 'Brasenose' into the Google box which led him directly to the college website. The home page showed a handsome beige stone building backed by a classical, leaded dome. To Rafi, it stank of antiquity, establishment and privilege – all the things that he despised most about England but that was because of his 'background' he was always being told. Rafi clicked onto *'college information'* but that was purely practical stuff and then he tried *'bnc society'*. This offered the latest edition of the college journal *The Brazen Nose* which he clicked on.

At once, the index shouted at him *'Iran warms to Hamid Saiyeidi'* – its old alumni, now famous among the alumni no doubt. Oh shit, thought Rafi, this one I missed. Typing 'Villarosa' into the 'Find' box, Rafi apprehensively hit the return key.

And there it was *'Hamid's nephew, Jules de Villarosa, also an alumni ... '*. Rafi felt the universe implode, swallowing him whole, white heat surging through his veins. Game over but he should have been at this point days ago if only he'd thought about it. It wouldn't even have been necessary to make the trip to Paris. Now he was in no doubt whatsoever Kleiner would make a real meal of it!

His nephew! That would explain everything. Game over! He packed up his computer and hurried outside, speed dialing Kleiner as he went.

WEDNESDAY 24TH APRIL, 09:45 LOCAL, (08:45 GMT)
Room 383, Hotel Georges V, 31, Avenue George V, 75008 Paris, France

Jim Barber was momentarily embarrassed as the bell boy carrying his suitcases deposited them carefully on the waiting stand in the bedroom and turned unpresumptuously towards him, just slowly enough to emphasise that he was about to leave and, respectfully, expected some appreciation of his efforts. Greg Ramirez, his colleague from the CIA, who had met him at Charles de Gaulle Airport, had disappeared directly into the bathroom and shut the door thereby cutting off Jim's access to the operational supply of Euros.

Jim pursed his lips into a smile, shrugged and handed the man a $10 bill which he took with apparent but regretful understanding of Jim's dilemma and departed. 'Jet lag!' Jim murmured to himself.

Jim stripped off and luxuriated briefly in the massaging throb of the powerful shower as the effects of the journey and the time change began to dissolve. His body clock was already in a state of confused suspension having crossed the Atlantic twice in two days. He wanted his breakfast and was heartened to see the tray of fresh croissants, baguette, homemade quince jam and fresh orange juice awaiting him as went back to the bedroom. The opulent aroma of rich, dark coffee spurred him into his change of clothes.

All the while, Greg continued to call round his various agents that had been staked out at the obvious entry points, Charles de Gaulle, Orly, the main stations as well as more predictable places such as de Villarosa's apartment, the offices of International Herald Tribune's in Neuilly and *Le Monde* in Boulevard Auguste Blanqui. Greg explained between calls that if the guy was really this hot, he would hardly be about to show up in broad daylight where he might be expected to! It was as close to looking for a needle in the proverbial haystack as any assignment he'd been given. He hoped Mr Watts back in SIOC in D.C. realised that.

Half way through melting a croissant in his mouth, the main telephone in the room rang. It was Charlie Cuyper calling from a taxi in Neuilly. 'Wagons roll'. He'd just scrambled into a taxi following the target who had emerged from the IHT offices and had himself caught a taxi and was now heading for the Périphérique in pursuit. He wanted back up and soon. 'Tell Greg to get off his cell phone!'

Within five minutes, Greg had them both inside one of the embassy's service vehicles, working its way up the Champs-Élysées towards the Arc de Triomphe. Cuyper's taxi had now crossed the Seine and was heading towards them up Avenue Charles de Gaulle in slow-moving traffic. As Jim stuffed the last of the croissant he had grabbed as they raced out of the hotel bedroom into his hungry mouth, the shower of loose pastry flakes went unnoticed as Greg hissed impatiently that de Villarosa's taxi was stuck in a jam at the Porte Dauphine. Greg looked decisively at Jim and announced 'If he comes off the next exit, he's heading for his apartment and then we've got him!'

But he didn't and the taxi apparently exited at the Place de Paraguay before turning briefly into Avenue Bugeaud and then into Rue des Belles Feuilles. During the same time, the embassy car had hardly moved. Greg Ramirez was looking anxiously at his file. 'When you get round the Etoile' he directed the driver, 'take

Avenue Kleber – the traffic will be lighter than Victor Hugo.'

'Apparently de Villarosa has paid off the taxi and has entered an apartment block in Rue des Belles Feuilles, a couple of doors down from the back of the Gallerie Saint-Didier' snapped Greg.

'God knows where he's going, just stay outside and wait for us' he directed Cuyper.

At least Greg had been right about the traffic and after what had seemed like an eternity of six minutes, Greg spotted Cuyper standing by the entrance to an apartment block.

'Been in there nearly ten minutes now. Should we move in?' Cuyper demanded immediately.

'We don't know where he's gone – this is not an address we know so he could be doing anything here. We'll grab him when he leaves, as discretely as possible and I really mean that. This is the centre of Paris and this government does not like its citizens being abducted – and certainly not by us!' he said turning to the driver. 'Jack, you take Jim here and get the car down into the garage. Charlie and I will intercept him and bring him down to you. And for Christ's sake' emphasised Greg severely 'only use your weapons as a last resort. It is absolutely imperative that we take this man alive. If it can't be done here, then back off. We'll be bound to get another crack at it later. Clear? He's no goddam use to us dead!'

Jim and the driver went back to the car and nosed down into the garage which offered a number of empty spaces but the driver got as close to the door into the building as possible and then checked his weapon. Jim did the same reflecting momentarily that it was the first and only time he had ever handled his weapon with intent in his seven years with the Bureau. He had never actually fired it.

After a couple of minutes, a shiny looking, metallic grey Audi S8 drove down into the garage and parked round the corner. Jim could see the driver, a man with dark hair as he sat in the car for a few minutes apparently on his cell phone. Then he left through the door to the stairs or lift without looking round.

Another couple of minutes and two expensive looking women emerged, crossed in front of the car and stood chatting under one of the overhead lights to the left of them. Both were stylishly dressed and somehow impeccably French and Parisian. Jim realised that he needed to spend more time here sensing perhaps for the first time that there was more to life than jeans and tee-shirts.

'Not bad eh!' said Jack. Jim nodded knowingly and smiled back.

Then suddenly things all seemed to happen very fast.

As the ladies continued to chat, a battered-looking, green Triumph TR4 roared into life and accelerated up the ramp and out of the garage. At the same moment, Greg and Cuyper burst through the garage door waving their guns, urging Jim and the driver to help them.

As they left the car and started to run after their colleagues, one of the women screamed and threw herself to the floor. Pausing fleetingly to look, Jim saw the dark haired man raising what looked like a small submachine gun which seemed to cough out a silent spray at Greg and Cuyper.

As Jim watched in stunned disbelief, they fell slowly to the floor. In that instant, time seemed to slow, the gravity around him was suddenly intense and his bones heavy. It was so strange; he knew he had to take out their killer quickly and yet he could hardly move now. All he could see as he turned towards the man with dark hair was a couple of flashes and a distant boom, as in a cavern.

As Jim felt his head meet the concrete of the garage floor, it was painless, surreal and he passively watched as their driver too fell beside him spraying a red mist over him as he fell. Rolling over, the last thing Jim saw was the tyres of the Audi gushing smoke as they sped up the garage ramp.

WEDNESDAY 24TH APRIL, 15:40 LOCAL, (14:40 GMT)
Hotel de Calais, Rue des Capucines, Paris 8e

Rafi had been waiting nervously in his hotel room for Kleiner to call him back for what seemed like an eternity. Kleiner had a reputation for being unswervingly ruthless in pursuit of the Zionist cause and his own personal goals. His ambitions had indiscriminately destroyed a number of careers along the way and Rafi knew he was in trouble. The fact that de Villarosa and his uncle had obviously been to considerable trouble to hide their connection was not going to help him explain away his complete failure to pick up on the Brasenose connection. The worst thing was that Rafi knew how pivotal his position had been in the whole affair and how excruciating the standards expected of Mossad operatives were – and he had failed, potentially jeopardised his country's position and its relationship with its most powerful ally.

The buzz of the secure mobile was not loud but it still startled Rafi. He braced himself for the inevitable onslaught and answered it.

'I'm sorry not to have got back to you sooner Hermesh.' Kleiner's voice was eerily level. 'The cabinet had a crisis meeting which I was ordered to attend. Your message was passed on to me immediately and I was able to portray your revelation as real progress. We both know that you blundered badly but this whole situation is turning into a full-blown crisis for the Prime Minister and indeed the country and so we will deal with that first.'

Rafi was not off the hook but he sensed a chance of redemption.

'I think we have to assume that the Americans have made the family connection too or will do shortly' Kleiner continued. 'Either way, the race is on in earnest to locate de Villarosa, establish the location of the bombs and identify any failsafe mechanisms they have employed. But finding him is not going to be a pushover.'

'I have the phone number of his apartment' said Rafi trying to sound on the ball, 'but there is just a voicemail message saying that he is away until May and suggesting contact by email. The email address was the same as that attached to the article in *L' Expansion*.'

'Ok Hermesh, given that we have to assume that time is extremely limited thanks to your oversight, what do you suggest? He's wandering around somewhere. If he's gone to ground in Iran with his uncle until Wilmington's wretched security conference (which is what I would do in his position) we are dead in the water anyway. If, however, for whatever reason, he has chosen to ignore the sanctuary of his uncle's protection and say come back to France then we may still have a chance.'

'There are two ways we could go,' said Rafi still trying to sound positive. 'I have the name of a senior journalist here in Paris who is our *katsa* in the French Press. Thanks to some recent help from us, he is currently enjoying a rich vein of material and I am sure that he would be more than pleased to try and contact him 'for an urgent assignment' shall we say. If that does not elicit a response by tomorrow morning, I think we will have to risk going directly to his family here in France. I could always pretend to be an old friend from his Oxford days for example.'

'I doubt that de Villarosa is going to be answering the call of journalism quite so soon after what he's just been up to but it's worth a try before going to his family' said Kleiner again sounding dismissive. 'In the meantime, I will get our people here to see what they can come up with on passenger lists in and out of Tehran, although the odds of him travelling under a name that we would recognise are remote.'

WEDNESDAY 24TH APRIL, 18:15 LOCAL, (17:15 GMT)
Chateau Marzotte, Selles-sur-Cher, Loir et Cher

Jules knew he'd caused something of a panic at home and he felt faintly buoyed up by it like a small boy playing a trick. He had thought about making his return a total surprise but, stuck in traffic as he approached the Porte d' Italie, he wondered whether it might be thought uncaring, even rude – his mother hated surprises.

His journey from Tehran had been complicated by his uncle's

insistence on maximum security and he had therefore flown first to Copenhagen and thence into Charles de Gaulle. Farid Karzam had insisted that anyone looking out for him would not bother with the Nordic arrivals and he appeared to have been right. He touched base with his most productive contact at the International Herald Tribune on his way into Paris to warn him that he would not be looking for freelance work anytime soon and had then picked up his car from the garage of one of Karzam's 'safe houses' where he'd left it during his travels.

Now, as the TR4 sped down the A6 towards his family, he felt a warm glow growing within him. His fight was over; it looked like the Americans had little option but to capitulate; now his future beckoned, a new start and one within the family curtilage, if he was lucky. The heartbreak and horror of Zahra's murder would always be there but life was for the living and he had more to be grateful for than many. Now, after all that had happened, after all his uncle had promised, after everything, he wanted the embrace of his family.

As the car scrunched through the high, black iron gates and up the cobbled drive set between the two ornamental canals, Jules could see his parents, his two younger brothers and his sister appearing at the top of the stone horseshoe stairway that led down from the front door. Jules threw open the car door and, two at a time, bounded up the steps to the waiting kisses, handshakes and hugs. It had been a long two months for everyone but his homecoming radiated the magic of a strong family, united again. The trauma of the last few months seemed to evaporate or at least recede in the warmth of his welcome wrapping around him, once more in the familiar balm of home.

A shower and a change, a celebratory glass of champagne

before dinner and a habitual family bun fight through a magnificent dinner that his mother had managed to rustle up from somewhere. Jules told them that Uncle Hamid's best chef had prepared an Iranian banquet a couple of nights back when he was passing through but that it didn't hold a candle to home cooking!

Everyone round the table kept instinctively away from Jules's immediate past or his future, filling the gap with all the news and gossip that a family in motion picks up – until after dinner when Jules's father suggested that they might take a *digestif* together in the library. Strangely, it was the only room in the house with a fire; it was nearly May and it seemed to Jules unnecessary but he guessed that his father wanted to mellow the atmosphere as a background for their chat. His father poured some dark Calvados from an old, dusty looking bottle into two oversized brandy balloons, giving one to Jules before he too settled into the depth of an armchair.

'Well Jules, welcome home' he said raising his glass slightly.

'It's very good to be back, Papi,' said Jules raising his own glass in salute 'it was a long trip.'

'So how long have we got you for?' his father enquired gently.

'Not long at all, I'm afraid. I've exorcised some of the demons from Zahra's murder but, equally, in the course of doing so I have come to understand something of why Uncle Hamid felt he had to go back to Iran.' Jules recounted the conversation they had had about the economic potential Iran possessed, about the opportunities for early stage investment and the nascent characteristics of the economy. Jules described Hamid's hopes to incorporate the Saiyeidi fortune within the Villarosa interests worldwide, particularly given his uncle's lack of progeny.

Jules then turned to his personal aspirations, his realization that the time had come to get serious about the family business and his gratitude for the lack of pressure that had been applied to bring him to this point.

'It might have been actually counterproductive Papi. In the end, I would probably have come into the fold but, this way, I come to it with a burning desire to dedicate my life to something new and dear to the family, to meet the challenge and build on what you have already achieved.

The immediate downside is that I need to be back in Tehran on Sunday to meet some people at a reception – you may have noticed that I didn't have much luggage! But please, it's a secret surprise for Uncle Hamid. He thinks that I am going to be here for a bit but, as it is, I will probably be there trying to sketch things out for another three or four weeks and, once I have an idea of what could be done, I will come back and make you a presentation – if you agree that is.'

'Jules' said his father fondly, 'I've waited patiently for this moment and I'm delighted that you've come to it your way. Welcome!' he said and raised his glass again.

'Your mother and I haven't discussed what you may or may not have been up to with Hamid – quite deliberately. Either you would come back alive or not. There was no point in speculating. You've finished the report that you were commissioned to do and I have no intention of asking what you might have been up to in, well – let's call it, 'your spare time'. That subject will remain dead forever and I don't actually want to know. You're back and now we can start to plan the future.'

A pause and his father smiled at him and then laughed. 'Your mother is going to kill you for leaving again so soon but I think I'll be able to square it for you!'

'I hope so Papi because the bad news is that I have to abandon you tomorrow as well. Tomorrow is the anniversary of the day Zahra and I found each other and it would also have been her 27th birthday so I am going to throw some flowers in the river at Grez-sur-Loing. Whatever comes in the future, she'll always be a part of me but tomorrow is our first anniversary.'

WEDNESDAY 24TH APRIL, 14:20 LOCAL, (19:20 GMT)
The Oval Office, Washington

After the frustrations of Manokawi, the shock of Jim's massacre alongside the CIA agents in Paris hit Norman Watts like an apocalyptic wave. Suddenly everything seemed doomed; the work that had led to identifying de Villarosa's link with President Saiyeidi and the advantage that it had bestowed on his team in their race against Mossad appeared to be nullified by the killings in Rue des Belles Feuilles. Worse still, it appeared to be the Israeli's doing.

The dark suited man opened the door to the Oval Office as Watts approached, nodding respectfully as the Director of the FBI passed him. Wilmington was seated at the large desk in the window looking grave with Fairburn and Porter seated in front of the desk. The President rose as Watts approached and clasped his hand in both of his.

'Norman, I'm so sorry to hear about your man. I never met him but I understand that he was good at what he did and enthusiastic. It's always hard to lose those sort of people.'

Wilmington returned towards his seat ushering Watts to the third chair in front of the desk. 'So, take us through it.'

Watts recounted the CIA's success in picking de Villarosa up when he emerged from the Tribune's offices in Neuilly and passed quickly over the shooting of the four Americans in the basement car park.

'They had been on the trail of de Villarosa and I have to assume that they followed him into the apartment block. We don't know what happened then but one has to assume that de Villarosa somehow jumped them in the car park. They must have been taken unawares as not one of them fired a shot despite their guns being drawn when they were found.

And here's the difficult bit.' Watts paused and looked at his President. 'The spent bullet cases that were recovered, 25 in all, were all of the type used by Mossad in their Heckler & Koch MP7 submachine guns. That doesn't mean that they assassinated them for sure but it is one hell of a coincidence.' Watts paused briefly to let it sink in.

'We may know more if Jim's driver pulls through. He is the only man to have survived but he is in a coma and has a bullet lodged in his brain while another hit his spinal cord. At best he is expected to be paralysed.'

'Holy Mother of God!' exclaimed George Fairburn. 'Shit Tom, I always had a strange feeling about this. There is a lot at stake for Tel Aviv as they got us into this whole thing as I said before. I never thought that they could go that far in pursuit of their advantage. They're our allies for Christ's sake!'

'My problem' said Wilmington trying to weigh the revelation up as he spoke, 'is that it sounds too blatant. We all know what Israeli special forces are capable of – Entebbe and then again

Nairobi, but this would just be beyond the pail – even for the most hardened Zionist.'

'Militarily, as a special Op' began the soldier Secretary of State, 'it seems downright idiotic for Mossad to have been so obvious, to have left such a clear trail. It almost looks as though someone is trying to set them up.'

'The only person who that could have been, would have been de Villarosa himself' interjected Fairburn, 'and where on earth would he have got a weapon like that in Paris?'

'Same place as he got the fissile material to hide as bombs' said Wilmington laconically.

'Well Mr President, Sir' interrupted Watts, 'there could be a number of angles here. We do know that Kleiner and his people have not been telling us the whole story. Jim called Rafi Hermesh, his sort of counterpart on the Israeli team, on my instructions before he left on Tuesday and was told that he would be out of the office for a couple of days. He asked to speak to Kleiner but he too was unavailable. They know that they have to move heaven and earth to dig up the location of the bombs before we do. They will have seen the reaction in the media and the public over here since this broke. They are in arguably the most uncomfortable strategic position they have ever found themselves since the declaration of their State in 1948. What they will do with the information if they get it before us, Lord only knows but we do know they are masters at exploiting leverage and that knowledge would certainly give them just that.'

'Guys' said Wilmington definitively, 'worst case, in the circumstances, is that de Villarosa is scared off and runs straight back to the security of Tehran. What induced him to go to Paris is hard to imagine. It was an incredible risk and we must take advantage of it.'

'Our problem now, Sir 'Watts said, 'is a lack of resources on the ground that know their way around. Those were the CIA's best agents in France and I think we have to assume that Kleiner's people are hot on de Villarosa's trail now. We have to make up a huge amount of ground Sir.'

'Second worst case' continued Wilmington, 'is that Mossad get their hands on de Villarosa before we do. We don't know what is in that Pandora's box and I don't want to be the one to open it!

'No' he said, 'we have to make a virtue out of a necessity. I'm afraid we need to pull the French into this. We stand too small a chance of pulling this off by ourselves now, so let's have the French take him into safekeeping. That'll at least keep him out of Kleiner's hands and give us time to work something out.

Their new President seems keen to play a wider role on the world stage, he appears to want to be our friend and he has an established focus on the Middle East. We can do a deal.

Wilmington looked for affirmation from his colleagues. Each nodded. 'Good' he concluded, 'Norman, set it up and let me know before you go live.'

WEDNESDAY 24TH APRIL, 20:00 LOCAL, (THURSDAY 25TH 01:00 GMT, 03:00 TEL AVIV)

Dean Armitage's apartment, Wisconsin Avenue, NW, Washington, DC

In his 71st year, Dean Armitage was alone. His wife of 48 years had passed away 18 months previously and his solitary evenings wore increasingly heavily upon him.

Dean was a respected member of the D.C. community having personally advised no fewer than three occupants of the White House during his career. An esteemed lawyer, he still had an advisory role with the State Department and sat on a distinguished selection of committees accustomed to patronage by the good and the great of the nation's capital. But really he was alone now, the impetus of his life's work fading with the passing months, his influence increasingly ceremonial.

He was a proud man, scarred briefly by his proximity to the Nixon team during Watergate but rehabilitated by his contribution to keeping Israel out of the conflict during *Desert Storm* under George H W Bush. He had laurels but they were evermore brittle with age and so it had been a clarion call to him when Joe Kleiner had asked to meet him shortly after Wilmington had been inaugurated.

Now he was torn between the vanity of his re-engagement with top echelons of government, in support of his friend Joe Kleiner, and the ominous consequences for the safety of his beloved country that had flowed from that reunion. No one could have foreseen the Iranian response to Wilmington's stand but now Dean was inwardly, deeply ashamed of his role. He saw himself as, first and foremost, a patriot and if Iran was ever to trigger one of its hidden bombs in anger, it would obliterate him. Ultimately, he had been responsible for opening the door to Wilmington for Kleiner's people and now all he could do was to wait to see how the tangle unravelled.

The telephone broke into his recurring thoughts.

'Good evening Mr Armitage' said the voice, 'this is Norman Watts from the FBI. You may remember that we met at the White House when your friend Mr Kleiner briefed the President on events surrounding the death of Radin Ivanovic.'

'Of course' replied Dean 'what can I do for you?'

'Mr Armitage, this is an unofficial call and I want to make that clear. However, I am calling you because I want you to know that one of my senior agents was gunned down this morning in Paris alongside three agents from the CIA who were close to apprehending our chief suspect for the seeding of our towns with the hidden nuclear devices. The bullets that killed them in that parking lot were those normally used exclusively by Mossad.'

'Are you a student of our history, Mr Armitage?'

'Obviously a little' replied Dean sounding unnerved.

'Well Mr Armitage, in my opinion, you have displayed what George Washington, in his farewell address labelled 'a passionate attachment' for a foreign nation that produced 'a variety of evils', as he put it, for the our nation. Do you recall that speech?'

'I'm afraid that I do not' replied Armitage defensively.

'Well, he goes on to say, and I quote, that 'sympathy for the foreign nation, facilitates the illusion of an imaginary common interest, in cases where no real common interest exists… and it gives to ambitious, corrupted, or deluded citizens, (who devote themselves to the foreign nation) facility to betray or sacrifice the interests of their own country, without odium, sometimes even with popularity.' You may not recognise the speech Mr Armitage but I'm sure that you understand what I am getting at.

Mr Armitage, you should be aware that I know that you met Kleiner and his Mossad chief last November in the British Virgin Islands prior to their visit here that we both attended. If it transpires that this outrage in Paris was in any way linked to your friends in Tel Aviv, I promise you now that we will come after you and expose your duplicity to the full scrutiny of the American people and its system of justice. I hope you can live with that.

Oh, and you probably should know, if you don't already, that the Shahab-8 ICBMs that you were told about have yet to make a successful test flight let alone go into service. You were conned Mr Armitage and, because of you, so was our nation.'

As the phone went dead, Armitage felt a cold wave of fizzling panic sweep through his aging body. He sat staring at his shoes for an eternity. Conned? Those missiles not even in service? A wave of anger slowly replaced his panic and he picked up his Blackberry, retrieving Kleiner's number.

'Kleiner?' he demanded. 'You and your colleague Ben-Ezra deliberately deceived me when we met on Tortola.' It was a statement not a question. 'You knew that those Iranian missiles weren't a threat; they're not even in service today!'

'Good evening Dean. You seem to be very upset about something!' Kleiner said as if surprised. 'Why don't you explain?'

'You know very well what I'm talking about. Your friend Ariel Ben-Ezra told us that the US mainland was about to be threatened by this new missile system and I gather that, today, it hasn't even finished its testing let alone being in service. You lied!'

'Listen Dean' said Kleiner now sounding agitated, 'we told you what we understood to be the case. I assume that, at the very least, you ran our information past your own people. You did, didn't you?'

'I have no idea. At that point, it was sent over to Defense for Edwin Rich to deal with. But it's well known you know, that he's a part of your mosaic over here in Washington so it would fit if he had backed up your story with Wilmington wouldn't it.' Again it was a statement and Armitage was becoming audibly angry.

'But that's not the half of it, Kleiner' he continued. 'The Director of the FBI has just spoken with me and I understand that Mossad has just killed four of our people in Paris this morning – just as they were about to arrest the chief suspect in this bomb plot. Murdered in a parking lot they were and apparently by your people' Armitage was shouting down the phone now. 'Left their dirty, spent bullets everywhere; you dirty bastards, I can't believe you did this, you dirty bloody bastards – don't ever, ever call me again!'

Slamming the phone down, Armitage dropped his hands to his sides, hanging his head, engulfed by despair. It was the end; he knew he was finished, his reputation destroyed for ever, he was done for; there would be no redemption – not in today's circumstances! Such stupidity, such vanity!

He remained staring at his shoes for several minutes. Then Armitage went to the kitchen, carefully filled a glass with water and picked up a large packet of paracetamol. He opened the packet very deliberately and counted out 30 tablets.

***

In Tel Aviv, Joe Kleiner made a call to Ben-Ezra advising him to call Edwin Rich to make sure that he was ready for all eventualities.

Then he called Rafi Hermesh in Paris to tell him that de Villarosa was definitely home but that the FBI were close on his tail. His time was limited and he must find de Villarosa before the Americans did. 'Call his parents, make sure that you portray him in the light of having let you down in some way rather than as an enquiry. It will start fewer alarm bells that way. Don't fail me Hermesh. If you do, don't bother to come home.'

THURSDAY 25TH APRIL, 11:05AM *(10:05 GMT)*
Chateau Marzotte, Selles-sur-Cher, Loir et Cher, France

Jalileh de Villarosa clattered through the stone hall towards the telephone. The voice at the other end asked in English to speak to Jules.

'Unfortunately, you've missed him.' she said, 'He left about a couple of hours ago.'

'Oh that'll be all right then.' said the voice. 'We're having lunch together in Paris and I just wanted to make sure that Jules was on his way.'

'Who am I talking to?' asked Jalileh

'Oh, I do apologise, my name is James Trenchard. Jules may have mentioned me. We rowed together at Oxford?'

'Oh dear,' Jules's mother said instinctively, 'I'm afraid there might be a problem. He's actually gone to Grez-sur-Loing to mark his poor girlfriend's birthday so I'm afraid he may have forgotten. She died you know. He's also left his mobile phone here so you won't be able to contact him either. Although, I suppose you could always try calling the restaurant there; I think it's called the Moulin. If not, he should be back here in time for dinner.'

'That's very unlike him,' said Trenchard beginning to sound put out. 'We arranged it in January but Jules knew that it was a special rowing club reunion. But you're right, it does sound as though he must have forgotten. Anyway, you've been most helpful and I'll try calling that restaurant.'

The phone went dead.

THURSDAY 25TH APRIL, 11:40AM
Chateau Marzotte, Selles-sur-Cher, Loir et Cher, France

Hugo de Villarosa listened to his wife with equanimity. Jules's ordeal after Zahra's brutal murder, his evident repression of all natural emotion and the deafening silence surrounding his departure and absence had jarred badly with her deepest maternal instincts. Jalileh always worried.

'Hugo, you know, I really do think something's very wrong' she fretted. 'Jules is back less than 24 hours and this man, whom he has never, ever mentioned rings up like a long-lost friend claiming a lunch appointment today that was made in January when Jules wasn't even here.

I know that I worry but it's just that we know so little about the past couple of months when so much must have been happening. Jules has been up to something with Hamid even though he told me he was just passing through Tehran on his way to New Zealand. We just don't know what he's been up to, we don't know what's happening!'

'Jalileh, I know it's hard but we've just got to trust him. He's been through a terrible ordeal and has been dealing with it in his own way. We cannot wrap him in cotton wool for ever – there are things that he has to do for himself. And I told you that he had seemed so much recovered during our talk last night, he's looking to the future again now and he's coming in, back to the family fold again, to join the business, to take his proper place.

Now I take that to mean that he has expunged his demons, that he has taken a long hard look at where he's going and, thank God, made the right choice. How he made that choice and what he did during what I would call his 'time in the wilderness', is not our business. The important thing is that he's back on the road again, looking to the future and that future is with us.

I have no intention of jeopardizing his welcome embrace by delving into what may or may not have happened in the immediate past. If there is anything that threatens him from that journey he took, Jalileh, you can be sure that we will all be there to protect him, whatever it takes.

What did you say his friend's name was? I'll just look him up in the college register.'

Somewhat mollified, Jalileh de Villarosa left he husband playing with the Brasenose website and returned to her duties planning the weekend festivities.

Just after midday, the direct, private line on Hugo de Villarosa's desk rang.

'Bonjour Monsieur, this is Inspector Lépine; you may remember I was handling the regrettable affair of Mousavi murders back in November' the voice said as a shard of apprehension flashed through Hugo de Villarosa.

'Indeed Inspector, naturally I remember you well' he replied, a model of calm politeness. 'What can I do for you?'

'I will come straight to the point Monsieur; we have received reliable information that Mossad, the Israeli spy agency, has operatives in France seeking to kidnap your son. We are not aware of why they should want to do such a thing merely that they are urgently seeking to do so. Irrespective of their motives, foreign agents trying to kidnap French citizens on French soil is completely unacceptable and will not be tolerated under any circumstances.

Therefore Monsieur, if you have any idea about your son's whereabouts, I think we would all be well served, not least your son, if you could enlighten us so that we may offer him protection. Mossad has a ruthless reputation as I expect you are aware.'

'I see Inspector' said Hugo cautiously, 'and when did you come by this information?'

'Early this morning apparently Monsieur, from an impeccable source.' Lépine answered.

'Right!' said Hugo without hesitation. 'It sounds from what you are saying that neither you nor your informant knows where he is. Well I can tell you that. He arrived last night and this morning, he's gone to mark his dead girlfriend's birthday at Grez-sur-Loing, up near Fontainbleau.

More to the point, about an hour ago, my wife took a call from an apparent friend of his from their days at Oxford University in England. I looked him up and the odd thing was that he was nearly four years older than Jules. It seemed a large age gap although they had rowed together in the boat that beat Jesus College in Jules's first year. However, in the light of what you now say, it sounds too much of a coincidence, I'm afraid. It also sounds as though Mossad are ahead of you and, what's more, we have no means of getting hold of Jules as he left his cell phone here!'

'*Merde*!' exclaimed Lépine, 'If you'll excuse my English, Monsieur. The Mossad agent, if that is what he was, was probably calling from Paris.' The Inspector paused and de Villarosa looked urgently at his watch. 'We have absolutely no margin for delay' Lépine said with a note of alarm in his voice. 'Our best chance is to mobilise the CRS units stationed at Fontainbleau. They'll get to him first; let's hope it's in time! Monsieur, could I suggest you meet us there and keep your mobile phone on in the meantime?'

THURSDAY 25TH APRIL, 12:05
Hotel de Calais, Rue des Capucines, Paris 8e

Rafi Hermesh had made another mistake. Now he was pacing nervously up and down the pavement outside his hotel waiting for the hire car to come.

It was coming from the depot near the Gare de l'Est and he had calculated that it would be quicker to take up *Location Bleu's* offer to deliver it to the hotel than risk the semi-permanent traffic jams first going north to pick it up and then all the way back, virtually to the hotel, before continuing south to the Porte d' Italie and the A6 to Nemours.

But that was 40 minutes ago and Rafi was acutely aware that he was in a race with the Americans. He had to get to de Villarosa first or his job was history – Kleiner did not forgive or forget. He had taken Kleiner's advice – it had actually been more of an instruction – and taken the risk of calling the family home outside

Paris. The ploy had worked and de Villarosa's mother had told him exactly where he could find him. She hadn't seemed reticent or concerned and if they were to check they would see immediately that Jules had rowed with a James Trenchard during his first year at Oxford. But, with the contact made, he had now laid out a hostage to fortune.

Rafi was about to call *Location Bleu* for the third time when a white Peugeot 205 drew up in front of the hotel and the driver got out clutching the paperwork. Rafi virtually carried the man to the nearest table ignoring his explanations about the traffic, signed wherever he was asked and then grabbed the ignition key and his bulky computer case and disappeared. It was midday and he needed to head de Villarosa off at the Moulin. Otherwise it would come down to stalking him and the longer it took the bigger the risks became.

By the time he got the Peugeot wheels on the '*Autoroute de Soleil*', Rafi was glad that he had not actually been too rude to the *Location Bleu* driver as he had fared little better himself threading his way through the Parisian traffic jam to the Ports d'Italie. He had barely got out of third gear before he passed Orly airport.

It was going to be touch and go. He would ring the *auberge* when he got within striking distance.

THURSDAY 25TH APRIL, 12:45PM
Moulin de Grez, Seine et Marne, France.

Claudine saw Jules walk through the front door and come towards the desk. She remembered him immediately from whenever it been had and then she remembered how the Patron had shown her the newspaper cutting about the grisly murder of his girlfriend and her father. She remembered how, when they had stayed at the Moulin together, she had been more than a little jealous of her despite the fact that she had appeared so nice and open.

Monsieur de Villarosa had changed. He looked now as though he was a well worn 35-year-old; gone was the boyishness that she remembered and that had first caught her eye.

'Bonjour Monsieur' Claudine said with her biggest smile.

'Claudine, I'm flattered that you remember me' he replied sounding genuinely surprised.

'Oh Monsieur, we were all so sad and terribly shocked to read about your poor girlfriend. It must have been unbelievably horrible for you' she said as sympathetically as possible.

'How very kind of you. Yes, it was an awful business.' Jules agreed. 'You know Claudine, it's exactly a year ago that we were here. Today would have been her 27th birthday. It seems like yesterday but so much has happened. I brought flowers for her and I thought that I'd drink to her memory, here where she and I were so happy together.'

'Of course, Monsieur a very beautiful thought. If you would please take a seat in the bar, I know that we would be most honoured to offer you that drink.'

Watching him disappear into the bar, Claudine suddenly realized that a tear was rolling down her left cheek as she dialled the bar. 'If the Patron objects, I'll pay for it myself' she snapped to Henri the barman. She was never this emotional she told herself!

Ten minutes later Jules emerged from the bar. He came straight up to her, round the desk, flung his arms round her and gave her a big kiss. 'You're a really lovely lady Claudine' he whispered, tears welling up as he fled. Claudine watched him go and she realized that she too was crying again.

Closing her mind to the unexpected rush of emotion, Claudine settled into the daily, mindless task of preparing the guest registration forms for the authorities. A little more than ten minutes later, she answered the telephone to a man with a strong English accent who asked to speak to Monsieur de Villarosa in very broken, almost theatrical French. Claudine explained that he had just left to put flowers on his girlfriend's grave. He asked if she was sure and then rang off.

As Claudine bundled the week's registration slips neatly into an envelope for dispatch, she heard the approaching cacophony of police sirens that grew louder and closer until a succession of tyres crunched rapidly to a halt on the gravel outside and running feet clattered into the hall. Claudine had never seen CRS officers except on television and their brusque arrival startled her.

'Bonjour M'selle, I am Captain Argenot of the CRS and I need to speak to Monsieur de Villarosa urgently' ordered the officer apparently in charge of the men in uniform.

'I'm very sorry monsieur, I'm afraid you've just missed him' replied Claudine, her maternal instincts rushing to defend him. 'As I told the Englishman who rang just ten minutes ago, Monsieur de Villarosa went to the church to put flowers on his dead fiancé's grave.'

'English? And where is that church please, m'selle?' Argenot commanded.

'It's not far at all, monsieur. Go to the top of the road and turn left into Rue Wilson, go past Rue de Vieux Pont and you'll see the tower of the church and a high stone wall on your left, just before the Mairie.' Claudine replied.

'Merci M'selle!' the captain cried, already heading for the front door again.

'Good Luck!' whispered Claudine as the tyres sprayed the gravel outside.

THURSDAY 25TH APRIL, 12:55PM
Notre Dame church, Grez-sur-Loin, Seine et Marne.

Rafi could see the monolithic, almost Norman looking bell tower of the church dominating the village as he approached. Parking his car by a small wooden door in the high wall, Rafi debated whether to see if the church was open to the street from a door under the arch of the tower. If it was locked, as many French churches were, he would lose valuable time and there was no way of knowing if another door gave directly onto the graveyard behind the wall. Too risky. Instead, he opted for the door nearest to where he had parked. Its risk was a loss of surprise but then he barely needed it as de Villarosa would not be expecting him or anyone else with malicious intent.

Opening the computer case, he retrieved the primed syringe and the compact pistol and secreted them in his blue bomber jacket.

With all his senses now heightened, Rafi turned the rusting door handle easing the door open as quietly as he could. Once inside he could see a man with dark hair and about the right height, kneeling by a grave with a headstone that looked recent.

Taking his time, conspicuously studying anything that would confirm his role as a tourist, Rafi worked a circuitous route around the churchyard drawing slowly closer to his prey. De Villarosa remained oblivious to Rafi's presence, busying himself with meticulous weeding and tidying of the grave.

When he was some 20 yards from his victim, Rafi was aware of the sound of cars stopping and footsteps running down the street away from the church. His senses were now alert. On the face of it, there should be nothing in it but you never knew. Better make this fast. Within two quick strides now, Rafi moved behind de Villarosa as if looking at the carved inscription on a plaque in the wall.

Slowly, with his left hand, Rafi eased the plastic cap from the tip of the needle in his pocket, applied a little pressure with the palm of the hand and felt the liquid flow. Just as he moved in to administer the knockout dose, the door through which he had entered, clattered open and five men in dark uniforms ran through it taking up firing positions in an arc in front of what Rafi took to be their commander who was carrying a megaphone. De Villarosa was transfixed but Rafi knew immediately that this was too much of a coincidence, this was an ambush, someone had followed him, someone had known he was coming, someone protecting de Villarosa. Or was it the Americans?

Either way, his exit was blocked. Suddenly, not only was de Villarosa his quarry but now he was also his only ticket out of here and he lunged forward wrapping his left arm round his neck, yanking de Villarosa backwards hard so that he fell prone against him now acting as a human shield. With his right hand he now held the pistol to de Villarosa's head.

'Come any closer and he's dead!' yelled Rafi. 'Stand up slowly' he calmly instructed de Villarosa and together they rose, Rafi's forearm pressuring his victim's throat.

'It's no good, you're surrounded' Argenot said into the megaphone, 'you'll never get out of here alive with de Villarosa. We have orders to kill you if necessary and that will become the case unless you release your prisoner. You should be aware that we are the anti-insurgency unit of the CRS and we don't make idle threats.'

'Mr de Villarosa and I are going to walk out of here now,' retorted Rafi 'and if you want to stop us, you'll have to kill him first and that, I'm sure, is against your orders. Please stand aside now and let us pass.' Rafi nudged him forward tightening his grip around his throat.

'I will count to three' said Argenot dispassionately as Rafi began to move towards them.

As Argenot very deliberately annunciated the word 'Three', he glanced up at the bell tower and nodded. Too late thought Rafi as he turned his head up to where the captain had nodded in the same split second that the marksman pulled the trigger. A flash from the shadows of the opening at the top of the tower was all that Rafi saw.

His prisoner screamed as the debris from Rafi's skull exploded like a watermelon behind him and, still gripped by the forearm, he fell to the ground on top of the cadaver, gasping and gulping air as he went. The CRS rushed forward and pulled him off the body, lifting him to his feet again, supporting his sagging knees.

'Monsieur de Villarosa, it's over, you're alright now!' said Captain Argenot trying to sounds reassuring.

The man stared at him simultaneously terrified, bewildered but relieved. After a few seconds, the peasant in him recovered sufficiently to vent his shocked anger at the captain 'My God! Imbecile! Are you mad? Who the fuck is de Villarosa?!'

THURSDAY 25TH APRIL, 12:55PM
North bank of river Loing, between Grez and Montigny-sur-Loing, Seine et Marne.

Turning right at the top of the road, out into the countryside towards Montigny, Jules left behind the cosy familiarity of the cobbled, narrow streets and white-shuttered houses of the village. He felt the knot in the top of his stomach turning to a lump. Claudine's kindness at the hotel had begun breaching the dam that had held his emotions in such disciplined check for months. He had known it would happen, even wanted it to; it was a hurdle that he had to cross to rejoin the real world and now that his crusade to redress the viciousness of Zahra's suffering, to bring honour and rectitude to her memory and to expunge his own sense of guilt having outlived her, now that it had run its course, he could let himself go, let it rush, ranting out of him. He was alone, the river bank would be deserted, it was the way he had planned it. He needed so badly to be able to grieve on this, her birthday.

The irony of the beautiful afternoon was not lost on him as he parked the TR4 at the bottom of the track above her favourite walk, just as they had a year ago today. Clutching a single, dark red rose, Jules retraced their steps down towards the river. He felt the sun on his back and he could see the waves of bluebells and jonquils once more lighting up the river bank.

How ironic Jules thought, catching sight of the point with a small run where the river narrowed, where Zahra had confessed her awful secret that had so worried her, how ironic that it was now he that was going back to Iran and not her. Carrying their torch but without the flame, he thought, without his beloved Zahra.

Through eyes weary with the hollowness of grief that had for so long been submerged by his need for action, Jules looked once more on the scene of springtime colour bordering the swelling river that had greeted them at the pinnacle of their zeal. This was the same place where Zahra and he had pledged themselves to each other, to a lifetime together – exactly a year ago.

The searing pain of Zahra's agony and the engulfing guilt of what he had done in vengeance suddenly poleaxed him.

He sank towards the damp ground below, covering his eyes to suppress his guilt, to smother the hurt. He stayed kneeling in the wet grass, his grief and conscience bursting together, flowing unchecked down his cheeks, his hands still covering his face as if in prayer. But Jules could not pray, he had never learned the skill. Instead, emptiness and longing howled inside him for redemption.

He never felt a thing. The soft-nosed bullet tore away the upper, right side of his head with pinpoint efficiency. His body slumped forward over the edge of the riverbank, his blood mingling with the swirling river that washed over his limp right arm, carrying away the red rose on its flow.

Above him, some 75 metres away, the gunman in full camouflage kit watched for 30 seconds to make sure that no life signs remained. He already knew Jules was dead as he had seen the bullet hit its target through the powerful telescopic sight. But he had to be absolutely sure this time.

Noureddin Siaz was a trusted member of Hamid Saiyeidi's personal bodyguard and renowned to be among the best rifle shots in the country. The President had personally instructed him that his nephew should be neither aware of anyone stalking him nor suffer for even a split second. The trauma was to be kept to an absolute minimum.

Justifying his orders, as much to himself as to Noureddin, Saiyeidi had explained simply that Jules's demise was the only way to guarantee and safeguard Iran's national security. He had knowledge that simply couldn't be allowed to fall into the wrong hands, ever, at any price. If only he had chosen to stay in Iran, he could have been protected. But he hadn't. And now, reliable intelligence had been received that both the CIA and Mossad were separately racing to pick Jules up. The risk of his capture and inevitable torture had to be eliminated, permanently. And, if possible, seeds of confusion and mistrust should be sown between the two predatory allies.

Therefore, as instructed, Noureddin ejected the single, spent case from the .293 bullet and left it lying randomly in the grass under the thin hedge that he had used for cover. It was bound to be found and would later be identified as manufactured exclusively for Mossad by Rafael & Co, the Israeli arms manufacturer.

Back in the hired, metallic grey Audi S8, Noureddin sent the code verifying the final execution of his orders to the private number the President had given him. 'The bitter irony of his own extraordinary success' Saiyeidi had called it.

As he drove north towards Orly airport and home, Noureddin, a father himself, wondered how his childless President, alone in the darkness of the night, would live with the everlasting guilt of the calculated death of his own nephew and sole heir.

END